George

The Christians of St. Thomas and their Liturgies

SALZWASSER
VERLAG

George Broadley Howard

The Christians of St. Thomas and their Liturgies

Reprint of the original, first published in 1864.

1st Edition 2022 | ISBN: 978-3-75259-496-6

Verlag (Publisher): Salzwasser Verlag GmbH, Zeilweg 44, 60439 Frankfurt, Deutschland
Vertretungsberechtigt (Authorized to represent): E. Roepke, Zeilweg 44, 60439 Frankfurt, Deutschland
Druck (Print): Books on Demand GmbH, In de Tarpen 42, 22848 Norderstedt, Deutschland

THE

CHRISTIANS OF ST. THOMAS

AND

THEIR LITURGIES:

COMPRISING

The Anaphoræ of St. James; St. Peter; The Twelve Apostles; Mar Dionysius; Mar Xystus; and Mar Evannis; Together with the Ordo Communis.

TRANSLATED FROM SYRIAC MSS. OBTAINED IN TRAVANCORE.

BY THE

REV. GEORGE BROADLEY HOWARD, B.A.,

LATE ASSISTANT CHAPLAIN IN THE DIOCESE OF MADRAS.

"In illis igitur (*sc.* Liturgiis Ecclesiæ) non Doctoris alicujus eximii, non Concilii, sed totius Ecclesiæ vox auditur."—RENAUDOT, *Lit. Orient. Coll.*, tom. i. p. lii.

OXFORD and LONDON:

1864

The Invocation of the Blessing.

(*See p.* 122.)

PREFACE.

THE present volume will be found to consist of two distinct parts; the first containing a sketch of the history of the Christians of St. Thomas from the earliest times to the present day, and the second a translation of the six Anaphoræ mentioned in the title-page.

The principal sources of information of which I have availed myself in preparing the first part of the work are mentioned at p. 8, and are frequently referred to in the notes. Besides the writers there specified, there are several others, as Duperron, Hamilton, and Moens, whose works might be consulted with advantage by those who are disposed to trace as far as possible the records of this interesting people. To attempt anything of this kind was beyond my present purpose, and I have contented myself with giving a general sketch of their history, in the earnest hope that it may tend to re-awaken the sympathy of English Churchmen for these native Indian Christians, some few of whom may not improbably be subjects of the British Crown.

Those who are able to turn to the learned work of Eusebius Renaudot, will there find all the Anaphoræ which are here translated, with very many more besides; and it is interesting to observe the close agreement between the contents of MSS. obtained in India, and those of the MSS. which he found in the libraries of Europe.

An English translation of a very considerable portion of the Syriac Liturgy of St. James is given in the "Madras Church Missionary Record" for the years 1835, 1836. This translation has been useful in elucidating some interesting points in connection with the service, but, as it consists only of "Extracts from the Liturgy," it cannot be accepted as a complete and satisfactory representation of the Eucharistic Office, as celebrated by the Syrian Christians in Malabar.

I was not aware, however, until I had nearly finished my labour, that the same translation had been reprinted in a revised and complete form in an appendix to one of the volumes of Hough's "Christianity in India[a]." Had I known this at first, the present volume would probably never have been undertaken; and, as it was, I felt much disposed to abandon my design: but, considering the object I had in view, and especially that one of the MSS. which I had obtained enabled me to present a translation of five other Anaphoræ, which, I believe, have not yet been made known to the English public, except in the costly work of Renaudot, I ventured to hope that this would be ac-

[a] The lateness of the time at which I obtained access to Mr. Hough's volumes, and the little opportunity I have had of consulting them, will explain the comparatively slight reference which has been made to that laborious and valuable work.

cepted as a sufficient motive for proceeding with the work, which I had all but brought to a completion.

The last-mentioned consideration had the more weight with me, because a comparison of the six Anaphoræ together brings out a feature of the most striking character, in regard to the structure of that large class of Liturgies which are founded on the model of the Syriac Liturgy of St. James. Compiled, as they have been, in different countries, and in ages widely separated from each other, they are nevertheless all cast in the same mould, they observe the same order,—the very terminations of the prayers are strikingly similar, and the variety which exists is due rather to the language employed, than to the main subject of the prayers.

This remarkable identity of structure—and it comes out yet more forcibly in the work of Renaudot—indicates a deep traditional reverence for the ancient model on which the Anaphoræ are severally framed, and shews how little success may be expected to attend the labours of any who may attempt to sweep away these time-honoured offices, and to substitute some other form of the Eucharistic service in their place.

This observation leads me to speak generally of the value of the Anaphoræ themselves. Many persons, I fear, will think that the time devoted to what they will deem a profitless subject of inquiry might have been far more usefully employed, and I am not without anxiety on this point; but the study of the liturgy of an ancient Church has far higher objects than the gratification of a mere idle curiosity. If, by God's mercy, we may ever be permitted to make any advance towards the recovery of external unity,—I will not venture to say throughout Christendom, but among *any* of those branches of the Church which have been so deplorably severed from each other,—surely one preliminary step towards the attainment of this end must lie in the careful examination of the doctrine and discipline of those with whom we hope that we may eventually hold communion.

But the Anaphoræ here translated will, I believe, be found to possess a value of their own, in addition to that which appertains to them as testimonies of the faith and practice of the Syrians in Malabar; and I may say this with the more confidence, because it is of the merits of the Anaphoræ themselves, as distinct from the translation of them, that I am now speaking. Although the MSS. from which I have translated are of comparatively recent date, they nevertheless correspond so nearly, both in form and matter, with the ritual of the ancient Church, that they may serve at any rate as an *introduction* to the study of those valuable monuments of Christian faith and practice, which we possess in the Liturgies of the first few centuries.

The Syriac Liturgy of St. James, indeed, is traceable to a period at least antecedent to the Council of Chalcedon; for it is used, says Renaudot, by both orthodox and Jacobite Churches at the present day. Of this Liturgy there are two forms, both of which are given in Renaudot's work. The "Liturgia Minor," as he calls it, appears to be a slightly abbreviated version of the older form, and its arrangement is attributed to Gregory, Catholic of the East, in the year A.D. 1591. It is this form with which my MSS. most nearly correspond; but the two are much alike, and the substance of them is, as we have seen, traceable to a high antiquity.

I may here observe, by the way, that much of the Office which is given by Renaudot in the *Ordo Communis*—i.e. that portion of the Service which is used with all Anaphoræ alike, and consists (i.) of the Office preceding the *Prayer of the Peace*, and (ii.) of the *Post-communion*—is here found in its natural place; thus preventing the confusion which renders his versions somewhat difficult to understand.

It remains that I should speak briefly of the MSS. themselves, and of the translations which I have ventured to offer in the following pages.

The MSS. are two in number, and both of quarto size. The larger of the two (which for distinction's sake I have called MS. A.) consists of 175 pages in excellent preservation, and, with the exception of the Anaphora of Evannis, is written in a clear Estrangelo character. The paper is evidently of native manufacture, resembling that of several MSS. in the British Museum, and is remarkably strong and opaque.

Pp. 150, 159, present good specimens. The Curators of the Bodleian Library at Oxford have done me the honour to accept this MS. for that Library, where the Malabar MSS. obtained by Dr. Mill, (M.,) in or about the year 1820, are also to be seen.

The smaller manuscript, MS. B., consists of 72 pages, and contains only the Anaphora of St. James, with the Ordo Communis, which forms a part of that Anaphora. This MS. is much eaten or worn away, and is incomplete, three of its leaves being wanting, besides any that may have been lost at the end. It is written in a fair Estrangelo character, but is not nearly so legible as the other. The paper on which it is written is a poor thin paper of European make, bearing a water-mark consisting of three fleurs-de-lis; or, a large fleur-de-lis and a crown; or, in some instances, a fleur-de-lis, with the letters SAPS introduced above.

Inaccuracies frequently occur, as may be expected, in both of these MSS.; and in numerous instances, some of which are mentioned in the notes, I have been able to correct one of them by the other.

In the translation of these manuscripts I have been anxious, above all things, to adhere as faithfully and closely to the original as possible. For in a work of this kind, in which the main object is to shew what forms of worship, and what expressions, are really used in the Eucharistic Office, it seemed the most satisfactory course to render the Syriac into English as nearly word for word as possible. A similar rule appears to have been observed by Renaudot; and I felt that it would be unwise to depart from it, even in cases in which a little freedom of translation might have been adopted without any danger of misinterpreting the sense. This must be my apology for many a clumsily turned passage, and for the apparently capricious insertion or omission of a preposition, a conjunction, or a phrase, which, I am sure, will frequently surprise the reader.

It is with sorrow that I am compelled to acknowledge that the feeling of eager anticipation with which I entered on the study of these Offices—though rewarded beyond all hope in respect of their general contents—has been followed by much keen disappointment, occasioned by some of the passages which they contain, and by the reflection that, among the members of my own Church, there will be not a few who will consider the existence of such passages decisive against the value of the Liturgies, except as bearing testimony to the corruption of the Church.

These passages—from whatever source they may have been derived—will be read with pain by every English Churchman: and there are others, which, I am well aware, will provoke disapproval or the contrary, according to the theological bias of the reader. I must, however, leave the Liturgies to speak for themselves; merely observing that there are certain portions of the Office which are not common to all MSS. alike, and which, we may therefore presume, form no part of the ancient Office, and are not generally adopted in the ritual of the native Church.

On the other hand, it may be hoped, I trust without presumption, that a perusal of these Services will, in some cases, lead to a quickened apprehension of the great Catholic verities which are the common heritage of the Church throughout the world: and that, should they fall into the hands of any who have hitherto been strangers to Liturgical study, they may serve to bring out the beauties and catholicity of our own Office, the arrangement and purport of which is so forcibly illustrated by comparison with those primitive Liturgies from which it is in a great measure derived.

I beg to offer my sincere thanks to several friends who have afforded me very kind and valuable assistance in the preparation of this work. Among these I should especially mention the Rev. Dr. Neale, Warden of Sackville College, who has laid me under deep obligation by the loan of the works of Raulin, Asseman, and Renaudot; the Rev. R. Payne Smith, Sub-Librarian of the Bodleian Library; and Dr. E. J. Waring, late Physician to H.H. the Rajah of Travancore, to whose kindness, in an early stage of my undertaking, I am indebted for an introduction to sources of information of which I have largely availed myself. My best thanks are due also to those who have so kindly subscribed for copies of the work, and have thus enabled me at length to put it into a printed form.

CROYDON, *Sept.* 17, 1864.

[POSTSCRIPT.]

On the Ancient Inscriptions mentioned at p. 17.

The "Journal of the Royal Asiatic Society," vol. vii. pp. 343, sqq., contains facsimiles of the Inscriptions on the ancient copper tablets belonging to the Christians of Malabar; but, unfortunately, I was not aware of their existence until the first sheets of this work were passing through the press, and it was too late to modify what I had written, except by a reference to the preface.

There are, as stated at p. 17, six copper plates in all, five of which are engraven on both sides, thus forming, so to speak, eleven pages altogether. A memorandum is prefixed to the facsimiles, in which the writer states that the inscriptions on five of the plates are in the ancient Karnataka character, with the exception of a name in Devanagari, which occurs three times. These five plates are not all of one size, but they bear a general resemblance to each other, and being written in one character, may not improbably form one continuous document. I must beg permission, therefore, to recal the statement upon which I hesitatingly ventured, in consequence of the rather ambiguous language in Capt. Swanston's description of these tablets, that they were written apparently in six different languages.

The sixth plate, which is one of those engraven on

both sides, is thought to contain the signatures of witnesses; eleven of them being in Cufic,—the nail-headed character mentioned by Dr. Buchanan and Capt. Swanston,—ten in a cursive form of Syriac, and four in an old Hebrew character, resembling that of the Palmyrene inscriptions. The Cufic signatures have been rendered into Arabic by Mr. Shakespear, and his reading is subjoined to the memorandum referred to.

In the "Asiatic Journal," N. S. vol. vi., will be found facsimiles of two other very interesting documents, the property of the Jews of Cochin, with whom they remain, I believe, to the present day. One of these has been translated by Mr. Whish, and appears to be a grant of privileges to a certain Jewish family. The article in which these facsimiles and translation are given, contains much interesting matter connected with the early chronology of the Jews and Christians in Malabar. It contains also the foundation of the statement made in a note to Capt. Swanston's Memoir, and reproduced by myself with reference to a *portion* of the Christian inscriptions—for the brevity of the Jews' document compared with the "closely written[b]" inscriptions on the *six* plates belonging to the Christians was a strong argument against its applying to the whole of the latter—that "a copy, purporting to be made from the Christians' grant, proved, on examination by Mr. Whish, to be word for word the same as that of the Jews."

[b] Buchanan.

7

This statement, I am happy to say, seems little likely to affect the value of the Christian tablets. Indeed, it does not appear to have any concern with them at all; and only shews, either that the native who presented the "copy" had been misinformed, or that he was guilty of attempting a fraud. Mr. Whish seems to have known nothing about the six tablets belonging to the Christians, but, hearing some rumour of a grant having been made to them, and finding that a document, which was forwarded to him as a *copy* of this grant, was in fact (errors of the copyist only excepted) word for word identical with that belonging to the Jews, he was naturally led to doubt the existence of any grant to the Christians at all.

A hasty examination will suffice to shew that the Christian tablets are all of them longer than those belonging to the Jews—supposing, that is, that the latter are duly represented in size as well as in substance; and although many of the characters in both documents bear a near resemblance to each other, it is not easy to detect a correspondence between any consecutive portions of the several inscriptions. This point, however, is one that can now be easily determined by a careful examination and comparison of the two.

CORRIGENDA.

P. 53, note, *for* "12 copper pie" *read* "16 cash."
— 87, l. 3, *for* "Middleton" *read* "Heber."

The Author would be thankful for any communications upon the subject of this volume, addressed to the care of MESSRS. PARKER, 377, STRAND.

CONTENTS.

INTRODUCTORY NOTICE.

CHAP. I. Sketch of the early traditions and history of the Christians of St. Thomas previous to the year A.D. 1502 1
CHAP. II. The Synod of Diamper 23
CHAP. III. Subsequent history of the Church.—The Church Missionary Society's Mission at Cottayam.—Proposals for a renewed effort to restore the Church 44
CHAP. IV. Personal observations among the Syrians in Travancore 114

APPENDICES.

A. ON THE DOCTRINE OF THE CHRISTIANS OF ST. THOMAS 168
B. ON CEREMONIAL IN THE EAST 177
C. ON THE ORDO COMMUNIS AND ANAPHORA, &c., WITH ANALYSIS AND CONSPECTUS 179

TRANSLATIONS OF THE LITURGIES.

THE ORDO COMMUNIS 191
THE ANAPHORA OF ST. JAMES 222
THE ANAPHORA OF ST. PETER 267
THE ANAPHORA OF THE TWELVE APOSTLES 279
THE ANAPHORA OF MAR DIONYSIUS BARSALIBI . . 291
THE ANAPHORA OF MAR XYSTUS 301
GOSPELS UPON SEVERAL OCCASIONS—DEDICATION OF ALTAR VESSELS, &c. 311
THE ANAPHORA OF MAR EVANNIS 317
SEALS AND SEDRAS 327

INTRODUCTORY NOTICE.

CHAPTER I.

General Description of the Malabar Coast.—Antiquity of the Church in Malabar.—Its Foundation ascribed to St. Thomas.—The Mission of Pantænus.—Thomas Cannaneo.—Introduction of the Nestorian Heresy into Malayala.—Transition to Jacobitism.—The Christians elect a King.

THE part of India to which the reader's attention will be directed in the following pages is a narrow district stretching along the south-western coast for about two hundred miles or a little more, between the ninth and twelfth parallels of north latitude, and bounded on the east by a range of lofty mountains, called the Anamullays, or Elephant Hills.

The direction of this mountain range may be said to be, upon the whole, nearly parallel to that of the coast-line, its highest peaks being found at a distance averaging from thirty to fifty miles from the sea. The intervening country is more or less undulating, except that portion of it which borders upon the coast from Chaukad in lat. 10° 37′ in the north, to within a few miles of Trevandrum in the south.

This district is for the most part flat and low, and presents a geographical peculiarity in the distribution of its water-courses, which gives a distinctive character to the country, and of which a short account may not be uninteresting. It is watered by numerous streams which descend from the mountains towards the sea; but these little rivers, instead of pouring their waters separately into the ocean, spread out before they reach it into wide channels which communicate with one another just within the coast-line, and form what is called the Backwater—a land-locked lake of ever-varying depth and width, with an outlet here and there through which the water finds its way into the ocean.

It must not be supposed that these lagoons extend along the coast in one unbroken sheet of water, but they are so connected with each other by natural channels, or where these do not exist, by artificial canals, that you may pass from Chaukad to Trevandrum, a distance of about one hundred and sixty miles, with but a single change of boat—a change rendered necessary by an unkind spur of the mountains which interrupts the navigation, though but for a distance of five miles, causing no little inconvenience to the burthened traveller.

The canals are monotonous, but the more open parts of the Backwater are often very beautiful. They are separated from the sea by a strip of land, generally of considerable width, but contracted in some places to a mere bank of sand, so narrow as to form, in outward appearance at least, but an insecure barrier against the roaring surf beyond, the spray of which may occasionally be seen dashing over it almost into the very waters of the lake, whose gentle ripple forms a striking contrast with the restless ever-heaving ocean, so near yet so completely dissevered[a].

The eastern banks are broken into a continual variety of outline, rising into low cliffs or sweeping gently down to the water's edge; now abruptly terminating where a stretch of the Backwater recedes far inland, now presenting a long line of shore clothed with perpetual verdure, amid which a shrub much resembling our British holly, and the feathery pinnæ of the cocoanut palm, are conspicuous. Beyond these, where a wider range of view is obtained, tower the summits of the Anamullays, raising their broken outline in the far distance against the eastern sky.

This Backwater is the great highway of the country. Villages dot its sides here and there, and the traveller as he passes along will scarcely fail to notice the contrast which is occasioned at intervals by the whitewashed façade of a Roman or a Syrian church standing out in strong relief from the deep-toned foliage by which it is surrounded.

The waters teem with fish; and an alligator may occasionally be seen creeping among the reeds or drift-

[a] There are two points especially where I have noticed this phenomenon; one a few miles south of Quilon, and the other a little to the south of Anjengo. At one place where the Backwater ends,—I forget its name, but it is about six or seven miles south of Quilon,—the inland water approaches that of the ocean so closely, that when you step out of your boat, you are in fact on the sea-shore; not a tree or blade of vegetation is to be seen between the two; high-water mark reaching to within some fifty feet of the Backwater, and the highest part of the bank being elevated only seven or eight feet above the level of the lake. Yet the sea appears to cast up the bank, rather than to wash it away. At Quilon itself the sea is encroaching on the land.

ing over the surface, his head alone being visible, and easily mistaken at a distance for a piece of floating timber. As the evening closes in, the water exhibits the phenomenon of phosphorescence in a remarkable degree, the spray falling from the oar-blades like showers of diamonds returned to the dark depth from which they are momentarily withdrawn by every stroke of the boatmen. I have observed this phenomenon more particularly in the neighbourhood of Quilon, where the water is unusually clear.

The mountain jungles afford shelter to such wild animals as are commonly found in India, especially elephants, tigers, and cheetas; and the plains seem to contain an average number of jackals and mosquitoes, and more than an average number of snakes. It is said that a species of the boa-constrictor is found here, and I have twice seen enough to satisfy me that the country is infested by snakes of enormous size. Yet these are by no means so dangerous as the smaller species of the serpent tribe, especially the deadly cobra, which is only too common. The domestic animals are oxen, fowls, ducks, and goats, to which should be added the snarling ill-fed pariah dogs, which abound in every village, many of them appearing to have no particular owner. And I feel much disposed to add crows to the list, for they are at least as useful as the domestic cat in England, and the bold impudence of an Indian crow is so great as to present a strong claim to this distinction. He is the constant attendant of the cook-room, and is always ready, if only your back be turned, to hop on to your breakfast-table, and make off with the bread and butter, or any other eatable.

Abundant fertility characterizes this well-watered region. The shore is fringed with cocoa-nut palms, which strike their roots deeply into the sandy soil, and grow so close to the sea as to be washed, and sometimes undermined, by the waves. The low lands yield paddy, a coarse kind of rice, in great abundance, while the firmer ground is clothed with fine timber trees, such as the teak and jack-tree, round the latter of which may often be seen the beautiful pepper-vine clinging like ivy to its stem. This plant, which much resembles ivy in appearance, forms one of the most important productions of the country, and, with the cardamom and other spices, contributes materially to the value of its commerce[b].

The climate, however, exercises by no means so happy an influence upon the general system, as that which is produced by external nature upon the eye. It is, on the contrary, peculiarly trying to the European constitution, and is regarded with apprehension even by natives of other parts of India. The south-west monsoon blows from April to September, and is accompanied by an abundant fall of rain, which renders the atmosphere perpetually damp; and the land winds which prevail more or less during the remaining por-

[b] Cosmas, an Alexandrian merchant of the sixth century, surnamed Indicopleustes, from his having made voyages to India, makes an allusion to the growth of pepper in Malabar in the following interesting passage:—"In the Malabar country also, where pepper grows, there are Christians, and in Calliana, as they call it, there is a bishop, who comes from Persia, where he is consecrated." I take the passage from Hough's Christianity in India. A very similar quotation is given by Capt. Swanston, in the Journal of the Royal Asiatic Society, 1833.

tion of the year are still more injurious. A dry cold wind, blowing violently and continuously from the north-east, and laden with the exhalations which it collects in its passage over the decaying vegetation of the hills, is productive of much disease and mortality. So great is the danger incurred by exposure to this wind, especially during sleep, that it is better to endure any amount of discomfort from the heat, than to repose subject to its baneful influence.

Whether it be owing to the unusually deleterious effect of the climate, or to the habits of the people, I know not, but certainly one cannot have resided many days in this part of India without being struck by the terrible forms of diseased humanity which constantly present themselves. Cases of elephantiasis, and of leprosy too hideous for description, often meet the eye, and create a sensation of mingled horror and astonishment, which however soon gives place to the more wholesome feeling of compassion for the poor afflicted sufferers. Cholera and small-pox do their work here, as well as in other parts of India, and must annually carry off many of these poor creatures, but their number is so great that the lepers in Quilon alone may, I believe, generally be counted by scores.

The natives of the lower castes are, generally speaking, slight in build, but, like most Indians, wonderful for their power of endurance; and the boatmen will, if required, row for two or three nights and days together, with a short interval occasionally for food and sleep. In conclusion, I should observe that the country is inhabited by men of all castes, and of almost all

Eastern religions, except Buddhism and that in which fire is regarded as an object of worship; the former finding its stronghold in Ceylon and the far East, and the latter, I suppose, in Persia and in the north of India, but having few votaries in this country.

Such are the more prominent features of the Malabar coast, a country which may claim no small share of interest on the part of the ecclesiastical student, as the locality of a Church which, planted perhaps in apostolic times, certainly in times of remote antiquity, has borne in her isolation a noble witness to the Christian faith amid the various forms of false religion by which she has ever been surrounded.

It is well known to readers of ecclesiastical history that when Vasco de Gama reached India in 1498, or at any rate on his second arrival in 1502, he found there a people who already professed the Christian religion, which they said had been the faith of themselves and their ancestors for many generations.

But although the discoveries of De Gama led the way to a more intimate knowledge of the Church in Malabar, he was by no means the first to make its existence known to the people of Western Europe. Marco Polo, in the thirteenth century, had visited the rock on which St. Thomas suffered martyrdom, and says that his tomb was frequented by Christian and Saracen pilgrims from all parts, but especially "from the pepper coast of Malabar." We have, however, yet earlier and more interesting testimony of the existence of the Church in Malayala; for it is stated that, full six centuries before Vasco de Gama set foot in India, an Anglo-Saxon bishop named Swithhelm had been sent from the court of our own Alfred, to bear presents and congratulations to this distant people [c]. The testimany of Cosmas, in the sixth century, has been already mentioned, and it is thought that a trace of the same Church may be found among the records of the Council of Nicæa, (A.D. 325,) in the signature of a Bishop Johannes, who bears the title of *Metropolitan of Persia and of the great India.*

These indications of the extreme antiquity of this Church—and they do not stand alone—are sufficient to excite a strong desire to know something of its history; and although the destruction of books at the Synod of Diamper almost precludes the hope that its early history will ever be satisfactorily recovered, much interesting information is still to be gathered from the traditions of the people and the labours of those who have investigated the subject [d].

[c] See Turner's Hist. of the Anglo-Saxons. The account is given in the Saxon Chronicle, and by William of Malmesbury. Swithhelm was Bishop of Shireburn, and it is said that he returned in safety from what must have been, at that period, a most difficult and perilous journey.

[d] For the historical portion of the following sketch I am indebted mainly to an able paper by Capt. Swanston, contained in the Journal of the Royal Asiatic Society for 1834; and to Raulin's History of the Synod of Diamper, published at Rome in 1745. Further information may be found in a work by one Michael Geddes, Chancellor of Sarum, 1694; and in La Croze's *Histoire du Christianisme des Indes,* 1723; "Indian Conferences," translated by the Dutch, 1719; and Hough's "Christianity in India." The large quarto by Raulin is occupied chiefly with the history and decrees of the Synod of Diamper, translated from the Portuguese work of A. Gouvea, but it contains several interesting dissertations on other matters connected with the subject. There is also a French translation of Gouvea's work, by De Glen, said

The foundation of the Church in Malayala is generally ascribed to the Apostle Thomas, who, after having laboured in Arabia Felix and the island of Socotra [e], is said to have passed over to Cranganore, on the western coast of India, (N. lat. 10° 13′,) where a large colony of Jews then resided, towards whom he may have felt drawn by a natural sympathy, as being himself of the stock of Israel. Here his zeal was crowned with success; converts were made from both Jews and heathen, churches were built, (the remains of which it is said are yet to be seen in some places, especially Paroor and Neranum,) and Christianity spread through a large portion of the country [f].

Having thus witnessed the fruit of his labour on the Malabar coast, St. Thomas delegated the care of these infant Churches to others, and continued his apostolical journey to the opposite side of the peninsula, selecting Mailapoor, then a rich and populous city, and

to have been published at Brussels in 1609,—I think the date must be wrong,—but neither of them is easily procurable. For a general description of the country and people, the reader should consult Mr. Day's "Land of the Permauls," lately published at Madras.

[e] Socotra is an island lying at a little distance from the most eastern point of the coast of Africa. It thus lay in the direct line of trade between India and Egypt, through which much of the merchandize of the East passed into Europe, and is said to have been a mart of considerable importance. Its high volcanic peaks are often seen by passengers on the Peninsula and Oriental Company's steamers.

[f] Baldæus, the Dutch traveller, says, "On the rocks near the seashore of Conlang (Quilon) stands a stone pillar, erected there, as the inhabitants report, by St. Thomas." See his Description of Malabar and Coromandel, c. 20. Mr. D'Albedhyll, the Master Attendant at Quilon, told me that he had seen this pillar, and that it was washed away only a few years ago. The shore *at* Quilon is all sand, and has no rock or cliff, but there are rocks *near* Quilon.

one to which great multitudes of heathen were attracted from every side by the reputed sanctity of its temples, as the head-quarters of a new mission [g].

Here, therefore, he remained for some time, and then, in obedience to the command of his Divine Master, to "go into all the world, and preach the Gospel to every creature," he again left the care of the Church to some of the converts he had made, and extended his labours yet further eastward, reaching, according to some writers, even the distant city of Pekin, and there, as elsewhere, he planted the standard of the Cross. Those who may be disposed to examine the grounds for this statement may do so in the work of Raulin above alluded to, and perhaps more satisfactorily in a treatise by Eusebius Renaudot concerning the origin of Christianity in China.

From China, if he ever went there, St. Thomas returned to Mailapoor, where his preaching became so successful as to excite intense hostility on the part of the Brahmins, who naturally began to fear that they should lose their power and prestige. It has, indeed, been suggested that the division of time into *Man-*

[g] Mailapoor is now a suburb of Madras. There is a story of a pillar erected here by the Apostle, on which he inscribed a prophecy that the religion he had planted would be restored by a race of foreigners when the sea should reach its foot. Mailapoor is said to have been forty miles inland at that time. Vasco de Gama, it is further added, found this pillar with the sea washing its base. Bruce's Scenes and Sights in the East, p. 75. The story, which with this addition seems to be manifestly burlesqued, may have originated in some trick of the Portuguese missionaries, who were not always very scrupulous as to the means they employed. Was Vasco de Gama ever on the Coromandel coast at all?

wantaras, or patriarchal ages, which they introduced about this period, was intended to counteract the teaching of the Apostle, by the assertion of a claim to antiquity beyond that of the Mosaic account, which had then just become known in India. The Manwantaras were formed from computed conjunctions of Saturn with the sun, and were nine in number, the earliest commencing with the year 4225 before Christ[h].

However this may be, the Brahmins, it is said, at length stirred up a tumult against the Apostle, who deemed it expedient to retire for a time until their malice should have spent itself, so that he might return to his flock without danger. There was a cave in a rocky hill, some two or three miles from Mailapoor, which seemed to offer a secure retreat; and here accordingly he secreted himself for three days[i]; but his enemies having at length discovered his hiding-place, advanced towards the cave in great numbers, being resolved upon his death. St. Thomas, having been warned of their approach, fled to a larger hill, about two miles off, but failing to secrete himself, was overtaken and slain, being first stoned, and afterwards thrust through with a javelin. Thus did he receive

[h] See Capt. Swanston's Memoir &c., note ‡, p. 174. If this epoch referred to the date of the first creation of man, the discrepancy would not be so great as to be of much use to the Brahmins: and the chronology of the Samaritan Pentateuch and of the Septuagint would be in favour of the Christians. The expression *Conjunctions of Saturn with the Sun* is evidently incorrect, for these conjunctions occur yearly, when Saturn and the Sun have the same right ascension.

[i] This cave may yet be seen in the "Little Mount." The traveller should look for the hollow which St. Thomas cleft in the rock for water, and for the Apostle's footprint on a stone near the bottom of the hill.

his crown of martyrdom: and the place where the deed was done is still called St. Thomas's Mount.

It has been objected to this account of St. Thomas's martyrdom that it is inconsistent with the alleged forbearance of the Brahmins towards the preachers of all religions. This, however, is but a poor reason to assign in opposition to so time-honoured a tradition. The Brahmins will not patiently submit to interference with their religion or with their temples: and the people, once excited, may be easily supposed to have proceeded to any length of violence [k].

I regret that, owing to the difficulty of the language, it has not been in my power to make much enquiry into the foundation of this tradition among the people themselves, and it is improbable that the question will ever be satisfactorily determined. Some writers are disposed to father the whole story upon the Portuguese, who fabricated it, they presume, in order to promote the accomplishment of their own designs. Others, as Tillemont, the Abbé Fleury, and Renaudot, (whose religion did not tempt them to make so gratuitous an assumption,) while admitting that the common tradition of the Malabar Churches points to St. Thomas as their founder, yet acknowledge that the whole subject is involved in the greatest uncertainty. Others, again, are inclined to consider the account as by no means improbable. Dr. Buchanan expresses his conviction "that we have as good authority for believing that

[k] Mr. Day, in his "Land of the Permauls," gives an account of a Brahmin convert in Travancore who was put to death on account of his apostacy from the faith and customs of his fathers. I am sorry that I cannot refer to the page, not having the volume at hand.

the Apostle Thomas died in India, as that the Apostle Peter died at Rome[l]:" and Capt. Swanston goes so far as to assert that the story "unites in its favour all the proofs which can warrant its correctness; the accumulated testimonies of the first ages of the Church; of St. Jerome; St. John, surnamed Chrysostom; Athanasius, and Eusebius[m]."

Still, however anxious we may be to establish so interesting a fact as the visit of St. Thomas to India, (especially interesting in its presumed connection with the history of a Church which was for so many centuries independent of Western influence,) I fear it must be admitted that we are not yet in possession of sufficient evidence to be entitled to claim the account as a matter of well-ascertained historic truth. Documentary evidence of early date may possibly yet be forthcoming[n]; but it should be considered that written documents, although the strongest, are by no means the only authentic evidence of *general fact;* and when the

[l] Christian Researches, p. 137.

[m] Capt. Swanston's Memoir. I have not been able to ascertain the passages to which the gallant author so confidently refers.

[n] It is much to be desired that *all* the plates at Cottayam (of which some account will be given presently, see p. 17) may be deciphered and translated, particularly that in the cuneiform character, which is said to be the oldest. It is worth while to observe that, by one of the provisions contained in this charter, "the right to rule over the Church in Malayala was vested in the families out of which the Apostle Thomas had ordained priests." So at least Capt. Swanston's Memoir seems to imply. One of these families was that of Palakomatta, of which we shall hear afterwards. It may be added here that, according to Mr. Whish, (Asiatic Journ., N. S., vol. vi.,) the Jews say that St. Thomas arrived in India in A.D. 52, and themselves in A.D. 69. See also Buchanan's Christian Researches, p. 137, and Heber's Journal, iii. 212.

constant traditions of a country are confirmed by the support of collateral circumstances, they must at least command attention. Upon the whole, it may not unreasonably be held that, in this case at least, the balance of probability is strongly in favour of the supposition that St. Thomas was the founder of the Church in Malabar.

Before taking leave of this subject, it may be worth while to mention that there is another tradition (derived from I know not what source) of the manner in which St. Thomas met his death. According to this account, he was accidentally killed by the arrow of an Indian who was engaged in shooting peacocks. This tradition is so utterly unlike the other, as to escape any suspicion of collusion, or of its being only another form of the same narrative. It is, moreover, unlike a story made up for ecclesiastical purposes, and is therefore of some independent value as a testimony that St. Thomas died in India.

The Church in Mailapoor continued, according to Capt. Swanston's "Memoir," to flourish for some time after the death of St. Thomas; but its members were at length dispersed by persecution, and such of them as escaped death were glad to take refuge with their more fortunate brethren on the coast of Malabar.

But this Church was also destined to meet with its share of reverses, which were owing rather it seems to internal decay, than to oppression from without; and it is thought that the mission of Pantænus may have been undertaken in order to restore the Churches of Malayala to the purity of the faith. Some Eastern

Church, the locality of which is not clearly ascertained, had sent to Alexandria towards the close of the second century, praying that teachers might be sent to them from the celebrated Christian school at that place. A mission was accordingly established under the charge of Pantænus, to whom this important work was specially assigned, and he is said to have proceeded to India, where he found the Christian faith already professed by the inhabitants of the country[o], and obtained a copy of St. Matthew's Gospel, written in Hebrew, (? Syriac[p],) which had been left with them, as they said, by the Apostle Bartholomew. But it is uncertain what country is here signified, the term *India* having been formerly applied to the greater part of south-western Asia.

Those who reject the tradition which assigns the foundation of the Church in Malayala to St. Thomas the Apostle, find an explanation of the term *Christians of St. Thomas* in the mission of one Thomas Cannaneo, who had much intercourse with the nations of the western coast in the pursuit of merchandize, and being filled with zeal in the cause of Christianity, used every effort to promote its adoption or restoration among the people. At length, it is said, he gave up his secular calling altogether, and devoted himself entirely to the service of the Church in Malabar, of which he assumed charge, about the year 345, by direction of Eustathius, Patriarch of Antioch.

[o] Eusebius, v. 10.

[p] The words are, *αὐτοῖς τε Ἑβραίων γράμμασι τὴν τοῦ Ματθαίου καταλεῖψαι γραφήν, κ.τ.λ.*

"Up to this time," says Capt. Swanston, (who gathers his information from the 'annals and traditions' of certain 'native historians,') there had been "no foreign bishops or priests among the Christians in India; they had but few places of worship, built after the form of the Hindoo pagodas of the country, till Mar Thomas assumed charge of their Church, and introduced among them 'several bishops and priests, as also many Christians, men, women, and children, from foreign countries.'"

Whether this Thomas were the original founder of the Church in Malayala or not, it is certain that he acted a very important part in its history. He is said to have introduced, or re-introduced, the Syro-Chaldaic ritual, and must have exercised great influence on the doctrine of the Church; for evil, it must be feared, rather than for good, if, as it is affirmed, he was himself a supporter of the Arian heresy [q].

But the name of Mar Thomas is associated in history as much with the temporal affairs of his diocese, as with those of a spiritual nature; and he is said to have been eminently successful in promoting the external prosperity of the people committed to his care. He built many churches in the country, and established schools for the education of the clergy, especially at Mahadevapatam, which he founded as a settlement of the foreign Christians whom he induced to take up

[q] Asseman (vol. iv. 443) endeavours to shew that Thomas Cannaneo lived some four and a-half centuries later than the date here assigned. He calls him an Aramæan, i.e. a Syrian, and not an Armenian, as La Croze states him to have been.

their abode in Malabar. But the act by which he was pre-eminently remembered in after times was the obtaining of a charter from the Perumal princes, whereby certain privileges were secured to the Christians, which gave them a position of great social importance. They were acknowledged to rank on an equality with the highest castes, and were exempted from the jurisdiction of the Hindoo judges and governors; all authority in civil as well as in ecclesiastical causes, with the exception of criminal cases only, being vested in the Metropolitan. These privileges were recorded on six copper plates, apparently in as many different languages, one of them being written in cuneiform characters, and bearing four signatures, engraven, it is said, in a character similar to that of the Palmyrene inscriptions. The plates themselves, after having been lost by the Dutch or Portuguese, were recovered by Col. Macaulay when resident in Travancore, and delivered for safe custody to the college at Cottayam. There seems, however, to be some doubt as to the real purport of these curious documents, one of them having turned out to be a copy, word for word, of the writing contained on the ancient plate belonging to the Jews of Cranganore. See an article by the late C. M. Whish, Esq., in the Asiatic Journal, N. S., vol. vi. page 6, and the Preface to this volume.

A long blank now occurs in the history of the Church of Malayala, relieved only by occasional records which testify to its continued existence, under extreme vicissitudes of adversity and prosperity, until at length we become better acquainted with its actual history in the records of the sixteenth and following centuries.

Capt. Swanston, whose allusion to the "annals of native historians" has been already noticed,—it is deeply to be regretted that he has not more definitely referred to them,—draws a most gloomy picture of the condition of the Church after the death of Thomas Cannaneo. "Discord and insubordination," he says, "took possession of the people. They split into factions; communities ceased to acknowledge the authority of their lawful bishops; priests usurped the authority of their prelates, laymen of their priests; and anarchy and schism reigned throughout the Church of Malabar. All communication with their Syrian Patriarch was obliterated; the seed of the gospel was quickly eradicated; and the coast of Malabar was on the brink of losing all traces of the language and religion of Syria, when they were saved by the zeal of the Nestorian missionaries, who, overleaping the limits which had confined the ambition and curiosity both of the Greeks and Persians in the fifth century, diffused the doctrines of their Church from China to Jerusalem and Cyprus."

Thus early, it seems, were the tenets of Nestorius introduced into the Church of Malayala; and the testimony of Cosmas, who visited the country in A.D. 522, shews that it was then in communion with the Nestorian Patriarch; the Bishop or Metropolitan of Malabar receiving his consecration from the Catholicos of Babylon[r].

But it is doubtful whether the Nestorian heresy ever took a deep hold in this branch of the Church; for

[r] See note, p. 25.

although, on the arrival of the Portuguese in the sixteenth century, the liturgies which they found in use were of a Nestorian character, there are indications that the creed of the Church had not been continuously Nestorian, but that it had suffered more than one transition in respect of its tenets regarding the Natures and Person of our Lord.

Thus we have Mr. Day's statement, that "according to one authority," which unfortunately he does not mention, "a bishop of the Church of the Jacobites arrived in India from Alexandria, about A.D. 696[8];" a statement the probability of which is supported by the consideration that communication with Egypt (which had ever been a stronghold of the Monophysites) was at this period constantly maintained for the purpose of merchandize.

But after the lapse of little more than a century, the Nestorian Patriarch found an opportunity of regaining the ground which he had lost, and in the year 825 sent two Syrian ecclesiastics, Mar Saul and Mar Ambrose, to take charge of the Church in Malabar. These distinguished prelates were introduced into the country through the instrumentality of a merchant named Job, who persuaded the people of Quilon to receive them and submit to their rule. They governed, it is said, for many years, and were highly respected by the rajahs and nobles of the country, from whom they obtained a yearly revenue for the support of the Church, and a confirmation of the charter which had been granted in the time of Thomas Cannaneo, and

[8] Land of the Permauls, p. 216.

which was again engraved on plates of copper in four Indian dialects. In addition to these privileges, they obtained permission to build churches, and to convert to Christianity all who might be persuaded to embrace that religion.

In the ninth and tenth centuries, however, the Melchites and the Jacobites began to acquire a general ascendancy in the East. "They obtained great privileges," says Mr. Hough[t], "from the caliphs and sultans, and soon became the dominant sects, the Nestorians either uniting with their neighbours or becoming extinct. The Patriarch of Antioch adopted the Jacobite creed about the same period, and it is said in the *Notitia* of Nilus Doxapatrius that his authority extended over all Asia, the East, and the Indies, whither he sent a Catholic, bearing the title of Romogyris." See the work of Eusebius Renaudot, on "The Origin of the Christian Religion in China," pp. 114—119. It

[t] Christianity in India, i. 87. The three parties here mentioned are distinguished from each other mainly by their respective tenets concerning the nature of our Lord.

The Nestorians, so called after Nestorius, Patriarch of Constantinople in 429, are said to hold that there are TWO PERSONS as well as TWO NATURES in Christ; and strongly object to the term *Mother of God*, as applied to the Blessed Virgin, though they have no objection to the term *Mother of Christ*.

The Jacobites, taking their name from James Baradæus, an eminent promoter of their tenets,—though Eutyches is regarded as the founder of their doctrine,—acknowledge after the Incarnation but ONE NATURE and ONE PERSON. Hence they are called Monophysites. Their tenets are more fully described in Appendix A.

The Melchites (or Orthodox), so called from the fact that the Emperor (Melech) favoured their part at the great Council of Chalcedon, acknowledge the TWO NATURES joined together in ONE PERSON.

is remarkable that this *Jacobite* suffragan is here called Catholicos, not Maphrian, which was his ordinary title.

How far the doctrine of thé Church in Malabar was affected by this change in the relative supremacy of the Nestorian and Jacobite communions, it is not possible to ascertain; but the external prosperity of the Church continued to increase. The distinguished prelates who had contributed so largely to this result were succeeded by others of equal zeal and integrity, under whose administration discipline was enforced and learning encouraged, insomuch that the Christians obtained a very influential position among their heathen neighbours. Their reputation for sobriety and truthfulness led to their being employed in offices of the highest trust and honour in the state; and the strength of a pagan rajah was estimated by the number of Christians he could reckon among his warriors.

It must have been about this time that the Bishop of Shireburn was despatched to Malabar from the Court of Alfred, who appears to have entertained some design of opening a more direct communication between his own kingdom and the distant Eastern land whose riches were said to be almost inexhaustible. Swithhelm returned, laden with precious gifts and spices, and the success of this enterprise contributed no small share to the fame of the illustrious Anglo-Saxon.

So elated were the Christians by their continued prosperity, and by the fame which they had obtained among distant nations, that they became ambitious of still greater power, and at length ventured to throw off the yoke of their Hindoo rulers, and to elect a king of their own. This bold design was successfully carried into effect, and one Baliarte was elevated to the regal dignity. His authority was maintained for some generations in the direct line of succession; but one of the kings dying without an heir, the crown passed first to the Rajah of Diamper, and then to the Rajah of Cochin, under whose sway the Christians lost much of their former prestige, (though still retaining their ancient privileges,) and relapsed into a condition of dependence from which they have never yet recovered [u].

[u] The duration of the dynasty is unknown; but the deputation which was sent to Vasco de Gama in 1502, informed him that the last of their kings had died not long before the arrival of the Portuguese.

CHAPTER II.

VASCO DE GAMA AND THE PORTUGUESE. THEIR EFFORTS TO CONVERT THE CHRISTIANS.—MAR ABRAHAM.—MAR SIMEON.—ARCHBISHOP MENEZES.—MAR ABRAHAM'S DEATH.—ARCHDEACON GEORGE.—MENEZES VISITS THE DIOCESE.—THE SYNOD OF DIAMPER.

SUCH was the condition of the Christians in Malabar when Vasco de Gama visited Cochin in 1502. At this period they were estimated to number about two hundred thousand souls; and it is said that they had fifteen hundred churches[a], under the jurisdiction of a single Metropolitan, who resided at Angamalé, a town situated at some distance from the sea coast.

Their religion would probably have rendered them the most cordial allies of the Portuguese, had not the latter discovered in this unfortunate people the existence of two grave offences which could not be overlooked. They were charged with maintaining the heresy of Nestorius on the one hand, and on the other, with the equally fatal sin of schism, in not acknowledging obedience to the See of Rome; for they recognised no higher spiritual authority than that of the patriarchate to which they belonged.

The Portuguese laboured diligently to persuade the people to abjure Nestorianism, and to admit the claims of the Roman Pontiff; and with this object in view they established missions, preached and held disputations in

[a] These numbers represent an *average* of one church to about a hundred and thirty-three souls. But I suspect a mistake in the number of churches, though it is twice given in Captain Swanston's Memoir.

the churches, and founded two colleges, one at Cranganore and the other at Vaipicotta, near Cochin, by means of which they hoped to imbue at least the younger portion of the community with the doctrines and principles of Rome.

These measures however did not produce the desired effect, and at length they resolved upon a bolder course, in which they aimed at nothing less than sending the Metropolitan himself to Rome. This appeared a matter of some difficulty, especially as Mar Joseph, who then presided over the Church, was (as they confess) a man of irreproachable character. He was however cited to Goa, on the charge of having taught some Portuguese youths to use the words *Mother of Christ* in their addresses to the Blessed Virgin; and from Goa he was sent to Portugal and Rome, there to answer this charge of heresy [b].

This monstrous interference, on the part of the Jesuits, in the affairs of an independent Church, was only the commencement of a series of similar acts, which became more and more violent, until at length they culminated in the atrocious horrors of the Inquisition.

The citation of Mar Joseph seems to have occurred about the year 1564 or 1565, and from that time down to the present the history of the Church in Malabar presents a scene of continual turmoil, rivalry, and confusion, the perusal of which leaves a most painful impression on the mind. In a brief sketch, however, like the present, only the leading events can receive atten-

[b] Raulin, Hist. Syn. Diamp., ch. i. § 3.

tion; but they will be sufficient, it is hoped, to enlist the reader's earnest sympathy and Christian love in behalf of this oppressed and suffering people.

When the Christians of St. Thomas found that their Metropolitan had been sent to Rome, they not unreasonably despaired of seeing him again, and sent to the Patriarch of Babylon [c], praying for a successor. The choice of the Patriarch fell on one Mar Abraham, who was accordingly commissioned to take charge of the Church, and was received with joy. This prelate, however, did not long retain the quiet possession of his dignity, for Mar Joseph unexpectedly re-appeared in Malabar, having so satisfactorily cleared himself before the authorities in Portugal, that he was allowed to return to his diocese without going to Rome at all.

A faction among the people was the result; and Mar Joseph appealed to the Portuguese, shewing the commendatory letters he had received from their Queen, and entreating their interference in his behalf. The

[c] This title is of frequent occurrence, and requires some explanation. The ancient see of the Nestorian Patriarch was that of Ctesiphon, afterwards called Bagdad. He himself seems to have been called either *Patriarch*, or *Catholicus*, or to have had both titles applied to him together. Asseman, ii. 249. Castell, however, explains the title *Catholicus* (ܩܬܘܠܝܩܐ) as that of an assistant to the Patriarch,—"Nestorianis secundus a Patriarchâ." Moreover, Asseman tells us that Bagdad is often called Babylon by the writers of this period, though the two cities were on different rivers. ii. 123. The Patriarch or Catholic of Babylon will therefore signify either the Nestorian Patriarch or his suffragan; and the title might probably be retained after the removal of the see to Mosul by the Patriarch of the Nestorians of the Plains, after the schism in 1551. Among the *Jacobites*, Maphrian was the title of the Patriarch's suffragan. Asseman, ii. 215.

appeal was not made in vain; for the Portuguese were only too willing to have the question referred to their arbitration. Mar Abraham was therefore in his turn cited to Goa, from whence he was sent to Portugal, and from that country to Rome, where he appeared before Pius V., who then occupied the Papal see. Here he not only managed to clear himself of the charge of heresy, but obtained the Pope's sanction to his return to Malabar, with the title of Archbishop of the Mountains, after having again received ordination and consecration, on the ground that his former orders were invalid.

In the meantime, the proceedings of Mar Joseph had been carefully watched by the Portuguese, and not being considered satisfactory, he was delated to Pius V., by whose orders he was again seized and despatched to Rome, where he died.

Mar Abraham reached Goa on his return in 1568, the year following that of Mar Joseph's deportation; but the Portuguese refused to permit him to proceed to his diocese, alleging that he had imposed upon the Supreme Pontiff, and he was placed in confinement in the monastery of the Dominicans at Goa. Not long afterwards, however, he contrived to effect his escape, and was received with incredible delight by the people of his diocese, who had begun to despair of his return.

Ten years were now passed in comparative quiet; but in 1578 the Portuguese determined to make another effort to reduce the refractory Metropolitan to obedience. A council was accordingly held at Goa by command of Pope Gregory XIII., and Mar Abraham was summoned to attend its sittings. The Metropolitan, hoping to conciliate the Portuguese by a show of compliance, obeyed the summons, and having, as it is asserted, given the assurances of reformation which were required by the council, was suffered to return to Angamalé, from whence he never again emerged so far as to place himself within reach of such very doubtful friends.

About this period there arrived in Malabar one Mar Simeon, consecrated, as he declared, by the Nestorian Patriarch to take charge of the Church in the place of Mar Abraham, in whom the Patriarch had no longer any confidence. Hence arose another schism among the people, of which the Portuguese were not slow to take advantage. They espoused the side of Mar Abraham, considering it to be in some degree identified with their own cause, inasmuch as Abraham had been confirmed in his see by the Pope; and having obtained possession of the person of Simeon, they recommended him to seek the confirmation of his claims at the hands of the Supreme Pontiff by appearing personally before him. Thus he too was persuaded to take the now customary journey to Rome[d]; where he was tried and condemned, Raulin says only to imprisonment in the convent of the Franciscans at Lisbon; but other accounts add that he was subsequently brought before the Inquisition, and expired under the tortures inflicted by its authority.

The archbishopric of Goa fell vacant in 1594, and the opportunity which thus presented itself of infusing

[d] "Tritum iter," Raulin.

new vigour into the struggle between the Portuguese and the native Christians rendered the question of the succession one of unusual interest and anxiety. The King's choice fell upon an Augustinian monk, Alexius de Menezes by name, who was accordingly appointed to the see, and proceeded to his diocese, armed with stringent orders from the Pope (Clement VIII.) to imprison the incorrigible Metropolitan, and to purge the diocese of Angamalé of its heresy. The new Archbishop, who belonged to a noble family in Lisbon, was now in the prime of life, (having been born in 1559,) and entered with the utmost ardour upon the task assigned to him. He was indeed just the man for the work; and the measures which he took for its accomplishment are marked by a degree of perseverance, courage, and determination worthy of a better cause.

Mar Abraham, whose age now rendered him extremely infirm, continued to reside at Angamalé, whence the threats and persuasions of the Archbishop were alike ineffectual to withdraw him; and as his place of retirement lay too far inland to be securely approached by the Portuguese, unless they had gone in large numbers, Menezes was unable to obtain possession of his person by open violence. But this was considered of little consequence, as it was improbable that the old man would survive much longer.

The necessary precautions were however taken to prevent the arrival of a successor; and as Ormus, which appears to have been a necessary rendezvous for all who passed between India and Ctesiphon, was then in the hands of the Portuguese, the matter was accomplished without difficulty by the arrest and examination of any suspected travellers who passed that way.

At length, in 1597, Mar Abraham died, and the Archbishop determined to act with vigour in the crisis which his death was sure to occasion. The Metropolitan had designated George, the Archdeacon [e], to succeed him in the government of the diocese, until a new metropolitan should arrive; and as this man was of high rank, and had great influence among the people, Menezes thought it prudent to confer upon him the dignity of a Vicar Apostolic, together with authority to conduct the government of the Church, in conjunction with two assessors, one of whom was Francis Roz, a Jesuit, and the other the Principal of the College at Vaipicotta.

The Archdeacon was induced by motives of policy to declare his acceptance of the office thus conferred upon him, but the laconic remark, *Id accipio quod præhabebam*, ascribed to him on this occasion, shews plainly the sense he entertained of the officious interference of the Portuguese. He trusted, however, by a temporizing policy to avert the danger which so imminently threatened the independence of his Church; and during the delay thus gained he used every means in

[e] The Church in Malabar was, in old times, governed by a single Bishop, or Metropolitan, consecrated by the Patriarch, Catholicos, or Maphrian, as the case might be; and he was assisted in his government by an Archdeacon, who was always taken from the family of Palakomatta, from which it was said the Apostle Thomas had selected one to fill this office.

his power to resist the encroachments of the Romanists. This conduct exasperated Menezes, who now saw that his own presence would be indispensable to the success of his design, and he was only dissuaded from going at once to the Malabar district by the intelligence of a war between two of the petty rajahs, which would probably render his journey ineffectual.

But moved by a fresh instance of evasion on the part of the Archdeacon, towards the close of the year 1598, he determined to delay his journey no longer, and on December 28 of that year he left Goa for the south.

It was no easy task to which Menezes now applied himself. It had baffled the efforts of his predecessors for upwards of half a century, but he was resolved on its accomplishment; and the knowledge that the Christians of St. Thomas were bitterly opposed to his interference, and that they were united under the direction of an able leader, only urged him to more determined exertion. And it must be confessed that the character of Menezes was one which eminently qualified him for the work that he had undertaken. A man of consummate tact and of untiring patience, little scrupulous as to the means he employed, unmoved by danger, and ready to undertake any amount of personal fatigue, he added to these qualities an iron will, which broke down all opposition, and contributed in no small degree to his success.

Convinced that little result could be expected from the measures which had hitherto been tried, he had formed the bold design of assembling the whole Church in council, and there insisting on the rejection of all heresy, the admission of the dogmas of the Church of Rome, and entire submission to the Roman Pontiff.

In order, therefore, to prepare for the accomplishment of this design, he landed at various places on the coast, and endeavoured by laborious and constant preaching to convince the people of their errors, and to set forth the Catholic faith. In this he was assisted by a staff of priests well acquainted with Malayalim, (the vernacular language of the country,) whom he sent round to the churches in the neighbourhood, while he occupied himself with preaching and other acts of episcopal visitation.

On February 1, 1599, Menezes arrived at Cochin, whither he summoned Archdeacon George to meet him. The latter judged it prudent to obey, but provided for his safety by a retinue of three thousand armed men, some of whom were sworn to defend him to the last. The interview, however, passed off without any very serious disturbance, though there were some indications of the temper of the people which might have frightened a less resolute man; and George, reluctantly yielding to the Archbishop's superior will, at length agreed to comply with his demands.

But he had not yet overcome the difficulties by which he was surrounded. The people were everywhere sternly opposed to him, and on more than one occasion his life was exposed to the most imminent peril. The Archdeacon also, finding evasion no longer possible, now openly expressed his hostility, and anathematized the Archbishop, who in turn was not slow to use the same spiritual weapon against all who presumed to oppose his measures.

The country was at this period under the jurisdiction of several petty rajahs, whose aid was sought by both parties; but these applications were productive of little result, for although most of the princes were disposed at heart to espouse the side of the Archdeacon, they were deterred from lending him any effective support through fear lest, should they offend the Portuguese, they would suffer not only by the loss of commercial intercourse with them, but perhaps also by more active measures of retaliation on the part of the powerful foreigners.

Menezes, however, continued his arduous labours, travelling from place to place, and preaching, arguing, and persuading from time to time, whenever an opportunity presented itself. No means were left untried which seemed likely to promote the object he had in view, nor did he scruple to assert and to use the episcopal authority with which he was invested, not only over the Portuguese Churches in India, but over the whole of this district likewise, in defiance of existing rights, and of the general constitution of the Christian Church throughout the world.

Or rather, doubtless, it should be said that he acted in accordance with that principle which the Church of Rome so strenuously asserts,—if not in express terms, at any rate by her actions,—that she is the mistress of the universal Church, and that no community of Christians, no matter how pure their doctrine or how regular their orders and their discipline, can be recognised as a part of that Church, unless they be in external communion with herself, and acknowledge her supremacy. This principle, the continual assertion of which has (in accordance with a well-known metaphysical law) led to its being *heartily believed*, as a vital article of the faith, by members of the Church of Rome, and even by her clergy, notwithstanding it has been shewn to have no real foundation either in Holy Scripture or in the history of the primitive Church, is the key which renders intelligible the proceedings of Archbishop Menezes and his colleagues in their dealing with the Christians in Malabar; and forbids our entertaining too harsh an opinion of their conduct, even though from our point of view it savours of the utmost arrogance and presumption.

Regarding the question from his own stand-point, De Menezes would not consider his proceedings as an unwarrantable intrusion into another diocese; but would feel himself, let us rather believe, actuated by a conscientious zeal in behalf of immortal souls, which had been committed to his care by the vicegerent of Christ upon earth, and which, unless they could be brought within the true fold, must be regarded as altogether beyond the pale of salvation. What other motive could have induced him to undertake and to persevere in such incessant labour in that fever-laden climate, at the constant peril of his life, and with little prospect of worldly fame to look forward to in compensation for his toil?

I have been led into this digression by the necessity of mentioning in this place an act of the Archbishop which strikes us with astonishment as we read it, until we examine the real motives by which he was actuated—the ordination of thirty-eight native catanars who were devoted to his cause, notwithstanding the indignant protest of the Archdeacon, and the threatening attitude of the people of the place.

Let us beware lest, prompted by a similarly mistaken zeal, we rush unbidden into a course of action, the effect of which can only be to break the unity of Christ's Church, and to introduce confusion where there should be order and peace.

At length, after incredible toil, the tide began to turn in his favour. He had gained many adherents, it is said, by the show of humility which he displayed in the ceremonies of the Great Week, especially in washing the feet of the catanars on Holy Thursday, and by the unflinching reiteration of his claims to supreme authority as the legate of the Roman Pontiff. The Archdeacon himself began to waver. He had been thrown into a state of the utmost consternation—it is said that he even fainted away—on the receipt of a letter, in which the Archbishop dwelt upon the terrors of everlasting perdition into which he was hurrying himself and his people by his obstinate resistance to the truth; and finding that the Rajah of Cochin was no longer able to afford him even the underhand support which he had hitherto received, he was at length persuaded to tender his submission, and to sue for a reconciliation with the Archbishop, promising to render active assistance in convening a synod of the Church, in compliance with his demands.

The manner in which the Rajah's change of policy was ultimately brought about affords a good illustration of the determined and overbearing temper of Menezes, and shews the power which the resolute will of one man exercises over the mind of another. He had returned from the south to Cranganore, and there received a visit from the Rajah of Cochin,—the most powerful prince in the country at that time,—who came to signify his loyal attachment to the interests of the Portuguese Government, and to consult the Archbishop about the conclusion of a truce with a neighbouring Rajah. This matter having been disposed of, the conversation turned upon the condition of the Christian population of Malabar, and Menezes took occasion to express his surprise and displeasure at the part which had been taken by the Rajah in the struggle between the Archdeacon and himself. He represented the advantages that His Highness derived from his alliance with the Portuguese, and said that, under such circumstances, it might have been expected that he would do all in his power to further their humane efforts in behalf of the Christians.

"As for myself," he added, "I have voluntarily come to this country, where I endure all kinds of privation, and have been in frequent peril, insomuch that I have often despaired even of life, in order that I may restore these misguided people to the unity of the Catholic Church. I might have lived in my own country in honour, affluence, and prosperity; but these things I have gladly given up for the love of Christ and of those for whom He died. Yet I find that you, who owe so much to our nation, are secretly encouraging the Archdeacon in his opposition to the truth and to me. And, as if this were not enough, we have from time to time to treat with you, a heathen man, wholly devoted, alas! to your worthless idols, concerning the most sacred mysteries of our faith. This is a state of things which I will not endure; I have therefore appointed the ensuing Sabbath as the limit beyond which I will brook no further delay; and should the Archdeacon not have complied with my demands by that time, I shall punish him by curse and deprivation."

Hereupon the Rajah grew angry, being indignant at the contempt with which his idols had been alluded to, and declared that the Archbishop's wish should be acceded to neither on the following Sabbath, nor on the second, nor on the third. Menezes immediately replied with warmth,—striking the ground with his crozier as he spoke,—"But I say it shall! not on the third, nor on the second, but on the very first."

The Rajah, alarmed by his firmness, and being a great adept at dissimulation, pretended to take the matter as a joke, and smilingly promised that all should be as he wished; and so they bade each other farewell[d].

The long-desired Synod was at length convened. It met at Diamper, a few miles south-east of Cochin, on June 20, 1599, and was attended by the Archdeacon with 153 of his catanars, and 660 delegates from the

[d] Raulin's Hist. Syn. Diamp. The term *Sabbath* would be familiar to the Rajah, from the large colony of Jews in his dominions. But the word might perhaps be translated *week*.

different Churches, besides numerous deacons and others connected with the Church.

The Mass *Ad tollendum Schisma* having been celebrated by the Archbishop, robed in full pontificals, a sermon was preached by the Jesuit Francis Roz, and the prayers *Ad inchoandam Synodum* were recited according to the Latin rite; after which De Menezes, enthroned on the faldistorium, addressed the assembly, and demanded whether they were pleased to hold a synod for the extirpation of heresies, the correction of their books, the eradication of simony, a general reformation of the whole Church, both in faith and morals, and for their restoration to the unity of Christendom by submission to the Roman Pontiff.

Having received the assent of the catanars and delegates, Menezes proceeded to publish a sentence of excommunication against any who should presume to discuss the questions before the Synod in any private assembly, so long as the Council should continue to hold its sittings; and it was ordered that no one should be permitted to leave until he had signed the acts of the Synod, and had made the required profession of faith.

On the following day, after the celebration of Mass, a particular confession of faith was proposed, in which Nestorius was anathematized as a heretic; the title *Mother of God*, and the decrees of the Council of Ephesus, were expressly admitted; submission to the Church of Rome as the head and mother of all Churches, and to the Pope as Christ's vicar upon earth, was openly avowed; all communication with the Patriarch of Babylon renounced; and obedience promised to the

Metropolitan designated by the Pope, and to none other.

This confession, the acceptance of which was required without deliberation or delay, although it contained the very essence of the questions before the Synod, was not received without a murmur; but the opposition was presently overborne, and the articles having been read from an ambo by the interpreter of the Synod, it was formally accepted by the catanars and delegates, who ratified their assent by oath, as they severally touched the cross and the book of the Holy Gospels upon the altar.

This done, the business of the Council proceeded. Its acts are nine in number, and comprise no fewer than two hundred and sixty-seven sections, many of them of considerable length: yet the whole were disposed of, and the Synod dissolved, by the 26th of June. No further proof would be required, even were it wanting, to shew that this Synod was assembled, not for the purpose of deliberation, but of compelling the entire submission of the whole Church to whatever demands Menezes should think it desirable to make.

The principal subjects treated of were:—

The rejection of Nestorianism and other heresies;

The recognition of the Papal supremacy;

The reception of the rite of Confirmation, of which (strange as it appears) this ancient Church is said to have been ignorant[e];

[e] This is denied by Joseph Aloysius Asseman, who gives the "Form of Confirmation" in use among the Nestorians. He admits, however, that the chrism was consecrated by a priest, whereas it should be

The extirpation of simony, and other abuses in respect of faith and morals;

And the expurgation of all books which were declared to contain heretical doctrine.

Dr. Buchanan, in his "Christian Researches," p. 108, states that the Christians of St. Thomas were accused of having no other orders in their Church than the priesthood and diaconate. This statement, though partially explained in a note, seems to lay too much stress upon the matter. The passage on which the statement is founded is contained in the 14th Decree of the 3rd Action, where, in the catalogue of books proscribed, mention is made of one "ubi docetur .... nullum haberi ordinem in Ecclesiâ præter Diaconatum et Presbyteratum." It is probable that this treatise was of recent origin and of little influence, as it is notorious that the catanars of this Church had always received episcopal ordination.

The correction of the Liturgy and other Offices of the Church required, of course, especial attention. Besides the three Liturgies of the Nestorians which are commonly known, it is asserted that a fourth, bearing the name of one Diodorus, was found in use among the Christians of St. Thomas. The form, however, most revered among them was that of the Blessed Apostles, Adæus and Mares, and this was accordingly taken as the basis of the emended Liturgy. This Liturgy, as expurgated and altered by Archbishop Menezes for

consecrated by a bishop. Codex Liturgicus, tom. iii. c. v. p. 136. Compare also the work of his uncle, to which he alludes, tom. iii. Bibliot., part ii. chap. vii. § 10.

the use of the Malabar Christians, is given by Raulin in Latin, and has been recently translated by Dr. Neale.

The most notable of the alterations confessed by the Portuguese editor Gouvea are the following:—

The substitution of the name of the Roman Pontiff for that of the Patriarch of Babylon:

The substitution of the names of Cyril and other orthodox doctors for those of Nestorius, &c.; and of the term *Mother of God* in place of the Nestorian term *Mother of Christ*, throughout the Liturgy:

The substitution of the terms *Bread* and *Wine* for *the Body* and *the Blood*, before the act of consecration:

The insertion of the words, *God of God, Light of Light, Very God of very God*, in the Nicene Creed, (for in the Malabar copies these words were wanting); and the substitution of the words *consubstantial with the Father* for *the Son of the Essence of the Father*, which was the Malabar reading:

The direction to elevate the Host at the time of consecration:

And particularly, the transposition of the Invocation of the Holy Ghost from its former position *after* the words of consecration, so as to *precede* those words: and the alteration of its terms, so as to make it refer solely to a fruitful reception of the Eucharist[f].

These and other corrections were made in accord-

[f] This was done, as the Roman censors confess, in order to prevent the idea that the words of Christ uttered by the priest are not sufficient by themselves to effect the consecration.

ance with the first three decrees of the fifth session of the Synod.

One thing yet remained to be done, and that a matter of no little importance. It has already been mentioned that certain books and writings which were found among the Christians were declared heretical. These were twenty-one in number; and two of them, at least, viz., that *De Synodis*, and the *Liber Homiliarum*, appear from the description to have contained more or less historical matter; another, corresponding to the *Flos Sanctorum* of the Roman Church, must have contained much from which information might have been gleaned; but most of the books were probably of a dangerous tendency, and more or less directly heretical. The last mentioned in the catalogue, called *Parisman*, is described as a book of instruction in charms and magic, and full of blasphemy.

All copies of these books, wherever they might be found, were now to be delivered to the Portuguese, in order that such as would bear it might be expurgated[g], and the rest destroyed. Menezes himself committed many of them to the flames in the course of the visitation which he again made after the synod had been

[g] The use of this expression, if it were employed with a *bonâ fide* intent, and not merely in order to coax the people to deliver up their books, renders it just within the bounds of hope that some of the better class of these books may have been preserved. Yet the hope of our being able to recover any of them after so many years have passed is very small. Mr. Day made every enquiry in his power as to the existence of any of the books or records which must have passed into the hands of the Dutch, when they took Cochin and Cranganore from the Portuguese, but unfortunately without success.

held; and Francis Roz, of the Jesuit College at Vaipicotta, was charged with the task of completing this important business.

Archbishop Menezes at length returned to Goa, which he reached on Nov. 19, 1599, having witnessed the complete accomplishment of the object with which he had left it little more than ten months before, and in which the utmost efforts of the Portuguese had hitherto been unsuccessful.

It is impossible not to feel some astonishment at the success with which Menezes was able to carry out these sweeping measures of reform. The extraordinary qualities with which he was endowed are hardly sufficient to account for it, when we consider the bitter hostility with which he and his party were regarded. But the great power of the Portuguese, and the fear of their armed interference, ought to be taken into account in their influence upon the native princes, and through them upon the Christians of the country; and if it be true that the Rajah of Cochin had been bribed to support De Menezes with an army of fifty thousand Nairs, in case their assistance should be required[h], we shall have less difficulty in understanding the secret of his success. Yet the result was no doubt mainly attributable to the personal efforts and determined character of this remarkable man; and however indignant we may feel as we peruse the history of his proceedings, we can scarcely fail to be convinced that he was actuated by the most earnest zeal for the spiritual

[h] See Captain Swanston's Paper, and Mr. Day's Land of the Permauls, p. 225.

welfare of the Malabar Church; nor can we withhold our admiration of the skill, courage, and perseverance of the man who, against such difficulties, and almost single-handed, bowed a whole people to his will. O that the reformation he effected had been in accordance with the purity of the ancient faith!

CHAPTER III.

The Metropolitan See removed to Cranganore.—The meeting at Alanghat.—Ahatalla.—Dissension among the Syrians after their Secession, and the result.—A Native Episcopate re-introduced into Malabar.—Transition to Jacobitism.—Subsequent condition of the Church.—Drs. Kerr and Buchanan.—The Syriac Bible printed.—The C. M. S. College established at Cottayam.—Breach between the Syrians and the C. M. S.—Proposals for a renewed effort to promote the Restoration of the Church.

THE Synod of Diamper was followed by other proceedings all of which were calculated to render the subjection of the Malabar Church as complete as possible. The episcopal see was removed from Angamalé, its ancient seat, to Cranganore on the sea-coast, which was more easily accessible by the Portuguese. The dignity of the office itself was lowered, by the loss of the title of Metropolitan, which had been attached to it from time immemorial; and by being made subject to the archbishopric of Goa; and the first four bishops who were appointed to the newly-erected see were either Spaniards or Portuguese, the first of them being Francis Roz, of the Society of Jesus, who had already taken so prominent a part in the subjugation of the Church.

But the attachment of the people to their ancient faith and customs was not subdued; and no sooner had the power of the Portuguese begun to decline, than they entertained the design of throwing off the detested yoke to which they had been compelled to submit.

Accordingly they watched with increasing interest the course which events around them now began to take, being determined to seize the first opportunity for the accomplishment of their design. Such an opportunity at length appeared to present itself; and in the year 1653, fifty-four years after the Synod of Diamper had been held, a number of their leading men assembled in the church of Alanghat, and there solemnly bound themselves by oath, sworn upon a copy of the Holy Gospels, to renounce obedience to the Archbishop of Cranganore. They then elected one Thomas, of the archidiaconal family of Palakomatta, (for the Archdeacons were always taken from this family,) to be their chief, twelve leading catanars taking part in the ceremony of his appointment.

The next thing to be done was to obtain a Metropolitan from one of the Eastern Patriarchs, but the watchful jealousy of the Portuguese rendering communication with Babylon impracticable, the Syrians applied to the Coptic Patriarch at Grand Cairo, who sent to them a Syrian Bishop named Ahatalla[a] to take charge of their Church. Ahatalla (who seems to have been a Nestorian) went first to Mousul for confirmation by the Patriarch, and from thence, in the disguise of a mendicant, made his way to Surat, and thence again, as a pilgrim, to the shrine of St. Thomas at Mailapoor.

Here he was seized, and embarked in fetters for Cochin, but not until he had found means to communicate with his flock, approving of the appointment of

[a] Captain Swanston and Mr. Day call him Attila. In the Syrian MSS. he is called Mar Ignatius.

Thomas, and directing that four assessors should be nominated to act with him, but enjoining him on no account to consecrate the holy oil, or to presume to confer orders.

The tidings of Ahatalla's capture, after he had escaped so many dangers, and had arrived within a comparatively short distance of his adopted country, was a sad blow to the Christians over whom he was appointed to preside. They determined, however, to make an effort for his liberation, and anxiously watched for the arrival of the vessel at Cochin. It was at that time, as indeed it is still for the country vessels, a tedious and somewhat perilous voyage from the Coromandel coast to that of Malabar; for the monsoon which produces fair weather on one coast occasions violent storms on the other, and the distance round by Ceylon cannot be much under a thousand miles; so that weeks, and often months, are required for its accomplishment. At length, however, it became known that the vessel was in the roadstead, and the Christians, having assembled to the number of two thousand five hundred men, marched to Cochin, and demanded their Metropolitan's release. The Cochinese manned their walls, and prepared for an assault; but feeling themselves too weak to resist by open force, they embarked their unhappy victim on board a galliot—for he had been brought on shore—and setting sail in the dead of night, either drowned him at sea, or, according to Raulin, conveyed him to Goa, where he was condemned to the flames, and having been delivered over to the secular arm, suffered the execution of that terrible sentence, as a warning to any others who might venture to promote the liberation of this unhappy Church.

It now became an object of the utmost anxiety to the Roman party to reduce these rebellious Churches to submission; but as it appeared improbable that they would listen to any proposal from the Portuguese, whose conduct had rendered them objects of extreme suspicion and abhorrence, and whose power was already shewing symptoms of decay, it was thought a wiser course to entrust the execution of this important and difficult matter to one who had hitherto been unconnected with the country. A Carmelite Friar, Jose de Sancta Maria by name, was accordingly despatched to India, as the legate of Pope Alexander VII., and it was hoped that by the union of firmness and moderation he would ultimately succeed in accomplishing the object of his mission. He was instructed to avoid, as far as possible, everything that would unnecessarily irritate the native Christians; not to interfere with their customs and ritual, (except where interference might be essential to the preservation of the faith in its integrity); but to make it his especial object to regain the allegiance of the Church in Malayala to the see of Rome.

The efforts of Fr. Jose were, however, ineffectual, so long as the Christians of St. Thomas remained at unity among themselves; but after an interval of two years, a grave dissension arose between some of the leading members of the native community, and the dispute at length ran so high as to result in the disaffection of two out of the four assessors who had been appointed to act with Thomas of Palakomatta, and who now separated from their colleagues, and tendered their submission to the Apostolic delegate.

The dominion of the Portuguese was meanwhile rapidly declining before the advancing power of the Dutch. Quilon had fallen to their arms in A.D. 1661; and in the following year they laid siege to Cranganore, the see of the Jesuit Archbishop, and the stronghold of the ecclesiastical authority of the Portuguese on this part of the coast. This fortress, the remains of which are yet to be seen, though they only add to the general appearance of its desolation [b], surrendered towards the close of the same year; and its fall was succeeded in 1663 by that of Cochin, which put an end to the power of the Portuguese on this coast.

One of the first acts of the Dutch, on becoming masters of the Portuguese settlements, was to insist on the departure of the Jesuits from Malabar; a proceeding which could not fail to influence the Christians of St. Thomas, though it unhappily occurred too late to prevent the disaffection which has been already mentioned.

Alexander of Palakomatta, one of the renegade assessors, was now rewarded by the archbishopric of Cranganore, (which the Jesuit Garcia was unable to hold any longer,) and was supported by the adhesion of forty-five of the Syrian Churches, whom he persuaded to return with him to the obedience of Rome.

[b] These ruins are frequently passed by travellers on the Backwater. I saw them in 1860, and again in 1861; and was much struck by the picturesque appearance of a small ruined bomb-proof tower which stands close to the water, in bold relief against the western sky.

He retained this position till his death, which occurred in 1676, when he was succeeded by a Portuguese, one Don Diego, as Archbishop of Cranganore.

Don Diego, being unable to take immediate possession of his see, appointed Archdeacon Matthew his commissary, a choice which was disapproved by a large number of the people, who thereupon proffered their allegiance to the Carmelite Friars of Verapoly, thus forming a new party in this miserably divided Church.

We must now return to the remaining body of the Syrian congregations who, under Archdeacon Thomas, were struggling to maintain and to consolidate their newly acquired liberty. They were exposed to enemies on all sides; for the Romanists, considering their secession as an act both of apostacy and of rebellion, regarded them with unrelenting animosity; and the native princes, it is said, were in too many instances disposed rather to take advantage of their defenceless condition, than to protect them in the undisturbed possession of their rights. Mar Thomas however defended his Church with courage and success, and every effort was made to procure the re-establishment of a native episcopate, so that ordinations might be continued, and the Church be governed in accordance with Apostolic rule, and with their own ancient custom.

The unwearied exertions of the people were at length rewarded by the arrival in Malayala of Gregorius, Bishop of Jerusalem, about the year 1665, or perhaps a little earlier. In that year, according to Captain Swanston, he consecrated Archdeacon Thomas to be their Metropolitan, and continued to render the assistance of his counsel in the government of the Church, until his death, which occurred shortly afterwards.

The arrival of Gregorius introduces us to a period in the history of the Church in Malabar not more remarkable for the restoration of the episcopate to the remnant of the native Church, than for its adoption of the Jacobite liturgies and ritual in place of those of the Nestorians which had been in use previously to the Synod of Diamper.

This transition meets with but little notice in the history of the period, beyond the bare mention of the fact that it was brought about by the influence of Gregorius. There is, however, no indication that it was occasioned by a recoil from repugnance to the distinctive tenets of Nestorianism, pushed to their legitimate conclusion; or, again, that it was violently forced upon an unwilling Church. On the contrary, it appears to have been admitted with little or no opposition by a people among whom the profession of Jacobitism or Nestorianism was but a secondary consideration; their main desire being to secure the independence of their Church from the foreign and overbearing dominion of Rome. Thus they were prepared to accept the boon they longed for at the hands of either the Nestorian or the Jacobite Patriarch, and the opportunity which now presented itself appears to have decided their choice. Yet the very readiness with which they were willing to pass from the tenets of Nestorius to those maintained by the Jacobite doctors—from pole to pole as it were of the theological compass—is itself remarkable, and affords matter for grave reflection. It appears doubtful indeed whether the distinctive tenets of the Nestorians had ever taken any very strong hold in the Church in Malabar; and the present remarkable instance shews how feebly they maintained that hold in the hearts and affections of a people who were resolved to be free.

From the year 1663 the Christians of St. Thomas have been a divided people. About half of their Churches, following the renegade Alexander, have since that period continued to recognise the supremacy of Rome, acknowledging, some the Archbishop of Cranganore, others the Carmelite Bishop of Verapoly, others the Vicar-Apostolic of Quilon, as their local head; but all designated by us under a common term, as *Romo-Syrians.* The remaining body, i. e. that which succeeded in throwing off the yoke of Rome, were branded as *Schismatics, Jacobites,* or *New Christians,* but are by us commonly known simply as *Syrians,* in contradistinction to the *Romo-Syrians* before mentioned.

The history of the Syrians, subsequently to the time of Gregorius, consists of little more than a record of the emulation and efforts of rival competitors for the metropolitan throne, which from time to time disturbed the peace of the Church, and must have exercised a most baneful influence on the spiritual welfare of its members, or, at least, of such of them as were drawn into the vortex of the contending factions. An account of these dissensions would be of little interest to the general reader, unless it could be given with a minuteness of detail which the materials before us are insufficient to supply; nor, perhaps, could its perusal result in any practical benefit, except as affording examples of the depravity of human nature, and drawing out feelings of deep commiseration for the low estate to which this ancient Church had fallen. It may be proper, however, to give a brief *résumé* of the leading events which mark this unhappy period.

Mar Thomas, whose consecration by Gregorius, Bishop of Jerusalem, has been already mentioned, was succeeded, in 1678, by Mar Andrew, and on his death, in 1685, two foreign prelates, Mar Basilius and Mar Gabriel, came to reside in the country, and had a church assigned to them for their residence. They did not, however, interfere in the government of the Church, which rested with Thomas, the native Metropolitan, who had been consecrated to succeed Mar Andrew.

But on the death of Basilius, Mar Gabriel raised a faction, and endeavoured to depose Thomas, consecrating a priest of the Palakomatta family to be Metropolitan in his room. Mar Thomas, however, outlived his adversaries, and placed the mitre on the head of his own nephew, whom he appointed to succeed him. His authority, however, was rejected by a considerable party in the Church, and the dissension was only appeased by the interference of the Rajah of Cochin, and by an appeal to Antioch, which, it is said, was made through the medium of the governor of the Dutch colony on the coast.

In the year 1750 Mar Basilius, Maphriana, Mar Gregorius, Metropolitan, and Mar Johannes (Evanius) were conducted with much honour into Travancore. The Maphrian, who it will be recollected was the suffragan of the Patriarch of Antioch, brought with him crozier, ring, and crucifix, with the intention of consecrating one Thomas to be Metropolitan ; but a quarrel arose between them, and a new faction was the result ; the Maphrian preferring one Cyril, whose character for scholarship and piety is highly spoken of, to the metropolitan chair, in the place of Thomas, who died in 1757. He had, however, appointed his nephew Thomas to succeed him in the government of the Church ; and as this man was not disposed to waive his claim in favour of Cyril, the factions continued to rage with unabated violence. At length, after nineteen years of turmoil and confusion, the dissension was put an end to by the interference of the Rajah of Travancore, whose power now extended over a great part of the Malabar coast. His award was given in favour of the native Metropolitan, and the opposing faction was punished by a fine of 72,000 chuckrums, or about £253 of our money [c].

The restoration of order was followed by the consecration of Mar Thomas, or at any rate by his public recognition as Metropolitan of the Church—for it is probable

[c] The chuckrum is the ordinary coin of Travancore. It is about the size of a small shirt button, and is said to be made by letting drops of molten silver fall into water. The drops are then flattened under a die. The value of a chuckrum is $\frac{12}{14\cdot25}$ of a penny ; and each of these small coins is equivalent to 12 copper pie—so minute is the division of money in Travancore. Chuckrums are counted with ease and rapidity by means of a board, in which several rows of small holes are sunk just the depth of the coin ; and a heap of chuckrums is readily shaken over its surface, until each coin occupies a separate hole, and the rows are quite filled up. Some of these boards contain a hundred such holes ; others two, four, or five hundred, or a thousand of them.

that the validity of his previous consecration was admitted—under the name of Mar Dionysius. He was adorned with the crozier, crucifix, and ring, which had been brought by the Maphrian for the decoration of his uncle; and was invested with the full powers which in ancient times had been attached to the office to which he was raised. The Maphrian had died in 1765, apparently some years before this event took place; and the two remaining bishops, Gregorius and Johannes, retired to a church which had been assigned to them as a residence, where they were maintained by an allowance daily supplied to them from the revenues of the diocese.

In the year 1772 a fresh dispute arose, originating, it is said, in some question respecting the maintenance of the foreign prelates; and Gregorius, finding himself left without support, retired to Cochin, where he conferred the full metropolitan dignity upon Cyril, whom he had consecrated in 1757. This appointment was recognised by the Dutch authorities at Cochin, as well as by the Rajah of that state; but Cyril was unable to assert his claim beyond the Rajah's dominions, and being shortly afterwards betrayed into the hands of his rival, he was placed in confinement and compelled to give up the insignia of his office. At length, however, he contrived to effect his escape, and took refuge at a place called Agugnúr, where he built a church, and lived in strict seclusion, without attempting to re-assert his authority. He died in the year 1811, having previously consecrated his successor under the name of Mar Philoxenus.

Cyril's retirement was followed by the death of the two foreign prelates, and Mar Dionysius now ruled in peace. He lived to a great age, and his firm and gentle government afforded the Church a breathing time from the violence of party strife, by which it had been so grievously wasted during the early part of his career. He exercised his power with moderation and justice, and exerted himself to promote the revival of practical religion among his people, recommending it by the influence of his own pious example no less than by precept and exhortation.

It had been the ancient custom of the Church, as we have seen, to obtain their Metropolitan from the Patriarch of Babylon, Antioch, or Mousul, as the case might be; but in the sad confusion of later years this custom had been set aside, and the Metropolitan himself consecrated his successor, by virtue of his own episcopal authority. Moreover, the Metropolitans were always selected from that family in which the office of the archidiaconate, and afterwards of the primacy, had been hereditary from the earliest times; but as this family had gone over to the Roman Church with Alexander of Palakomatta, it was customary (says Captain Swanston) "to get a youth from that family, and place him with the Metropolitan for the time being, to instruct him, and eventually to consecrate him:"—a remarkable arrangement certainly, considering that the Syrians were regarded as schismatics by the Roman party, and therefore cut off from the body of the Church which alone possesses the covenant of salvation.

The successor nominated on the present occasion was

one Thomas, of the family of Korrovolanghat; and as Dionysius was now getting into years, he was consecrated in 1797.

The venerable Metropolitan, however, continued to live for many years, and in 1806 received a visit from Dr. Claudius Buchanan, who has left a most interesting memoir of his interview in his "Christian Researches in Asia." It took place on the 23rd of November, at Candenad, where the Metropolitan then resided, in the presence of several of the leading catanars, who had been invited to meet the Scottish malpan. Dr. Buchanan seems to have been much impressed by the personal appearance of the Metropolitan, strongly suggestive, as it might well be thought, of the appearance of an Eastern bishop in the early days of the Church's history. "He was dressed," he says, "in a vestment of dark red silk; a golden cross hung from his neck, and his venerable beard reached below his girdle. Such, thought I, was the appearance of Chrysostom in the fourth century." "I found him," he adds, "to be far superior in general learning to any of his clergy whom I had seen. . . . He descanted with great satisfaction on the hope of seeing printed Syriac Bibles from England, and said they would be a treasure to his Church."

On the following day the Doctor had some conversation with the catanars and malpans on the important subject of "union" with the Church of England. The term, as employed by Dr. Buchanan, appears to signify much the same thing as intercommunion, a mutual and friendly recognition of one another on the part of the two Churches, without any idea of advancing a claim on the part of either of them to authoritative interference in the affairs of the other; each being acknowledged to be an independent branch of the one universal Church. Could a union be established on such principles—they are not indeed expressly mentioned in his work, but are evidently consistent with the language he employs—he conceived that it might tend much to the advancement of pure religion.

The catanars, however, appear to have entertained some doubt as to the possibility of such a union, on account of their uncertainty as to the validity of English orders. "They acknowledged that there might be salvation in every Church where the name of Christ was named; but as to *union*, it was to be considered that they had been a pure Church from the earliest ages: that, if there were such a thing as Apostolic succession, it was probable they possessed it, ... and they expected that in any official negotiation on the subject, the antiquity and purity of Syrian ordination should be expressly admitted [d]."

This conversation was reported to the Bishop, and in a subsequent interview between them, he asked the Doctor what would be the advantages of a union? "One would be," he replied, "that missionaries ordained by the Church of England might . . . . preach in the churches of the Syrians, ... and aid them in the promulgation of pure religion, against the preponderating . . . influence of the Romish Church. The Bishop said, 'I would sacrifice much for such a union: only let me not be called upon to compromise anything

[d] Christian Researches, pp. 131, 132.

of the dignity and purity of our Church.'" He confessed, however, "that some customs had been introduced during their decline in the latter centuries, which had no necessary connection with the constitution of the Church, and might be removed without inconvenience[e]."

The visit of Dr. Buchanan was the second which the Syrians had received from an English clergyman in the course of the year 1806; for, a few months before his arrival in Malabar, the Government of Madras had sent Dr. Kerr, then senior chaplain of that Presidency, with instructions to examine into the condition of the several Christian communities on the western coast. Some extracts from Dr. Kerr's official Report are given in Dr. Buchanan's "Christian Researches," and although they do not add much to our knowledge of the history of the native Church, they are valuable as affording evidence of the interest with which it was beginning to be regarded, and as shewing that the idea of a union with the Church of England was already entertained, and had even been submitted to the consideration of the Metropolitan.

Dr. Kerr's testimony as to the moral character of the Christians of St. Thomas at this period is of the most favourable kind; and since from his position as senior chaplain of the Presidency, one would infer that he must have resided at least some years in India, long enough at any rate to be able to form an estimate of the general character of its inhabitants, his report should be allowed to have its due weight. "The character of

[e] Christian Researches, pp. 132, 133.

these people," he writes, speaking of the Syrians, "is marked by striking superiority over the heathens in every *moral excellence*, and they are remarkable for their veracity and plain dealing. They are extremely attentive to their religious duties, and abide by the decision of their priests and Metropolitan in all cases, whether in spiritual or temporal affairs." He then mentions the high respect in which they are held by the nairs, or nobles of the country, and closes his report with some observations on the prospects of Christianity in this part of India.

Dr. Buchanan's sympathy was largely drawn out in behalf of this interesting people, and his labours in promoting the restoration of their Church were continued with unwearied zeal and ardour until his death. He had observed the want of complete and accurate copies of the Scriptures in the churches which he visited, and endeavoured to ascertain the feeling of some of the leading catanars in regard to a proposal which he made to send them printed copies of the Syriac New Testament from England. "They would be worth their weight in silver," was the reply; and the Doctor promised to see what could be done; adding that if a translation into the vernacular could be prepared, he would be able to get it printed, so that a complete copy might be procured at a very trifling expense. "That would indeed give joy," said the old catanar, and there was a murmur of satisfaction among the people.

Dr. Buchanan remained among the Syrians until the commencement of the year 1807, and was fortunate enough to obtain several MSS.[f], including one of the

[f] Bagster's Bible of Every Land, p. 44.

Old and New Testaments in Syriac, which appears to be of very great value. It had been deposited in one of the remotest of the mountain churches, and was presented to him by the Metropolitan. The remark with which this precious gift was accompanied shews how greatly the volume had been esteemed, and how carefully it must have been preserved from generation to generation. "It will be safer perhaps with you," said the Bishop, "than with us: yet we have kept it, as some think, for near a thousand years." To present a foreigner with such a MS. was indeed a mark of confidence and esteem; and we may imagine the sensation of extreme delight with which he handled and bore off the precious tome.

Laden with these treasures the worthy Doctor returned to England in 1808, and devoted his energies to the promotion of the cause in which he was so deeply interested. Yet there appears to have been considerable delay—however it may have been occasioned—in the appearance of a printed edition of the Syriac New Testament; and it was not until the year 1815, within a short period of his death, that the first sheets were issued from the press. These contained the four Gospels and the Acts of the Apostles, which were printed at Broxbourne under the eye of Dr. Buchanan. At his death the British and Foreign Bible Society, for whom the work had been originally undertaken, appointed Dr. Lee, of Queens' College, Cambridge, to complete the New Testament; and the whole of it left the press in the following year. The Old Testament was printed in 1823, under the care of the same distinguished Orientalist; and in 1826 a complete edition of the Syriac Scriptures was published by the Bible Society, especially for the use of the Syrians in Malabar. Copies of this Bible may be had at the College at Cottayam for the small sum of two rupees, but there is now very little demand for them[g].

This excellent work, though it was probably the most satisfactory in its ultimate results, was not the only fruit of Dr. Buchanan's labours. The earnestness with which he advocated the cause of the Syrian Church, and the description he had given of its "Scriptural liturgy," and of the simple manners of the people, induced the Church Missionary Society to take measures for the establishment of a mission in Travancore, with the object of promoting the education of the people, and especially of the clergy, and the general restoration of the Church in accordance with the purity of evangelical truth.

But in the meantime dissension had again sprung up and had borne its bitter fruit in this unhappy Church; and the Society consequently found much difficulty in carrying out their designs. The dissension originated, as before, in a dispute connected with the succession to the primacy. Mar Dionysius, as we have

[g] This is easily accountable for under the unfortunate relations which at present exist between the Church Missionary Society and the Syrians. I met with a torn copy of one of these Bibles at the ruined church in Quilon, and saw the New Testament at other churches. Notwithstanding the great value of *printed* copies of the Holy Scriptures, it is impossible not to see that the continual production of MS. copies among such a people could not but be attended with beneficial results in promoting the careful perusal of the inspired volume.

seen, had consecrated Mar Thomas in 1797 as his coadjutor, *cum spe successionis:* and he in his turn nominated a nephew to succeed him in the government of the Church. This appointment was unsatisfactory to a certain faction, who lost no opportunity of traducing the poor nominee—although he is said to have been a man of simple inoffensive habits—and at length succeeded in obtaining his rejection. But year by year rolled on, and no other successor having been appointed, the friends of Mar Thomas (for such was his name) brought him to the bedside of the dying Metropolitan, and causing him to kneel down, persuaded the old man to perform as far as possible the office of consecration.

Mar Thomas accordingly assumed charge of the Church; but the irregularity of his ordination only added to the objections that were entertained against him; and the dissatisfied party appealed to the British authority, making application at the same time to the Patriarch of Antioch for a legitimate successor. The discord was happily not of long duration, for Mar Thomas died soon afterwards, and was succeeded by the Remban Joseph, a man of eminent piety and conciliatory demeanour, who was fortunately able to unite the interests of both parties, and to restore concord to the Church.

Mar Joseph had already been eminently successful in gaining the concurrence of his countrymen in the friendly proposals of the Church Missionary Society and the British Resident in Travancore; and at length there seemed to be a prospect of their being able to carry out the accomplishment of their design. The scheme which they entertained included as its especial nucleus the establishment of a Syrian College, in which those who were intended for holy orders, and the young deacons of the Church, might receive a sound education, in the hope that the light of pure evangelical truth might thus be diffused throughout the diocese.

An appropriate site was obtained at Cottayam, a village some thirty miles south-east of Cochin, and the necessary buildings were erected; the Ranee nobly assisting the enterprise by a grant of twenty thousand rupees, a considerable amount of land, and a hundred slaves to till it. The instruction of the boys was provided for by a considerable staff, comprising two English missionaries, two malpans (Syrian doctors), a Professor of Hebrew, himself a Jew, and two native teachers of Sanscrit; while the Metropolitan resided at the College as its head. I have not been able to ascertain the exact date of the establishment of this College; but it is clear from the Madras Church Missionary Record, that the first missionary of that Society reached Travancore in 1816[h]; and from the heading of the fourth and fifth chapters of Captain Swanston's Memoir it would appear that the arrangements had been completed the year before.

It will be remembered that Cyril, upon whom the title of Metropolitan had been conferred by Mar Gregorius in 1772, had retired to Agugnúr, after his escape from confinement; and that in or about the year 1805 he had consecrated another priest to succeed him, by the name

[h] See the Madras Church Missionary Record, November, 1837.

of Philoxenus. He again, in 1812, consecrated his successor, who also bore the same name, and lived quietly in the retirement of Agugnúr, as his predecessors had done.

At the death of Mar Joseph, however, with whom it is admitted that the direct line of Metropolitans had become extinct,—and it is not clear how he himself had been consecrated,—Mar Philoxenus was called from his retreat to rule over the Church in fact as well as in name. He was a man of the most abstemious habits, and is described by Captain Swanston as "pre-eminent for a simple dependence upon God, for an unaffected simplicity of manners, and for a most intimate knowledge of the character of his countrymen."

The elevation of Philoxenus gave rise to a fresh disturbance. No sooner had he exchanged the privacy of Agugnúr for the residence of the Metropolitan than he found himself opposed by a strong faction, the leaders of which had originally endeavoured to prevent his consecration to the episcopate, and now strove to throw doubt upon its validity. In order, therefore, to settle this untoward controversy, it was thought good that a synod should be held, in which the question might be openly and fairly examined. The catanars were accordingly summoned to meet at Balghatty, near Cochin, and there the matter was tried in the presence of the British Resident, the Dewan of Travancore, and the whole of the clergy of the diocese. The validity of the consecration was supported by the Rambans Philippus and Joseph, and opposed by the Malpan Konatta; but it was shewn that, although, as in the case of his predecessors, there had been no Metrans (Prelates) to *assist* in the consecration, as the holy Canons require[1], Mar Philoxenus had been really and sufficiently consecrated in the presence of the catanars and congregation of the Church of Chatakulum and its appendant Churches of Paraqui and Konankalakare.

As these facts were incontestably proved, the Synod admitted the legality of his consecration; and order being thus restored, Philoxenus appointed one George to be his colleague, and having consecrated him (under the name of Mar Dionysius), committed the charge of the diocese into his hands, feeling himself too infirm to discharge efficiently the onerous duties of his office. Having thus provided for the government of the diocese, Philoxenus retired to Agugnúr, where he had been educated, ordained, and consecrated; and where he purposed to pass the remainder of his days in seclusion and prayer. But he was shortly afterwards summoned from his retreat to perform the last offices over the grave of his coadjutor, whom it pleased God to take to his rest not long after his consecration.

The selection of a successor to fill the place of the deceased coadjutor now occupied the attention of the Church, and it was determined that the decision should be made by lot, after the manner in which it is recorded that Matthias was chosen to the apostleship. An assembly was held of the presbyters and chief laity of the diocese, and three catanars were put in nomination—two of them, Philip of Chapaud and Abraham of Ma-

[1] "The Patriarch shall then consecrate him: there shall be two other Metrans with him, that the words of our Lord may be fulfilled, which He spake to His disciples, 'When two of you shall agree,' &c."—*Canons*, ch. vii. ii. § 1.

malacheri, being eminent malpans (doctors), and the third, Joseph of Kallupar, having been recommended by the deceased Metran. Two papers were then put in for each candidate, one of them bearing the words, "If it be the will of God that Malpan —— be raised to the office of Metropolitan let this paper come up;" and the other, "If it be not the will of God that Malpan —— be raised to the office of Metropolitan, let this paper come up;" the name of each candidate being properly inserted in his respective papers. These papers were then folded up and placed upon the altar, and Mar Philoxenus having implored the Divine guidance and determination, a young deacon was sent to draw one of them. It was found to be that containing Malpan Abraham's name, but rejecting him. The other paper containing his name was then looked for, and removed; and further prayer having been made, another paper was withdrawn as before, which on examination turned out to be that in favour of Philippus. He was therefore consecrated under the same designation as his predecessor, and assumed the direction of the diocese, Mar Philoxenus retiring to Agugnúr as before.

The College at Cottayam was now in fair working order, and appears to have been regarded with general satisfaction, "the missionaries conducting themselves with great prudence, and being respected and beloved by the people[k]." In 1817 the Society found itself able to extend the field of its operations, by establishing a branch mission at Allepy, a large and important town on the sea-coast, inhabited by a vast number of

[k] Capt. Swanston's Memoir. Date A.D. 1826.

people of different races and religions, and so affording ample room for mission work among the heathen, as well as among the Syrians and Romanists of the place.

But the diocese was not long permitted to enjoy the blessing of peace and order; for the party which had opposed Philoxenus at first, though silenced in the country, yet appears to have made its influence felt abroad; and (grievous as it was) to have received the support of certain foreigners, whose strictures, originally published in Europe, seem to have found their way into Syria about the year 1825. These "publications,"—for so Bp. Heber termed them, observing, by the way, that they were "said to be marked with scandalous exaggerations[1],"—at length attracted the notice of the Patriarch of Antioch, who thereupon sent two Syrian monks, named Athanasius and Abraham, with the titles of "Metropolitan" and "Ramban" (or Archdeacon), to assume charge of the Church in Malayala.

These ecclesiastics reached Bombay on the way to their destination while Bishop Heber was there, and caused him some anxiety as to the effect which their arrival might produce upon the Church: but as they had "regular appointments from the Patriarch, 'sitting in the seat of Simon Cephas, which is at Antioch,'" and as it had always been his endeavour to conciliate and befriend such Eastern Christians as found their way into India, he shewed them all the respect and kindness in his power, furnishing Athanasius with a small viaticum for the rest of his journey, and with letters of recommendation to the English missionaries

[1] Heber's Journal, iii. 447.

at Allepy and Cottayam, advertising them at the same time, by a post letter, of the visitor they had to expect.

While Athanasius and his Archdeacon were at Bombay, they attended church, unasked, and received the Sacrament at Bishop Heber's hands: "On which occasion," he writes, "I placed the Metropolitan in my own chair, and we embraced in a most brotherly manner at the church door after service." This interview afforded the Bishop an opportunity of exhorting Mar Athanasius to use all becoming moderation in the advancement of his claims, and of this he did not fail to avail himself. At the same time he earnestly enjoined the missionaries "to take no part, if they could possibly help it, in any disputes which might arise, and to recognise implicitly, with all due marks of respect and confidence, which ever patriarch the majority of the Malayalim Churches might receive[m]."

Athanasius reached the diocese in the month of November, 1825, and the worst apprehensions of Bishop Heber were but too well realized. So far from adopting such measures of conciliation as a spirit of Christian love would have dictated, he is said to have acted with the most unseemly violence; demanding the immediate deposition of the native Metropolitan and his coadjutor, forbidding the catanars to make mention of their names in the public liturgy of the Church under pain of his severe displeasure, and suspending all who continued to acknowledge their authority.

The native prelates, alarmed for the safety of their persons, took refuge in the College at Cottayam, where

[m] Journal, vol. iii. pp. 448, 449.

they presently received a summons from Mar Athanasius to appear before him in the neighbouring church without delay. This arrogant citation was rendered yet more offensive by being addressed to them as ordinary presbyters, so that they could hardly accept it without waiving their claim to the episcopal office, and with it to the rights and privileges belonging thereunto; but Athanasius would permit no hesitation, and on their refusal to appear, he fulminated a sentence of excommunication against them in the presence of the astonished congregation, who were not prepared for so terrible a display of the prelate's anger.

An attempt was then made to obtain the signatures of the principal men to a declaration acknowledging Athanasius and rejecting the native Metropolitan and his coadjutor, but it was resisted with indignation; and Athanasius, finding himself unable to prevail by threats or persuasion, left the church with his adherents, and causing the doors to be immediately closed, offered liberty to the unfortunate assembly within the building only on condition that they would submit to his demands. A compromise was eventually agreed upon, and a document drawn up and subscribed, in which Athanasius was acknowledged as having been deputed by the Patriarch of Antioch to assist the native metropolitans, and obedience promised accordingly.

But the proceedings of the Syrian Archbishop became more and more violent. He pronounced all ordinations void which had been held since the decease of Mar Dionysius in 1810; conferred fresh orders on those already possessing them, priests as well as deacons, threatening all recusants with excommunication; he annulled marriages, altered the interior of churches, and listened to no advice but that of his Archdeacon (who is said to have been his chief instigator to these proceedings) and of the disaffected Malpan Konatta, who had all along headed the opposition to Philoxenus.

The position of the English missionaries was no enviable one in the midst of all this turmoil and confusion. I have no means of ascertaining the course which they took under the difficult circumstances by which they found themselves surrounded; but their influence appears to have been used, as would be most natural, in favour of the native metropolitans; and they may perhaps have carried their interference rather too far. Complaints were made to Bishop Heber that, although extremely well-meaning and correct men, they had been somewhat prejudiced by their friendship for Philoxenus, by whom they had been treated with so much kindness, and to whose efforts they were much indebted for their success in the establishment of the mission. And however ready to make allowance for the difficulty of their position, he could not help feeling some apprehension that there might have been some ground for complaint, though as yet he had been unable to enquire into the matter, and could only judge from such rumours as he heard, and from the decided tone assumed by the President and the Ranee, who forbade Athanasius to exercise his functions, (although he was acknowledged, as the Bishop had been assured, by the great majority of the people,) and threatened to send him from the country.

A general desire appears to have been expressed by members of the Malayalim Church, that the English Bishop should come and settle the question ; and Bishop Heber had reached Trichinopoly on his way southwards, with this very object in view, when his career was suddenly terminated by death. The following letters, which I have ventured to extract from the third volume of his Journal, are of much interest in connection with the history of this remarkable struggle, and derive a peculiar charm from the quaint simplicity of the Eastern style in which they are composed; but the reader will not fail to notice, as a still more pleasing feature, the high tone of Christian courtesy and moderation by which the Bishop's letters are so strongly marked, and which might have exercised a very beneficial influence upon the affairs of the diocese, had they not unfortunately failed—at any rate in the case of Athanasius—to reach their destination.

1.

" *March* 22, 1826.

"To the honoured among Bishops, Mar Athanasius, Metropolitan of the Churches of India which follow the Syrian confession, my dear brother in the Lord Jesus, Reginald, by Divine permission, Bishop of Calcutta, wisheth health, peace, and increase of prosperity in this world and the world to come. Amen!

"This second letter I write unto thee, my brother beloved in the Lord, to let thee know that by God's mercy I have reached the country of Madras, whither thy letter, which arrived in Calcutta after my departure thence, hath been sent after me. I was comforted to learn thy safe arrival and good health among the Churches of thy people; yet I have much grief and heaviness of heart to hear that the enemy hath sown trouble between thee and our brethren Philoxenus and Dionysius, which in time past had guided and governed the Churches of Travancore in their desolation, when no tidings came from Antioch for many years, and the people of the Lord (but for them whom God raised up to feed His flock) had been scattered on the mountains as sheep having no shepherd. Let this, my brother, incline thine heart to shew them favour, and may the good Spirit of God move them to render thee all worthy honour and obedience, both for thine own sake, and His that sent thee!

"Furthermore, I have spoken concerning thy business to the most excellent Governor of the English nation which is in the city of Madras, who had heard divers things reported against thee; to whom I said, 'Athanasius is my brother, and while he sojourned in Bombay, appeared (? approved) himself in all things blameless, and of a truth he brought letters with him from the honoured father in Christ, the Patriarch of Antioch; perhaps the things are not true which are reported; why then should he be sent away from the land? And now, behold, I go southward, even to Trichinopoly and Quilon; it may be that I shall reconcile him to his brethren. I pray thee write thus much to the Queen of Travancore and the deputy that dwelleth in Quilon;' and the Governor has written as I desired. Wherefore my honoured brother, when I come into your borders, as, by the grace of God, I hope in forty days to come thither, my desire is to be allowed to be a maker of peace between you, not as having authority, for I am a stranger in your Church, neither desire to rule over any but my own people; not as having wisdom, for I would gladly learn of you in things pertaining to the truth, but as your brother in the Lord, and the servant of the Churches of Christ; and as desiring, like Mordecai, to speak peace to all the children of God, and to say unto you that strive together, as Moses said unto the Israelites, 'Sirs, ye are brethren, why do ye wrong one to another?' But my counsel is, that all the malpans and catanars of the Church, also thou thyself, and the brethren Philoxenus and Dionysius, should come together to meet me in one place, even at Cotym, and testify unto me concerning the customs of the Church, and all things belonging to the same. And that all men may speak their mind freely and without fear, I will bring with me learned men, who speak both Arabic and the language of the Malayalim, (but who are not of the number of the priests sent heretofore for the College of Cotym,) and I can hear both what is said, and what thou desirest to speak unto me in secret. And whereas there are some which say that Philoxenus is no bishop, and some which say that he was consecrated by laying on of hands and the Holy Ghost, even as thou wert, this thing may be enquired of at the mouth of many witnesses, and the will of the Church be made known whom they choose to obey. And in the mean time, my brother, forasmuch as it hath been said of thee, 'he is a violent man, and seeketh to change times and hours;' let me pray thee to be patient, if in the days of darkness and trouble anything have been done amiss, awaiting the time that thy power shall be strengthened, and the Lord shall cause all thy ways to prosper. But I speak as unto the wise. Thou knowest that the priests of the high places were not at once cut off from Israel; how much less those whom a bishop hath ordained, though in the absence and without leave from Antioch. Likewise, in the days of King David, Zadok and Abiathar were both high priests in the tabernacle, though the true priest, having Urim and Thummim, was Abiathar son of Abimelek only; and thus it may be that the anointing shall be on thy head, and the government shall be on thy shoulders, and yet the place of honour next to thee may be given to them that kept the flock before thy coming. (But of these things we may discourse together when there is opportunity.) And further, if any man have wronged thee, speak to me thereof without fear; am I not thy brother? Even if he be of my own people, as far as I have power, he shall not go without correction. Salute the Bishops Philoxenus and Dionysius in my name. I call them bishops, forasmuch as they have been so reported unto me by divers sure tokens, and I trust they may be found bishops indeed. Salute the Rabban Isaac, thy fellow traveller and mine, whom I met in Bombay. Salute the malpans and catanars. The priests, Thomas Robinson and John Doran, (concerning whom I wrote unto thee,) salute you. Verily John was sick at Madras, wherefore my letter was not hastened on. Nevertheless, he is now restored by God's blessing, and is with me on my journey.

"The Abuna Mar Simeon, the Armenian, who was with us at Bombay, and who has been now again with me at Madras, salutes you. Grace and peace be with you all, from God and our Lord Jesus!

"If thou hast anything to write, let thy letter be sent unto me, in the city of Palamcottah.

"Written in the land of Coromandel, nigh unto the city of Alambura."

(Signed) "REGINALD, Bishop."

2.

"*Sent March 27th,* 1826.

"To the honoured among bishops, Philoxenus, raised up of God to be a guide and shepherd to the Churches of India which hold the Syrian confession, Reginald, by Divine permission, Bishop of Calcutta, wisheth health, grace, and much prosperity from God and our Lord Jesus.

"I have heard from many witnesses, my brother beloved in the Lord, of the works which thou hast wrought, and thy deep tribulation, and thy labour of love which hath been shewn towards the Church of Christ among the Malayalims, at a time when no tidings came from the Church which is at Antioch, and there were many dangers and much sorrow without and within, on the right hand and on the left, from the idolatrous people and the false brethren. Likewise how thou hast made choice of a wise and holy man, even the brother Dionysius, to judge the people in thy room, and to teach them the pure and certain doctrine of the Lord, and that thou hast sealed him to the work by the laying on of hands, to the intent that the grace which was given thee might not perish, but that after thy decease, a witness of the truth might not be wanting in Israel, until the time that the Lord of the vineyard shall return to reckon with His servants.

"Which thing also was made known to the blessed father in God, Thomas Middleton, who, before my weakness came hither, was Bishop of Calcutta and the Churches of the English in India, who beheld also your order and the grace of God which was among you, and was glad, and spake thereof unto all the chief of our nation. Insomuch that in the land of Feringistan, which is Chittim, and Ashkenaz, and Gomer, the glory of the Lord was made known, not there only, but in Britain also, which is our own land; where the blessed Apostle Paul, after he had been in Spain, in times past preached the Gospel, even as the Apostle Thomas did with you, whose memory is at this day blessed among the Churches of India.

"For which cause also, the holy father in Christ, the Patriarch of Antioch, having heard of your love and the truth and patience of your brethren, sent our brother Athanasius to carry his letters to you, and to testify unto you all the things which were in his heart as a faithful bishop and evangelist; at whose coming, when I heard the same in Bombay, my heart greatly rejoiced, hoping that, by communication with him, yourself and your flock might be the more established in faith, and that love might increase more exceedingly with all knowledge. Whence then is it, my brethren, that there are wars and envyings among you? God is a God of peace, not of division; a God of order, not of disorder; and by all these things the name of God is blasphemed among the Gentiles, and the souls of many shall be turned into perilous heresies, such as are taught by the priests of the Bishop of Rome, which are in Cranganore and Verapoli, from whom in time past great sorrow hath arisen to this people. Let me entreat you then, my brethren, on Christ's behalf, that you be reconciled one to another, in honour preferring one another, and each desirous to take the lowest room, to the end that ye may reap an exceeding weight of glory hereafter. And forasmuch as the people are divided, and this man is of Philoxenus and that followeth after Athanasius, my counsel is that the multitude must needs come together, and that the priests of the order of Aaron and the holy Levites, which are the deacons, be called into one place, to declare openly, according to the knowledge given unto them, what hath been the custom of your fathers, and whom they will obey as their bishop and faithful shepherd. Like as it is written, 'If thou hast anything against thy brother, tell it unto the Church, and he that will not hear the Church, let him be unto thee as a heathen man and a publican.' At which time I also, if it seemeth good unto your discretion, will be present with you in Cotym, not as a ruler, for I am a stranger among you, nor as a judge, for who am I that I should judge any but mine own people? but as a brother in Christ, and a faithful witness of that which shall be determined, and who may plead the cause of your nation with the Queen of Travancore, and with the most excellent Governor whom the King of England hath set over his cities in India. And forasmuch as it is slanderously reported of thee that thou art no bishop indeed, let this thing be also enquired into at the mouth of two or three witnesses, and let not thy heart be troubled in that I have known our brother Athanasius in Bombay; for I have purposed, by God's grace, to know no man after the flesh, but to walk in these things according to the will of God and the tradition of the Churches, and to speak peace, if it may be so, to both of you, (are ye not both brothers?) and to acknowledge him, if difference must be made, whom your people shall freely choose to rule over them; and within forty days I trust to be strengthened to come unto you.

"Brethren, pray for me! Salute our brother, Bishop Dionysius, in my name; salute the brethren which are with you, the malpans, catanars, and deacons, with all others of the Church. Salute our brother Athanasius.

God grant that ye may be at unity with each other. The brethren which are with me, even Thomas Robinson (which was in time past known unto the Bishop Dionysius) and John Doran, salute you.

"Grace, mercy, and peace be with you, and in the Israel of God! Amen."

3.

"1826.

"The Presbyter, Thomas Robinson, Ramban to the blessed Mar Reginald, Bishop of the English Churches in India, sendeth greeting and reverence.

"I am not worthy to write unto thy Eminence, forasmuch as thy order in the Church of our Lord Jesus is the highest and mine the most humble, yet since God hath thought me worthy to serve His honoured and blessed servant, Mar Reginald, the Bishop of our Church in India, I pray thee to receive my words as the words of him who was my master and my brother. The rather is it my duty to write to thee, because there were many things which were in his heart to say unto thee, and he was meditating a letter of peace to thee at the very time when the great Master of all, the Chief Shepherd, called him to his eternal reward. With thy permission, therefore, I will relate to thy wisdom what things he had already done towards thy Churches in India, and what was farther in his mind to do. It is not unknown to thee, most reverend father, from the information of the reverend legate and Metropolitan of thy Churches in Malabar, Mar Athanasius, that he met our blessed father Mar Reginald at Bombay soon after Pentecost, in the last year, (1825,) and, as one bishop with another, partook of the holy mysteries with him at the altar of the English Church dedicated to St. Thomas in that city. Mar Reginald shewed great affection to Mar Athanasius in return for his love to him, and gave him letters to several persons of distinction among the English in this country, commending him to them as Metropolitan and supreme Bishop of the Syrian Churches in India. After that time he saw his face no more, but he always remembered the brotherly intercourse that was between them; and when he wrote an account of his diocese to the Most Reverend and excellent Mar Carolus, Archbishop of Canterbury and Metropolitan of all the Churches of the English nation, he made mention therein of Mar Athanasius, and his mission from your Eminence, and how, by his means, an end would be put to the irregularities that had heretofore prevailed in the Church of the Apostle Thomas at Malabar. Also, when an English priest, Johannes Doran by name, came to him at Calcutta, five months after, desiring to proceed to Malabar, our blessed father gave him a letter to Mar Athanasius requesting him to allow him permission to reside among his people, and to receive him as a son for his own sake. This letter I have now at length the satisfaction of sending to the care of your Eminency, and I will now relate from what cause, and in what manner, it was most unfortunately detained so long from the hands of Mar Athanasius, for our blessed father most earnestly desired it should be delivered without delay, since it would, in all probability, have prevented his departure from the country, and healed the disorders and schisms that now so wretchedly divide your Church in India.

"When the priest, Johannes Doran, had gone from Calcutta to Madras, on his way to the country of Malabar, he heard, for the first time, that there were dissensions between the Indian bishops and the Metropolitan from Antioch, and being a stranger, he was advised by some persons that he should avoid taking any part in such controversies, even such as might seem just to him. Therefore, and on account of his health, he remained at Madras for two months, till the end of the month of February in this year, when Mar Reginald arrived there on his visitation to the southern part of his diocese. It gave him great grief to find that Johannes had delayed his progress, although he had given him letters to Mar Athanasius, as the head of those Churches, in which also he had included another letter written by Abrahim Abuna, a legate from the Armenian Patriarch of Jerusalem to Mar Athanasius. As soon as he obtained these letters again from the hands of Johannes, on the 4th day of March, he sent them to Travancore, to be delivered into the Metropolitan's hands. He also sent answers to letters he had received from that land, in which he exhorted all who were subject to his authority to reverence the ancient canons and usages of the Syrian Church, and to know him as the rightful head and Metropolitan of the faithful Indians in Malabar, who had been received as such, agreeably to your Eminency's letter, in a general convocation of the Church summoned at Cotym on December 29th, 1825, by the Bishop Mar Philoxenus. He also expressly and earnestly desired all these his children, not to interpose the authority of the heathen government in Travancore, as defining anything in the affairs of the Church, but to suffer all things to continue as they were from the old time, even since the heathen princes gave the Syrian Churches of Malabar independent privileges, the people choosing their ecclesiastical governors according to the rites and usages which they held from the day of the blessed

Apostle St. Thomas to this time, the Government allowing their elections, and receiving those they elected, while they thus rendered to Cæsar the things which were Cæsar's, and to God the things which were God's.

"And forasmuch as it had been reported to Mar Reginald, that Mar Athanasius had acted violently in the Church, depriving those that had been formerly accounted bishops, and despising the authority of the rulers of the land, our blessed father was very careful to enquire into this matter, that he might represent it truly to all the deputies of the governors of the English in that land. In the meantime, the letter of Mar Athanasius to him, written one month before, which had been ignorantly sent to Calcutta, was given to him at Madras, and to this letter he sent an answer in the Syriac language on the 22nd of March, which also I now enclose to your Eminency, wherein he assured him of his unaltered friendship, exhorted him to mildness and forbearance till he should come, and, with his permission and good-will, mediate between him and those in Travancore who supported the Indian bishops; assuring him also that he would not leave unpunished those who behaved unjustly or unkindly to him in any way. And Mar Reginald acted even as he had wrote, and he obtained a promise from the excellent Governor of the English at Madras, that he would confirm whatever appointment he thought good respecting the peace of the Church in Malabar. And your Excellency will see, by his letters to both sides, that he intended that Mar Athanasius should be acknowledged as Metropolitan by all those who had power, and that the Indian bishops, when it should be seen they were truly such, should receive honour and maintenance as his suffragans. In this belief and intention he wrote also a letter of friendship and brotherly love to Mar Philoxenus, as one bishop to another, exhorting him to receive Athanasius, as sent by your Eminency, to rule them. I send a copy of that letter to your Eminency. I beg your Eminency's wise and careful attention to this account, and of the truth of it I myself am witness, for I wrote with my own hand the two letters to Mar Athanasius, and have been near to our blessed father as his Ramban and Secretary during all these transactions. Your wisdom will judge from this, with what grief and surprise Mar Reginald heard the events that took place at the same time at Travancore. These events there is no need that I relate, as your Eminency has heard them clearly from Mar Athanasius himself; but the thing which gives most grief to the hearts of all who love the memory and rejoiced in the plans of our late blessed father in Christ, is that his two letters to Mar Athanasius were not received.

"The first letter, which, as I have mentioned, was sent on the 4th of March, must have arrived at Travancore either on the same day Mar Athanasius was arrested by the Divan and banished the country, or at least the day after[n]; yet the letter was not sent after him to Cochin, where he remained many days. Nor was it told to Mar Reginald that his letter had not been delivered till many days after it had arrived at Travancore, and this news not coming to the Bishop till after Easter at Tanjore, no remedy was found for the evil, much less was the second letter delivered, which was written, as I have mentioned, twenty days

[n] The first letter is not given here; it may be seen in Bishop Heber's Journal.

later than the other. But as soon as Mar Reginald heard, as he did in the Passion-week, that the Metropolitan had been arrested by order of the heathen Government, he immediately wrote a letter to the British Deputy in Travancore, Colonel Newall, who was then living at some distance in the mountains of the north. In that letter he supplicated him to stop all these proceedings against Mar Athanasius, to wait for his coming before he listened to any accusation against the person bearing the commission of your Eminency, and recognized in that character, as he had no doubt he soon would be, by all of the faithful in Malabar. He reminded him, moreover, how infamous it would be to the English nation, if we should admit, in any degree, the accursed practices which we all condemn in the disciples of the corrupt Church of Rome, in their conduct towards the legates from Syria, who came to the ancient Churches which Divine Providence had now placed under our civil government and protection.

"Our blessed father Mar Reginald lived not long after the writing of that excellent letter. It was his mind to have followed it up by a letter to your Eminency, and by other acts calculated to ensure the peace of your Church at Malabar, when it pleased his heavenly Father to call him to Himself. The letter was, however, received by Colonel Newall, who immediately sent orders to the Divan of Travancore, to stay all further proceedings against Mar Athanasius, and to authorize his return to the country. That letter arriving after the death of Mar Reginald, was opened and read by me. But, alas! the news had already arrived from Travancore, that Mar Athanasius had already sailed from Cochin, and consequently that these orders of the Resident came too late. It would ill become me, most reverend father, to obtrude any counsel of mine upon your Eminency, in an affair where the peace of your Church is so nearly concerned. Suffer me, however, to give you what are not mine, but the ideas of my honoured father in the Lord, whose nearest wish after the prosperity of his own children, and the extension of the Gospel of the Lord by their means, was to preserve the integrity of the Church, subjected to your Eminency's rule in the land of Malabar. It appeared, then, to Mar Reginald, from very strict and accurate enquiries made into the truth of the circumstances, not only from those resident in Cotym, but from others also, that when the last prelates (on whom be the peace of God) came from Syria to Malabar, Mar Gregorius of Jerusalem, Mar Basilius Maphrian, and Mar Johannes, they encountered the like opposition from the ambition of the Indian Bishop, Mar Thoma, and his nephew, that Mar Athanasius has to encounter from the ignorance and prejudice of those opposed to him. Nevertheless, as disciples of Him who was lowly and meek in heart, and who by His own mouth and that of His holy Apostles has taught us not to render evil for evil, but to overcome evil with good; they, after more than eighteen years quarreling, procured the younger Indian bishop to be submissive to their will, and (Mar Basilius being dead) Mar Gregorius consecrated him, and honoured him with the title of Metropolitan by the name of Dionysius. All this is not unknown to your Eminency, but besides this it is also true that there was a young Indian priest, who, during all these troubles and contentions, remained faithful to the just cause of the Syrian prelates from Antioch. Him, therefore, during those troubles, Mar Basilius had consecrated bishop, by the name of Cyrillus. And it is said also, though with what truth I know not certainly, that when Mar Gregorius had given the title of Metropolitan to Dionysius, and when Mar Dionysius afterwards refused to give him the maintenance he agreed to give, then Mar Gregorius gave the same title of Metropolitan to the aforesaid Cyrillus. However this may be, as to his dignity of Metropolitan, or whatever right this may have conferred upon him, it is the confession of all in Malabar, of every party, that he was truly a bishop by the consecration of Mar Basilius. That Cyrillus, as is sufficiently attested, consecrated another priest before his death, A.D. 1805, by the name of Philoxenus; who again, in 1812, consecrated in the same manner him who now lives, and is called Mar Philoxenus. Now, though the title of Metropolitan is wrongly assumed by that prelate, and the others whom he has consecrated, and ignorantly allowed them by the heathen governors of the land, it will not be doubtful to your Eminency that they are real bishops, though there were not the number of prelates present at the consecration which the holy Canons ordinarily require. But in a barbarous land, where bishops are very few, where intercourse with the see of Antioch was interrupted and difficult, it may seem perhaps to your Eminency, as it did to Mar Reginald, that it were better for a bishop before his death to provide successors for himself, provided the real form of ordination be duly observed, than that the Church should be left entirely destitute of bishops. More especially when at the demise of the true Metropolitan, more than twelve years ago, there was no provision for the continuance of lawful pastors among the people of Malabar, unless the other successions from Mar Basilius were admitted as true, which continued from Cyrillus to those who are now in Malabar. It was therefore in our blessed father's mind to entreat your Eminency, and also his right reverend brother Mar Athanasius, to lay aside all prejudices from the reports of ambitious men in India, who often decry in their brethren those things which they only desire for themselves; and that you would consult in these matters what is conducive to the peace, security, and welfare of the Church, not indeed giving place, even for an hour, to those prejudiced or wicked brethren who pretend to set up the right of the heathen magistrates to name Church governors against that of the see of Antioch, but not denying, even to the gainsaying and the prejudiced, that character which is allowed them by the nation, if it should appear on due examination and trial by the faithful, the priests and doctors of Malabar, that the character of bishop does of right belong to them. By these mild means, and by inviting a fair and impartial trial of all doubtful matters, the peace and order of the Church will be best promoted. Our brethren and fathers of the English Church all look with the greatest interest and affection on the state of the Church of the Apostle St. Thomas in Malabar; all desire earnestly to see it in peace and prosperity, and its connection with Syria unimpaired, and they all will hear with sorrow of the violent removal of your legate from this country. I am now engaged, as is my bounden duty, in giving an account of these transactions, with the whole of the wishes of our blessed father concerning them, to our venerable father and lord, Mar Carolus, Primate of England.

"THOMAS ROBINSON,

"Priest and Ramban of Mar Reginald the Blessed."

The expulsion of Mar Athanasius was a decided measure on the part of the Government, and (as Bishop Middleton appears to have thought) had perhaps been resolved upon somewhat too hastily. In one respect, however, it operated beneficially upon the interests of the Church, inasmuch as it put an end to the disturbances which had been excited by his arrival. Konatta the Malpan, and certain others, who had taken a leading part in kindling the flame of discord, were punished by a fine and a short imprisonment, as well as by the spiritual censures of the Church; and if any disaffected party still existed, it was overawed by the strong arm of the secular authority, which was little disposed to permit any renewal of the agitation.

The English missionaries were now able to carry on their designs under the most favourable circumstances. With a friendly Metropolitan to support their efforts, and possessing considerable influence with the British Resident, and through him with the native government, it is not easy to conceive more hopeful conditions of success. And, whatever opinion we may entertain regarding the character of some of their proceedings, it must be admitted that they applied themselves to their work with unsparing energy and devotion.

The first missionary reached Travancore in 1816. He was joined in the course of a few months by a second clergyman, and in the following year (1817) two stations were occupied, one at Allepy on the sea-coast, and the other at Cottayam, where the College had already been established by the efforts of the

British Resident, Col. Munro. In the year 1819 the staff was again reinforced by the arrival of two more missionaries, who heartily co-operated with their brethren, and contributed in no small degree to the progress of the work.

In order to render the course of studies at the College as effective as possible, three preparatory seminaries were formed in different parts of the diocese; and schools were established in many of the parishes, with the view of promoting the general education of the people. These measures were favourably received by the Syrians, who were not slow to perceive the advantages they might derive, not only from the education of their children, but also from the protection of the missionaries, whose influence with the Government was known to be considerable; and they were soon able to reckon thirty-seven of these parish schools, containing, it is said, 9,000 scholars[o].

The circulation of the Holy Scriptures, both in Syriac and in the vernacular language of the country, was one of the chief objects with which the mission had been originally established, and the measures necessary for its accomplishment were undertaken with as little delay as possible. Copies of the Syriac version were, as we have seen, supplied from England by the British and Foreign Bible Society; but the translation into Malayalim had yet to be made, and was entrusted to the missionaries who resided in the country. This important work was commenced as soon as circumstances would permit, but many years appear to have

[o] Mullens's Missions in South India.

elapsed before the whole was completed[p]. The difficulty of printing was at first very great, and was not overcome without the exercise of admirable patience and ingenuity. Application had been made at Madras for a fount of Malayalim type, and, after long delay, it had at last reached its destination at Cottayam. But after all it was found to be useless. The missionaries however were bent upon the accomplishment of their purpose, and one of them undertook to cast a fount of type himself. His efforts were eventually successful, and the first sheets of the Malayalim Bible were printed with the types and press which his own skill had produced.

In addition to these labours, the missionaries were engaged in the preparation of multitudes of tracts, which they diligently circulated, and in assiduous preaching in the churches and bazars[q]; new ground was occupied from time to time, and the mission re-

[p] From the report in the Madras Church Missionary Record for Sept., 1834, it appears that the translation of the Old Testament had been recently finished "in plain intelligible Malayalim." The writer adds, "I am only anxious for the day when we shall possess the whole of the sacred volume complete in the native tongue." But other passages in the report seem to imply that what is here spoken of is, in part at least, a revised translation. Under date Dec. 15, 1833, he writes, "Yesterday an old man came to solicit a Malayalim Testament. He entreated so earnestly that I could not refuse him." And a little further on, "During the year (1833) I have been able to revise the Psalms, Proverbs, Ecclesiastes, Canticles, and Isaiah, to translate and 'revise Jeremiah and Lamentations. Now I am going on with Ezekiel."

[q] The bazar is an essential part of every Indian town. It is simply a collection of shops, or rather stalls, in which the goods are displayed. Allepy, it should be remembered, contains a vast heathen population, who of course will not come to church to hear the Gospel.

inforced by the arrival of clergy and lay assistants, as occasion demanded. The press was furnished with a liberal supply of the necessary plant, and some idea of its activity may be gathered from the two following reports, taken from the "Madras Church Missionary Record" for September, 1834, and June, 1835, respectively. The first states that the preceding year, 1833, had been "fruitful in the products of the press, as from it had issued nearly 30,000 tracts, 55,000 hand-bills, 300 hymn books, and 1,500 copies of the Psalter." The second consists of the following table:—

"*Malayalim works published at the Church Missionary Society's Printing Press at Cottayam, during the year* 1834.

"No. of Copies.	Names of Works.
3,000	Tahiti, No. 4, 12mo.
2,000	Accepted Time, No. 9, 12mo.
3,000	Lord's Supper and Mass, No. 10.
3,000	Sixteen Short Sermons, No. 12.
3,000	The Brahmin, No. 11.
5,000	Accepted Time, No. 9.
5,000	On Idolatry.
5,000	Good Pearl, 12mo.
2,000	Proverbs.
1,000	Ecclesiastes and Canticles.
2,000	Isaiah.
2,000	Jeremiah and Lamentations.
2,000	Ezekiel and Daniel.
2,000	Minor Prophets.
500	Family Prayers in Malayalim."

Under the peculiar circumstances in which the missionaries were placed at Cottayam, some account of their public worship may not be uninteresting. It appears to have consisted of some form of daily prayers with exposition of Holy Scripture or catechizing, conducted apparently, not in the Syrian Churches, but in one of the missionaries' houses, or occasionally in the grammar-school attached to the College. The Sunday services are thus described in a report contained in the November Number of the "Madras Church Missionary Record," for 1834:—"On Sunday morning I collect all the boys from the grammar-school at 10 a.m. into the college, where we are going through the Bible in the presence of all the teachers and boys of the college and grammar-school. At these lectures I speak the pure truth in love; and often, when they have closed, have taken the malpan and other catanar teachers aside to ascertain whether they have comprehended all that has been said, and what has been their opinion about it. On Sunday afternoon we have full service in Malayalim in the grammar-school; I or a deacon read the Morning Prayers, as I am so partial to the Litany; and a catanar preaches, as it was not till last month that I was enabled to perform full service; on which occasion after reading, I commenced my preaching course by addressing them from the words, 'Behold the Lamb of God,' &c. After this service is concluded, I have been in the habit, for the last six months, of collecting the teachers, boys, &c., who know anything of English, and preaching to them in English in a familiar style. The whole number at this service does not exceed nine."

While one of the missionaries was thus employed at the College, others appear to have found opportunities of preaching to the congregations in the Syrian churches, after the Corbano (or Eucharistic service) had been offered. At the Corbano itself, however, they seem never to have been present, except as mere spectators; indeed, it would have been altogether inconsistent with their principles to have given any support or countenance to a service which one of them has not scrupled to call "a most wretched piece of buffoonery."

Yet the celebrations of Holy Communion among themselves appear to have been few and far between. We learn from the Journal of the Rev. Mr. Woodcock, who joined the Mission in 1834, that for nearly three months after his arrival in India he had had no opportunity of Communion. The passage is so significant in its naive simplicity that I cannot forbear quoting it. He had landed at Madras on the 9th of June, and reached Cottayam on the 30th of July. On the 5th of September he writes, "As I have had no opportunity of partaking of the Lord's Supper since my arrival in India, and as Sunday is the day for its administration at Cochin, I intend, in company with brother Peet, to-morrow (D.V.) to proceed thither." And so they did accordingly. But why not celebrate at Cottayam, where there were at least two English priests, besides the lay-assistants of the Mission, who were employed at the press and elsewhere? I find in another report the equally significant expression, "We have a meeting on the Saturday evening preceding the first Lord's Day *in the months on which the Lord's Supper is administered;*" language which plainly indicates a more than monthly interval between the celebrations [r].

The Report which has been already quoted from the "Madras C. M. Record," for November, 1834, gives an account of the number of students at the College, and of the studies pursued at that period. The number in the College was then "73 deacons and boys and 2 catanars, making in all 75 students." "Of this number," says the writer, "about 50 learn English, from the alphabet to works of the highest order; 2 read Greek; the rest learn Syriac and Malayalim; 4 write tolerably correct English and Malayalim; 12 learn English geography; 15 Malayalim geography, for whose use I have constructed a Malayalim globe; 9 or 10 are learning English arithmetic, the rest Malayalim arithmetic; 4 read Letters in Chemistry, accompanied by such experiments as the poor apparatus we possess will allow. The time for learning is divided as follows: those who only learn Syriac and Malayalim study the former daily in the morning, the latter in the afternoon, when they read and translate into common Malayalim Mr. Bailey's Testament, which for giving them a good knowledge of Sanscrit words is excellent; besides which they daily commit to memory Watts's and the Assembly's Catechism in the same

[r] It was with deep regret that I noticed similar lukewarmness—is that too harsh a word? let me rather confine my expression to the simple fact, and say infrequency—in regard to the celebrations of the Holy Communion in other Missions of our Church, (one of them, I grieve to say, an S.P.G. Mission in a large town,) where the Lord's Supper is administered once in three months! How can we expect vitality in our Missions under such circumstances as these?

language." The Assembly's Catechism had been translated into Malayalim the year before, and henceforward formed a staple article of the education given in the Mission schools.

About this period a cloud began to gather over the Mission, and symptoms of uneasiness began to manifest themselves, threatening to disturb the amicable relations that had hitherto existed between the missionaries and the Syrians. The former had never entered heartily into the feelings of the people, or even of the clergy; they believed them sunk in ignorance and superstition, and directed their efforts, not so much to restore that which might be wanting, as to persuade them to abolish, *en masse*, all that was offensive to their own prejudices,—and this comprehended apparently the entire Syrian ritual,—and to substitute what are technically called Evangelical principles, both in doctrine and in worship, in place of the ancient usages and doctrines of the Church.

The Syrians, on the other hand, with few exceptions, were strongly attached to the forms of worship and the customs which they had received from their ancestors, and complained that "what the missionaries said about the Bible was partly good, but that they wished to overturn Mass-service altogether[s]; that it is highly improper, and therefore the people ought

[s] Report for 1835, Madras Church Missionary Record, March, 1836. The terms *Mass* and *Mass-service* are entirely unknown to the Syrians, but are gratuitously used by the missionaries, in order to signify their sense of the identity between the Syrian Eucharistic Office and the Roman Mass. In one instance the term is altogether misapplied by them, being used for the consecrated bread itself.

not to listen;" and the English clergy found themselves powerless to arrest the progress of the soul-destroying error which they deplored.

"By degrees," says Dr. Mullens, who, although an agent of the London Missionary Society, writes with a strong partiality for the Church Missionary Society's missionaries, "they gained a clearer estimate of their true position." He had been describing the success which attended their earlier efforts, and the favour with which they had been received;—but now the light began to dawn upon them:—"They saw that in relation to the Syrian Church they were absolutely without authority; they were mere volunteers in the attempt to get rid of existing evils; . . . . . they saw that the spiritual worth of the Church, and the task of raising it up, had been much overrated. They found the people careless about real religion; they found the priesthood unconverted, looking after their fees, formal in their service: the whole body was lifeless and cold. They found enmity gradually excited, especially in persons of influence, by their pure doctrine. While they preached Christ crucified, the priests in power taught regeneration by Baptism, and the efficacy of prayers for the dead. . . . They found themselves entirely in the hands of the Metran: all the priests were ordained by him: all their priests, all their scholars and students, were under his ecclesiastical authority. If any were obnoxious to him, or to the priests generally, by peculiar excellence or fidelity, he could refuse ordination, or he could forbid them to preach, or by himself he could keep up the error of ordaining boys as deacons. As head of the Mission, he could check, or alter, or refuse to sanction, measures for the improvement of the people.

"In the course of time, all this opposition was experienced in fact. An irreligious Metran was appointed, who cared nothing for the spiritual progress of the Church; and on more than one occasion a missionary in charge of the College returning suddenly to his class-room after going homeward, caught the Metran or one of the native professors in the very act of teaching some doctrine the very opposite of that which he had just laid down, and purposely undoing all the good which the missionary had just endeavoured to do[t]."

A coldness naturally arose between the Metropolitan and the missionaries, and at length developed into an open breach. I have not made it my object to examine step by step the progress of this deplorable quarrel, but it is easy to gather from the published records of the Society, brief and fragmentary as they are, what was the *tone of the proceedings* at Cottayam and elsewhere shortly before the final outbreak; and to see that, under such circumstances, a rupture was all but inevitable.

Thus we find that in the year 1833 the Assembly's Catechism had been translated into Malayalim by one of the missionaries, and that towards the close of the year it had become a text-book at the College, some

[t] Mullens's Missions in South India, pp. 129, 130. It will I hope be understood, that I merely quote Dr. Mullens's language, and by no means adopt his sentiments.

portion of it being "daily committed to memory" by the students, many of whom were in deacon's orders, two of them being catanars. So high indeed was the estimation in which this Presbyterian Catechism was held by the missionaries, that we find one of them—not the translator, who might be supposed to be enamoured of his own work—using it, alternately with the Word of God, as the basis of his Sunday lectures[u].

Another example is found in the record of a transaction which, taken as it is from the voluntary statement of the chief actor concerned, is at least somewhat startling. This is described in the following language, penned the year after all intercourse between the Syrians and the missionaries had been forbidden:—"On rising to leave, I went into the church and looked around me, and recollecting that after a sermon preached here several years before I went to England, I had, by the help of my own servants chiefly, removed from the altar-piece a large image of George and the Dragon, I said, it then occurred to me, that I did once commit an act of violence to an individual there, in that I removed the image alluded to out of the church[x]." It is but fair to add this gentleman's statement, that "one of the churchwardens" admitted that the act had been done with the consent of the people, and that he himself had lent a helping hand. We have but to try to realize such a proceeding as this, and we shall see no cause to wonder that it should

[u] Madras Church Missionary Record, March, 1836.

[x] Ibid., August, 1837. If the words *to an individual* have any meaning, do they not signify a recollection of at least *some* opposition?

make a deep impression, and one not favourable to the missionaries, even though a "churchwarden" had assisted in the work. How should *we* feel it, if some reforming foreigner were to come to England, and having been courteously admitted into our churches, should, under the impulse of excitement, straightway leave the pulpit and proceed to tear down an altar picture or the carved work of a reredos!

The scene of this transaction was Chenganoor, a village in the Cottayam district, and therefore in the very heart of the Syrian population. Unhappily it is not a solitary example of the iconoclastic zeal by which the missionaries and their agents were actuated; for we find from a report dated a few months earlier, that a similar instance had occurred shortly before July, 1836, at Corencherry, (also in the Cottayam district,) where, at the instigation of one of the native readers employed by the Mission, "an image and a shrine" were dragged out of the church and "hewed to pieces" by the people. In this instance the reader declared that the image and shrine "had long been objects of superstitious regard, if not of actual worship," among the people of the place. "They were said to be worth two hundred rupees[y]."

A third example, of a different kind, but hardly less characteristic and suggestive, presents itself in the letter of a young missionary, fresh from Islington, who tells us how, on the third day after his arrival at Cottayam, he entered into discussion with the Metropolitan with regard to certain reforms which he (the mis-

[y] Madras Church Missionary Record for 1837, p. 39.

sionary) appears to have intimated as desirable; and expresses regret that, on the occasion of his *first* visit, the day before, the Bishop's courtesy in making inquiries about the missionaries and their wives who had returned to England, would not permit him "to introduce his church as the topic of conversation, though I tried," he says, "several times." The return visit with which this young missionary was honoured by the Metran gave him a third opportunity of urging the necessity of reformation, of which he did not fail to avail himself. "After conversing on general subjects," he writes, "I endeavoured to bring his attention to the state of his Church." Unfortunately, however, while in close conversation, the church bell rang; and as this was the signal for commencing what he calls, with an ill-concealed sneer, "the prescribed number of evening prayers," the Metran instantly rose and took his leave. Mr. —— (I do not care to proclaim his name) of course entered freely into controversy with the catanars, obtaining from them admissions that their Church was in error, though as yet he was wholly ignorant of Malayalim, and must have been indebted for the means of conversation either to the intervention of an interpreter, or more probably to their own knowledge of English.

Different people will probably take widely different views of these transactions. Some will see in them indications of an evangelical love of truth, a righteous indignation, a burning zeal, such as characterized the reformers of the sixteenth and seventeenth centuries in Scotland. Others will hardly be able to view them with approbation. They are here adduced, however, only to illustrate the tone of the proceedings of the Church Missionary Society and its agents in Travancore, previous to the disruption in 1836.

It would be easy to multiply instances from the same source from which the above are taken, all tending to shew that there was little disposition on the part of the missionaries to enter into the feelings of the native Christians, or to make any allowance for their habit of thought, and the customs which they had received from their forefathers. The offices of the Church were declared to contain heresies which a careful examination of their language fails to detect; the Eucharistic Service, which the Syrians regarded as the great act of public worship proper for the Lord's Day, and which they were wont to celebrate with the highest ceremonial, was, in the missionary churches, dragged down to a cold uninviting performance, once in so many months; and customs, however venerable for their antiquity, were denounced as objectionable and superstitious if they did not accord with the received usages of Western Protestantism.

Such were the relations between the missionaries and the Syrian Church, when, in November 1835, the late Bishop Wilson paid a short visit to the Mission stations at Allepie, Cottayam, and Cochin. He had been invited by the Metran a little more than two years before, but had been unable to accept the invitation. Now, however, he was anxious, if possible, to compose the misunderstanding which every day became more serious between the English clergy and the native

Church; and to impress upon the Metropolitan the necessity of adhering to the stipulations which had been mutually agreed upon when the College was first established. A conference was accordingly arranged at Cottayam, and took place on the 21st of November. An interesting account of this interview will be found in the second volume of Mr. Bateman's "Life of Bishop Wilson," from which it appears that the Bishop submitted six points for the consideration of the Metropolitan and his clergy. These were the following:—

1. A recommendation "that those who should in future be ordained by the Metran should be so only after they had been instructed and examined (at the College), and had obtained certificates of learning and good conduct."

2. A recommendation "that all the lands, funds, property, belonging to the Church, being examined, an account should be sent to the President, in order that, being looked into, he might see that all was proper and correct."

3. A suggestion that "some means should be devised to increase the incomes of the Rev. catanars, and to support them respectably"—"some permanent endowment, instead of uncertain fees;" e.g. those for "prayers for the dead."

4. A suggestion in regard to the establishment of schools all over the Syrian Churches.

5. A request that the Metran would direct the catanars to expound the Gospel to the people on Sundays, in Malayalim.

6. A proposal that the prayers should be inter-

preted; and that "being thus rendered into Malayalim, they might have, from all their various liturgies, one of moderate length arranged for the use of those who do not understand Syriac."

The brief discussions which followed each of the foregoing proposals were conducted with courtesy on both sides, and the Metran promised "that the Church should assemble and take them into consideration." Bishop Wilson seemed hardly satisfied with this, and appeared anxious that some definite pledge should be given by the Metran, of his own proper authority; but the Metran replied that "in peculiar matters all must meet; that only a few of his clergy were present at the conference, and that time would be required for deliberation." "Our Liturgies," said he, "have been formed by great persons: we are weak ones, what can we do?" He promised assent, however, to the Bishop's reiterated desire "that the agreement originally made by the Metran and Col. Munro should be scrupulously adhered to in its main features:" and Mr. Bailey, the senior missionary, took the opportunity of reminding the assembly that this agreement provided for the joint signature by the Metran and one of the missionaries of all official letters on Church affairs and to the Churches,—a plan which had been adhered to up to the period of the then Metran's death, and for some time afterwards.

On the day following the conference, the Bishop (with the Metran's permission) addressed an attentive congregation of from 1,500 to 2,000 persons in the large church at Cottayam, after the celebration of the Eucharist, according to the Syrian rite. The Bishop himself was not present at the Corbano, being fatigued by his previous service with the missionaries, but he took care to be in time for his sermon. Its delivery and interpretation occupied an hour, and at its close, the Metran took him by the hand to the church door, and thanked him, saying, "What you have preached is what we want." The subject was taken from the 7th and 8th verses of Rev. iii.,—the message to the Church in Philadelphia.

Next day the Bishop proceeded on his way northwards; but before leaving Cottayam he signified his good-will towards the native Church by a donation of a thousand rupees (£100), "out of love, and as a mark of love to the Church of Malabar, to be administered by the Resident, the Metran, and the Church missionaries."

The Charge which he delivered subsequently at Bombay, shews how deeply the good Bishop had been impressed by his visit to this venerable Church, and with what tenderness and sympathy he was disposed to regard it. He calls particular attention to the points in which the Syrian Church is free from those distinctive features of the Church of Rome, which, so long as they are rigorously insisted on, must present an insuperable obstacle to external re-union with her; and speaks of some of the customs of this primitive Church, as not unworthy of regard and even of imitation. Thus he speaks of the respect for antiquity which is manifested by the Syrian Church; of her synods, consisting of bishop, clergy, and laity; of the parishioners' consent to the appointment of pastors, (a matter, by the way, which would require the most careful limitation;) of the choice of the bishops by the clergy and laity; of the preparatory diaconate, in which the younger members of the ministry serve for many years before being admitted to priest's orders; of excommunication and admonition, administered by a court which meets in the church porch, and consists of the catanar and four lay-members; of the less severe, but marked ecclesiastical censure conveyed by the omission of the blessing in the case of the offender, when the remaining members of the congregation receive it, on passing out of the church; and lastly, of the provision for constant services by a numerous staff of clergy, residing in chambers closely adjoining the church, built in fact over the verandahs or cloisters which generally form a portion of the fabric.

"But I hasten," he continues, "to remark generally, on all which I have now been stating, *what charity and tender sympathy* we should cultivate towards these and similar relics of Apostolical Churches. How readily should we acknowledge what is good in them; without requiring of them conformity to our Protestant models of liturgical worship, or our Western notions [z]."

Well might it have been, if the missionaries had acted in conformity with the spirit of this advice: but, alas! they appear to have aimed at nothing less than an entire assimilation of the ritual of the Church to their own peculiar standards. What Archbishop Menezes

[z] See extracts from this Charge in the July number of the Missionary Register, 1838.

had attempted in one direction they sought to accomplish in another. As early as the year 1820 (or thereabouts) there appears to have been a disposition to introduce the English Communion Office in place of the Syrian ritual; but it was overruled by instructions from the Committee at home[a]. In the year 1836, however, if not earlier, another effort was made in the same direction, by inducing some of the catanars to adopt an Office modified—"much modified"—from their own[b]; and, to use the expression of one of the missionaries in his report for the year 1838, it was hoped "that the people would be willing ere long to substitute our English Sacrament service in its stead[c]."

To alter the Liturgy of a Church is a matter of the gravest consequence, even when alterations are made under the sanction of proper authority: but that men in the position of the missionaries at Cottayam should tamper with and "modify" the liturgy of an independent Church, into connection with which they had been admitted by mere courtesy, is a height of presumption almost incredible—unless they and the catanars who were associated with them were acting as a committee duly appointed to carry out such a work. It is just possible that they may have been acting under such general permission as they may have construed into some sort of sanction from the Metran; but there is not the slightest hint of anything of the kind in

[a] See Hough's Christianity in India, vol. v. p. 386.

[b] Madras Church Missionary Record, vol. iv. p. 60. See also p. 118, and vol. v. p. 39.

[c] Ibid., vol. vi. p. 45.

their Reports; and remembering the position which he steadily maintained at the conference with Bishop Wilson, that these and other grave questions affecting the interest of the Church could be decided only by a council of the whole Church, the probability of such an explanation will be seen to be extremely small.

The opposition which the missionaries had experienced from time to time since the year 1833, had gradually increased in its intensity, and was met by them with characteristic determination. It is impossible to give an idea of the scenes which occurred in some of the churches, as at Cottayam[d], Neranum[e], and Manucattee[f], without quoting lengthy extracts from the Reports: it is enough to observe that, in one instance, the "saying of Mass" by the catanar, and the missionary's preaching to an excited assembly from the chancel steps, appear to have been carried on in horrible rivalry in the same church and at the same hour; while, to add to the confusion of the scene, jugglers were exhibiting their performances outside[g]. It is but just, however, to add that the missionary's prayer and sermon were first commenced, and that the catanar passed him and began the "Mass," while the former was giving out his text. On another occasion he writes, "The people fled from me as from a tiger, as I entered the doors of the church." These events took place in 1835, two or three months before Bishop Wilson's arrival.

Under such circumstances it was hardly possible that

[d] Madras Church Missionary Record, vol. iii. p. 35.
[e] Ibid., p. 37. [f] Ibid. [g] Ibid.

the missionaries should continue to act in harmony with the Syrians, or the Syrians with them: and the rupture, which had so long been imminent, at length became a grave reality. This deplorable result occurred early in the year 1836, and is thus noticed by Mr. —— in his Report, dated April 29th of that year:—"On leaving the church (of Puttencar), the deacons came to tell me that the Metran, who had just left an adjoining church, had sent for the friends of the deacons of the several surrounding churches, and had forbidden them, upon the pain of his heavy displeasure, to send the deacons to the College." He does not state what particular act or acts had led the Metran to take so important a step; but it is remarkable that it is announced in the same Report in which allusion is made to the introduction of the modified Liturgy of which mention has been already made.

But the missionaries, although foiled in the original object of their mission, had no thought of retiring from the field, or of confining their labours to the conversion of the heathen; but went on with the work they had set themselves, in spite of the opposition of the Metropolitan and catanars. They built churches in close proximity to those of the Syrians, as at Cottayam, Mavelicare, Mallapalli, Colatta, and elsewhere; and persisted in a system of proselytizing, undeterred by the sentences of excommunication which were pronounced by the Metropolitan against all who joined them. They encouraged the people to disregard his injunctions, and not to fear his threats; they induced some of his catanars to adopt their modified ritual, and to serve the congregations which they formed here and there among the Syrians, giving them "express instructions" as to the performance of their Office[h]; and the lamentable spectacle of this new schism is continued to the present day. Yet they do not urge the plea lately urged at Manchester in defence of the Irish Church Missions. They do not deny that "saving Christianity" is to be found in the Syrian Church of Travancore. On the contrary they write, "Her errors are grievous, but she is not an apostate Church, and we doubt not but that she has in her 'a seed which shall be counted unto the Lord for a generation[i].'"

Hitherto, however, the labours of the missionaries do not appear to have been attended with much practical result, so far as the Syrians are concerned. "For many years," says the present Bishop of Madras, "nothing has occurred to revive those bright anticipations of reformation which Bishop Wilson and many others for a time entertained[k]."

It has been with extreme reluctance, and under a sense of grave responsibility, that I have felt constrained to enter upon this very painful subject: and in so doing I am conscious of no other motive than a most earnest hope that some further effort may yet be made, WITHOUT BREAKING UNITY, to promote the restoration of this venerable but fallen Church.

There is doubtless a great work to be done in this

[h] For my authority for the above statements see Madras Church Missionary Record, vol. vi. 109, 110, 128; iv. 60, 118; vi. 45, 197; v. 39; iv. 118; and vols. iv.—vi. *passim*.

[i] Madras Church Missionary Record, vol. iv. p. 1, (for January, 1837).

[k] Charge, 1863.

part of the vineyard. One may hope, indeed, that in many cases the missionaries may have misapprehended what they saw and heard, either through prejudice or deficient information; yet it is impossible to read their Reports without being convinced that there *is* a sad amount of ignorance and superstition among the people; and a perusal of these Liturgies will shew a state of feeling with regard to the faithful departed, and especially the Blessed Virgin, which we cannot regard without the deepest anxiety. While *fully* admitting the sweet doctrine of the Communion of Saints, and all that it implies, and remembering that it was the practice of the early Church to mention the faithful dead in their Liturgies[1], we can hardly help feeling that some passages which are found in these Offices not only go beyond the warranty of Holy Scripture and early practice, but are derogatory to the majesty of God and the office of our ascended Saviour.

The tenacity with which the Syrians, in common with all other Eastern nations, cling to the customs of their fathers, will doubtless render the work of reformation one of no little difficulty; but as the earnest setting forth of the TRUTH has in all ages, under God's blessing, produced marvellous results, so where He pleases, it will certainly continue to do so.

And there are, at the present time especially, many sources of encouragement. It must be remembered that with the Syrians Christianity is not a novelty, but the faith which they have received from their forefathers from time immemorial. And to the ca-

[1] See, for instance, St. Cyprian's Ep. i. 3, and other passages.

tanars *at least*, whose very office requires a knowledge of Syriac, the whole dispensation of the Gospel must be well known, including the fall of man, his restoration through Christ, and the hope of eternal life through Him. See this beautifully expressed in the Consecration Prayer of the Anaphora of St. James, (p. 50). Again, the statement of Dr. Buchanan that the Creed of this Church accords with that of St. Athanasius, is one of no light importance. I have seen nothing in the Reports of the missionaries to overthrow this statement, which, as the reader will see, is on the whole remarkably supported by the Liturgies before us [m]. Indeed, the Nicene Creed, with the exception of some clauses, forms part of the Eucharistic Office. Here, then, in these all-important fundamental subjects, we should I trust find ourselves able to meet them on a common ground, and the great work to be done would be, *just what is so urgently required in this Christian country of England*, the teaching of the masses. In many respects, indeed, the English Church is, as a visible body of so many baptized people, analogous to that of the Syrians, regarded in the same light:—the Church holds the right faith; but the *mass* of the people are miserably ignorant, and, it must be feared, miserably superstitious.

Another source of encouragement to which we might point, is the renewed anxiety which has been so strongly manifested of late on the part of the Episcopal Churches of America and Scotland, and of the Church of England, to promote the restoration of intercommunion

[m] P.S. This language is perhaps too confident. See Appendix A.

with the orthodox Eastern Church. This, one would hope, is not unlikely to become known to the Patriarch of Antioch, to whom the Syrians look as their spiritual head; and would tend to dispose them to receive our advances with favour, if made in a truly Catholic spirit. At present, indeed, we are looked upon with great suspicion, and not without reason; but surely this need not always be the case.

Lastly, the *character* which the Syrians still retain as a simple honest people, remarkable for modesty and truth [n], and the respect with which they are consequently regarded by the heathen, is a most important fact, the value of which can hardly be over-estimated. The census of Travancore, made in 1854, and that of Cochin in 1849, represents the number of the Syrians in those two states as amounting to 116,483, far more than twice the number of baptized natives *in the whole of our missions* in the diocese of Madras [o]. Their churches are numerous, and in different parts of the country; and are served by an abundant staff of native clergy, thoroughly acquainted with the language and

[n] This testimony is borne by every writer I have seen, except Raulin, who states nothing to the contrary. The latest witness is Mr. Day, Land of the Permauls, p. 263.

[o] In his recent charge, the Bishop of Madras gives this number as 48,252; 17,589 being connected with the Gospel Society's Missions, and the remainder with those of the C.M.S.

Bishop Gell makes an interesting statement regarding the *Romo Syrians*. He says, "Amongst those who have been subject to the Latin bishop, i. e. in the Syro-Roman Church, there is a dissatisfaction with Romish rule. They have very recently received a new bishop, a native of Travancore, *consecrated by the Syrian 'Patriarch of the East,'* and are desirous of being allowed to read the Scriptures."—*Charge*, p. 6. The italics are mine. The number of Romo-Syrians is about 119,000.

manners of the people. Even in the present depressed condition of the Church, its influence must be widely felt among the heathen; what would that influence be if the Church were restored to the purity and zeal of early times?

Any effort which may be made in this direction will require not merely piety and zeal, but much wisdom, tact, and forbearance, and, of course, considerable theological attainment, especially in reference to those questions which are so constantly interwoven with the history of the Eastern Church. It should be remembered that these questions are not identical with those which have so grievously distracted the Churches of the West, and which are I believe for the most part unknown as matters of controversy to Eastern Christendom [p].

The great points to be attended to will probably be, to guard against venality in the appointment to holy offices; to teach the masses of the people by earnest evangelical preaching, and in every way to encourage the practice of this important duty by the catanars, for it would be mainly in the native clergy that, under God, our strength would lie; and lastly, to induce the Church in synod to revise her Offices, amending them where necessary, in conformity with the most ancient models.

[p] This caution does not seem altogether unnecessary. I remember reading of a missionary who went out to teach some of these benighted Christians of the East, and while busy in setting them right on the subject of Transubstantiation, Prayers for the Dead, the Sacraments, &c., was asked, in turn, his belief concerning the *natures of Christ*. This question utterly puzzled him, as he had never heard of it before! I am glad to say, this gentleman was not a member of the Church of England, or of any Episcopal Church.

Should such an effort be made, in a spirit of reverence for the "old paths" of early Christendom; with an earnest desire to make the most of points of agreement wherever they are to be found; and, *at least*, a kindly forbearance in regard to ceremonial[q], when not plainly at variance with the faith and practice of the early Church; if, in those points of doctrine which are *really* opposed to the truth of the Gospel, it were sought to conciliate and *convince*, by reference to the Holy Scriptures, and the general consent of primitive antiquity; and all were done in the spirit of meekness, and with the most heartfelt longing for external as well as internal unity; if the native Christians should see that there is no disposition on our part to subvert the independence of their Church, or to withdraw its members from allegiance to their own Metropolitan[r];—surely in such a case we might hope for ultimate success; and by God's blessing such a light would then shine in that dark and distant land, such a standpoint would be gained for the pure doctrine of the Gospel, as might become an effective centre for the evangelizing of the whole of south-western India.

[q] See Appendix B.

[r] Dr. Buchanan, in his Christian Researches, pp. 132, 133, bears testimony to the extreme anxiety with which the Metropolitan, though willing to entertain a proposal for the union of the Syrian Church with that of England, and "to sacrifice much for it," yet protested against being called upon to compromise anything of the dignity and purity of his Church.

CHAPTER IV.

PERSONAL INTERCOURSE WITH THE SYRIANS.—KANUNKALUM.—CATANAR JACOB.—CHATTANOOR.—KAYENCOLUM.—DESCRIPTION OF THE CHURCH.—THE CORBANO.—CURIOUS MODE OF RECEIVING THE BREAD AND WINE.—MAVELICARA.—THE SUNDAY EVENING SERVICE.—THE MISSION CHURCH.—A STORM ON THE BACKWATER.—COTTAYAM.—VISIT TO MAR ATHANASIUS.—THE TRISAGIUM.—ASPECT OF THE COUNTRY.—MAR KOORILLOS JOACHIM.—THE WHITE JEWS AT COCHIN.—A TRAVELLING CANVAS CHURCH.—PALM SUNDAY AT PAROOR.—CONCLUSION.

THE foregoing sketch has far exceeded the limits I originally proposed to myself; and I have still to beg the indulgence of my readers while I lay before them some account of my own intercourse with the Syrians, and of their services, churches, and any other points of interest that seem worthy of notice.

The first place at which I met with the Syrians was Kanúnkalum, a large town in the north of Cochin. I was then on my way to Quilon, the station to which I had been appointed, and after travelling all night, had reached the bungalow shortly after sunrise on a Sunday morning. While strolling about in the neighbourhood of the bungalow, which is beautifully situated on a rising ground to the east of the town, the gable of a pretty building higher up the hill met my view, looking just like the gable end of a village church in England. Assuming that this must be a Mission church, I made my way towards it, in the hope that I might be able to attend the service, and see something of the Mission. On enquiry, however, I found that the missionary was absent, and that the services would be conducted by a native catechist, who usually took charge of the Mission in the absence of the priest. The church was closed, and I could see little of the internal arrangements, but my interest in it, and in the Mission generally, was much diminished when I learned that converts were invited not only from among the heathen, but from the Christian population around, and that the Holy Communion was celebrated only once in three months.

To confess the truth, it had not hitherto occurred to me that the part of the country I was now entering was the abode of the Christians of St. Thomas, and when I found Kanúnkalum described in the Road Book as "a large Syrian Christian village," I wondered what it could mean, not being then aware that these people went by the name of Syrians. I had indeed made some enquiry about them on my arrival in India, four years before, but having been sent first to Burmah, and then to Trichinopoly, my thoughts had been directed into other channels, and on the present occasion were occupied mostly by anxiety on account of a sick child whom I had left behind, and by the difficulty of making my way to Quilon in the teeth of the S. W. monsoon.

It was then a most unlooked-for pleasure to find myself now actually among the Christians of St. Thomas, and I determined not to lose the opportunity of "seeing their devotions" as I passed by. I set out therefore immediately after breakfast, under the guidance of a little boy, who undertook to lead me to one of the principal churches in the town. Our way lay through the narrow by-lanes of the place,—little alleys enclosed with mud walls on either side, and often presenting the appearance of a water-course rather than of a road. In about twenty minutes we reached the Bazar, where the combined effect of loose pigs, fowls, mud, and rain, made it difficult to choose one's path. A few more steps, however, brought us to a doorway in a high dingy mud wall, and passing through it, I found myself in a courtyard, in the midst of which stood a plain massive church.

It was evident from the sound of many voices that the service had begun, and I lost no time in entering. The church was *crowded,* and although I met with much politeness, it was some little time before I could get beyond the door; for of course I felt anxious to disturb the worshippers as little as possible.

Here first I saw the veil, screening the chancel from the nave, and the wonderfully impressive service of the Corbano,—the offering of the Eucharist,—celebrated by a native priest, according to the rites of this ancient Church. I will, however, defer the description of it for the present, merely remarking that in this church, as elsewhere, the priest was richly vested; the noise of the responses almost deafening; and the sexes separated from each other, the eastern part of the nave being occupied by the men, and its western portion by the women. There was no reception by the laity on this occasion.

At the conclusion of the service I sought and obtained an interview with the catanars, of whom several were present, but Hindustani being the only medium of communication, and that being but little understood either by myself or by the good man who undertook the office of interpreter, I could not succeed in obtaining much information, beyond the fact that they had printed copies of the New Testament in Syriac, and that (if I understood them rightly) they did not attribute the foundation of their Church to St. Thomas the Apostle. I observed that most of the people in the congregation had books in their hands, but I did not succeed in my attempt to purchase one of them.

As it was important that I should reach Quilon as soon as possible, I was unable to see anything more of the Syrians on my way thither; but not long after my arrival I had the pleasure of receiving a visit from a catanar whose church was about eight or ten miles distant. This was Catanar George Jacob, whom I have already mentioned as the friend to whose kind assistance I am indebted for the MSS. which I so much value. He was apparently about thirty years of age, or a little more perhaps, and was habited in the usual dress of catanars when not officiating, a long white vesture something like a cassock, but with turn-down collars like a countryman's smock-frock.

Catanar Jacob's visits were repeated at occasional intervals, and he was twice kind enough to join us at our meals. On these occasions curry and rice was, as might be expected, the dish he preferred,—indeed there was little else to be had at Quilon,—but the good man ate it I fear not so much from relish for the food, as from motives of politeness: he used a fork and spoon not without effort, but tolerably well, considering that he was probably little accustomed to these accessories of Western civilization, or at any rate of the use of both of them together. But notwithstanding this mutual disposition to be on friendly terms, it was not easy to obtain much information respecting the Syrian Church, the difficulty of language rendering free conversation impracticable. English was the only language we knew at all in common, and of this he understood so little as to express himself with the utmost difficulty; indeed he often failed altogether to make me understand his meaning. On such occasions he would turn to the servant behind his chair, and put a number of questions in Malayalim, asking how many rupees he got a month, what he had to do, and whether he liked his place, &c., finding apparently a vast relief in holding conversation in his own native tongue.

The distance between Quilon and Chattanoor [a], where Catanar Jacob resided, was not great by land, but the route was intersected about midway by a deep river, which flows down from the mountains, and pours itself into the Backwater a little to the south of Quilon. This river was easily crossed by foot-passengers, by means of a small canoe, but it presented a serious obstacle to one travelling on horseback or by palanquin, and rendered it difficult for me to return the catanar's visits, especially as my own duties demanded efforts which my health was hardly equal to.

On one occasion, however, I determined to accept

[a] Pronounced *Sartanoor*.

his invitation. It was my great object to be present at the celebration of the Corbano, and this could be accomplished only by going over on one of their holydays, as Sunday was of course occupied by my own duty. I went accordingly on the Feast of the Purification, in 1861. This was not held on the 2nd of February, as with us, but on the corresponding day according to their reckoning, which with us was the 14th of that month.

It seemed the best plan to travel as far as possible by water, as I had determined to go on from Chattanoor to Trevandrum, my out-station, without returning to Quilon. Leaving my house therefore about 7.30 A.M., my palanquin was taken to the Backwater, and there placed on a jungárum—a sort of stage formed by tying two canoes together side by side, with an interval of about eighteen inches between them: this is done by means of stout poles, which keep the boats apart, and make a very steady platform, on which the palanquin rests.

Our course lay at first along a shallow canal which connects the Backwater at Quilon with another portion of it about three miles to the southward; then, turning towards the interior of the country, we made our way up the river which I have already mentioned as intersecting the road to Chattanoor. About two hours of this kind of travelling—punting, rowing, or sailing, or all three together—brought us to the landing-place, and we reached the village a little before 11 o'clock.

I found my arrival anxiously expected, for this place is out of the usual track of Europeans; and as the "ho-ho" of the bearers announced my approach, I observed peeping eyes from many a doorway, eager to see something of the English catanar. When we had nearly reached the church, we were met by a little boy carrying a sort of flag—a streamer with a cross worked into it at the top—and a hand-bell, which he rang as he ran before the palanquin.

Having alighted at the entrance of the church compound, (which was marked, as usual, by a fair stone cross erected just outside,) I was received with much courtesy by Catanar Jacob, who led the way to the western door, where he introduced me to his aged father, who was also a catanar. We then passed through the church to a verandah on the south side of the nave, where a table was laid out with viands for my refreshment. I cannot too warmly acknowledge the hospitality with which I was received. No little pains had been taken to render the entertainment agreeable, and to set it out as much in the European style as possible: indeed, I found that, in order to do the thing correctly, my host had specially retained the services of a Quilon cook, whose acquaintance with English customs (or such a knowledge of them as he had obtained in the service of a half-caste family) was supposed to qualify him for the important duty now required at his hands. The dishes consisted of fowl-curry and roast goat's-flesh; and port wine, claret, and brandy were each in turn pressed on my acceptance. The only cause for regret on my part was my inability to do justice to this profuse hospitality; but I explained that, having breakfasted in my boat as I came along,

I was not disposed for anything more than a light refreshment.

Catanar Jacob and his father sat at the table with me, the remainder of those present, who might be ten or twelve in number, either standing by to look on, or serving the table. But this remark should not be understood as indicative of any great degree of luxury. On the contrary, everything indicated the rudest simplicity, if not absolute poverty. The verandah was so narrow as to admit only the table and the benches on which we sat; the rafters and bamboos which formed the framework of the roof were exposed to view, no attempt having been made to conceal them either by cloth or by plaster; and the crowd of by-standers consisted mainly of such as, having the privilege of *entrée*, had been drawn thither by curiosity.

When my host found that he could not prevail upon me to take anything more, be begged permission to retire—for it was already somewhat beyond the usual hour of service—and left his father to do the honours of the table. We did not, however, sit long; for hearing the sustained murmur of a voice, I enquired whether the service had not been commenced. They said that the public service had not begun, but that the Catanar was making the necessary preparations at the altar. Being anxious to see all I could, I asked to be allowed to go into the church, and found it empty, so far as the nave was concerned, and as the chancel was screened off by a curtain drawn across the arch, I was unable to see within. In the course of a few minutes, however, all was ready, and the congregation having assembled, the curtain was drawn aside, and the public service began.

The vestments worn by the Catanar were very handsome, the stole and outer robe being of silk damask, shewing a yellow pattern upon a scarlet ground. But the change in his dress was not by any means so striking as that in his manner. Hitherto he had appeared shy and uneasy; but now, as he stood at the altar, and performed the several functions of his office, reciting the well-known prayers meanwhile, I could not but be impressed with the dignity and reverence of his manner, and the solemnity of the whole scene.

At one time he stood beside the throne, with his left hand on the book, and his right across his breast; at another he knelt low before it; at another he prepared the incense, and gave the sign of peace: he would be seen now to veil the mysteries; now to raise them up on high, or perfume them with incense; then turning towards the people, with uplifted arm he invoked upon them the blessing of the Almighty[b].

The Anaphora used on this occasion was that bearing the name of Mar Xystus, which will be found at p. 132 of the MS. translated. The Catanar was assisted by two lay clerks, no deacon being present. There was no reception by the laity, but the church was very full, and the service was quite intelligible in its commemorative aspect.

The church itself presents few features worthy of

[b] See the frontispiece, which is copied from a photograph of Catanar Jacob in his eucharistic vestments, kindly taken for me by Lieut.-Col. Stevenson.

notice. It consists of nave and chancel, both of them of the plainest structure. The latter contains one altar; but two smaller tables, which at the time I took to be side-altars, stand against the east wall of the nave, one on each side of the chancel-arch, and are furnished with a cross placed in the centre. Although outside what we should naturally call the chancel, they are within a small space railed off from the rest of the nave, and therefore perhaps properly belonging to the sanctuary[c]. The chancel-arch is decorated with a wreath of leaves and flowers painted on plaster, and at the apex is a small fresco representing two angels kneeling beside a cross. The south wall of the nave contains a larger fresco, in which St. George is seen on horseback, pinning a ferocious dragon to the earth, while a woman prays under a tree in front of the horse. Next to this stands the calendar, in three columns, gay with its red and black characters and ornamental bordering.

Having spent a short time in making a sketch of the church, I was invited to return to the verandah for dinner. The bill of fare was much the same as before, and the several dishes were pressed upon me with the greatest hospitality. They were not how-

[c] I am not at all clear as to the use of these quasi-altars. The missionaries mention an instance of a "châtam upon three thrones," i. e. "Mass performed by three priests upon as many altars at the same time," (Madras Church Missionary Record, vol. iii. p. 35); but Renaudot declares that there is no trace of a second altar in the sanctuary in any books of the Oriental Church, and that the structures which might from their appearance be taken for additional altars, are only protheses, or credence-tables. (Lit. Or. ii. 54.)

ever very tempting to the palate of one in indifferent health, and it required a good deal of effort to eat at all.

The verandah was now crowded with visitors, mostly of the male sex, and outside there sat a great many impotent folk, blind, lame, or maimed, who had crawled thither to solicit alms. I do not remember seeing any lepers among them, though leprosy is so frightfully common in Travancore, but there were many afflicted with elephantiasis, and one, on the contrary, so extremely emaciated, as to present the appearance of a skeleton covered with shrivelled copper-coloured skin.

For some weeks after this I saw little more of the Syrians, nor was I able to renew my intercourse with them until I had finally left Quilon on medical leave. But Catanar Jacob kindly came over several times to see me, and made his visits more welcome by bringing with him a printed copy of the Syriac New Testament, and the two MSS. mentioned in the Preface to this work. These were the more acceptable by reason of the difficulty of procuring them; indeed, my subsequent experience has convinced me that I should have had little prospect of success in obtaining any MSS. at all, but for Catanar Jacob's kind assistance. He had negotiated their purchase for a small sum, ten rupees being paid for the larger MS. He was also good enough to give me two or three lessons in Syriac, which I found of the greatest service, though to some extent they were a source of confusion, as the names and pronunciation of the vowels, and of some of the letters, as he gave them, were often very different from those given by the grammarians.

At length I left Quilon on the night of the 20th of April, and, although in very poor health, I determined to see as much of the Syrian churches in my way northwards as circumstances would permit; for I felt it extremely doubtful whether I should ever again return to the western coast.

Accordingly I made a detour from the usual route, which passes few Syrian churches, and proceeded a little more towards the interior of the country. The Backwater is the great highway in these parts, and a pull of nine hours brought me by daybreak of the 21st to Kayencolum, the first Syrian village which I had been recommended to visit.

This village stands at a little distance from the open Backwater, with which it is connected by a channel, once, it is said, capable of admitting vessels of a considerable size, but now barely sufficient for the passage of small boats. A sudden turn in this channel brought into view a beautiful stone cross about sixteen feet high, which marks the landing-place. Here therefore I left the boat, and after having walked about two hundred yards, found myself within a large enclosure, or compound, the centre of which is occupied by the church. It is a large substantial building, divided into nave and chancel, and standing east and west, as ours do; but, as viewed from the outside, it presents few architectural features of much interest.

The Syrian churches are generally much alike, being all built on the same plan, and in the same style of architecture, the principal care being bestowed on the west front, and on the interior decoration of the chancel. The roof is generally high-pitched, that of the chancel being always a little higher than that of the nave; and both gables are usually surmounted by a cross of stone or iron, which is often of beautiful design. The west front consists of three stories, and is always whitewashed, presenting as its most prominent features an arched doorway in the centre, two or three recesses in the tier above, like windows that have been built up, and above the centre window an open one, square or arched. Besides the west door, there are always one or two entrances on the north of the nave, which, being furnished with projecting porches, add considerably to the architectural effect of the building.

My first enquiry was for the catanar, who was presently pointed out standing in the compound. He was an old man with fine features, and a good beard grey with age, and he stood apparently astonished at my appearance, and waiting to see what I would do. Having made my salam, I signified that I was come to see the church and the church service, and presented a letter of introduction with which I had been furnished by Catanar George Jacob. This was read aloud by one of my boatmen who had accompanied me, but, to my regret, it did not seem to satisfy the old man, who I thought looked upon me with increased suspicion, on finding that I was a priest of the Church of England. Language failing, there seemed nothing more to be done, so I left him, and went into the church, after having ascertained that the Corbano would be offered about 11 o'clock.

As the interior of this church may be taken as a fair specimen of the appearance of the Syrian churches generally, a description of it may not be uninteresting. It consisted of a nave and chancel, without transepts, the eastern portion of the nave being railed off from the rest at about twelve feet from the chancel-arch. Within this railing the floor was raised one step; and here was the font, on the south side near the wall. A handsome brass lamp was suspended in the centre, hanging low down before the chancel steps. There were two other lamps on the ground, and a small table stood near the font. The remainder of the nave, which has an earthen floor, is without furniture of any kind, if we except two large bells, which are hung *within the church*, just over the rails before mentioned, one on the north side, and the other on the south. The western part of the nave is covered by a gallery, which is reached by steps in one corner.

The whole interest of the church thus centres in the chancel, which is raised about four feet above the nave, and contains three altars of stone[e], the central and principal one standing eastward of the other two, about twenty feet from the chancel steps. This altar is ornamented by a carved framework of wood, which, standing on its edge, surrounds it on the north, east, and south, being carried up to a height of nearly three feet. On the eastern side the carved work is carried up yet higher, the whole being surmounted by a cross.

[d] See note, p. 123.

This reredos, so to call it, is divided into four tiers, of which the two lower consist merely of little pillars, forming a sort of basement to the rest, to give it height. The third contains seven angels, the outmost pair blowing trumpets, and the five others all alike, their wings touching each other, and their hands joined in the attitude of prayer. The fourth tier contains open crosses and other devices, and above all stand a pair of nondescript carvings, half elephant half flower, supporting an arch, over which stands the cross. The whole of this carving is picked out in colours and gold.

The two side altars have a less elaborate framework, supporting a cross in each case; and on all three altars a wooden or metal cross is placed in the middle, that on the great altar having star-like rays diverging from the centre. The chancel roof is semicircular internally, and richly ornamented with carved bosses at the intersections of the beams and cross-pieces. After having spent some time in examining and sketching the interior of the church, I returned to my boat for breakfast; and the heat being now intense in that close canal, shut in as it is by trees on either bank, I was glad to return about half a mile to a more open space.

As the natives have no clocks, I took care to be at the church again in good time, and found a seat in one of the porches already mentioned. Here I was presently surrounded by a great crowd of men and boys, who peered at me through the open woodwork, and over one another's shoulders, with evident curiosity and delight, and I found it necessary to ask them now and then to keep back a little, so that I might have air to breathe, a request which was always complied with with much good-nature for a time, until curiosity brought them gradually closer again. They said that many of them had never seen a white man before.

The other porch, more to the west, was full of women, who, I presume, were at least as inquisitive as the men; but custom apparently prevented their coming within twenty or thirty feet of the men's porch. They were all habited in their Sunday costume, a veil (of such beautiful whiteness as is only attainable under the bleaching power of a tropical sun) passed over the head, and reaching completely down to the feet.

Thus passed nearly an hour, during which the heat was very trying. At length my attention was aroused by a voice rising sharp and clear above the general hum, and, on entering the church, I found that it proceeded from the old catanar, who was standing near the door, engaged in loud conversation with one of his lay assistants.

They passed up into the chancel as I entered, and the curtain was immediately drawn, so as to shut them out from view. This screen or curtain is invariably found in the Syrian churches on the Malabar coast, and is closed and opened at stated periods of the service. It hangs across the arch which separates the chancel from the nave.

The congregation now began to enter the church, and I at once took my place just outside the railing already mentioned, so as to be as close to the chancel as possible. One of the men however kindly invited me to come within the railing, and brought a seat, which I thought it no harm to use so long as the curtain remained drawn. I was glad to avail myself of my seat for another reason besides that of resting, for it enabled me, without the difficulty or unmannerliness of continual stooping, to get my eyes nearly on a level with the bottom of the curtain, which did not quite reach the chancel floor; and thus, by peeping under it, I was able to see something of what was being done by the catanar and his attendants within; not much, however, for the view was most provokingly cut off about half way up the altar, and all that I could make out at the time amounted to an impression that the catanar was vesting, and making other preparations for the service. When he prostrated himself, as he did once or twice, I could of course see the whole of his person, and was thus enabled to notice the change of vestments which will be spoken of presently.

I deeply regret that I was not then familiar with the structure of these Offices; for had I known their contents, it would have been possible I think to trace more clearly what was done in regard to a very interesting and important part of the service, which presents no little difficulty in respect of its position and arrangement.

If the reader will turn to the *Ordo Communis* he will observe that almost at the very first, the elements are brought and with much ceremony placed on the altar, the water mingled with the wine, and the bread, here called *the Seal,* and *the First-Begotten,* solemnly offered to God.

This portion of the service is said by Renaudot to correspond to the Great Entrance of the Eastern Church[e]; and although not conducted with the elaborate ritual of the Greek Office, it is thought to have a similar intention, setting forth the Incarnation of our Lord. The ceremony, he tells us, is not fully represented in the Syriac MSS., but that it is retained, at least in substance, is evident from the testimony of Barsalibi, who thus alludes to it in his Commentary on the Liturgy. "The Mysteries or Sacraments," he says, "are brought forth, and are carried from the altar"—so he here calls the prothesis—"round about the sanctuary, before the illation (or entrance) of the sacrifice." He declares that this rite signifies "the descent of Christ into the world, and the period of His conversation upon earth,—*τῆς ἐνσάρκου οἰκονομίας*;" and that the bringing of the mysteries to the altar represents His ascent to the Cross. Renaudot, *Lit. Or. Col.*, ii. 60.

The reader will be surprised to find that the Order of Vesting is placed in the Ordo Communis *after* this important part of the Eucharistic Office. For it cannot be supposed that a ceremony so full of meaning would be conducted by the priest in his ordinary habit. Yet

[e] A description of the Great Entrance will be found in Dr. Neale's "Translations of the Primitive Liturgies." It consists of a grand procession from the prothesis (or credence table) in one of the parabemata, through the holy doors to the altar, the priest and deacon bearing the Divine gifts, "with great pomp of readers, deacons, and priests, with the lamps and holy vessels preceding and following;" and is intended to represent mystically the Incarnation and Second Advent of our Lord. In the Greek Liturgies it is introduced much later. See p. 141.

the order in both of my MSS. is the same, and they agree herein with the MS. which Renaudot followed in the second form of the *Ordo Generalis* given by him.

On the other hand I find that, in a partial translation of the Liturgy of St. James published in the Madras Church Missionary Register in the years 1835, 1836, and in the MS. obtained by Dr. Mill, the vesting comes first, and *then* the oblation of the elements, in accordance with the order which we should expect to be observed.

Renaudot has himself noticed this difficulty, (vol. ii. pp. 53, 54,) and disposes of it by the supposition that the prayers are not in this instance placed in the order in which they are used. "Verisimile videtur, orationes non eo ordine collocatas fuisse, quo dicuntur in Liturgia." His conjecture may probably be correct, but it is worth while to observe that, on the occasion which I am now describing, I noticed that *two sets of vestments were used.* I made a memorandum of this circumstance at the time, long before I had any distinct idea of the nature of the service which was being conducted behind the curtain, and it may be that one set of robes is used for the Office of the Oblation, and another for the remainder of the service. At the time I took the change to be a mere matter of caprice on the part of the catanar.

The prayers which are to be used while the priest is robing will be found in full at pp. 13—15 of the MS. I append here a brief account of the vestments themselves, which are the following:—

(1.) A pair of shoes. The use of these is contrary to the ordinary custom of the East, where the natives look upon the act of putting off the shoes as a token of respect. Their adoption therefore is remarkable, and seems to refer to the *preparation of the gospel of peace*, wherewith to crush the power of the enemy, and to tread down all carnal affections, and every high thing which exalteth itself against the knowledge of God.

(2.) A robe of black serge or coarse calico, which it seems "is not reckoned as part of the officiating dress, but is worn in compliance with the former custom of the Syrian priests, whose common costume it was. And in this common dress the rubric of Antioch directs its clergy to commence their service; but as the common dress of the Malabar Syrian is white, they put on the black gown in imitation of their spiritual progenitors." (Madras Church Miss. Reg., vol. ii. 165.) It is not therefore, strictly speaking, one of the eucharistic vestments, but rather the "private dress" mentioned on p. 13, and is assumed in order to be put off at the proper time.

(3.) The cuthino, the *χιτώνιον* of the Greek Church, a long white linen robe, corresponding to our surplice, but with narrower sleeves.

(4.) The orro or stole, the Greek *ὠράριον*, made in one piece, with a hole for the head to pass through.

(5.) The zunro, a girdle or cord, the object of which, according to Catanar Jacob, is to signify that at the time of ministering at the Corbano, all worldly thoughts must be bound down.

(6.) The zando, sleeves or maniples. These are made to fit pretty close to the arm, and extend a little beyond the elbow. The material is generally the same as that of the phaino.

(7.) The phaino, or chasuble as I suppose we should call it, though some think it corresponds rather to our cope. This question I must leave to those who are more learned in regard to our English vestments than I am. Renaudot, however, calls it "casula, vel planeta," and says that it corresponds to the *φαινώλιον* or *φελόνιον* of the Greeks. It is made sometimes of handsome silk damask, sometimes of velvet, and of different colours, according perhaps to the taste or means of its owner. In shape it is nearly square, the corners being rounded off, and it is fastened over the shoulders by a loop and a button in front like a cloak.

(8.) The cap.

On this occasion, as I have observed, the phaino, zando, and stole were removed, and others substituted for them. The colour of the robes last assumed was a deep crimson, the pattern being seen only in certain lights. The phaino had a handsome cross embroidered on the back.

At length the curtain was drawn aside, and the public service began. I would gladly have taken notes of its most striking points as it proceeded, but, knowing the suspicion with which I was already looked upon, I feared to give offence, and was obliged to trust to memory alone, until I could find an opportunity for jotting down a few memoranda of what I had witnessed. I am conscious, therefore, that the following description may be liable to some modification, nor can it pretend to be more than a general account of those parts of the service which were most likely to strike the eye of an uninitiated spectator. I have, however, endeavoured to bring my notes into harmony with the MS., and trust that they may serve to illustrate the translations which form the more important part of this volume, and to which I must refer the reader for a closer acquaintance with the Office itself.

Before proceeding further with the description of the service, let us briefly review what had been already done, gathering our idea of it from the MS. itself, and such other sources as are available for our purpose.

First, then, the catanar, standing before the step of the throne, had repeated the *Gloria* and prayer for worthy ministration, with the Sedra following.

Then, putting on the black dress, (No. 2,) he had recited the 51st Psalm, and so, kneeling before the altar and kissing it, he had approached with reverent and humble ejaculations. (MS., pp. 4—7[f].)

Having then, assisted by his deacon, lighted the tapers on the altar, first that on the south, and then that on the north side,—each of these acts being accompanied by its appropriate prayer, for which see p. 7 of the MS.,—he had "set the Sedra of Penitence," viz. those prayers which will be found at pp. 9—12.

The Trisagium and the Lord's Prayer were then said, and thus ended "the first service."

The second portion of the service begins apparently with the vesting, (pp. 13—15,) after which—for I feel compelled to follow here the *order* of Dr. Mill's MS. and the Church Missionary Society's translation—the Bread and Wine, the latter a *mixed* cup, are brought from the prothesis and placed on the altar, with their

[f] The pages of the MS. are given in the margin of the translation.

respective ceremonies and words of worship. (MS., pp. 7—9.)

The paten and chalice, it may be observed, are not to be set down at random, but each in the place assigned to it, the paten on the north and the cup on the south; and the same remark applies to the veils and other furniture of the altar.

When the oblation has been made, the vessels are covered with their respective veils, and a large veil is thrown over all. This veiling is not distinctly mentioned in the MSS. before me, but it is implied by the rubrics at pp. 9 and 16, and is expressly mentioned in the Church Missionary Society's translation.

Having veiled the Mysteries—for so they are continually called both before and after consecration—the catanar prostrates himself before the Table of Life, and prays awhile in secret. Then rising from his knees (MS., p. 16) he removes the veils, reciting meanwhile the rapid prayers; and crossing his right hand over his left, takes up the paten and the cup, and raising them on high says the *General Prayer*, commencing with the words, "The Memorial of our Lord," &c., in which he commemorates the living and the dead, and especially him for whom the Liturgy is celebrated.

It must have been, I think, at about this part of the service, perhaps when the celebrant had ended his private prayer, that the curtain was withdrawn, so as to open the chancel to the sight of the people. The Church Missionary Society's translation puts it somewhat later, but I cannot reconcile the later withdrawal with the memoranda and recollection of what I saw.

There may probably be some slight variation in this matter in different churches.

Assuming, then, that the curtain was now withdrawn, I will endeavour to continue my description of the service. When the commemoration was ended, the deacon having made the exhortation indicated by the initial words Στῶμεν καλῶς, i.e. "Let us stand in seemly order," &c., the people immediately answered with a loud voice, *Kurielison, Kurielison, Kurielison,*—I give their pronunciation of the well-known words,—drawling out the last syllable with a peculiar and most disagreeable flattening of the voice; and as the response died away, the catanar put down the Mysteries, placing the cup on the east and the paten on the west, (an arrangement which it will be seen forms a cross, when considered together with the direction in which they had been previously disposed,) and taking the veil, spread it over them with a slow deliberate movement, repeating the accompanying words meanwhile. I have still a recollection of the light veil, which may have been of silk perhaps, floating as it were over the elements, as it gradually settled down upon them, so deliberate and gentle was the action of the priest.

After a short interval, occupied it would seem by the recitation of the Sedra, (pp. 23—26,) or rather perhaps during its recitation, incense was placed in the censer, and then followed that impressive ceremony described at p. 26, from which it will be seen that the altar is perfumed in the centre, and at the north and south horns, in honour of the Father, Son, and Holy Ghost; then on the east, west, north, and south sides;

and lastly in a circle over the mysteries themselves, the censer being passed round them three times, doubtless in honour of the Trinity.

The Nicene Creed[g] and some short prayers followed; and, as they were being said, one of the men near me made as if he would come where I stood. Stepping therefore a little aside, I observed that he unfastened a rope which was connected with the large bell above my head, and had been tied round the railing to prevent it from swinging about.

As soon as the catanar had finished the prayer, this man began to ring the bell with great energy, and the people at the same time raised as it were with one voice that glorious hymn, *Kadisha Aloha,* &c., which on subsequent inquiry I found to be the Trisagium of the Jacobite Church. No description can convey an adequate idea of the effect produced by the singing of this hymn. It was accompanied by the clash of cymbals as well as the ringing of two large bells just over head, but the sound of human voices was so loud as to render these accompaniments comparatively indistinct, their clash and clang only adding to the amazing discord of the whole. Yet it was very impressive and

[g] Renaudot's translation gives no hint of the recitation of the Creed at this place; but A., M., and the Church Missionary Society's translation agree in representing it as used here; and A. and the Church Missionary Society's translation give it again after the words Σοφίᾳ πρόσχωμεν, where Renaudot places it. B. presents no trace of the Creed at all, but a leaf is apparently wanting in the second place where it might be looked for. On consulting my abstract of Dr. Mill's MS. (M.), I find it mentioned only once, that is, at this part of the service; but I may have overlooked it the second time, in my necessarily hasty examination of that MS.

exciting, and the effect was heightened by the perfume of the incense, which, wafted from the chancel, now filled the whole church, and brought forcibly to mind the prayer of the holy Psalmist, and the words of the Prophet Malachi, "In every place incense shall be offered unto My name, and a pure offering: for My name shall be great among the heathen, saith the LORD of hosts." Who shall presume to say that this was but a dead and empty form, that it was not accompanied by the devout aspirations of a thankful heart? The hymn was afterwards recognised by the repetition of the word *Kadisha*, "Holy," (which occurs nine times in all,) and will be found with the melody to which it is sung at p. 157.

When it was ended, the curtain was drawn across the chancel-arch, and a short pause ensued, during which two clerks brought down a small table and set it in the middle below the steps. It was about eighteen inches square, and covered with a hanging of red cloth, the side towards the people being ornamented with a rude figure of a metran, or bishop, about half life-size, represented in the attitude of blessing. Having set this little table in its place, the clerks returned to the chancel, and brought from it a small cross and bookstand and two lighted tapers, which they placed upon the table, the cross on the west, and the book-stand on the east, with the tapers on either side.

All being thus prepared, the curtain was drawn aside, and the catanar came down to read the Scriptures to the people, first using the appointed prayer, and then making the sign of the cross as he gave out the place at which he was about to read. Thus were read first "the Apostle," that is, what we should call the Epistle for the day, and after that "the Evangelion" or Gospel, which was given out as before, and preceded by its proper prayer, the people making a short response.

I may here mention that at Chattanoor, the candles were held by the lay clerks, one on each side of the catanar, while he read "the life-giving preaching" of the Evangelist. In either method, the special honour with which the reading of Holy Scripture was distinguished is worthy of all attention; and (though I regret to say it did not occur to me to make the inquiry for myself) it is pleasing to hear that it is read in the vernacular of the country as well as in Syriac. I am assured by Dr. Neale that this is the case, his authority being the express statement of Dr. Mill, who visited the Malabar Syrians about the year 1820.

As the catanar returned to the altar, the bells and cymbals were again sounded, and a short prayer was uttered by the people, the purport of which, according to the Church Missionary Society's extracts, was that his ministry might be acceptable, and that they might receive assistance through his prayers.

Then followed the Sedra, with its accompanying Procemium, which will be found at the thirty-second and following pages of the MS. It will be observed that the Sedras are not alike in both of my MSS., that in A. (which is far the longer of the two) being cast in the form of a Litany, while the shorter one is a simple prayer. They agree however in the purport of some of the petitions, e.g. those for a worthy participation in the Mysteries, and for the descent of the Holy Spirit upon the oblations of bread and wine[h]. The prayers are recited rapidly, but without any appearance of haste, and in an easy flow of utterance, modulated for the most part upon the first four notes of the key pitched upon, and, as it seemed to me, just as the voice and ear suggest.

The preparation of the censer, which followed next in order, was, if not a particularly striking ceremony, at any rate worthy of notice. The catanar, standing at the south horn of the altar, looking southwards, had the censer presented to him by the deacon, who held it up on high, while the former touching some part of it with his left hand, made the sign of the cross with his right; then put in incense; signed it again; lighted the incense; and signed it a third time. Then, holding one of the suspending chains with his left hand, with his right hand he touched first the top of the hook, and secondly some part of the thurible, and crossed himself, saying, "Holy is the holy Father." Again, taking hold of the second chain, he repeated the former ceremony, saying, "Holy is the holy Son;" and so again a third time, as he held the third suspend-

[h] Renaudot does not give this Sedra in either of the two forms of the *Ordo Communis* translated by him; but it seems to be alluded to in the second form, in the three words *Sedra Illationis Oblationis*. He offers no explanation of the passage; the remarks which he had made with regard to the Great Entrance referring to the oblation of the elements in the earlier part of the service. Yet it is remarkable that *this* is the position of the Great Entrance in the Greek Liturgies, and that our own Office, which retains a vestige of this ceremony in the Oblations following the offertory, places it much in the same position.

ing chain, saying, "Holy is the Living and Holy Spirit." He then took the censer from the hands of the deacon, and having perfumed the front of the altar, commenced the Nicene Creed. The remainder of the Creed was repeated by the deacon, who, during the repetition, took the censer from the priest, and passing quite round the altar, perfumed it at each corner, bowing and kissing them after he had waved the perfume. This done, he returned to his usual station a few paces behind the catanar, who, having washed the tips of his fingers in water, was now kneeling, or rather prostrating himself, in silent prayer before the altar.

Thus ended the *Ordo Communis*, or Ante-Anaphoral portion of the Eucharistic Office, so called because it is always used, whatever be the Anaphora that is to follow. There is, however, little or no apparent break in the service, and as the several Anaphoræ, though differing in the language of the component parts, are always of one and the same form, the outward appearance of the service is the same in all cases[1].

The ANAPHORA always commences with the Prayer before the Peace, a short collect preceding the Kiss, or rather the Sign, of Peace, which is made in the following manner. The deacon takes the censer to the catanar, and having received a fresh supply of incense, he waves it towards each horn of the altar as before, and then towards the catanar officiating, who takes a handful from the cloud of smoke, and puts it to his

[1] The departure of penitents and catechumens, which in olden times used to take place soon after the reading of the Gospel, has long been discontinued; a change noticed by Jacob of Uraha.

nose in sign of salutation. The boy then waves it in like manner to all who are in the chancel, bowing to each as he waves the censer; and they in turn bow and cross themselves, taking a handful of the smoke as it rises towards them. The deacon then descends from the chancel, and in a similar manner transfers the sign of peace to all the congregation, as he passes quickly round[k].

After this the people are called upon to bow their necks before the Lord, and, prayer having been made for a blessing on those who so humble themselves, the mysteries are unveiled, the catanar folding and kissing the veil before laying it down, and saying, "Thou art the hard rock," &c. (MS., p. 47.)

Having done this, he makes the sign of the cross six times,—first on himself, then with outstretched hand he makes it towards the north and towards the south, and thrice eastward over the people, blessing them in a form much resembling that of St. Paul in 2 Cor. xiii. 14, (p. 48); and they meanwhile devoutly cross themselves, thus (as it seemed to me) accepting and appropriating the blessing.

The next portion of the Office, the *Sursum Corda*, closely resembles our own in expression as well as in form; and impressive as it is in its effect upon the outward senses alone, it becomes doubly striking when one learns the inner meaning of what is done. Raising his hands on high toward heaven, the priest bids the

[k] At another church I saw the sign made in a slightly different manner, without the censer, the deacon receiving an imaginary handful of smoke from the catanar, and passing it on in like manner to each member of the congregation.

congregation lift up their hearts to that place where Christ sitteth on the right hand of God. To this the people respond in language similar to our own, "We lift them up unto the Lord." Again the words of exhortation are heard, "Let us reverently praise the Lord:" and the reply is almost verbally the same as our own, "It is meet and right (so to do)." Then, turning to the altar, the celebrant continues the words of adoration, saying, "Truly it is meet and right," &c., which, as with ourselves, are a sort of prelude to the Sanctus, or Trisagium, wherein the people take up the glorious song, together with angels and archangels, and all the company of heaven.

Immediately after this follows the Prayer of Consecration, with the words of Institution; the bells being rung at the taking of paten and chalice respectively. An impressive form of Commemoration follows; then the Invocation of the Holy Spirit, (which Bishop Wilson wished for[1], and against which the Romanists take such grave exception): and after it, the Great Intercession for Quick and Dead, which is usually divided into six portions. (pp. 54—61.)

The curtain is now again drawn across the chancel, while the deacon repeats "the Catholic," and the celebrant performs the ceremony of "the Breaking." This is fully described in the translation, but cannot of course be seen by the congregation. At its conclusion, the curtain is withdrawn, and the Lord's Prayer is said, being commenced, it would seem, by the priest, and taken up by the people at the words "Hallowed be Thy Name."

[1] *Sacra Privata*, edition of 1853. (Oxford: J. H. Parker.)

After this the priest again invokes the blessing of the Holy Trinity upon the congregation, making six signs of the cross as he had done before. Then having kissed the altar, he elevates the paten with both hands, and extends it to the four points of the compass, saying, "Holy things are given for the holy and the pure." The bells are meanwhile loudly rung, and the priest, having elevated the cup in like manner, takes up both paten and chalice, and extending his arms crosswise, holds them on high above the altar, while he invokes the three Persons of the blessed Trinity. (MS., p. 66.)

The act of participation follows: first that of the celebrant and assistant clergy, who receive in the chancel, the curtain being drawn close during their communion; and afterwards that of the people. This was perhaps the most interesting sight of all, not only from its novelty, and from the number of the communicants, but from the impressive grandeur of the whole scene. During the pause that ensued while the catanars and deacons were communicating, the lay clerks brought down the little table that had been used for the reading of the Gospel, and set it where it had been placed before, below the chancel steps, but within the space railed off at the east of the nave. The cross was placed in the centre, and then the curtain was drawn aside, and the catanar was seen, holding the paten in his right hand and the chalice in his left, and attended by two deacons or lay-clerks, bearing lighted tapers, one on each side. He advanced very slowly towards the people, and having made the sign of the cross with the paten in his right hand, crossed his arms one over the other, and so raised the mystéries on high; using meanwhile the appointed prayers, which will be found at p. 72. It was indeed a striking scene, and was rendered yet more impressive by the energy with which the bells and cymbals were sounded, while the congregation repeatedly bowed and crossed themselves, singing, or rather shouting, the *Kyrie eleison* with the greatest apparent earnestness.

The paten was placed on the little table, and the tapers on each side of it; but the wine appears to have been transferred to a brass vessel furnished with a spout like a teapot, and was now in the hands of a lay-clerk, such at least I took him to be, for he was a full-grown man, without the tonsure, and clothed only with a white cloth, such as laymen use, passing about the loins and over the left shoulder. I missed this incident, however, my attention being caught by a rustle in the crowd caused by the communicants coming forward to receive. The men came up first, one by one, and passing to the north side of the little table, stooped, or rather sat on their heels, as low as possible, throwing the head back. The priest then, laying his left hand on the cover of the paten, (which was beautifully embroidered,) raised one corner just so much as to enable him to take out a portion of the wafer between the finger and thumb of his right hand; and placing his left hand on the communicant's forehead, pushed his head with a sudden jerk so far back that I wondered the man could keep his balance, and so placed the bread in his mouth. The recipient then moved a step to the left, and stooping as before, received the wine by its being poured into his mouth through the spout. I observed that it was often spilt.

The women received in like manner, a vast number of them,—there had been about twenty male communicants,—and during the whole time the lay clerks, deacons, and people kept singing a short hymn over and over again. See note at p. 73.

The posture of the communicants, when in the act of receiving, was grotesque in the extreme, and can be appreciated only by those who have seen the contortions of a horse-keeper's body as he hangs on behind a buggy when the hood is down. I have no doubt it was intended to be as reverential as possible.

The Sunday which I spent at Kayencolum was with us the third Sunday after Easter, the Paschal full moon having occurred on the 26th of March, and Easter-day having fallen on the 31st of that month. With the Syrians, however, Easter-day had not yet arrived, this Sunday being with them the last but one in Lent. On this Sunday, and on that which followed, Palm Sunday with them, I witnessed the reception of the Holy Communion by the laity[m].

As there was some difference in the manner of reception in the two cases, I may as well mention it here. At Paroor, where I witnessed their communion

[m] It is stated by Mr. Day (Land of the Permauls, p. 260) that the laity receive the Communion only three times a-year. If so, I was particularly fortunate in witnessing their communion on two out of the four occasions in which I was present at the Corbano. But he may probably have mistaken his authority. The Syrians, like ourselves, are (Dr. Neale informs me) bound to communicate three times a-year; but this does not prevent their communicating oftener.

the second time, both men and women *knelt* in a row, as we do. The bread was administered just as at Kayencolum, but they received the wine from a spoon, and I did not observe that any was spilled on this occasion.

From Kayencolum I proceeded to Mavelicara, which I reached about 4 P. M. Long before I reached it, the grey tower of the Mission church appeared through the trees, or where an open bend of the river permitted an uninterrupted view; but beautiful as it was, I felt distressed to think that it was associated with a course of interference, of which, although I knew little about it then, I could not but see that the result was very deplorable. Having reached the landing-place, I took the liberty of sending my card to Mr. Peet, the missionary, as being a minister of my own Church, and a fellow countryman; and he very kindly pressed me to stay the night.

In the evening he took me to see the Syrian church, where the service would probably be said about sunset. Our route lay along a cart track which had once been a well-appointed road, and it was curious to see how the trees that had formed an avenue, had extended their trunks downwards as well as upwards, as the ground had been washed away from their roots. A few minutes' walk brought us to the Christian quarter, where a large stone cross, some twenty feet high, bore its mute testimony to the love and suffering of our Saviour. It stands, if I got a correct impression of the locality, in what we might call the main street of the town, abutting into the road at a place where four ways meet, and appearing to great advantage among the small trees which skirt the road on either side. That, at least, was my idea of it in the dim twilight of a tropical evening; but there was little time to look around, for the daylight was almost gone, and the evening service had already commenced when we reached the church.

It appeared to be a very large building, and of good height, the chancel being higher than the nave, as is generally the case in the Syrian churches. The interior was feebly illumined by the light of two or three oil lamps; and the general gloom and indistinctness contrasted forcibly with the white dresses of the catanar and his deacons, who stood near the lamps. But there was little reason to regret one's inability to examine the detail of the church, for the service itself was a scene of passing interest. It was conducted by the catanar, who stood within the rails at the north-east of the nave facing the people, while a choir of some six or seven deacons stood in a line before him, and were from time to time heard in the responsive parts of the service, or in those which, like the Creed and Lord's Prayer, were said by priest, deacons, and people together. These little fellows had much the appearance of choristers in our own churches, for they seemed to be from twelve to fourteen years of age, and their long white dresses were just like surplices; but the tonsure gave them a more thoroughly ecclesiastical appearance. At one part of the Office, they went to a small table within the railing, and sung together from a book; but their usual station was in the body of the church, where they either responded by heart, or followed the utterance of the priest.

The most interesting portion of the whole was the ceremony with which the service was concluded. After the last prayer had been said, the priest came to the centre of the railing, where an open space was left for entrance, and while he stood there, the deacons, and after them the congregation, went to him one by one, and putting their hands in his for a moment, received the sign of peace before they left the church.

On our way home Mr. Peet spoke a few words to an old man who had been among the worshippers. "I asked him," said he, "how he thought he must get to heaven?" The old man replied, "By going to church and doing what is right," or something to that effect. This Mr. Peet told me as illustrating a want of saving knowledge among the Syrians; but who should presume to say that under the old man's expression there did not lie the thought of Christ as the foundation of all our hope, through whose merits alone we are accepted before God?

Next morning Mr. Peet shewed me *his* church, a large building, with a good height of roof, and, though too nearly square to be of good proportions, possessing more pretension to architectural merit than the majority of Anglo-Indian churches that I have seen. It was of course without pews, and the font had been placed in front of the altar rails, regard being had to edification, he said; probably it had not occurred to him that this end might perhaps have been attained in a yet higher degree by making the very *position* of the font symbolical of *entrance* into the church. There was nothing that could be called a chancel, and the holy table, which was without a cover, was raised only a few inches above the floor of the nave. Indeed the whole east end was bare and paltry, and by no means equal in effect to those of the Syrian churches.

I left Mavelicara next morning at 7 A.M., and steered for Cottayam, which I hoped to reach before night; but, owing to the winding and interlacing of the rivers, with which the boatmen did not appear to be at all familiar,—for their accustomed route lay much closer to the sea,—it was nearly sunset when we reached the open part of the Backwater opposite Allepie. Here, favoured by the sea breeze, we spread our sail, and were borne delightfully along, the water making a low soothing gurgle as it rippled up against the side of the boat. Such an opportunity of getting the air was not to be lost, and I mounted the cabin roof that I might enjoy it to the full. We were now in the middle of the Backwater, which is here quite ten miles wide. Cottayam lay before us, some seven or eight miles off, its position being marked by a white building about two or three hundred feet above the water; and beyond it rose the hills, higher and higher, and becoming more and more hazy and indistinct, until at length they blended with the dark sky above. Behind us, to the west, was a broad expanse of rippling water; and in the dim distance one could just discern the fringe of palm-trees on its western shore. They were so indistinct as scarcely to interrupt the line of the horizon, and as the sun was now dipping into the ocean beyond, I amused myself with trying to get the time by watching for its disappearance.

But I could not help casting a look occasionally at a threatening cloud-arch that was bearing up rapidly from the north-east, and that, while it added greatly to the picturesque character of the scene, shewed plainly enough that we should not enjoy the sea breeze much longer. In a few minutes the first symptoms of the storm began to exhibit themselves, and we had scarcely time to take down the sail when it burst upon us in all its fury, and changed the surface of the lake from a pleasant ripple to a boiling furious sea. So violent was the motion of the boat, that it required the utmost effort on the part of my servant and myself to keep the crockery, water-bottle, &c., from being thrown down; and the crew had as much as they could do to keep the boat's head to the wind. It was a mere open tub, and heavily laden, so that it did not rise properly over the waves, and seemed in great danger of being swamped. The lightning was very vivid, and the rain poured down in torrents. The crew, however, encouraged by a rupee or two, kept well to their work, and at length, taking advantage of a slight abatement of the storm, succeeded in getting into a sheltering creek. But we could not gain the intended river, and did not reach Cottayam till nearly midnight.

The next morning broke fair and clear, but I was detained a prisoner in my boat by indisposition until the evening, when I sauntered forth in quest of the Mission station. It was my object to pay my respects to the Rev. Mr. Baker, formerly one of the missionaries, who had kindly called on me in Quilon, and then to return to my boat; but it was nearly dark when I reached his house,—for the storm had driven us into the wrong creek, and the landing-place was nearly three miles from the station,—so that I was by no means unwilling to accept his kindly offered hospitality, and to pass the night in a comfortable bed, instead of sleeping in my boat in the midst of fog, mosquitoes, and jackals.

The early part of the following day was devoted to the examination of two Syrian churches, which presented the usual features in architecture and arrangement, except that in both of them the font was a mere hollow recess in the wall of the nave near the west end, and was covered by a door, closing, like that of a cupboard, flush with the wall.

One of these churches contained some good pictures, arranged on the east wall behind the altar. They had become so indistinct through neglect and damp, that it was difficult to make out their subject; but enough was still left to shew that they belonged to no mean order of art, and even in their decay they presented a striking contrast to the daubed frescoes which commonly adorn the walls of a Syrian chancel. These paintings, I was told, had been brought from Goa, at a time when the building was in the hands of the Romo-Syrians, and were probably of European origin. To the Goa party also, I presume, is to be attributed the introduction of an image of the Virgin and Child in the west front of this church. This was the only instance in which I noticed an image in or upon the

Syrian churches, though I examined nine[n], if not ten, of them in different parts of the country.

The Mission church stands on a hill not many minutes' walk from the Syrian churches. It is built in carpenters' Gothic, and is, of course, exceedingly ugly.

There were at this time two ecclesiastics in Malabar, each of whom claimed the right to preside over the Church as its Metropolitan, the allegiance of the several Churches being given to one or other of them, according as locality or other circumstances might influence their choice.

Some of my readers will perhaps recollect that in the year 1856 a certain Mar Athanasius Stephanos made his appearance in England, claiming to be the rightful Metropolitan of the Christians of St. Thomas. He was in some way connected with the quarrel, but I could never ascertain the precise nature of his claim. He did not, however, return to Malabar; nor, indeed, had he been heard of since he left for England. The two claimants now in the country were another Mar Athanasius, and one Mar Koorillos Joachim, who had been sent from Syria to supersede Athanasius in the government of the Church. But the latter had succeeded in gaining the ear of the British Resident, and so far as the authority of the Travancore Government could settle the matter, he was acknowledged

[n] At Kanunkalum, Chattanoor, Quilon (in ruins), Kayencolum, Mavelicara, Cottayam (two), Cheray, Paroor, and another on the Backwater of which I am doubtful whether it belonged to the Syrians or not.

as the rightful owner of the title, and was permitted to reside in the old College at Cottayam, which for some years past had been the abode of the Metropolitan.

As I had come round by Cottayam mainly with the object of seeing Mar Athanasius, I took counsel with Mr. Baker how this was to be effected, and was recommended to send my card with the request that I might be permitted to call in the afternoon. This I did accordingly, and having received a polite message in reply, I walked over to the old College about five o'clock. The Metropolitan received me very courteously, and having led the way to a couple of chairs in the verandah, we entered at once into conversation. He was a man of middle height, a burly figure, and a somewhat portly carriage, and had a very intelligent and agreeable expression of countenance. His dress consisted of a handsome purple silk robe of ample dimensions, buttoned down the front with a row of many buttons, and reaching nearly to the feet. Besides this, he wore trousers and shoes, and a large collar, folded down over the robe. A cross about four inches long hung from his neck by a ribband, and a skull-cap, ornamented with crosses embroidered on it in gold, completed his costume.

Our conversation turned chiefly on manuscript copies of the Services and Calendar of his Church, or of any books connected with it; but the hope that I might obtain some MSS. was not realized. "Our friends the missionaries," said he, "have taken most of our books." While in conversation with him, I took the opportunity of enquiring the rule of the Syrian Church on the subject of sponsors, and was told that *one* sponsor only is required, who must be of the same sex as the child, but not one of the parents; and that the *spiritual affinity* thus established was considered so close as to form a bar to marriage within certain degrees for several generations. I understood him to say *seven*, but must, I think, have been mistaken.

Towards sunset I took leave of the Metropolitan, and proceeded to my boat, (which had been brought round to the river hard by,) being accompanied on my way by a deacon of about fourteen years of age, and a young man a few years older. I was, however, unable to start immediately, as one of the boatmen had gone to a considerable distance to get some milk, an article which is of great value when one is on a journey.

But I had no reason to regret this little delay, as it enabled me to improve my acquaintance with these two lads, who on their part seemed nothing loth to take a turn with me up and down the sandy bank of the river. It was not unnatural, under such circumstances, to speak of the ministry of the Church, of the love of Jesus, and the dignity of the office of those who are called to serve Him, and to tell of His love to the people. This was done in the simplest language that could be used, something in this kind of way:—

"You know Yeshua? the great God, Yeshua Christ, God and Man: What *you* call Him?"

"Yeshua Meshiha, Aloha dilan."

"What is that?—Aloha dilan? Tell English."

"Yeshua Meshiha, our God."

"Yes: He plenty love man. He die for us. It is great business to serve Him; and to tell His love."

I know not how much might be understood by my companions, but I was much struck with the earnestness of the elder boy, who told me he longed to become a deacon, and to serve in the Church.

This led to our talking of the Corbano, and I asked what that was in which the word *kardisha* was so often repeated, especially when the whole congregation sang together. The deacon at once answered in some rapid words of Malayalim, speaking to his friend, and then sang the words,—I write them just as he pronounced them, making no attempt at orthography:—

"Kardisha Aloha, Kardisha Heilsarnar, Kardisha Lămaiosa; Detstalev halapein, Meshiha, Aloha dilan."

This little anthem he was kind enough to sing six or seven times, till I was sure I had both words and melody, and I wrote them down immediately on returning to my boat. The melody was the following; (I cannot persuade myself to alter the Malabar pronunciation, though the Syriac seems to require it in one or two words):—

This is, as I suspected at the time, the Trisagium of the Jacobite Church, differing from that used by the Orthodox and Nestorians, just as the elder boy informed me, by having the words "Who was crucified for us" in place of "Ethrakham alain," "Have mercy upon us °."

The melody is given below with a harmonized accompaniment, which will perhaps be more interesting to the majority of readers; but it should be understood that such a rendering does not represent the effect of the hymn as it is sung in the Syrian churches; for there it is sung in *unison*, and accompanied not by the harmonious chords of our music, but by the clang of two large bells and the clash of cymbals, which, in concert with the shout of a large congregation, produce such utter discord as we never hear in this country. I should explain that the first and second bars in the unharmonized melody stand just as I wrote them down *at the time*, and therefore represent the air more cor-

° Subsequent examination of the Liturgies leads me to doubt whether I carried away with me the correct pronunciation of the first word. This in the Liturgies is written either *Ka-dishth, Thou art Holy*, or *Kadish, Holy*, (the adjective in its absolute state, as it is called). But I am certain the word was pronounced as a trisyllable in Malabar, and there was no sound of *th* in it. This letter, however, is, in that country, commonly pronounced like *s*. Kadisha, or Kadisho, is the adjective in its emphatic state.

The reader will notice a grammatical difficulty in another part:—*Who was* (not wast) *crucified*. Similar instances of change of person have been pointed out in the Liturgies. But I see Renaudot has "Qui crucifixus es," and the Church Missionary Society's Translator "Who didst hang upon the Cross." The difference between the two in Syriac is so great that I think I could hardly have mistaken the pronunciation in this instance.

rectly than the other. But they presented some difficulty in the arrangement of the harmony.

More than two years have passed since I learned this hymn in the manner I have described, but the circumstances under which I heard it produced an impression such as could not easily be forgotten. The scenery itself was very beautiful, for the river issues from between two lofty banks, that on the side of the College subsiding into a gradual slope down to the water's edge, while the opposite bank is continued in a high broken line, covered with foliage from top to bottom, under which the river sweeps with swift but silent flow, making perpetual eddies in its course. The eastern gable of a church, standing high above the water, amid the foliage on the summit, was a picturesque feature in the landscape, and when the moon rose and shed her calm light full upon the whole, it became a scene of unusual beauty, such as might have been well worth an artist's care.

The deacon was habited in the usual dress of his order, a simple white robe reaching to the feet, and confined at the waist by a band, with loose sleeves coming down to the wrist. His head was bare, and exhibited the ordinary tonsure,—that strange but not uncomely token of the crown of thorns,—and as he chanted his glorious song, the song of all Christendom in all ages, (or at least a form of it,) with his hand locked in that of his companion, and looking right on as if his attention were wholly absorbed in the thought of what he sung, I listened with admiration and delight, fancying that such might have been the melody in which the *Ter Sanctus* was raised in the time of Chrysostom or Cyril [p].

At length we proceeded on our way, having taken in a pilot to steer us past the dangerous sunken rocks that occur here and there in the course of that rapid

[p] I mean Cyril of Jerusalem, whose account of the Eucharist as celebrated in his time is so deeply interesting and instructive. But it is doubtful whether this hymn was in use so early, the tradition being that it was first sung in the Church of Constantinople in the time of the Patriarch Proclus, to whom it was delivered by an angel. Proclus was Patriarch of Constantinople A.D. 432—446.

stream. As we approached the Backwater the stream became more sluggish, and the character of the country wholly changed; and about midnight we were passing through one of the most desolate scenes that I ever beheld. Not a tree, not a stick, was to be seen, but, as far as the eye could reach under the full moonlight, water with tufts of reeds and giant grasses rising out of it here and there on every side. It was, in fact, a vast marsh, with a channel winding through it somewhere, but as every opening looked like another, I wondered how the men could find their way. Indeed, they did seem in doubt once or twice, but they held on, winding among the tufts of reed, or across an open space, till at length I had the satisfaction of seeing the weeds become more scarce, and an open channel leading into the Backwater. This was the more grateful as the exhalations from that horrid marsh were exceedingly disagreeable, and of course unwholesome.

We reached Cochin about 7 A.M. on the 25th, and here again I have to acknowledge the kind hospitality with which I was received by Mr. Day, the Civil Surgeon of that station, whose interesting volume, "The Land of the Permauls," has been frequently alluded to.

My object here was twofold: I wished, if possible, to see the Jews, who have for ages dwelt on this coast, and now occupy the town of Mattancherry, near Cochin, and some few other stations inland[q]; and especially to

[q] For further information concerning this interesting people, who consist of two classes, the White and Black Jews, see Buchanan's Christian Researches, and an Art. in the Asiatic Journal, N. S. vol. vi.

pay my respects to Mar Koorillos, who has already been mentioned as having been sent by the Patriarch to supersede Athanasius, in consequence of the charges preferred against the latter.

This venerable old man, after having vainly endeavoured to obtain the recognition of his title to the Metropolitan throne, had taken refuge at Cochin, whence he exercised his authority over such Churches as were disposed to admit his claim. He lived in a miserable hovel standing in a ditch, the remains of the old ditch of the fort. The walls were of brick, to be sure, but old and ruinous, and the building was more fit for a cart-shed than for a human habitation. When I entered it, the uneven mud floor and broken roof, together with the squalid look of everything around, betokened the utmost poverty. There was a rickety table in the centre of the room, but nothing to sit down upon, nor indeed any other furniture except a few pots, &c., used for cooking.

On being informed of my arrival, the Metropolitan emerged from behind a partition which screened off one end of the building. He was in the decline of life, painfully grave and dejected in his manner, and altogether, in personal appearance, no less than in the external circumstances of his dwelling, presented a marked contrast to his younger and more fortunate rival. His dress was a long white garment with many folds, confined at the waist by a band of the same material, and a turban of that peculiar shape represented in some illustrations of the Jewish priests, i.e. nearly spherical, with a hole scooped out of one side for the head.

Our conversation was carried on through an interpreter, and that so lamely, that I obtained no information of any importance. My enquiry for MSS. was fruitless here, as elsewhere; but the Metropolitan was so good as to present me with a copy of the Psalter of which he had just completed a (?) lithographed edition, and afterwards, at my request, signed his name in the fly-leaf. This he did in Syriac, in the form of a cross, thus:—

India. Ap. 27, 1861.
Koorillos J'huyakim
Metr. of

The date in the right hand corner is mere conjecture. It is not Syriac, and I was unable to enquire into its meaning.

Before leaving Cochin, I managed to get a peep at Jews Town, and fortunately just at sunset, as the Sabbath drew on, (for it was Friday evening,) so that I saw them at their devotions in the synagogue. The most noticeable features in the building were the women's gallery over the east end; the tiling of the floor in squares of glazed pottery with a blue pattern on a white ground; the rabbi's pulpit in the centre, facing west; and the copy of the Law in a recess at the west, reverently covered with curtains, which were drawn aside that we might see the writing. It was not in a book, but on a roll, or rather two rolls of a book, set upright, and worked by wooden rollers in the centre.

I know not whether their services are ever used in common, but so long as I was there every one seemed to be praying on his own account, independently of the rest, and standing or sitting, but never kneeling, the utterance of the voice being invariably accompanied by a restless swaying of the body to and fro. I was exceedingly struck by the manifest irreverence in the behaviour of many of them, as they entered into loud conversation with one another, in the synagogue, while others were engaged in prayer.

As I was desirous to see as much of the Syrian services as possible, I left Cochin on Saturday night, so as to insure being in good time at Paroor the following day. After having proceeded a short distance, my attention was attracted by a great many lights on the shore, and on landing to see what was going on, I found that a temporary church had been erected at the place, in preparation it seemed for some coming festival, possibly that of the following day, which, with the Syrians at least, would be Palm Sunday. This was, however, a Roman Church, and their Calendar and computation of Easter would probably coincide with ours. The altar was decked out with a profusion of candlesticks and tawdry ornaments piled one above another, in a manner offensive to English taste, but the church itself seemed well worth notice. It was, in fact, a large tent, with vertical canvas sides about six feet high, whereon were depicted in vivid colouring a number of scenes illustrating Bible history, which were sure to be very attractive. I did not, however, stay long enough to make any minute examination or enquiries.

The distance from Cochin to Paroor is under twenty miles, but as it lies among muddy tidal creeks, I came to an anchor for the night before leaving the more open part of the Backwater, and proceeded leisurely to my destination next day, having held some little communication with the catanar of Cheray on my way.

On arriving in the neighbourhood of Paroor, we were brought to a standstill by the want of water until the tide turned, which it fortunately did in time to enable me to reach the church just as the services began.

The first service began about ten o'clock, and was connected with the blessing and distribution of palms, the long slender pinnæ of the cocoa-nut palm being used on the occasion.

This was succeeded by a processional service, the exact nature of which I was unable to ascertain: and I regretted this the more, because the effect—especially that of the concluding ceremony—was exceedingly striking. In order to give some idea of this ceremony, it is necessary to explain the manner in which the procession was formed. It was headed by the catanar, bearing a small wooden cross, over which a veil was arranged so as not to conceal it entirely. He walked under a canopy supported by bamboos carried by four lay-clerks, and was followed by the deacons and the people. The procession formed at the porch on the north of the church, and proceeded, chanting as they went, to a small stone building in the churchyard like a large tomb, or a well roofed over, before which the service was continued for some minutes. At length they returned, singing as before, towards the great western door, which however was *closed against them.*

The canopy was then lowered, and one of the bamboos being levelled on the shoulders of two men, was thrust thrice against the door, as if knocking for admission. Meanwhile, the catanar standing before the entrance, sang a melody of a most plaintive character, (modulated I thought in a minor key,) some idea of which will be conveyed by striking the following notes on a piano:—

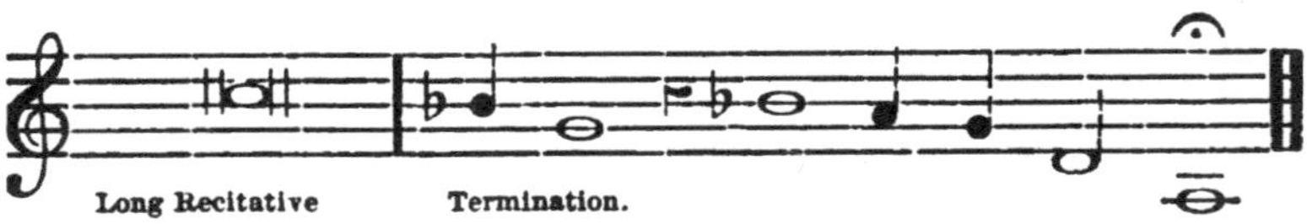

The door however was not opened, but a voice replied from the interior of the church in a strain equally plaintive. Then the bamboo was again made to beat against the door, and the priest repeated his "voice,"[1] and was answered from within as before. But the door was still closed. A third time the knock was made, the catanar repeating his words, and at the third beat of the bamboo the door slowly opened, and the procession entered the church.

After this the Corbano was offered, and the people communicated in the manner already described. On this occasion a great portion of the words were sung by a young deacon, standing about fifteen feet behind the catanar, with a twang of voice and a carelessness of manner that were very disagreeable. This boy wore a curious collar, made of some stiff material covered with embroidery, and rising in a peak behind so high

[1] So I venture to call it, using a Syriac term for supplication. MS. p. 10.

as to conceal all but the crown of his head and the tips of his ears. In other respects the service presented no peculiar features beyond those already noticed.

Paroor was the last Syrian village which I was able to visit. Here, therefore, I must take my leave, apologizing to my readers for the inordinate length to which this notice has grown. Those who have followed me in the sketch of this Church will have found that it has had a full share of those vicissitudes which have been the lot of so many others. They will trace with pain the worldly ambition, the intrigues and struggles for power, which, even to the present day, disfigure the pages of its history; but there are, I trust, not a few, who, remembering that features such as these must of necessity be the most prominent in any history, will love to cherish the belief that, from the day when it was first planted in Malabar, the Gospel has ever done its work in pious souls: that in many a village, such as Chattanoor, Kayencolum, and others, remote from the scenes of strife, men and women have lived quiet and peaceable lives in all godliness and honesty, and in faithful dependence on their Redeemer: that in the Church of Travancore, as elsewhere, beneath the troubled surface, there has ever been, and still is, a deep underflow of piety, which, from its gentle and unobtrusive character, is not chronicled in human records, but whose fruit will be found at the great day to the praise and glory of God.

APPENDIX A.[a]

On the Doctrine of the Christians of S. Thomas.

There are two points in connection with the doctrine of the Syrians of Malabar which seem to require special notice. They are said to be Jacobites; and to adhere to the doctrine professed by the Eastern Church generally in regard to the procession of the Holy Spirit.

1. The Jacobite heresy, as the reader has already been reminded, is said to acknowledge only *one Nature* and one Person in Christ; but it would be a gross misconception of the teaching of the Jacobite doctors, to understand them to affirm that our Lord had only the Nature of God by itself, or that of Man by itself. This is as far as possible from being the case. What they really held is thus gathered by Asseman (tom. ii. p. 25) from the writings of one Xenajas, who was Bishop of Hierapolis in the sixth century:—

"Filius, inquit, Qui unus ex Trinitate est, univit sibi personaliter corpus animâ rationali et mente præditum, in utero Dei parentis. . . . In hoc Christus natus, in hoc nutritus, in hoc passus, in hoc mortuus. Divinitas Filii nec passa nec mortua. Hæc autem omnia non apparenter, non phantasticè, sed vere et naturaliter gesta. Denique Verbum non in carnem conversum, aut cum eâ commistum, vel confusum, neque ab ea divisum; et vice versâ; sed eo modo humanitati unitum, quo anima rationalis corpori: et quemadmodum ex animâ rationali et corpore una conflatur humana natura; ita ex

[a] Referred to at p. 110.

humanitate Christi et divinitate una consurgit natura, non quidem simplex, sed composita, seu, ut recentiores Jacobitæ loquuntur, ܚܕ ܟܝܢܐ ܟܦܝܠܐ *Una natura duplex*, vel ut Xenajas loquutione S. Cyrilli in Epist. i. ad Successum abutitur, *post unitionem in Christo una tantummodò Verbi incarnata natura.*"

Thus then they hold "that there is one Nature in Christ, compounded of the Divinity and the Humanity, but entirely devoid of conversion, confusion, and commixture;" or, as the doctrine is briefly expressed in the title of an Apologetic Treatise by the Jacobite Patriarch Elias, written in the eighth century, "Unam Dei Verbi incarnati naturam in Christo post unionem, salvis proprietatibus, (ܘܢܛܝܪܝܢ ܕܝܠܝܬܐ) profitentur[b]."

These quotations from Asseman will serve to illustrate the bearing of such passages as those found at pp. 8, 62, and 110 of the Liturgies on this very important subject; and it may be interesting to compare with them the language of our own Article, which states the Catholic doctrine in the following terms:—"That two whole and perfect Natures, that is to say, the Godhead and the Manhood, *were joined together in one Person, never to be divided,* whereof is one Christ, very God and very Man."

The Jacobites, it will be observed, acknowledge the *two Natures* in Christ as plainly as we do; but whereas we are taught that they "are joined together" in the one Person of Christ, they maintain that they were so "united" in Him by the Incarnation, as to become

[b] Bibliotheca Orientalis, vol. ii. pp. 25, 95.

ONE NATURE, compounded of the two; *one*, yet two-fold—*Una Natura Duplex*—but "without any conversion, confusion, or commingling."

It is remarkable that two of the expressions last quoted are employed in the decree of the Council of Chalcedon declaring the Catholic faith; and, further, that the term "salvis proprietatibus," which has been already noticed as having been adopted by the Monophysites, has its counterpart also in the Greek of the same decree. The words are:—*Ἕνα καὶ τὸν αὐτὸν Ἰησοῦν Χριστὸν υἱόν, κύριον, μονογενῆ, ἐν δύο φύσεσιν ἀσυγχύτως, ἀτρέπτως, ἀδιαιρέτως, ἀχωρίστως γνωριζόμενον, οὐδαμοῦ τῆς τῶν φύσεων διαφορᾶς ἀνῃρημένης διὰ τὴν ἕνωσιν, σωζομένης δὲ μᾶλλον τῆς ἰδιότητος ἑκατέρας φύσεως καὶ εἰς ἓν πρόσωπον καὶ μίαν ὑπόστασιν συντρεχούσης, κ. τ. λ.*[c]

Whatever, therefore, may have been the distinctive features of the earlier form of the Eutychian heresy, the later Monophysites (though adhering to the general modes of expression with which this name is associated) appear to have guarded their language with the greatest care, by the use of terms intended to maintain the conception of a *distinct existence* of the two Natures in the one Person of Christ, while at the same time they asserted their *union*. They recognize them, not as co-existing only, but as actually united; neither Nature absorbed in the other, but the two together forming by their union a *tertium quid*, if we may reverently so speak, yet "without confusion," "and so that the properties of each are preserved."

[c] I take the quotation from Bishop Beveridge, on Art. II., p. 97.

If the foregoing be a correct description of the tenets maintained by the Jacobites, their heterodoxy would appear to consist, not so much in a denial of the Catholic faith, as in the addition which they have made thereto, by affirming more than it affirms.

It has been maintained however by some, and happily not without reason, that the difference between the orthodox and Jacobite doctrine on this subject exists rather in the mode of expression employed, than in real meaning; inasmuch as the union asserted by the latter is so limited by the use of qualifying terms, as to signify much the same thing as the conjunction or co-existence held by the orthodox Churches. The controversy (like so many others that have disturbed the Church's peace) appears to have been due, in a great measure, to an overweening love of logical precision, and a desire to define in terms what is beyond the reach of reason or language; and we may be heartily thankful that the Catholic doctrine has been handed down to us in the more cautious, and therefore more reverent, expressions of our own Article, and in the grand plain declarations of the Athanasian Creed.

The main point, however, with which we are concerned, is the practical question, whether the present creed of the Malabar Syrians on this vital point is such as to present a bar to intercommunion with them. That it has not been so considered by many eminent members of the Church of England, is plain from the historical sketch in the preceding pages; but perhaps only because their attention had not been closely drawn to the subject. Yet it may be found that the Syrians in Malabar are not so thoroughly committed to the opinions condemned at the Council of Chalcedon as to present an insuperable obstacle to intercommunion. "Notwithstanding their profession of Jacobitism," writes Dr. Buchanan, "they seem to explain it away in words; for they spoke of Christ's human nature." (Chr. Res., p. 129.) They clearly acknowledge both the divinity and humanity joined together in the one Person of Christ; and there is abundant evidence that they accept in its fulness the doctrine of atonement by His vicarious sufferings. See pp. 11, 33, 60, 62, 63, &c., the passages on pp. 62, 63 being especially remarkable.

Still, it becomes a question of deep anxiety whether we can, without danger of betraying the faith, hold communion with a Church whose clergy, it is affirmed, "renounce and abjure," in common with the worst heretics, "the Synod of Chalcedon," and Leo, who presided at that Synod; while at the same time they promise adherence to Gregory of Alexandria, Dioscorus, and Severus, who are said to have supported the Eutychian heresy [d].

It is possible that these and similar passages are retained by the Syrians in Malabar, not so much from a strong attachment to them as integral parts of their Offices, as by the habitual use of accustomed forms; and, if so, the prospect of their being induced to omit

[d] Address of the Metran to the Candidates for the Priesthood, at their ordination. See it in the Madras Church Missionary Record, vol. iv. 134, and (probably) in Hough's Christianity in India. Compare pp. 77, 78 of the MSS.

the objectionable names, in case they should consent to a revision of their Liturgy and Ordinal, is not altogether hopeless.

2. With reference to the Procession of the Holy Spirit, the Malabar Syrians, in common with the Eastern Churches generally, acknowledge, it is said, no more than this, that He proceedeth from the Father. But may it not be urged once again, that, on a subject so full of mystery, we are bound to exercise mutual forbearance one towards another? Is it not conceivable that, while the Western Church, gathering the doctrine from *the general sense* of Holy Scripture, affirms her belief that the Holy Spirit "proceedeth from the Father and the Son;" the Eastern Churches prefer to adhere to the *very letter* of Scripture, and while fully acknowledging that the Holy Spirit was *sent* by the Son, and *receiveth essentially of the Son*[e], yet desire to express their belief in the exact words of the Lord Jesus, (without any addition thereto,) viz., that He "proceedeth from the Father?"

The history of that deplorable controversy which was so long maintained on this subject, and which finally resulted in the disruption of the East and West, is thus concisely given by Bp. Beveridge. "The first General Council assembled at Nice, A.D. 325, having composed an excellent Creed or rule of faith, and having said no more in it concerning the Holy Ghost, than *καὶ εἰς τὸ πνεῦμα τὸ ἅγιον, and* (we believe) *in the Holy Ghost;* there being another General Council about fifty years after, held at Constantinople, they

[e] See the Anaphora of Barsalibi, p. 124, and of Xystus, p. 136.

thought good, for the better suppressing of the heresy of Macedonius, who denied the Divinity of the Holy Ghost, to confirm the same Creed, with this addition amongst others to it, *καὶ εἰς τὸ πνεῦμα τὸ ἅγιον, τὸ κύριον, τὸ ζωοποιόν, τὸ ἐκ τοῦ πατρὸς ἐκπορευόμενον.* Which Creed, with this addition, the next General Council at Ephesus, A.D. 431, not only continued, but also denounced an anathema against all such as should make any more additions to it.

"Yet notwithstanding, the controversy being started in the Western Churches, whether the Spirit proceed from the Son or no, as well as from the Father, the eighth Council at Toledo in Spain, A.D. 653, debating the question, and carrying it in the affirmative, they, after those words in the Constantinopolitan Creed, *ἐκ τοῦ πατρὸς*, put in *καὶ υἱοῦ*, and so made it run in Latin, ... 'ex Patre Filioque procedentem;' and not only so, but they caused this Creed so enlarged and altered to be put into their public liturgies, and so sung continually in their churches, the French joining with them, and afterwards the English too, as we may see in our public liturgy.

"But in the Council held at Akens, in Germany, the matter was after debate referred to Pope Leo III., but he was so far from allowing of that addition, that he desired it might by degrees be quite left out of the Creed. . . . . And that a true copy of the said Creed, without any such addition to it, might be recorded and perpetuated, he caused it to be graven in Greek and Latin upon silver plates, and placed in the church for every one to read. . . . . But afterwards these tables were neglected, and Pope Nicholas I. caused this clause *Filioque* to be added again to the Creed, and so to be read in all the churches under his power. But Photius, Patriarch of Constantinople, condemned him for it; and in the Council of Constantinople, A.D. 879, it was declared that the addition should be quite taken away again: and after that, Cerularius, Theophylact, and the Grecians generally, inveighed against it. For which the Popes of Rome branded them, and so all the Greek Churches, with heresy. And so the quarrel betwixt the Greek and Latin, or Eastern and Western Churches, began and hath been continued; the Eastern Churches condemning the Western for inserting the clause *Filioque* into the Creed of a General Council without the consent of the like authority; the Western Churches, on the other hand, condemning the Eastern for keeping it out." (Treat. on the Articles, pp. 174, 175.)

"The principal errors of the Syrian Church" are thus enumerated by the Editor of the Madras Church Missionary Record for Nov. 1835:—

"1. Transubstantiation.

"2. The Sacrifice of the Mass, in which it is said that the priest offers Christ for the quick and dead to have remission of pain or guilt.

"3. Prayers for the dead.

"4. Purgatory, or the possibility of transition from an unpardoned to a pardoned state, between the periods of death and judgment.

"5. Worship of the Virgin Mary, supplicating her intercessions, and observing a fast in her honour.

"6. Worship of saints.

"7. Prayers in an unknown tongue.

"8. Extreme unction.

"9. Attributing to the clergy the power to curse and destroy men's bodies and souls.

"10. The having pictures in their churches representing God the Father.

"11. Prayers to the altar and chancel.

"Connected with these," he adds, "are the elevation of the host, burning incense, ringing of bells at the time of elevation, the priest receiving the Mass alone, &c."

In reference to the foregoing charges, I would observe that a belief in the Real Presence does not necessarily involve a belief in transubstantiation; that the 1st, 2nd, 4th, 6th objections, and so much of the 5th as relates to worship, cannot, I believe, be substantiated by reference to any of their generally received Offices; and that while some of the remainder must be admitted, others are either frivolous, or probably capable of satisfactory explanation. The tenth very serious charge rests, I presume, on sufficient authority, (except, I would hope, in the use of the plural for the singular[f],) but, alas, we ourselves might not without cause be charged with this very offence, and yet it would be a gross libel on the Church of England to represent her as ordinarily chargeable with such things, because one or two instances of them are to be found.

[f] The only specified instance of which I find mention is that of a picture in one of the churches at Cottayam, probably one of those introduced by the Goa party, *and of Western origin*. Madras Church Missionary Record, vol. i. pp. 182, 183.

APPENDIX B.[g]

On Ceremonial in the East.

It would be as hopeless as it is unnecessary to attempt to force the Syrians into uniformity with ourselves in matters of ceremonial. What to many of us seems objectionable and superstitious "mummery," is with them oftentimes expressive of the most pregnant meaning. The lighting of tapers, censing the altar and people, mixing water with the wine, the careful ceremonial at "the breaking," &c., occur as instances in point. And as *words* are but the *signs of ideas* in LANGUAGE, so a proper and suitable ceremonial assists the expression and comprehension of them by the sight of an act performed. Ceremonial therefore may be, as it certainly is, a very useful handmaid in the service of religion, even the purest and most spiritual. It seems to have a special advantage in helping to teach those who are but little instructed, and exercises a marvellous influence in fixing the attention, and in "stirring up the dull mind of man" to a keener, heartier perception of spiritual things. Who that in humility and reverence has really attended to our services has not felt the power of those few but most significant ceremonies which still remain with us; the vesting of the minister, the imposition of hands, the cross at holy baptism, the standing of the priest, his kneeling at the prayer of humble access, the breaking of the bread, the act of consecration, and the final veiling of the elements?

[g] Referred to at p. 113.

There may be indeed a tendency to adopt ceremonial of such a kind, and to such an extent, as to distract the attention, rather than to assist the understanding and to promote devotion. Against such a danger—and it is one to which Eastern nations seem especially liable—a carefully revised Liturgy would be perhaps the surest safeguard. But to insist upon a near conformity with our English office, in case a revision should be undertaken, or to advocate the excision of the Church's ancient ritual, would assuredly lead to failure and disappointment.

For it should not be forgotten, that although, as a people, we are scarcely tolerant of high religious ceremonial, most other nations are wont to regard it as an essential part of their worship. A letter which appeared in the "Guardian" some years ago, from the pen of the Bishop of Brechin, forcibly presents this consideration with regard to the natives of India. His Lordship, whose personal acquaintance with the country greatly enhances the value of his testimony, points out the instinctive love of ceremonial which pervades all classes of natives, and the hopelessness that they will ever be brought in great numbers, and without motives of worldly interest, to join a communion which offers little that is attractive in this respect.

If this be the case in regard to the heathen natives of India,—and those who know anything of the country must be struck with the truth of the Bishop's remark,—it is at least equally so with the Christians of St. Thomas.

Would it be wise, therefore, to attempt to bring

them down to the cold unimpressive form of celebrating Divine Service which prevails so generally in our mission stations, and in so many parishes in England? Would it not be the truer wisdom to endeavour to persuade them so to *modify their existing ritual* (where such a course is absolutely necessary) *as to make it the exponent of a pure evangelical creed?*

APPENDIX C.

On the Ordo Communis and Anaphora.

Renaudot gives the following interesting summary of the Oriental Liturgies, as they are usually celebrated. (Vol. ii. xvi.)

"Observandum primo est, Liturgiam Syriacam, ut reliquas omnes orientales et occidentales, duabus partibus constare; quarum prima præparatoria est, altera, quæ Canoni nostro respondet, proprie *Anaphora* appellatur, ut apud Latinos veteres, *Oblatio, Illatio, Actio,* aut aliter vocata quondam fuit.

I. *The Preparatory Office, or Ordo Communis.*

"Præparato altari, Sacerdos diversas preces recitat, sacra vestimenta induit, et ita ad sanctuarium progreditur. Panis Eucharisticus, cum Calice, a Prothesi, ubi statim collocantur, ad altare deferuntur, eadem prope ratione, qua fit apud Græcos *magnus* ut vocant *Introitus.* Miscetur vinum aqua, ex vetustissima traditione: Dona, ubi ad altare illata sunt, duplici velo, majori et minori, teguntur, et incensantur. Dicuntur interea variæ orationes; Trisagium; Gloria in Excelsis; Psalmi aliquot; Hymni diversi secundum dies; Carmine Ephremitico vel Jacobitico; Procemia. Deinde leguntur sectiones ex Epistolis Pauli, et Catholicis; aliquando ex Actis Apostolorum, et ex Veteri Testamento; juxta indices qui habentur in singulari codice: neque enim, ut apud Latinos, Lectiones libris Missalibus inseruntur, sed petuntur ex Lectionariis quæ apud Syros et reliquos Orientales habentur, ut apud Græcos, *Ἀποστολοευαγγέλια*. Preces, benedictionesque Sacerdotis, hortationes Diaconi ad populum, singulis lectionibus adjunguntur; et eodem tenore, antea vel paulo post, dicuntur orationes *Εἰρηνικαί*, sive pro pace et aliis beneficiis quæ a Deo postulantur; præeunte Diacono: Sacerdote secretam orationem interdum pronunciante, et populo acclamante *Kyrie eleison*. Scripturarum lectio fit primum Syriacè, et postea Arabicè, quæ lingua est maximæ partis Orientis vernacula. His peractis, canitur Syriacè a populo Nicænum Symbolum: Sacerdos manus lavat; commendat se circumstantium precibus; et incipitur Anaphora, sive sacra Actio.

II. *The Anaphora.*

"Illius initium est oratio ante osculum pacis; et antequam dicatur superest in codicibus MSS[is] vetus formula ejiciendi audientes et pœnitentes, testis antiquæ disciplinæ. Tum benedictio antiquissima; *Caritas Dei Patris, &c.*; signum crucis super populum. Post osculum pacis, *Sursum corda* et reliqua, cujus formulæ ubique receptæ in omnibus cujuscumque linguæ Liturgiis extat memoria. Præfatio quæ est de gratiarum actione, laudibusque ad Deum referendis propter omnia in genus humanum beneficia, creationis, legis promulgatæ, missionis Prophetarum, tandem liberationis humani generis per Incarnationem, salutaremque Dispensationem Christi Domini. Sequitur in Præfationis fine Hymnus Cherubicus, *Sanctus, Sanctus, Sanctus*, qui canitur a populo.

"Sacerdos longam orationem pronunciat in Dei laudem, et pro Liturgiarum diversitate aliquando brevior, aliquando prolixior est illa oratio. Desinit autem in institutionis Sacramenti commemoratione, et pronunciatione verborum Christi, super panem, et super calicem: ad quæ populus acclamat, *Mortem Tuam Domine annunciamus, &c.* Sequuntur orationes sacerdotis in eamdem sententiam: et paulo post, *Invocatio Spiritus Sancti*, quam præcedit Diaconi exhortatio ad populum, ut oret attentius, expectando ejus illapsum in dona proposita. Ipsa Invocationis formula eadem omnino est, quæ in Græcis codicibus. Sequuntur Diptycha; tum commemoratio mortuorum; Sanctorum memoria: Oratio Dominica, quam Sacerdos incipit, populus alta voce continuat: Elevatio Eucharistiæ: et *Sancta Sanctis.* Tum hostiæ fractio, et particulæ in calicem intinctio; tum ex eadem, reliquarum quæ in sacro disco sunt, particularum consignatio: Sacerdotis communio: ejusdem distributio Sacerdotibus, Diaconis, et reliquis ex Clero. Deinde communio populo distribuitur per intinctam particulam, quæ cochleari præbetur: Gratiarum actio et Sacerdotis ultima benedictio.

"Atque hæc est totius Eucharistici Officii dispositio, secundum Jacobi Syriacam Liturgiam, Orthodoxis et Jacobiticis communem."

The following analysis and conspectus of the several Offices translated will, it is hoped, be found useful.

Analysis of the Ordo Communis.

Pages of the MS.		The work referred to in this column is the Second Form of the Ordo Com. [O_2] given by Renaudot, Lit. Orient. Coll., vol. ii. 12—21.
	The First Service, with closed curtain.	
1.	Priest stands before the Throne. *Glory,* and *Make us worthy*	O_2 12.
1—4.	Sedra with its Prooemium . . .	Wanting in R.
4.	Putting on the black dress, he repeats Ps. li.	O_2 12. Here R. inserts a clause.
6.	Approaches the Altar. *I will come* .	O_2 12.
6.	Kneels down. *To Thy house* . .	O_2 12.
6.	Kisses the Altar. *Bind, O Lord* . .	O_2 12.
7.	Lights taper on the south. *In Thy light*	O_2 12.
7.	Lights taper on the north. *O sacred* .	O_2 12.
9—12.	The Sedra of Penitence, with Prooem. .	O_2 13, 14, abbreviated.
12.	The Trisagium	Wanting in R.
12.	The Lord's Prayer	Wanting in R.
13.	End of the First Service . .	O_2 14.
13.	Service of the Corban, or Oblation .	O_2 14.
13.	Priest puts off his ordinary garments. *Put off from me, O Lord God* . .	O_2 14.
13.	Washes his hands. *Make us worthy* .	O_2 14.
14, 15.	The vesting	O_2 15, including the prayers to be used with the sandals, wanting in my copy.
7—9.	THE ENTRANCE[h], as follows . .	O_2 12, 13.

[h] For the reason of this transposition, see Introductory Notice, p. 131.

9.	The Priest arranges the sponge, spoon, *Coal*, and veil, on the altar . . .	O_2 13.
8.	Takes the *Seal* in both hands. *He was led*	O_2 13.
8.	Places the *First-begotten*. *O First-begotten*	O_2 13.
8.	Mingles water with the wine. *Make one*	O_2 12.
7.	Pours a draught into the cup. *Our Lord*	O_2 13.

The order in my MS. is confessedly misplaced. It varies in all the MSS. and Translations that I have seen.

[C.M.S.Tr.]	Covers the Mysteries with their veils .	
15, 16.	Kneels down before the altar. *O Lord God*	O_2 15, 16.
16.	Removes the veils. *The Lord reigneth* .	O_2 16.
17.	*O pure and spotless Lamb* . . .	O_2 16.
18—22.	Raises the Mysteries on high, crosswise. *The Memorial of our Lord* . .	O_2 16, 17.
22.	Στῶμεν καλῶς	O_2 17.
22.	*Kyrie Eleison*	O_2 17.
22.	Veils the Mysteries. *The heavens are* .	O_2 18.
23.	Incense. *To the glory and honour* .	O_2 18.
23—25.	The general Sedra	O_2 18.
26, 27.	Censing of the altar and Mysteries .	O_2 18, 19.
27, 28.	The Seal	Wanting in R.
28.	The Nicene Creed	Wanting in R.
28.	Responsory of Severus . . .	O_2 19.
28.	The Trisagium, and *Kyrie Eleison* .	O_2 19.
28—32.	The Epistle and Gospel, or other SS. .	O_2 19, 20.
32—41.	Sedra and Litany	Wanting in R.
41.	Incense. *The Holy Father is holy* .	O_2 20.
41.	Σοφίᾳ πρόσχωμεν	O_2 20.
41.	The Nicene Creed	O_2 20.
41, 42.	Priest washes his fingers. *Wash away* .	O_2 20.
	Asks forgiveness. *My brethren and* .	O_2 20, a different form.
42, 43.	Kneels before the Table of Life, and prays in secret. *O holy and glorious Trinity*	O_2 20, 21.
	Ascends the step; kisses the throne; and begins the Anaphora, "cantu gravi et tranquillo." [O_2.] . .	O_2 21.
43, 44.	Prayers on certain occasions . .	Wanting in R.

Conspectus of t

Pages of the MS.	St. James.	St. Peter.	XII Apost.
45.	The Prayer before the peace . .	. . . . .	. . .
46.	Peace	. . . . .	. . .
46.	*Let us bow our heads*	A slight varia	tion in the
47.	The Prayer of the Veil. *O God* . .	. . . . .	. . .
47.	*Let us stand*	. . . . .	. . .
47.	*Thou art the hard rock* . . .	. . . . .	omitted.
48.	*The Love of God*	. . . . .	. . .
48.	Sursum Corda	. . . . .	. . .
48, 49.	*Let us praise. Holy, Holy, Holy* . .	. . . . .	. . .
49.	Pr. of Institution, with the response, *Thy Death*	. . . . .	. . .
52.	*Have mercy. And we also* . . .	. . . . .	. . .
omitted.	*How terrible.* [Omitted in both my MSS. See note ad locum.] . .	. . . . .	. . .
52—54.	Invocation of the Holy Ghost . .	. . . . .	. . .
54—60.	The Great Intercession	. . . . .	. . .
60, 61.	*Put away. As. Peace. The Mercies*	. . . . .	. . .
61.	The Catholic	. . . . .	. . .
61—64.	The Breaking	. . . . .	. . .
64, 65.	The Lord's Prayer, with Introduction and Embolismus	. . . . .	. . .
65, 66.	*Peace.* Bowing the neck. Prayer for blessing. *Peace.* Blessing . .	. . . . .	. . .
66.	*Let us behold*	. . . . .	. . .
66.	Sancta sanctis	. . . . .	. . .
66.	*The One Father is Holy* . . .	. . . . .	. . .
67—73.	Here follows the Communion, the	order of which,	being appare
73.	Let us stand	omitted.	omitted.
73, 74.	Thanksgiving. *Peace.* Blessing .	. . . . .	. . . .
75—94.	The Seal, and all that follows, including the Dismissal of the P Dead, and the Farewell to the Altar, are given only once, being co found for the most part in Renaudot's Second Ordo Communis.		

: *Anaphoræ translated.*

Barsalibi.	Xystus.	Evannis.	Renaud. Tr. Lit. Jac.	Remarks.
. . .	. . . .	. . . .	. . . .	Explanation.—The dotted line indicates a corresponding form in the several Anaphoræ.
. . .	. . . .	. . . .	. . . . .	
words in	all the six Ana	phoræ.	omitted.	
. . .	. . . .	. . . .	. . . .	
. . .	. . . .	. . . .	. . . .	
omitted.	omitted.	omitted.	omitted.	
. . .	. . . .	. . . .	. . . .	
. . .	. . . .	. . . .	. . . .	
. . .	omitted, but implied.	. . . .	. . . .	
. . .	. . . .	. . . .	. . . .	
. . .	. . . .	. . . .	. . . .	
. . .	. . . .	. . . .	. . . .	
. . .	. . . .	. . . .	. . . .	
. . .	. . . .	. . . .	. . . .	
. . .	. . . .	. . . .	. . . .	
. . .	. . . .	. . . .	. . . .	The Deacon says the Catholic, while the Priest is occupied with the Breaking.
. . .	. . . .	. . . .	. . . .	
. . .	. . . .	. . . .	. . . .	
. . .	. . . .	. . . .	. . . .	
. . .	. . . .	. . . .	. . . . .	
. . .	. . . .	. . . .	Only in Lit. major.	
. . .	. . . .	. . . .	. . . . .	
mmon to all	Anaphoræ, is gi	ven only once.	See O_2 p. 23.	
. . .	. . . .	. . . .	omitted.	
. . .	. . . .	. . . .	. . . . .	

the Disposal of the Elements, the Sedra of the to all the Anaphoræ. Hence they are

Of the Altar, Holy Vessels, &c.

The Altar or Throne is generally about 4 ft. high, 6 ft. in length, and 3½ or 4 ft. in width. It is built sometimes of stone, sometimes of wood, and is placed so as to admit of a passage between it and the east wall of the chancel. At the time of the celebration it is covered with a white cloth, and the western side is usually ornamented with a frontal, bearing an embroidered cross in the centre. In front is a single step, on which the priest is directed to stand during certain portions of the Office.

The furniture of the altar comprises, in addition to the holy vessels, a wooden cross in the centre, sometimes bearing the image of the Crucified rudely painted upon it; two plain candlesticks, one on each side of the cross; a book-stand, which is usually placed on the south; and the *Tablitho*, or Table, a slab of precious wood or marble, about eighteen inches in length and twelve in width, which is placed on the throne in the centre of the west side, and is used as a stand for the sacred vessels at the time of celebration.

Besides the paten and the chalice, we find mention of a sponge and spoon, and three veils, two small ones for the paten and the cup respectively, and the third to cover the whole. This last is called the *anaphora*, and corresponds to the Greek νεφέλη or ἀήρ. The sponge (which, by-the-bye, is said to be made of silk, though it retains a name consistent with the Levantine origin of the Liturgy) is used apparently for the frequent washing of the fingers prescribed by the rubric, and for wiping out the cup after the celebration.

The bread is made of fine flour, with leaven, and ought to be prepared on the same day on which it is offered. It is said to be circular in shape, and to be stamped with a large cross, the centre of which coincides with the centre of the circle. The border is ornamented with smaller crosses, so that when it is broken up each fragment may bear the holy symbol. It will be observed that the bread is mentioned by various names, as *the Corbano* (or Oblation), *the First-begotten*, *the Seal*, *the Body*, and *the Coal*, the last probably in allusion to Isaiah vi. 6. The *Seal* is said by Renaudot to be the central portion, "major et media pars Oblatæ." The bread and wine are together called *the Mysteries*, a name which (like the others) is applied to them both before and after consecration.

THE LITURGY OF ST. JAMES, BROTHER OF OUR LORD.

"NEQUE sane aliter de eo judicaverunt veteres Christiani Syri, cum Jacobi Liturgiam sua lingua transtulerunt, sive formulæ illæ sacrorum Græce primo, sive lingua Hierosolymitana, quæ magnam affinitatem habet, scriptæ fuerint. Factum id fuisse ante schisma Jacobitarum, hoc est ante Concilium Chalcedonense, vel eo solo probatur, quod orthodoxi Syri, non minus quam Jacobitæ, eamdem Jacobi Liturgiam non servant modo inter recentiores multas alias, sed eam ut præcipuam sequuntur, veluti Canonem generalem, ut in Præfatione ad Syrorum Liturgias fusius exponetur."—*Renaudot, Lit. Orient. Coll.*, i. p. xxv.

ORDO COMMUNIS.

ܗ̄ p. of MS. 1

By the power of our Lord Jesus Christ we are beginning to write the Book of the Order of the Anaphora of Mar Jacob, Brother of our Lord.

First. The priest praising. Glory to the Father, and to the Son, and to the Holy Ghost: and may mercy and grace be poured forth on us who are weak and sinful in both worlds, for ever and ever. Amen.

The prayer of the beginning. Make us worthy, O Lord God, merciful and loving towards man, with knowledge, and reverence, and beauty of spiritual order to stand before Thee, purely and holily, and to minister unto Thee as the Lord and Maker, to whom is due adoration from all: Father, and Son, and Holy Ghost.

Proœmium[k]. Let us pray, all of us: let us ask mercy
and grace from the Lord. O merciful Lord, have 2
mercy upon us and help us. May we be made worthy to send up glory, and thanksgiving, and honour, and praise, and exaltation good that doth not cease, continually, in all moments and times, to Him who hath

[k] It will be observed that the Sedras are always preceded by a short introduction, or proœmium. The word *sedra* literally signifies *order* or *series*. This Sedra (with its Proœmium) is wanting in both forms of the *Ordo Communis* given by Renaudot, in Dr. Mill's MS., and in the Extracts from the Liturgy published by the Church Missionary Society. It is probably of a comparatively recent date. B. contained it, but the first leaf of that MS. is missing.

magnified the memory of His mother and of all His saints in His goodness, and pardoneth the faithful dead in His grace: to whom belongeth glory, and honour, and adoration in this time of this divine perfect eucharist, and in all feasts, and times, and hours, and moments, and all the days of our life, now and in all moments for ever and ever.

Sedra. May all who from the beginning have pleased
Thee make supplication unto Thee with us, and for us,
and because of us;—holy fathers and patriarchs; they
who served in the priestly office of the ministry of the
law: to wit, the prophets who declared Thy revelation;
3 the apostles who preached Thy gospel; the martyrs
who were killed for love of Thee; the confessors who
confessed Thy divinity; the doctors who held the
truth; the priests who served Thy altars; the deacons
who did Thy will; the upright[l] who laboured in Thy
vineyard; the monks, and cœnobites, and religious,
and styliti[m]; they who clung to Thy divine words and
life-giving commandments, and renounced kindred and
family, and took up their cross and followed Thee.
With these, and before these, and after these, she who
is the glory of the whole earth, and named the second
heavens[n], the Virgin immaculate, the holy Mother of

[l] ܟܫܝܪܐ, *prosperous, skilful,* perhaps *diligent.* Castell gives *rectus fuit* as the meaning of the root.

[m] ܐܣܛܘܢܝܐ, Styliti, probably a religious order. "Guards or watchers," according to Catanar Jacob. Cf. p. 71 of the MS.

[n] ܡܥܛܦܢܘܬܗ ܫܡܝܐ ܕܬܪܬܝܢ. Cf. "Per orationes .... matris amictæ justitia, cœli secundi, Virginis immaculatæ," &c.—*Renaudot, Lit. Or. Coll.*, ii. 25. The words occur in the *Seal,* in O_2. (Cf. p. 75 of the MS.)

God, Mary. By her prayers and [those] of all the saints,
do Thou avert and make to pass away and turn from
us all strokes and rods of wrath, which have been 4
brought upon us because of our sins; and lead us
quietly in tranquillity and in peace all the days of our
life; and heal the sick, O my Lord, by Thy power;
and enlarge the afflicted in Thy mercy; and make rest
and good remembrance to all who lie asleep in Thy
hope in the belief of the truth; so that we and they
may send up unto Thee glory and thanksgiving, and
to Thy Father, and to Thy Holy Spirit, now and in
all moments for ever.

He says[o] *the Psalm at full length.* Have mercy upon
me, O God, according to Thy goodness; and according
to the abundance of Thy mercies blot out my sins.
Wash me copiously from Mine iniquity: and cleanse
me from my sins. For I confess my faults: and my
sins are before me at all times. Against Thee, Thee
only, have I sinned, and done wickedness before Thee:
that Thou mayest be justified in Thy word, and mayest
conquer in Thy judgments. For I was conceived in 5
iniquity: and in sins did my mother conceive me.
But Thou takest pleasure in truth: and teachest me
the hidden things of Thy wisdom. Sprinkle me with
Thy hyssop, and I shall be cleansed: wash me with it,
(and) I shall be whiter than snow. Fill me with Thy
joy and Thy gladness: and my bones that are laid low
shall rejoice. Turn away Thy face from my sins: and

[o] Here ܠܐܡܪ̈ is doubtless an error, either for ܐܡܪ̈, 'he says,' or for ܘܐܡܪ̈, 'and he says,' which B. has.

blot out all my misdeeds. Create in me a clean heart,
O God: and renew Thy firm Spirit within me. And
cast me not away from before Thee: and take not Thy
Holy Spirit from me. But restore to me Thy joy and
Thy salvation: and let Thy glorious Spirit sustain me.
That I may teach the wicked Thy way: and sinners
may be converted unto Thee. Deliver me from blood,
O my God, God of my salvation: and my tongue shall
glorify Thy righteousness. O Lord, open my lips for
6 me: and my mouth shall sing Thy glory. For Thou
hast no pleasure in sacrifices: and art not appeased
by whole burnt-offerings. The sacrifices of God are a
lowly spirit: a contrite heart, O God, Thou dost not
despise. Be favourable in Thy pleasure unto Sion:
and build the walls of Jerusalem. Then shalt Thou
be pleased with sacrifices of truth and with whole
burnt-offerings: and then shall they offer bulls upon
Thy altar. And to Thee belongeth glory, O God[p].

When he goes up to the altar. I will come unto the altar of God: and unto God who maketh my youth joyful.

And he kneels down and says, To Thy house, O God, have I come up: and I kneel before Thy throne, O heavenly King. Pardon me all that I have sinned against Thee.

[p] Here Renaudot's translation has the following clause: "*Sacerdos petit remissionem et dicit.* Benedic Domine remissioni, seu absolutioni." B. contains a similar clause between the Sedra and the Psalm; thus: ". . . . and to Thy Holy Spirit. *He adds.* May we receive of God pardon of offences (debts) and remission of sins in both worlds, for ever and ever, Amen. *And he asks pardon of the presbyters and deacons.* And he says the Psalm, &c."

And he kisses[q] *the horn of the altar and says,* Bind,
O Lord, our feasts in chains even to the horns of 7
Thy altar.

And when he lights the wax taper on the south side[r] *:* In Thy light have we seen [or, do we see] light, O Jesus, full of light, Who art the true Light that enlighteneth all creatures: enlighten us with Thy glorious light, the splendour of the heavenly Father[s].

And lighting that of the north he says[r], O sacred and holy One, Who dwellest in the abodes of light, keep away from us evil passions and hateful thoughts: grant us with purity of heart to work the works of righteousness.

(C.) *And he takes in his two hands the Seal which has* on p. 8.
been prepared in the paten, and says[t], He was led as

[q] Here ܢܩܫ, 'knocks,' is probably an error for ܢܫܩ, 'kisses,' which is B.'s reading. So elsewhere, e.g., at p. 45.

[r] They are lighted by the deacon or lay-assistant.

[s] Or, O Beam of the heavenly Father.

[t] The order of the letters A, B, C, D, E, shews the order of this portion of the service as it stands in my MSS. I have ventured on this transposition in accordance with Catanar Jacob's express instructions, and with the arrangement in Dr. Mill's MS., the Church Missionary Society's "Extracts," and Renaudot's Translation. But the disagreement of MSS. in respect of this part of the service is very remarkable. In the first place, the preparation and oblation of the elements, which is here described, does not always form a part of the "first service." Indeed it is doubtful whether it ever does so. See Introductory Notice, pp. 131, 132, where this part of the question is more fully discussed. Secondly, its own particular arrangement differs in different MSS., and although the variation may be less in practice than it appears to be, judging from the MSS., (for the rubrics may be in some instances memoranda, as it were, introduced as an afterthought, and so

a lamb to the slaughter: as a sheep before the shearer was He silent; and in His humility He opened not

not strictly in order,) yet it is probable that the *Use* of some Churches is slightly varied in details from that adopted by others.

Thus, the mingling of water with the wine is everywhere performed, but not at the same time, nor (if the Church Missionary Society's rubric be correct) in the same manner. My MSS. represent the pouring of a libation of the *mingled* draught with the words "Our Lord Jesus Christ, &c." Renaudot has "Elevat calicem *vino et aqua mistum*, et dicit, 'Dominus noster,' &c." The act of mingling is mentioned before this in Renaudot's Translation, in my MSS. it is mentioned afterwards.

But the Church Missionary Society's "Extracts" represent it as follows: After the oblation of the *First-begotten*, the priest pours *wine* into the cup, and says, "Our Lord Jesus Christ, &c." Then, pouring water upon the wine, he says, "Make one, O Lord, &c."

The Seal which has been prepared in the paten. These words indicate some previous ceremonial, which is thus partially explained by a rather obscure rubric in B: *And if (it be) a large paten, he shall arrange crosswise, by four corners: and if small, one on another. Without two he shall not arrange yokes (pairs), unless when he desires to add (more). They shall be unequal. And he pours a libation part wine and part* —— [The word has been eaten away.] *And he takes, &c.* So Renaudot: "*Si discus magnus est, ad quatuor ejus angulos disponit* (particulas panis consecrandi) *in formam crucis: si minor est, super tres particulas unam super aliam collocat, aut duas ad minus, pari numero, aut impari, si opus est.*"

I quote from Renaudot partly for the sake of his translation of this rubric, but chiefly in order to point out that the rubric on p. 9 is here (in Renaudot's Translation) *introduced between the foregoing directions and the taking of the seal.* Thus, after the words *Si opus est* it goes on to say, "*Spongiam et cochlear in latere australi, supra tabulam consecratam, deponit; Oblatæ majorem particulam, et velum,* seu Anaphoram, *in latere occidentali, donec frangat Corpus prima vice. Accipit Oblatam, et postquam extersit manus, eam osculatur, ponitque in latere australi cum cochleari. Tum accipit Sigillum, sive majorem et mediam Oblatæ partem, ambabus manibus, et collocat in disco, dicens:* Tanquam ovis, &c." It is therefore not improbable that my rubric on p. 9 may have a retrospective bearing. The Church Missionary Society's "Extracts" do not give any of these directions except the last, in the fol-

His mouth. O Lord, Thou hast made Thy sanctuary ready for Thy seat. Establish it, O Lord, by Thy hands. The Lord shall reign for ever and ever.

(D.) *And when he places the First-begotten*[u]*:* O First-begotten of the heavenly Father, receive this First-begotten from the hands of Thy weak and sinful servant.

(A.) *And he pours a libation of the mingled (wine and* on p. 7.
water) in the cup, and says, Our Lord Jesus Christ was
crucified between two thieves on the wood in Jeru-
salem: He was pierced in His side by the spear; and
there flowed therefrom blood and water, the propitiation
for every creature: and he that saw it bare testimony;
and we know that his testimony is true. What shall 8
I render unto the Lord for all that He hath rendered
unto me? I will receive the cup of salvation, and will
call on the name of the Lord. My vows also will
I render unto the Lord in the presence of all His
people.

(B.) *And when he mixes the water, he also says,* Make one, O Lord God, this water with this wine, as Thy Divinity was made one with our humanity.

(E.) *And he places the sponge and the spoon on the south* 9
side upon the Table; and the Coal[x] *and the veil on the*

lowing words: "*After dressing, the priest ascends the step of the throne, and taking the bread in both hands says,* He was led, &c."

The interest attaching to this portion of the Office, corresponding, as it does, to the Great Entrance of the Greek Church, will I hope be accepted as an apology for this long digression.

[u] The bread is so called in allusion to Heb. i. 6, &c.

[x] Another name for the bread, in allusion to Isa. vi. 6.

north side, until he breaks [the Body the first time[y]*]. And he takes the Coal, and wipes his hands, and kisses it, and places it on the south side with the spoon.*

And he sets the Sedra of Penitence. Let us pray, all of us. Let us ask mercy and grace from the Lord. O merciful Lord, have mercy upon us and help us. Glory to the one merciful Father, who answereth the sinners who cry unto Him: to the one merciful Son, who receiveth the penitents who knock at His door: to the one living and Holy Spirit, who pardoneth the guilty who pray unto Him. To whom belongeth[z].

The Sedra. O God, who art gentle, and gracious, and kind, and loving to men; who takest pleasure in mercies and [not[a]] in sacrifices, and lovest a contrite
10 heart more than whole burnt-offerings, and receivest a humble spirit rather than the blood and fat of bulls and fat lambs; receive our spiritual sacrifice at this time on Thy reasonable altar, and make us meet to present ourselves unto Thee a living and acceptable sacrifice, that in reasonable service may be pleasing to Thy will; and to offer unto Thee reasonable and spiritual sacrifices, with contrite heart and humble spirit, upon Thy altar that is on high: and may we be unto Thee a flock bright and without stain; so that being changed the new change, and renewed, we may be sent to the new world, with reasonable and wise souls, with the bright torches of the faith: (and)

[y] Supplied from B. Observe the name for the bread.

[z] In B. this is called the Procemium to the Sedra.

[a] Supplied from B.

may be made worthy all of us to sing in Thy temple, Glory to the Father, and to the Son, and to the Holy Spirit, now.

Voice[b]. At Thy gate, O our Lord, do I knock; I
make supplication for mercies from Thy treasury. 11
I a sinner of years have declined from Thy way. Grant me to confess my sins and to forsake them, and to live by Thy goodness. At what gate shall we go and knock, but at Thy gate, O our gracious Lord? And what have we that shall plead with Thee for our offences, if Thy mercies do not plead with Thee, O King whose glory kings adore? *Glory.* Father, and Son, and Holy Ghost, be Thou to us a lofty wall and house of refuge, both from the evil one, and from the powers of him that fighteth against us. Hide[c] us by the wings of Thy mercies, when the good are separated from the evil. *From everlasting.* Let the voice of our ministry be a key that openeth the gate of heaven: and may the archangels in their orders say, How sweet is the voice of the inhabitants of earth! May the
Lord quickly answer their prayers. *The smoke*[d]. May 12
the fragrance of prayer[e] be sweet unto Thee, O my Lord, at all times: and may the smoke of our incense be for Thy reconciliation; and be Thou reconciled thereby to Thy creatures for Thy mercies' sake. Now.

[b] "Versus," Renaudot.

[c] ܛܠܗ̈ܝܢ, a probable error for ܛܠܠܝܢ, which B. has. So elsewhere repeatedly.

[d] These terms, Glory; From everlasting; The smoke; Examination; occur again in the course of a Sedra, pp. 90, 91. Here Renaudot has a short rubric, *Incensum adoletur*.

[e] B. has "our prayers."

Examination. I have sinned against Thee, O Thou that pitiest sinners: receive my prayer, and forgive me all my offences, and have mercy upon me. *Another.* O Christ, who didst receive the offering of the pure priest Melchizedec, receive, O my Lord, the prayer of Thy servant, and forgive the sins of Thy flock. *The Seal.* May we be made worthy to offer unto Thee, O Lord, sacrifices of praise for a sweet perfume, all our thoughts, and words, and works, and whole burnt-offerings; and to appear before Thee without fault, and well pleasing to Thy Godhead, all the days of our life: Father, and Son, and Holy Ghost, now, and at all times for ever.

Thou art holy, O God: *three times*[f]*:* and, Our Father, Which art in heaven, &c.

13 *The first service is finished.*

Again. *And putting off his private garments, he says,* Put off from me, O Lord God, the filthy garments wherewith Satan hath clothed me, by the loosing of my wicked works; and clothe me with choice garments, that are fit for the service of Thy majesty, and for the praise of Thy holy name, O our Lord, and our God, for ever.

And he begins the service of the Corban, [or *Oblation,*] *and washes his hands, saying,* Make us worthy, O Lord God, that having our hearts sprinkled and pure from

[f] The Trisagium. It appears to be sung at least three times in the course of the service. First, by the priest and deacon or lay assistants alone. Secondly, by the whole congregation, shortly before the Epistle is read; p. 28. Lastly, after the Sursum Corda in the Anaphora; p. 49.

all evil conscience, we may be made meet to ascend to Thy high and lofty Holy of Holies, [and [g]] may stand purely and holily before Thy holy altar, and offer unto Thee reasonable and spiritual sacrifices in belief of the truth: Father, and Son, and Holy Ghost, now and at all times, for ever [h].

And he makes three crosses on the Cuthino [i], *and says,* 14
Put upon me, O Lord, a robe of incorruption by the power (lit., by the hand of the power) of the Holy Spirit: and grant us that we may be led in pure and right conversation all the days of our life, in the belief of the truth: Father, and Son, and Holy Ghost, now and at all times for ever.

And he marks three crosses on the Orro [k], *and puts it on his neck, letting it down in front in the figure of a cross, and says,* Thou shalt gird me with power in the battle: and shalt subdue under me them that rise up against me.

[g] Supplied from B.

[h] Renaudot's translation introduces two prayers in this place, to be used with the left and right sandal respectively: "Calcea me, Domine, ad præparationem Evangelii pacis, ut conteram serpentes et scorpios, omnemque virtutem inimici, in sæcula. Amen." And (with the right sandal), "Deprime, Domine Deus, sub scabellum pedum meorum omnem sublimitatem extollentem se adversus scientiam tuam, ita ut per auxilium tuum conteram passiones carnales in sæcula."

According to the Madras Church Miss. Record, vol. iii. p. 82, there is a canon which declares that "it is not lawful for a priest or deacon to enter the chancel without clean shoes. It is better, if shoes can be made especially for the chancel." This canon is under the heading *Persians*. The same authority, vol. ii. p. 166, represents the sandals as being put on at the very commencement of the service.

[i] A linen vestment, corresponding to our surplice.

[k] A scarf: "orarium," Renaudot.

And he ties the Zunro[l], *and says,* Gird the sword upon Thy thighs, O Mighty One: Thy honour and Thy glory [and Thy glory[m]] triumphs.

And he takes the Zando[n], *and makes two crosses, and says,* Make my members instruments of righteousness, O Lord, and meet for all good and right-handed works:
15 manifesting us pure temples and chosen vessels, that are fit for Thy glorious service[o], and for the praise of Thy holy name: Father, and Son, and Holy Ghost, now.

And he vests the left arm, and says, Teach my hands to war: and strengthen my arms as a bow of brass.

And he makes one cross on the other, and says, Make my members instruments of righteousness, &c.

And he vests the right arm, and says, Thy right hand shall help me: and Thy discipline shall make me great.

When he puts on the Phaino[p], *he makes three crosses on it, and says,* Let Thy priests be clothed with righteousness, and Thy righteous with glory. For Thy servant David's sake, turn not away the face of Thy anointed[q].

And he kneels before the table of life, and says this prayer for himself, O Lord God Almighty, who pardonest guilty men, who delightest not in the death of

[l] A belt or girdle: "zona," Renaudot.

[m] Repeated in both A. and B., and in M.

[n] ܥܢܕܐ, no doubt an error for ܟܢܕܐ, as B. has it, adding ܐܘܟܝܬ ܟܦܝܬܐ, 'that is, the gauntlet.'

[o] Lit., Thy service of glory.

[p] A linen vestment; Castell. "Fainam (sive casulam)," Ren.

[q] Here follows the Oblation, or Entrance, according to the Church Missionary Society's Translation.

a sinner; to Thee, O Lord, do I stretch out the hand 16
of my heart[r], and I implore from Thee forgiveness of all my unlawful deeds, though I be unworthy; but I intreat Thee, keep my mind from the operations of the adversary; my eyes, that they look not incontinently; my ears, that they hear not vanities; my hands from the service of odious things; and my feet[s], that they may be moved in Thee; so that I may be entirely for Thee[t]; and from Thee may be granted unto me the gift of Thy divine mysteries: now, and at all times for ever.

Then he ascends the step, and removing the veils, that is, the covering of the mysteries, he places that of the paten on the south, and (that) of the cup on the north[u]. [*Over (that) of the paten he says*[x],] The Lord reigneth, and hath
clothed Himself with majesty: the Lord hath clothed 17
Himself with strength, and is strong. He hath also established the world, that it may not move. Firmly prepared is Thy throne from the beginning: and Thou art from everlasting. The floods have been raised up, O Lord; the floods have lifted up their voice[y]: the floods have been lifted up with the noise of breaking[z]. The Lord that is on high is more glorious than the

[r] Compare the Prayer of Manasses. Apoc.

[s] This should probably be ܟܘܠܝܬܐ, 'renes,' 'reins,' as B. has it. Mistakes of this kind, ܟܝ for ܩ, or *vice versa*, occur repeatedly. So below, note y.

[t] "Totus ad Te sim," Renaudot.

[u] "Ad Occidentale," Renaudot.

[x] Supplied from B.

[y] Here again ܟܝ for ܩ.

[z] The Syriac word appears to be borrowed from the Hebrew.

voice of many waters—mighty storms of the sea. Thy testimonies also are very faithful: and holiness, O Lord, becometh Thine house for length of days.

Upon (that) of the cup he says, O pure and spotless Lamb, who didst offer Thyself to Thy Father, an acceptable offering for the expiation and redemption of the whole world, make us meet to offer ourselves to Thee[a], a living sacrifice that may be pleasing unto Thee, and like [Thy[b]] sacrifice which was for our sake, O Christ our God.

Finding the paten placed on the north[c], and the cup on
18 *the south[c], he stretches forth his hands in the figure[d] of a cross, his right hand over his left hand, and takes the paten in his right hand, and the cup in his left hand, and lifts them up on high above the part where[e] the fixed table is; and he does not put them down until he has said this general prayer, that is,* The remembrance of our Lord, and our God, and our Saviour Jesus Christ, and of all His salutary dispensation on our behalf; that is, the message of the angel; and His glorious conception; and His birth in the flesh; and His baptism in the Jordan; and His fast of forty days; and His salutary passion; and His being lifted up upon the cross; and His life-making death; and His honourable burial;

[a] Lit., O pure * * * who offered Himself to His Father, &c., make us meet to offer ourselves to Thee, &c. A similar confusion occurs not unfrequently.

[b] Supplied from B.

[c] "Sinistra" in both these places. Renaudot.

[d] [Syriac] should no doubt be [Syriac], as in B.

[e] [Syriac] should doubtless be [Syriac], as B. has it.

and His glorious resurrection; and His ascension into
heaven; and His sitting on the right hand of God the 19
Father; according to His own command to us, we are
celebrating at this time upon this eucharist that is set
before us: Then by name, our father Adam, and our
mother Eve, and the holy mother of God, Mary; and
the prophets and apostles; preachers and evangelists;
and martyrs and confessors; righteous men and priests;
and holy fathers and true shepherds; and orthodox
doctors; monks and cœnobites; and those who are
standing and praying with us; with all those who from
of old have pleased Thee, from Adam even unto this
day. Again we commemorate our fathers and our
brethren; and our masters who have taught us the
word of truth; and our dead; and all the faithful
dead; especially and by name those who are of our 20
blood; and those who joined in the building of this
temple; and those who joined and are joining again in
the support of this place; and all that associate with
us, whether in word or deed, in little or in much; and
especially him for whom this corban is offered. *Here
he mentions him for whom*[f]. O God, make good remem-
brance to *such an one*, and pardon their offences and
their sins in Thy loving-kindness. *And if for a saint*:
and Saint Mar *such an one*, whose remembrance we are
fulfilling to-day[g]. *And if for the mother of God*: espe-
cially the holy mother of God, Mary, in whose honour

[f] The sentence seems to be incomplete. Renaudot has "propter quem Liturgia celebratur, et quemcunque alium commemorare oportet." This explains the plurals that follow.

[g] This clause is from B. A. reads, "the day of thy remembrance we are fulfilling to-day."

21 and for whom this corban is offered, peculiarly and dis-
tinctly: that she may be a suppliant unto Thee, O my
Lord, in behalf of all those who take refuge in the aid
of her prayers. O good and merciful God, by her
heard and acceptable prayers that are before Thee,
answer in Thy goodness the petitions of him who sepa-
rates and honours her remembrance. Cause to pass
from him temptations, and punishments, and rods of
wrath, and in Thy mercy forgive his offences and his
sins, by the prayers of Thy mother and of all Thy
saints. Amen. *Again.* O God, Thou wast the offering:
and to Thee is offered the offering. Receive this offer-
ing from my weak and sinful hands for the soul of *such
an one. And he repeats it three times. Again.* O God,
in Thy mercy, make rest and good remembrance to my
22 father, and to my mother, and to my brothers, and to
my sisters; and to the sons of the race of my family;
and to my teachers. *And if for the sick:* O merciful
God, have pity on *such an one*, and grant him healing
of soul and body. *And if for the dead:* O God, make
to *such an one* rest and good fruition of felicity [lit.,
sense] in Thy mansions of light, with all that have
done Thy will: and make rest and good remembrance
to my father, and to my mother, and to my teachers,
and to all my companions, and to every one that has
asked of our weakness that we would remember him in
this corban which is offered unto Thee by our sinful-
ness, whose names are known unto Thee.

Στῶμεν καλῶς [h].

[h] The reader will find a large number of instances in which some well-known form is indicated by its initial words alone. Such is the

Kurillison. (i.e. Kyrie eleison.)

*Here he puts down the mysteries, and places the cup on the east, and the paten on the west, upon the table, and he
extends the veil and covers the mysteries, saying,* The hea- 23
vens are covered with the splendour of the Glorious One: and His glory filleth all creation.

Here he places perfumes, and says, To the glory and honour of the holy and glorious Trinity we place perfumes.

And he begins the general Sedra. Let us pray, all of us: let us ask mercy and grace from the Lord. O merciful Lord, have mercy upon us, and help us.

Procemium. Glory to the beautiful Fruit which sprung from the Virgin's womb, and magnified and exalted the memory of her that bare it; to that adorable Lord whom the festival of His saints and the chorus of their companies in creation glorifies; to Him who liveth and giveth life; who by His sweet voice raiseth the dead, and maketh them joyful with Himself in blissful glory. To whom belongeth glory.

The Sedra. We adore, and confess, and glorify Thee,
the Creator of the worlds, and Disposer of created 24
things; the blessed Root that budded forth and ascended from the thirsty earth, Mary[1]: and all the

case here. Renaudot's translation supplies the rest of the form, as it stands in the first *Ordo Communis.* "*Diaconus.* Stemus decenter in oratione et precibus coram Deo Deorum, et Domino Dominorum, coram Rege Regum, coram altari propitiatorio, et coram mysteriis præclaris et vivis Salvatoris nostri: cum aromatibus impositis misericordiam tuam imploramus Domine."

[1] A probable allusion to Isa. liii. 2, and Gen. ii. 7.

earth was filled with the perfume of its glorious sweetness; and it drove away the fœtid odour of heathenism from all regions by its glorious doctrine[k]. We offer before Thee this incense, after the example of Aaron the Priest, who offered pure incense unto Thee in the temporary tabernacle, and thereby averted the plague from the people of Israel. So we beseech Thee, O Lord, receive this smoke of spices which our lowliness offers unto Thee because of our sins and our offences, in behalf of our father Adam and our mother Eve; in behalf of the prophets and apostles; in behalf of the just and righteous; in behalf of the martyrs and confessors; in behalf of the orthodox fathers and
25 doctors; in behalf of the monks and cœnobites; in behalf of the holy mother of God, Mary; in behalf of orphans and widows; in behalf of the distressed and the afflicted; in behalf of the sick and the oppressed; in behalf of all who have spoken to and have charged us to remember them in prayers before Thee, O Christ, our God; and for the living and the dead, and the rest of their souls in the heavenly Jerusalem; and we will raise glory, and honour, and adoration to Thee, O my Lord, and to Thy Father, and to Thy Holy Spirit: now.

He places spices and says, To the glory and honour of the holy and glorious Trinity we place spices with our weak and sinful hands. Let us pray, all of us; let us ask mercy and grace from the Lord. O merciful Lord, have mercy upon us and help us.

[k] All this is in the third person.

And he takes the incense, and adores, and gives incense to the midst of the table of life three times, which is a type 26
of the Father, saying, Adoration to the gracious Father.

And to the north horn [three times, which is a type of the Son, saying[1],] Adoration to the merciful Son.

And to the south horn three times, [which is a sacrament of the Holy Spirit[1],] Adoration to the living and Holy Spirit.

And he ascends the step, and raises the incense over the Mysteries on the east side, and says this voice[m], Praise the Lord, O ye righteous. With the smoke of spices let let there be a remembrance: to the Virgin Mary, mother of God.

And coming to the west side, he says, Praise Him, all ye people. With the smoke of spices let there be a remembrance: to the holy prophets, apostles, and martyrs.

And to the north side, saying, Glory be to the Father. With the smoke of spices let there be a remembrance: to the doctors, and the priests, and the just, and the righteous.

And to the south side, From of old. With the smoke
of spices let there be a remembrance: to the holy 27
Church, and all her children.

And he blesses[n] *the incense in a circle over the Mysteries three times, and descends from the step, saying this Atro*[o]. Receive, O my Lord, in Thy mercy, the in-

[1] Supplied from B.

[m] B. has, *this voice,—the clause* (*or section*) *Praise the Lord.*

[n] B. has the Aphel conjugation, 'causes to bow, or fall down;' 'dips.'

[o] Lit., Smoke: the technical name of this prayer.

cense of Thy servants; and be reconciled by the smoke of Thy priests; and be appeased by the service of Thy worshippers; and magnify thereby the remembrance of Thy mother and Thy saints, and of all the faithful dead: O Christ the Son, who, with His Father and His Holy Spirit, is worshipped and glorified, now, and in all times for ever[p].

The Seal. May the just and the righteous, the pro-
phets, and apostles, and martyrs, and confessors, and
Mary the holy mother of God, and all the saints who
in all generations have pleased Thee, O God, be inter-
28 cessors and suppliants unto Thee in behalf of the souls
of all of us; that by their prayers and supplications
wrath may cease from Thy people. And have mercy
upon the flock of Thy pasture; and cause Thy tran-
quillity and Thy peace to dwell in the four quarters of
the world; and to the dead grant pardon in Thy good-
ness, O our Lord and our God for ever.

He places spices. We believe in one God, &c.

And he says this examination. Let Mary who brought Thee forth, and John who baptized Thee, be suppliants unto Thee in our behalf; and have mercy upon us.

And he begins the responsory of the Oblation of Mar Severus:—Versicle. I will extol Thee, O my Lord the King, &c.[q]

[p] Observe the confusion of persons in grammar.

[q] The remainder is thus given in the Church Missionary Society's Translation: "My Lord the King, I will extol thee, through the prayers of Mary who brought Thee forth, and of John who baptized Thee: Thou art the only Son and Word of the heavenly Father: Thou art im-

Thou art holy, O God, *three times.*

Kurillison. 3. [i.e. three times.]

The Prayer before the Apostle. Receive, O Lord
God, our prayers and our supplications which are at
this time before Thee; and vouchsafe unto us that
with purity and holiness we may keep Thy command- 29
ments and those of Thy divine Apostles, and of Paul
the architect and builder of Thy holy Church, O our
Lord and our God for ever.

The Deacon. Paul the blessed Apostle.

The Prayer before the Gospel[r]. Grant unto us, O Lord God, the knowledge of Thy divine words, and fill us with the understanding of Thy holy Gospel; and vouchsafe unto us that with joy we may keep Thy commandments, and may accomplish and fulfil Thy will, and may be made meet for the blessings and the mercies that are from Thee: now and in all times.

And the Deacon reads the Apostle. Paul the Apostle. From the First Epistle to the Corinthians.

Bless, O my Lord[s].

mortal in Thy nature, but dost pity us, and in pity came (*sic*) down from heaven for the life and salvation of all mankind. Thou didst take a body, from a holy, blessed, and pure virgin, even from Mary who brought forth God, and didst become very man. Thou wast hanged on the cross for us: by Thy death Thou didst trample under foot and destroy our death. Thou art one of the holy Trinity. Our Lord Christ, who art equally worshipped and praised with Thy Father, and with Thy living and Holy Ghost, have mercy upon us all.

[r] This prayer appears to be out of place. In B. it follows the reading of the Epistle, after the words, *With silence, &c.*

[s] Perhaps spoken to the priest, *Sir, give the blessing,* and so in other instances.

My brethren (for) I received from the Lord that
which I delivered unto you; that our Lord Jesus, in
that night in which He was betrayed, took bread, and
30 blessed, and brake, and said, Take, eat of it, this (is) My
Body, which is broken for you. This do ye, in remembrance of Me, [lit., for My memorial]. In like manner, after they had supped, He took also the cup, and said, This cup is the New Testament in My Blood. So do ye yourselves, as often as ye drink [it], in remembrance of Me. For as often as ye eat this bread, and drink this cup, ye make remembrance of the death of our Lord until His coming.

Bless, O my Lord.
Halleluia and Halleluia.
Sacrifice to Him, [&c.[t]][u].
Bless, O my Lord.
With silence, [&c.[t]][u].
Priest. Peace to you all.
Make [us] worthy.

The holy Gospel of our Lord Jesus Christ. The life-giving preaching of the Apostle John, who proclaimed life and salvation for ever.

31 *And if Mark, and if Luke.* The life-giving Gospel of

[t] Supplied from B.

[u] These two forms, of which only the initial words are here given, are thus represented by Renaudot, in the first *Ordo Communis* translated by him:—"Immolate illi sacrificia, offerte oblationes, ascendite in atria Domini, et adorate eum in templo sancto ejus, confitemini et benedicite nomini ejus, a quo vita tribuitur. Alleluia." Again:—"Estote in silentio, Auditores, hoc est enim Evangelium sanctum quod legitur. Fratres mei, festinate, audite, et confitemini verbum Dei vivi."

Mark, *otherwise*, of Luke, the Evangelist, who proclaimed life and salvation for ever.

Blessed (is He) that cometh.

In the time therefore of the dispensation of our Lord and our God and our Saviour Jesus Christ, the Word of the Living God, who was incarnate of the holy Virgin Mary, these things thus were done.

Deacon. We believe and confess.

The Gospel of John. Verily, verily, I say unto you,
that whosoever heareth My word, and believeth on
Him that sent Me, hath eternal life, and cometh not to
judgment, but passeth from death unto life. Verily,
verily, I say unto you, that the hour is coming, and
now is, when the dead shall hear the voice of the Son
of God, and they that hear shall live. For as the Fa-
ther hath life in Himself, so hath He given also to 32
the Son to have life in Himself, and hath given Him
authority to execute judgment also, since He is the Son
of Man. Marvel not at this, that the hour is coming
when all that are in the graves shall hear His voice,
and shall come forth; they that have done good to the
resurrection of life; and they that have done evil unto
the resurrection of judgment. And Peace to you all.

Your prayers[x]. Our glory, and our thanksgiving, and our blessing to our Lord Jesus Christ, for His life-giving words to us; and to His Father, who sent Him for our salvation; and to His Living and Holy Spirit, who giveth us life; now.

Proœmium. Let us pray, all of us. Let us ask mercy

[x] *This prayer*, B.

and grace from the Lord. O merciful Lord, have mercy upon us, and help us. May we be made worthy to send up glory, and thanksgiving, and honour, and
33 praise[y], and exaltation good that ceaseth not, continually, at all times and in all moments, to Him who pardoneth offences, and giveth remission of sins; to Him who is the sanctifier of the filthy, and the receiver of penitents, and delighteth in the conversion of sinners, and desireth the salvation of the wicked; to Him that saith, Call, and I answer; and, Knock, and I open; and, I give My hand to you, and your sins and your iniquities I remit; to whom is due glory, and praise, and adoration, in this time of this divine perfect Eucharist, and in all feasts, and years, and hours, and moments, and all the days of our life; on this smoke [or, perfume] of spices, now and at all times for ever. *He continues.* Therefore, O Thou Propitiator, Purifier, Absolver, Thou that blottest out and doest away, not remembering our evil deeds, blot Thou out, O Lord God, in the pitiful-
34 ness of Thy love, O my Lord, my sins, many, and great, and unnumbered, and the sins of all Thy believing people. Spare, O Good, and have mercy upon us. Remember me[z], O Lord God, in the mercies that are from Thee; and remember therein, O my Lord, the souls of our fathers, and of our brethren, and of our

[y] ܘܫܘܒܟܬܐ has been corrected by the writer of the MS. to ܘܫܘܒܚܐ, and the correction is noticeable as affording a specimen of a class of errors of frequent occurence in the MSS., ܒ for ܦ, or *vice versâ*, and ܟ for ܚ, with which it is, in Travancore at least, almost identical in respect of pronunciation.

[z] 'us' in B.

masters, and of our teachers, and of our dead, and of all the faithful dead, the children of Thy holy and glorious Church. Give rest, O Lord God, to their souls, and their spirits, and their bodies; and sprinkle the dew of love and mercy on their bones; and be Thou the Propitiation and the Propitiator for us and for them, O Christ our King, O Lord our Lord, Lord of glory; and answer us, O my Lord, and come to our aid, and come to our protection, and deliver us. Re-
ceive our prayers and our supplications, O God, and 35
cause severe chastisements to pass away and to cease; and rods of wrath do Thou, in Thy loving-kindness, O Lord, turn from us and cause to pass away; and make us all meet for the good end which is for men of peace; and vouchsafe unto us a Christian close that is loved and honoured by Thee, and that pleaseth Thy divinity; and make us all meet for a good end; and to Thee we offer praise and thanksgiving, now and at all times for ever.

Sedra[a]. O Lord God, strong, and warlike[b], and

[a] Instead of this sedra and litany, B. has the following sedra:—"Before Thee, O God of gods, and Lord of lords; before Thee, O Judge of judges, and terrible above princes; at whose glory the fiery tremble, and at sight of whom the spiritual are moved; before Thee, O my Lord, do we worship, and we make supplication to Thy divinity, (and) that Thou wouldst make us meet for the service of the holy seraphim, and [for] our participation in the adorable mysteries of Thy divinity; and wouldst spare us in Thy abundant mercies, so that we may stand in holiness before Thee, and before Thy holy altar, and may perform the sacerdotal office gloriously unto Thee, upon Thy spiritual table; and wouldst send Thy Holy Spirit, and sanctify this bread and wine that is set before us, and wouldst glorify our bodies and our souls, and sanctify our minds and thoughts, and cleanse us from (lit., from us) all defilement of

powerful, and glorious, arise, help us, and deliver us
from the evil one and his powers, by Thy might and
by Thy uplifted arm. Thou, O my Lord, in Thy grace,
and in Thy abundant mercies, wast incarnate of the
36 holy Virgin Mary, and for our sake didst clothe Thyself
with a body, in Thy love towards man. O Lord, our
Lord, by that Throne which is in heaven, which beareth Thy majesty; and by the four-faced Beasts which
serve below Thy throne; by the multitude of Angels
and Archangels that glorify Thy deity; by the orders
of the Cherubim that bless, and celebrate, and magnify
Thy might; by the six-winged Seraphim that call out
and cry, and say, Holy, Holy, Holy [art Thou, O]
Lord, in Thy holiness; by all the Powers, and Orders,
and Bands which stand and serve Thy reverence with
the substance of Him that begat Thee; by the womb
which bare Thee, cast us not away from Thy pre-
37 sence, but shew unto us the way of life and of salvation,
that we may go in thereby to the house of the kingdom;
and grant us to give thanks for Thy grace, and to pray
and make supplication unto Thy sweetness, O my Lord.

O our Lord Jesus Christ, have mercy upon us.

O our Lord Jesus Christ, help us.

O our Lord Jesus Christ, look upon us with the eye of Thy loving kindness.

sin; so that we may perform the sacerdotal office unto Thee acceptably [one word is illegible, but this is clearly the purport] and without profaneness, and may be made meet for the beatitudes which Thou hast promised to Thy saints; and together with them, and among them, we will raise to Thee glory and thanksgiving, and to Thy Father, and to Thy Holy Spirit, now. *He continues,* May we receive, &c.," as on p. 40.

[b] Compare Exod. xv. 3.

O our Lord Jesus Christ, deliver us from our enemies.

O our Lord Jesus Christ, protect (or hide) us under the wings of Thy cross.

O our Lord Jesus Christ, deliver us from all the wiles of the devil.

O our Lord Jesus Christ, raise us from the ruin of sin.

O our Lord Jesus Christ, bring us up from the pit and lake of afflictions.

O our Lord Jesus Christ, deliver us from all evil 38
thoughts.

O our Lord Jesus Christ, deliver us from impurity and blasphemy.

O our Lord Jesus Christ, wash us from the filthiness and pollution of hateful things.

O our Lord Jesus Christ, cleanse us from wickedness and defilement.

O our Lord Jesus Christ, satiate us with good things and blessings.

O our Lord Jesus Christ, make us rich from Thy treasure-house which is full of mercy and pity.

O our Lord Jesus Christ, make us joyful in Thy chamber full of gladness.

O our Lord Jesus Christ, make us joyful with the companions and guests, the children of Thy kingdom.

O our Lord Jesus Christ, invite us together with the upright and righteous who have pleased Thee.

O our Lord Jesus Christ, set us with the sheep, the children of Thy right hand.

O our Lord Jesus Christ, shine upon us, together 39

with the elect and the saints in the day of the rising of Thy majesty.

O our Lord Jesus Christ, cause us to sit on Thy right hand side at that spiritual feast.

O our Lord Jesus Christ, be Thou friendly with us in Thy mercy.

O our Lord Jesus Christ, receive this offering from my hands.

O our Lord Jesus Christ, purify my mind by Thy mercy, and may I meet Thy adorable divine mysteries in purity.

O our Lord Jesus Christ, send forth to me at this time Thy living and life-giving Spirit, that He may come and dwell and abide in this offering, and in us.

O our Lord Jesus Christ, cleanse me at this time from all defilements of wickedness and of sin, and from all stains and corruptions.

O our Lord Jesus Christ, sprinkle me (with) Thy
40 hyssop, and life-giving dew, and let them cleanse me
from all those offences which I have committed before
Thee by night and by day.

O our Lord Jesus Christ, make rest and good remembrance by the hand of the smoke of the spices which we are now making to smoke before Thee: and we and our dead and all the faithful dead will send up glory and thanksgiving to Thee, O my Lord, and to Thy Father, and to Thy Holy Spirit, now, and at all times, for ever.

He continues, May we receive from God pardon of offences and remission of sins in both worlds, for ever and ever.

And adds, Peace to you all. May the pardon of the
Son of God be vouchsafed on our souls, and on the souls
of our fathers, and of our brethren, and of our masters,
and of our teachers, and of our dead, and of all the
faithful dead, children of the holy Church, in both 41
worlds, for ever and ever. Amen.

And he places spices, and makes three crosses on the incense, and says [c], Let us respond and say, Ho + ly is the Holy Father: Ho + ly is the Holy Son: Ho + ly is the Living and Holy Ghost, who sanctifieth the incense of His sinful servants, sparing and having mercy upon our souls, and upon the souls of our fathers, and of our brethren, and of our masters, and of our doctors, and of our dead, and of all the faithful dead, children of the holy Church, in both worlds, for ever and ever. Amen.

The Deacon, S. and P.[d]

[c] This ceremony is more fully described at p. 141 of the Introductory Notice.

[d] Probably the initial letters of the words Σοφία (or Σοφίᾳ) and Πρόσχωμεν. So in B. ⲁ̅ⲗⲟⲁ̅ⲗ stands for Hallelujah and Hallelujah.

The form itself—*Wisdom; let us attend!*—with the accompanying ceremonial, appears to be connected with different portions of the service in different Liturgies. In that of St. Chrysostom, it forms part of the Little Entrance, (that of the Gospel,) and is thus alluded to in the Commentary of Symeon of Thessalonica: "And when the torches are borne forth . . . and the holy Gospel is carried in procession . . . and the deacon, after the Prayer of Entrance, while he holds the Gospel in his hands, exclaims, *Wisdom; stand up,* the Resurrection and Ascension of the Saviour is shadowed forth." See it in Dr. Neale's translation of the Prim. Lit., Introd., p. xix. In the Liturgy of St. James (in Greek) the exclamation forms part of the Great Entrance, and its position corresponds with that which it here occupies.

The Priest begins, I believe.

And he washes the tips of his fingers in water, and says, Wash away, O Lord God, the filthy pollution of my
42 soul, and cleanse me with Thy dew of life, so that I may be made meet to ascend to Thy holy and sanctifying Holy of Holies in purity and in holiness, and may handle[e] Thy adorable and divine mysteries without defilement; so that with pure conscience I may offer unto Thee a living sacrifice that may be pleasing unto Thy divinity, and like unto Thy glorious sacrifice, O our Lord and our God for ever.

Again he asks for forgiveness, and says, My brethren and my masters, pray for me, that my offering may be accepted.

And he kneels before the Table of Life, and prays this prayer in silence, and says, O holy and glorious Trinity, have mercy upon me: O holy and glorious Trinity, forgive me my sin: O holy and glorious Trinity, re-
43 ceive this offering from my weak and sinful hands. O God, in Thy mercy, make rest and good remembrance on Thy holy and heavenly altar to Thy mother, and to Thy saints, and to all the faithful dead. O God, pardon and remit in this hour the sins of Thy sinful servant; and help my weakness which crieth unto Thee at all times; and by the prayers of Thy mother and of all Thy saints, pardon and remit, O God, in Thy loving kindness, the sins of those who are of our blood, our fathers, and our brethren, and our masters; and of

[e] ܐܡܫܫ, tractem, Renaudot. Castell gives *attrectavit blande;* it. *occurrit, obviavit,* as the meaning of the word. It occurs at p. 39.

him for whom and because of whom this sacrifice is offered.

Here he commemorates (or makes mention of) whomsoever he will.

[*The prayer that is said on the fifth evening of the Mystery*[f], *and on the Sabbath of the Annunciation in the*
place of the Oblation. O Christ our God, who in the 44
mystic supper didst bring to an end the old and typical service, and didst commit to us new mysteries of Thy grace; we beseech Thee, O Lord, to bring us in with Thee as companions and partakers of Thy holy and mystic supper; and make us meet to be made joyful by it, in holiness and without guilt; and in it may we be set free from all darkness of sin, and be pleasing unto Thee, in our secret (actions) and in our open (doings), here and in the life that does not fail. Make us joyful with the good things of Thy kingdom, and in Thy heavenly chamber, and by reason of all the goodness which is before us. Glory, and blessing, and adoration, and thanksgiving, shall ascend unto Thee, O my Lord, and to Thy Father, and to Thy Holy
Spirit, now and at all times, for ever. 45

People. Amen.

Priest. O Thou only merciful Lord.]

And he ascends the step, and kisses[g] *the throne, and begins the Corban*[h].

[f] Thursday in Holy Week. I have placed this prayer in brackets, as it is used only twice a-year.

[g] So I translate from B., which has ܢܫܩ. A. reads ܢܩܫ, 'knocks.'

[h] *Cantu gravi et tranquillo.* Renaudot's Translation.

The Anaphora of Mar James, the brother of our Lord. And this is the first Corban, which he said he heard and learned from the mouth of the Lord. And he did not add, and did not omit in it a single word. And it is proper to offer this on the days of the laying on of hands, that is, the giving of the degree[i]*. The new priest also should offer this Corban first. On the Lord's-days moreover it is proper to offer this.*

First. *The Prayer before the Peace.* O God of all,
and our Lord, make these our unworthy selves meet
46 for this salvation, so that without guile, and united by
the bonds of love, we may salute one another with
a holy and divine kiss, and may send up unto Thee
glory and thanksgiving, and to Thy only-begotten
Son, and to Thy all-holy, and good, and adorable, and
life-making, and consubstantial[k] Spirit; now and at
all times for ever.

People. Amen.

Priest. Peace.

People. And with Thy spirit.

Deacon. Let us give.

People. Before Thee[l].

[i] ܕܪܓܐ, dargo, our word 'degree'; the phrase probably signifies the right to minister at the *step* of the altar, i.e. ordination. Compare 1 Tim. iii. 13, where the Syriac version has this very word as the translation of the Greek *βαθμόν*.

[k] Lit., Equal to Thee in the essence. The reader will notice the change in the termination of the prayers.

[l] These are initial words merely, and incomplete. A MS. in the British Museum (14,493, supposed to be of the tenth or eleventh century) gives them a little more fully:—"*Deacon.* Let us give

Priest. O Thou only merciful Lord, who dwellest on high, and hast respect unto the lowly, send down blessings on those who bow their necks before Thee, and bless them by the grace of Thy only-begotten Son, with whom to Thee belongeth glory, and honour, and power, with Thy all-holy, and good, and adorable, and
life-making, and consubstantial Spirit; now. **47**

People. Amen.

Priest [m]. O God the Father, who, in Thy great love towards mankind, didst send Thy Son into the world to bring back the sheep that had wandered; do not reject, O my Lord, the service of this unbloody sacrifice; for we put our trust in Thy mercies, and not in our righteousness. Let not this mystery, which was appointed for our salvation, be to our condemnation (or, judgment), but to the blotting out of our sins and the rendering of thanks unto Thee and Thy only-be-

peace. *People.* Make us worthy. *Deacon.* Let us bow our heads before the Lord. *People.* Before Thee, &c."

"Osculum pacis apud Syros *Pax* vocatur simpliciter. Observatur eadem osculi sancti disciplina apud Ecclesias omnes Orientales, absque ullo discrimine. Canones qui de illa extant ex veteribus Conciliis leguntur similiter in omnibus collectionibus; observaturque præsertim, ut viri viros osculentur, mulieres sui sexus alias. Sacerdos sacra celebrans osculatur primum altare, tribus in locis, *ad captandam*, ut aiunt, *a mensa vitæ benedictionem.* Tum dat osculum Sacerdoti ministranti, si quis est, aut aliis dignioribus, qui se invicem osculantur: mox Diaconum, qui reliquis Ordinis Ecclesiastici dat pacem, a quibus Laici illam accipiunt." Abridged from Renaudot, pp. 76, 77. The manner in which peace is given among the Syrians in Malabar is described at p. 143 of the Introductory Notice. It is of course a sign of Christian love to the exclusion of all malice and hypocrisy, and is so explained by Barsalibi in his Commentary.

[m] This is called *The Prayer of the Veil* in some MSS., e.g. 14,493 and 14,498. Cf. p. 122 of this MS.

gotten Son, and Thy all-holy, and good, and adorable, and life-making, and consubstantial Spirit; now.

People. Amen.

Deacon. Let us stand [n].

People. Mercies.

The Priest lifting the veil. Thou art the hard rock
which sent forth the twelve rivers of water for the
48 twelve tribes of Israel. Thou art the hard rock which
was set against the tomb of our Redeemer.

[n] "Formula antiquissima, et ubique recepta in Officiis Liturgicis, Στῶμεν καλῶς, στῶμεν εὐλαβῶς, στῶμεν μετὰ φόβου Θεοῦ καὶ κατανύξεως. *Stemus decenter, stemus pie, stemus cum timore Dei et compunctione.*"—*Renaudot.* He observes that it was often pronounced in Greek, "ex antiquitatis reverentia,"—the Greek words being written in Syriac characters, as on p. 22,—and that, according to Barsalibi, the words have a simple and literal signification, in order that, should any of the congregation be sitting down, he may be instructed to stand up, as it was the ancient custom of the Church to do, during the celebration of Divine Service, and especially of the Liturgy.

Renaudot gives the entire text of the exhortation, of which these are the initial words, taking it from the *Liber Ministerii*, a book containing the text of such passages as are commonly indicated in the MSS. by their initial words. It commences thus: "Stemus decenter et oremus; gratias agamus; adoremus et laudemus agnum vivum Dei qui offertur super altare." It then speaks of the wonders of redemption, foretold by prophets, and accomplished in due time through the incarnation of the Son of God.—Vol. ii. pp. 29, 47, 75.

A second exhortation by the deacon, before the lifting of the veil, is equally remarkable:—"Stemus decenter orantes, stemus cum timore et tremore, stemus cum modestia et sanctitate: quia ecce oblatio infertur, et majestas exoritur. Januæ cœli aperiuntur, et Spiritus Sanctus descendit super hæc mysteria sancta et illabitur. In loco timoris et tremoris consistimus, et cum Cherubim et Seraphim circumstamus. Fratres et socii Vigilum et Angelorum facti sumus, et ministerium ignis et spiritus cum illis operamur. Nullus porro ligatus sit, qui audeat accedere ad mysteria hæc, quia velum tollitur, et gratia demittitur, misericordiæque effunduntur super unumquemque qui orat in corde puro et conscientia bona."—Vol. ii. p. 30.

And he signs six crosses: one on himself, and one on this side on the north, and one over against the south, and three on the people, saying[o], The love of God the Father, and the grace of the Only-begotten Son[p], and the communion and indwelling (*illapsus*) of the Holy Spirit, be with you all, my brethren, for ever.

People. And with thy spirit.

The priest stretches his hands equally towards heaven, and says, Up where Christ sitteth on the right hand of God the Father, be the thoughts, and minds, and hearts of all of us in this hour.

People. They are.

Priest. Let us praise the Lord with reverence.

People. It is meet and right.

Priest. Depression[q]. Truly it is meet and right that

[o] A rubric in O_2 is more explicit:—"*Postquam dictum est Stemus decenter, signat ter populum signo crucis. Tum imponit dextram super tabulam altaris, accipitque virtutem a mysteriis. Mox signat se ipsum, deinde eos qui sunt a parte Septentrionali, tum eos qui sunt ab Australi, facto ter signo crucis super populum. Si nullus sit ad dexteram ejus vel sinistram, ter signum crucis facit super se ipsum, ter super populum, et dicit,* Caritas Dei, &c."—Vol. ii. p. 21.

The following explanation of this passage is given by Barsalibi:—"Cum dicit Sacerdos *Caritas Patris,* significat quod Deus ex puro amore filium suum pro nobis morti tradiderit, ut ait Paulus. *Gratia Unigeniti Filii* significat quod ipse Filius, gratia sua et voluntate, gustavit mortem pro omnibus hominibus, eademque gratia fecit nos esse filios Patris sui. Ista autem *Communicatio et Illapsus Spiritus Sancti* designat quod per illapsum Spiritus Sancti perficiuntur sacrificia et oblationes suscipiuntur."—*Renaudot,* ii. p. 77. It may be worth while to observe that the reading of my MSS. agrees here with that of Barsalibi.

[p] A. reads "*Thy* only Son." B. omits *Thy*.

[q] i.e. The words are spoken in a low tone of voice, Greek *μυστικῶς*.

49 we should praise, and adore, and glorify the Maker of all creation:

And he raises his voice. Whom the powers of heaven, corporeal and incorporeal, glorify; the sun and the moon and all the stars; the earth and the seas; the Firstborn graven in the heavenly Jerusalem; Angels and Archangels; and primacies, principalities, thrones, dominions, powers; the many-eyed Cherubim; and the six-winged Seraphim, which being veiled, faces and feet, fly one to another, and sing the Sanctus, and cry and say,

People. Holy.

Priest. Depression. Assuredly Thou art holy; and Thou makest holy, O everlasting King: and holy is Thy Son, our Lord Jesus Christ; holy too is Thy Holy Spirit also, who searcheth hidden things. Out of the ground Thou didst create the son of man, and
50 didst place him in paradise; and when he had transgressed Thy commandments, Thou didst not leave him wandering[r], but didst guide him by the hand of the prophets, and at length didst send Thy Only-begotten Son into the world, who, when He had received a body by the Holy Ghost and from the Virgin Mary, renewed Thy image that was worn away.

And raising his voice[s], And when He was prepared to

In the preceding line, MS. A. has *Priest,* B. *People,* the latter being evidently correct.

[r] It is remarkable that six out of seven of the oldest MSS. of this Anaphora in the British Museum read ܛܒܐ, (one of them ܛܒܐ ܐܘ,) i.e. 'O Good,' in this place. One, the date of which is A.D. 1133, reads ܛܥܝܐ, 'wandering.' Renaudot has '*errantem.*'

[s] "Elevans vocem dicit, *Cum ergo, &c.,* simulque accipiens Oblatam

undergo voluntary death for us sinners, Himself without sin, He took bread in His holy hands; and when He had given thanks, He bless ✠ ✠ ed, and sancti ✠ fied, and brake, ʃ and gave to His disciples[t], and said, Take, eat of it: This is My body[u] which for you and for many is broken ʃ and given for the remission of sins, and for eternal life.

Amen.

In like manner also He took the cup, and when He
had given thanks, He bless ✠ ✠ ed, and sancti ✠ fied,
and gave to His holy Apostles, and said, Take, drink 51
ye all of it: This is My blood which for you and for
many is shed ʃ [x] and given for the remission of sins,
and for eternal life.

in manibus, eam ter cruce signat, &c."—*Renaudot, Observationes in Lit. Syriac.*, vol. ii. p. 80.

[t] Apostles, M.

[u] This is one of the passages in which Renaudot charges the editors of the "Chaldaic Missal" with tampering with the MSS. from which they prepared their work, in order to make it correspond with the Roman formula. The alterations, however, do not seem to be of much importance as affecting doctrine, for they are said to consist (1) in the introduction of the word ܕܝܢ, *autem*, [it seems to correspond rather to the Greek δέ, and to be equivalent to the Latin *vero, autem, tamen*, or even the Greek γάρ, according to the context,] in the words which, when translated, are *Hoc est autem corpus meum;* and (2) in the interpolation of the words *mysterium fidei* in the form of blessing the cup.

This then is one of the *Duæ insignes mutationes* especially mentioned by Renaudot. The other, which we shall presently notice, is of a more serious character. The Chaldaic Missal was published at Rome, apparently in Syriac, under the title *Missalis Chaldaici ad usum Ecclesiæ Maronitarum*, in the year 1592. It contains fourteen Jacobite Liturgies.

[x] These marks, which are found in B., and again in the Anaphora of

Amen.

This do ye for My memorial; when ye communicate in this mystery, commemorate My death and My resurrection until I come.

Thy death [y].

Commemorating Thy death and burial, O Lord, and Thy resurrection in three days, and Thy ascension into heaven, and Thy sitting on the right hand of God the Father, and further Thy second coming, wherein Thou wilt judge the world in righteousness, and wilt reward every one according to his works; we therefore offer unto Thee this unbloody sacrifice, so that Thou
52 mayest not make us guilty, nor reward us according to our sins. But according to Thy abundant mercies blot out the sins of us Thy servants; for Thy people and Thy inheritance make supplication unto Thee, and by Thy hands and with Thee to Thy Father also, saying,

People. Have mercy upon us.

Priest. And we also, O my Lord, Thy weak and sinful servants, render thanks unto Thee, and confess Thy benignity unto all, and for all.

* * * [z].

the Twelve Apostles, with six cross marks, (p. 111,) probably indicate the breaking of the Bread and the tilting of the Cup. So Gabriel of Alexandria: "*Eo loco Sacerdos calicem leviter inclinet, ad effusionem sanguinis Christi significandam.*"—*Renaudot,* vol. ii. p. 81.

[y] "*Thy death, O Lord, do we declare,* or *commemorate.*" Three MSS. in Brit. Museum.

[z] The omission of the exclamation of the deacon at this place is not a little remarkable, and I have therefore ventured to mark it by lacunæ.

Priest. The Invocation of the Holy Spirit[a]. Have mercy upon us, O God the Father, and send upon

The exclamation is thus given by Renaudot: "Quam terribilis est hæc hora; quam timendum tempus istud, dilecti mei, quo Spiritus vivus et sanctus ex excelsis sublimibus cœli advenit, descendit et illabitur super Eucharistiam hanc in sanctuario positam, eamque sanctificat. Cum timore et tremore estote, stantes et orantes. Pax nobiscum sit, et securitas Dei Patris omnium nostrum, clamemus et dicamus ter, Kyrie eleison."

It is represented in both forms of St. James's Anaphora given by Renaudot, and its initial words will be found in the remaining five Anaphoræ here translated. Renaudot, indeed, asserts that no Syrian Liturgy is without it:—"Neque in tanto Liturgiarum numero vel una reperitur, in qua primis vocibus non designata sit."

Yet no trace of it appears in either of my MSS. of the Anaphora of St. James, nor is it found in that obtained by Dr. Mill.

An examination of twelve MSS. of this Anaphora in the British Museum leads to the following result:—

Three, supposed to be of the tenth or eleventh centuries, read, "*Peo. We glorify Thee.*"—the invocation immediately following.

One, of the eleventh or twelfth century, has, "*Peo. We glorify Thee: et cetera.*"

Two, of the dates A.D. 1133, 1182, respectively, read, "*Peo. We glorify Thee. Dea. In silence and in awe.*"

One, of the year A.D. 1230, has, "*Peo. We glorify Thee. Dea. How terrible.*"

Three, inferior MSS. of the thirteenth century, have simply, "*Dea. How terrible.*"

In the remaining two, the passage is lost.

J. A. Asseman, in his Codex Lit., vol. v., gives "*Dea. How terrible,*" as his reading.

[a] The second of the *Insignes mutationes* made by the Roman Editors of the Chaldaic Missal was that of exciding from the Invocation of the Holy Ghost all reference to His operation in effecting or consummating a change in the elements, and of so framing its language as to make it apply solely to a fruitful and worthy participation by the communicants. We have already seen how, a few years afterwards, their example was followed by Abp. Menezes, in his recension of the Malabaric Liturgy. (See Introd. Notice, p. 40.)

This proceeding was grounded on the objection that the Invocation

these offerings Thy Holy Spirit, the Lord equal to Thee and to the Son in the throne and kingdom and essence eternal; who spake in Thy Old and New Testament; and descended like a dove upon our Lord
53 Jesus Christ in the river Jordan, and like tongues of fire upon the Apostles in the upper room.

Priest. Hear me, O Lord; hear me, O Lord; hear me, [O Lord[b];] and spare and have mercy upon us[c].

People. Kurillison, Kurillison, Kurillison.

Priest. So that He may come down, and make this

of the Holy Spirit, as expressed in the Syrian Liturgies, implies a denial of the efficacy of the words of institution alone; else why should the Holy Spirit be implored to effect or perfect that which has been already accomplished? Might it not be urged in reply, that the Invocation is simply an emphatic recognition of the Holy Spirit's office in consummating the mystery, without regard to the question of *time* at all,—time being as though it were not with the Eternal God? I trust I shall be pardoned for offering this suggestion, which I would offer with all modesty. The Invocation of the Holy Spirit is too deeply grounded in antiquity to be easily set aside by the exceptions of modern censors.

[b] Supplied from B.

[c] A rubric in MS. 17,128 gives the following direction: "*Here the priest falls on his face, and then extends himself:*" meaning, I suppose, that he prostrates himself at full length.

These earnest ejaculations are made, says Barsalibi, because the priest by faith perceives that the Holy Spirit is descending and consummating the mysteries; wherefore the people also, hearing the exclamation of the priest, cry out *Kyrie eleison,* the threefold repetition signifying their perseverance in deprecation. "There have been at times," he adds, "ignorant priests, who would at this time strike their foreheads with their hands, as though penitent for crime; but Moses Barcepha finds fault with such a custom as unsuitable to the occasion, seeing that the gifts of the Spirit are given with tranquillity, and not with clamour. For it was with tranquillity and gentleness that God the Word descended into Mary, and was incarnate of her, not with noise and tumult. In like manner He descends gently here also, and is personally united with the bread and wine upon the altar."—*Renaudot,* vol. ii. p. 90.

bread the life-making Bo ✠ dy, the saving Bo ✠ dy, the Bo ✠ dy of Christ our God.

Amen.

And may thoroughly-make this Cup the Blo ✠ od of the New Testament, the saving Blo ✠ od, the Blo ✠ od of Christ our God.

Amen.

So that they may sanctify the souls, and spirits, and A
bodies that partake of them; for the burthen of the
fruit of good works; for the confirmation of the holy
Church, which is made strong upon the rock of the
faith, and is not prevailed against by the infernal gates
[or, gates of Sheul]. And deliver her from heretical 54
offences even to the end; that she may raise to Thee glory and thanksgiving, and to Thy Only-begotten Son, and to Thy all-holy, and good, and adorable, and life-making, and consubstantial Spirit; now, and at all times, for ever.

People. Amen [d].

Priest. Depression. We offer unto Thee, O Lord, this unbloody sacrifice in behalf of holy Sion, the mother of all the Churches, and in behalf of the holy Church which is in all the world, that Thou mayest vouchsafe to her the gift of Thy Holy Spirit. Remember, O Lord, our just and upright fathers; our patriarchs Mar Ignatius and Mar Basillius, and Mar Evannis [e]; and our bishop Mar Thomas; and the presbyters and the

[d] B. adds here, "*Deacon.* Let us pray."

[e] If this portion of the *Diptychs* (or Great Intercession for quick and dead which follows the Invocation) have respect only to the living, which seems probable, we have here a clue to the date of this MS. See the Introductory Notice, pp. 52, 53.

55 deacons, and all the orders ecclesiastical, together with my humble self. Remember not against me the sins of my youth; but according to Thy mercies do Thou make me to live. Remember [also[f]] our brethren in bonds, the sick, the infirm, the afflicted, those who are vexed by evil spirits; and bless the air and the crown of the year; fulfilling Thy good pleasure unto all that liveth.

B *Elevation*. And deliver us, O Lord God, from every evil insurrection of the wicked sons of men, and assault and oppression of devils; and from every stroke which has been brought upon us because of our sins; and keep us in the observance of Thy holy commandments; for Thou art a merciful God, [and[g]] to Thee we send up glory and thanksgiving, and to Thy Only-begotten Son, and to Thy all-holy, and good, and ador-
56 able, and life-making, and consubstantial Spirit; now.

Depression. Remember, O Lord, the fathers and brethren who are standing and praying with us, and those who have journeyed from us, and those who willed to come and were not able; and grant to each one his proper (or, honest) petitions.

C *Elevation*. Remember, O Lord, all those whom we have remembered, and those whom we have not remembered; and receive their sacrifices in Thy broad heaven. Satisfy them with the joy of Thy salvation, and make them worthy of the aid that (comes) from Thee; make them strong in Thy might; arm them with Thy strength; for Thou art a merciful God, and to Thee we send up glory and thanksgiving, [and[h]]

[f] Supplied from B. [g] Ibid. [h] Ibid.

to Thy Only-begotten Son, and to Thy all-holy, and good, and adorable, and life-making, and consubstantial Spirit; now.

Depression. Remember, O Lord, kings and queens **57**
of honourable reverence; and aid them with the weapons of the Spirit; and make subject unto them all that hate them; that we may lead[i] quiet lives.

Elevation. For Thou art a Saviour and Defender, and **D**
givest victory to all them that trust in Thee, O Lord; and to Thee we send up glory and thanksgiving, and to Thy Only-begotten Son, and to Thy all-holy, and good, and adorable, and life-making, and consubstantial Spirit, now.

Depression. Forasmuch as Thou hast authority over life and death, remember, O Lord, our holy fathers; the prophets; the apostles; Mary, the Virgin Mother of God; Mar John the Baptist; the Martyr Stephen, with all the righteous.

Elevation. We implore of Thee, O mighty Lord, **58 E**
quickly[k] unite us to the multitude of the firstborn that are written in heaven; we remember them, so that they also may remember us before Thee, and may communicate with us in this spiritual sacrifice, for the preservation of those that live, and for the consolation of us that are in trouble; and for the rest of the faithful dead, our fathers, and brethren, and masters; by the grace and by the mercies of Thy only Son, and of Thy

[i] Lit., rest.

[k] ܠܐ ܡܠܟܡܠܟܢܝܬܐ, perhaps 'without delay,' 'quickly,' (ܡܠܟ) but B. and M. read ܡܠܟܡܚܢܝܬܐ, 'Who prevailest over that which is impossible.' So Renaudot.

all-holy, and good, and adorable, and life-making, and consubstantial Spirit, now.

Depression. Remember, O Lord, true shepherds, who, from James the chief of bishops unto this day, have maintained orthodoxy in Thy Church.

F *Elevation.* The doctrine of illustrious men and doctors
59 who bore Thy holy name before peoples, and kings, and the sons of Israel, do Thou confirm in our souls; and bring to nought the heresies that injure us; and make us meet to stand unaccused before Thy dreadful judgment-seat; for Thou art holy, and the sanctifier of the saints; and to Thee we send up glory and thanksgiving, and to Thy Only-begotten Son, and to Thy all-holy, and good, and adorable, and life-making, and consubstantial Spirit; now.

Remember, O priests, the sinner and the writer, and his dead[l].

Depression. Remember, O Lord, all the orders ecclesiastical which in the orthodox faith have gone before, and sleep, and are at rest; and all for whom they offered[m]; and those who now are named.

Elevation. O Lord, Lord God of spirits and of all flesh, remember all those who in
60 the right faith have gone from us, and give rest to their bodies, and souls, and spirits, and deliver them from the condemnation

[l] In B. we have, "Remember, O priests, the wretch who writes, and his fathers, and his brethren, and his masters, and his dead." I suspect that in A. the words should be "the sinner who writes," not "the sinner and writer."

[m] Here I follow B., and Dr. Mill's MS. A. reads "for whom they went before," a single stroke making all the difference. It is evidently incorrect.

that never endeth; make them joyful in that place which the light of Thy countenance visiteth; blotting out their misdeeds, and not entering into judgment with them, for there is none innocent before Thee, save only Thy only-begotten Son, by whose hands we also trust to find mercy and remission of sins, both for us and for them, for His sake [n].

People. Put away.

Priest. Depression. Put away, O God, pardon our misdeeds which have been in thought, and word, and deed: secret and open are open unto Thee.

Elevation. And keep our end without sin, O Lord;
and gather us under the feet of Thine elect, when and 61
where and as Thou wilt, only without the confusion of our sins, so that herein as in all things Thy all-glorious and blessed name may be praised and glorified, with (that) of our Lord Jesus Christ, and of Thy Holy Spirit; now.

As [o].

Peace.

People. And with thy spirit.

Priest. The mercies of our great God and Saviour Jesus Christ be with you all, my brethren, for ever [p].

[n] It will be observed that the Great Intercession always ends with this form of words. The word rendered 'Put away' also signifies 'to give rest;' but the former meaning is here chosen because it is presently repeated by the priest with the same signification.

[o] The initial word of the response, "As it was in the beginning," &c.; Renaudot has it thus, "Sicut est, et fuit, in generationes generationum, et futurorum sæculorum in sæcula. Amen."

[p] Here Renaudot's translation introduces the following form. Having invoked the blessing, the priest adds, "Credimus, accedimus, obsigna-

Deacon. The Catholic[q].

mus et frangimus Eucharistiam hanc: Panem cœlestem, Corpus Verbi Dei vivi, in calice salutis et gratiarum actionis, in crucis modum signamus, cum particula propitiatoria, mysteriisque supernis plena; in nomine Patris vivi, ad vitam; et unigeniti Filii; et Spiritus Sancti, principii, perfectionis, et sigilli omnium quæ sunt et fuerunt in cœlo et in terra; unius virtutis, unius potestatis, unius voluntatis, unius Dei veri, benedicti, excelsi, et indivisi, a quo est vita in sæcula sæculorum. Amen."

This, says Renaudot, is the ἁγία ἕνωσις, or *union* of the two species, testifying, in the words of Barsalibi, "hoc esse corpus istius sanguinis: hunc esse sanguinem istius corporis." It appears to be intimately connected with the ceremony of "the breaking," if not identical with it. See note r. towards the close.

It is remarkable that of the nine MSS. in the British Museum which contain this part of the Anaphora of St. James—in three fragmentary MSS. the passage is entirely lost—only one gives the words used in connection with *the Breaking*, while those of *the Catholic* are wanting in all. But they are represented in four MSS. by the initial words, "Deacon. The Catholic. The priest breaks and signs." In three others, only *the Catholic* is thus indicated; while one (17,128) passes over them without the slightest hint of their being said. But this MS. is characterized by numerous omissions, many of which have been supplied, between the lines, and in the margin, by a later hand.

The MS. which *does* contain the words—it is numbered 14,499, and is a small vellum MS. of the eleventh or twelfth century—supplies only the short form, "We break the true bread, and the holy and saving cup do we sign, In the name of the living Father, for life. *Amen.* In the name of the living Son, for life. *Amen.* In the name of the living and Holy Ghost, for eternal life. *Amen.*" Then follows the Catholic. This MS. professes to give the Anaphora of St. James according to the recension of James of Uraha, but it varies considerably from the normal form (so far as it may be represented by the general consensus of the rest) as well as from MS. 14,493, which also professes to be according to the same recension.

[q] The *Catholic* (or *Prodiki* as it is sometimes called) is a prayer uttered with a loud voice by the deacon, while the priest is engaged in the ceremony of the breaking. As soon as the blessing has been invoked, the curtain is drawn across the chancel, hiding the altar from the sight of the people, and the Catholic is said in order to occupy their attention, "ne mens populi in profundo silentio, quo sacerdos ministerium Sacramentorum perficit, alio evocaretur." (Barsalibi.) The prayer

The Priest breaks [r]. Thus truly did the Word of God

usually commences with the words "Again and again," &c., but it is not always of the same form, and, like the two succeeding portions of the Liturgy, appears not to belong strictly to the Anaphora of St. James, but to be of different origin. The form in Renaudot's translation is too long for insertion, but the general purport of the Catholic may be seen from the following specimen, taken from the Apostolical Constitutions, (see Ren. ii. 39, 110): "Again and again let us entreat God through His Christ, that the good God would receive this sacrifice, through the mediation of His Christ, unto His heavenly altar, for a sweet smelling savour. Let us pray for this Church and people, for all the episcopate, all the presbytery, all the diaconate and ministry of the entire complement of the Church, that the Lord would keep and preserve all of them. Let us pray for kings and for all in authority .... Let us make remembrance of the holy martyrs. Let us pray for them that have departed in the faith." J. A. Asseman gives the Catholic (which in his Syriac version is called *Brodiki*, Latin *concio*) much in the same terms as Renaudot. *Codex Liturgicus*, vol. v. p. 207.

[r] The following note from Renaudot (vol. ii. p. 111) will explain this interesting passage:—"De Fractione Eucharistiæ hæc habet Barsalibi. Accipit Oblatam sacerdos, eamque frangit in duas partes, quo significat Verbum vere passum esse in carne, immolatumque et fractum fuisse in cruce. Accipit deinde partem ex Corpore, eamque intingit in Sanguine, et cum ea signat super Corpus, etiamsi, cum parte quæ est in manu ejus prius leviter tetigerit sive pupugerit eam partem quæ est in disco. Ita significat transfossum lancea fuisse Christum in latere suo. Deinde, cum totum Corpus, sive omnes quæ in disco sunt particulas, signat, significat ipsum esse qui occisus, sanguine suo respersus est: ipsum qui dixit in cœnaculo, *Hic est sanguis meus:* et in cruce cum latus ejus lancea apertum est, exivit ex eo sanguis et aqua, quibus respersus est. Quando ex Sanguine Corpus signat in formam crucis, unionem facit animæ cum corpore, significans quod postquam separata est anima Verbi a corpore ejus, reversa est, eidemque rursus unita: quamvis nullatenus divinitas ejus separata fuerit a corpore ejus aut anima. Panis est corpus Verbi Dei: Vinum autem ejus anima: quia sanguis est typus animæ, sicut scriptum est, quod omnis carnis anima sanguis ejus est. Iterum, postquam signum fecit ex sanguine super corpus, unit et conjungit ad invicem duas illas partes Oblatæ: atque ita significat, Emmanuelem unum esse, neque divisum post unionem in duas naturas: significat etiam, quod postquam in cruce immolatus est, pacificavit per sanguinem crucis suæ, univit et conjunxit cœlestia cum terrenis, popu-

"Here he divides the Bread into two pieces, but holds the pieces together."

suffer in the flesh, and was sacrificed and broken on the cross: and His

"At the word separated, *he separates the pieces from each other."*

soul was separated from His body: though His divinity was in no wise separated, either from His

"At the word separated, *he again joins the pieces, after which, separating them, with the piece in his right hand he marks the wine with the sign of the cross, saying,* He was pierced, &c."

soul or from His body. ✠ And He was pierced in

62 *"Here he withdraws the Bread from the Wine, and wetting the broken parts of the other piece with the part that had been dipped with (in) the Wine, says,* From which flowed, &c."

His side by the spear, ✠ and there flowed from it blood and water, a propitiation for all the world;

"Again marking the top of the wine with the wet piece, he says, with which His body was covered."

✠ and His body was stained thereby. ✠ And

lum cum populis, et animam cum corpore. Oblatam quoque dum in circulum circumfert, significat quod pro peccato totius orbis immolatus est in cruce. Primo circumfert illam ad dexteram, secundo a sinistra refert ad dexteram, ut significet quod Dominus a sinistra, sive ab errore, ad dexteram nos reduxerit.

"Accipit particulam ex Corpore et mittit illam in calicem, ut intelligatur hunc esse Sanguinem hujus Corporis, et hoc Corpus hujus Sanguinis, non alterius, sed utrumque idem quod in cruce immolatum est. Significatur etiam, quod licet in vasis duobus posita sint Corpus et Sanguis, tamen unum Corpus dominicum est, Verbi Dei.

"Postea Corpus in plures particulas dividit, quia ita fecit Dominus cum Corpus suum fregit et divisit in cœnaculo: particula quoque, sive Margarita, quæ in calicem mittitur, significat, hunc Sanguinem esse hujus Corporis, unumque et eumdem esse occisum, in sanguine et corpore."

for the sins of the circle of the world ✠ the Son died upon the cross. ✠ And His soul came and was united to His Body: and He turned us from a left-hand conversation to (that of) the right-hand; and by His own blood[s] He reconciled and united and associated heavenly things with things of the earth, and the people with peoples[t], and the soul with the body. And the third day He rose from the tomb; and is One Emmanuel, which is not divided,

"*Marking the Bread as before*, For the sins of the universe, *here uniting the pieces in the form of a circle, and turning them round*, of the world, *again marking the top of the wine with the wet piece*, the Son died on the cross; *wetting the Bread as before*, His soul came and united with His body. He turned, *again joining the pieces in the form of a circle and turning them*, us from the left-hand works, &c."

"He rose — *elevates the Bread*, . . . one very Emmanuel, and joined in an union, which can never be divided, into two natures, *at the word* natures *he again separates the piece, and holding one part between the thumb and finger, and the other between the middle finger* (sic) *of the left*

[s] B. reads "by the blood of His cross."

[t] "Populum cum populis," Renaudot. "His people to the Gentiles," Church Missionary Extracts. There is no *His* in my MSS.

hand, so we believe, *here he touches the Bread with his right hand, and puts it to his forehead*, so we confess, *repeats the last form*, so we declare, that this Flesh is that which belongs to this Blood, *here putting one part of the Bread into the Wine*, this Blood is that which belongs to this Flesh, *here breaking one of the small pieces from the second piece, and laying them both on the plate, he repeats the prayer of the Doctor S. James.*"

"*During the repetition of
these words he divides the two
63 large pieces into four parts,
places them in the plate, then
elevating it, and dipping one
of the small parts into the
wine, and touching the other
parts with it in ten different
places twice over, he says,*
Behold, &c[z]."

after the indivisible union, into the two natures[u]. Thus we believe: thus we confess: thus we affirm. And this[x] Body appertains to (lit., is of) this Blood, and this Blood appertains to this Body[y].

Another prayer of the Breaking. O Father of truth, behold Thy Son, the sacrifice which propitiates Thee. Receive this One who died for me; and may I be pardoned through Him. Accept

[u] ܘܒܬܪ ܗܘ ܚܕܝܘܬܐ ܕܠܐ ܡܬܦܠܓܢ ܡܢ ܒܬܪ ܚܕܝܘܬܐ ܠܐ ܡܬܦܠܓܢܘܬܐ ܠܬܪܝܢ ܟܝ̈ܢܝܢ. These remarkable words express the distinctive tenet of the Monophysites. The negative form of the expression looks like an emphatic protest against the Nestorian heresy, rather than the addition of a new dogma.

[x] B. reads, "That this," &c.

[y] This form is attributed to Mar Jacob Barsalibi (who is also called Dionysius Barsalibi) in the Rubric of Renaudot's translation. That which follows is called in B. a Prayer of Mar Jacob the Malpan. It bears the same title in the translation by Renaudot, who places both in the *Ordo Communis*, as being used with all Anaphoræ alike.

[z] These marginal rubrics are taken from the Church Missionary Society's "Extracts from the Liturgy of the Syrian Church," already

this offering from my hands, and be Thou reconciled unto me. And remember not against me the sins which I have committed before Thy majesty. ✠ Behold the blood shed upon Golgotha by wicked men, and pleading for me: for its sake receive my petitions. As great as are my offences, so great are Thy mercies. If Thou shouldst weigh them, Thy mercies would weigh more than the mountains that are weighed by Thee. ✠ Look upon the sins, and look upon the offering for them; for the offering and the sacrifice is much greater than the sins: because I sinned Thy Beloved bore the nails and the spear: His sufferings are sufficient to reconcile Thee; and by them may I live[a]. ✠ Glory to the Father, who delivered His Son for our salvation; and adoration to the Son, who died on the cross, and restored us all to life: and thanks-
giving to the Spirit, who began and completed the 64
mystery of our salvation. O Trinity, exalted above all, have mercy upon us all. ✠

[*Another prayer of the Breaking*[b].] Thou art Christ the God: who was pierced in His side on the height of Golgotha for us. Thou art the Lamb of God which taketh away the sins of the world. Do Thou pardon our offences and remit our sins, and set us on Thy right hand.

alluded to. The last mentioned "form" (? ceremony) is said to be repeated with each of the first three clauses of the prayer, separated by a ✠.

[a] ܐܚܐ̤. B. has ܐܚ̈ܐ, which is observable as explaining numerous instances in the MSS. where the dots look like ribui, where ribui is inadmissible.

[b] Supplied from B.

And he raises his voice. The prayer of[c] *Our Father, which art in the heavens.*

O God and Father of our Lord Jesus Christ, who art blessed by the Cherubim, and hallowed by the Seraphim, and extolled by thousands of thousands and myriads of myriads of reasonable hosts, who sanctifiest and makest perfect the offerings and ripe fruits which are offered unto Thee for a sweet odour: sanctify also our bodies and souls and spirits, so that with a clean
65 heart and face that is not ashamed we may call upon Thee, O God, heavenly Father, and may pray and say, Our Father, which art in the heavens,

Ha llowed be .

Yea, O Lord our God, lead us not into temptation that cannot be endured, but deliver us from evil, making a way to escape to follow the temptation; and we will send up unto Thee glory and thanksgiving, and to Thy only-begotten Son, and to Thy all-holy, and good, and adorable, and life-making, and consubstantial Spirit; now. *Amen.*

Priest. Peace.

People. [And[d]] with thy spirit.

Deacon. Before.

People. We will bow our heads unto the Lord.

Priest. Unto Thee do (Thy) poor servants bow their heads, because Thy mercies are rich. Send forth blessings, O Lord, and sanctify our bodies, and souls, and spirits; and make us meet to partake of the life-giving
66 mysteries of Christ our Saviour, and we will raise to Thee glory and thanksgiving, and to Thy Only-begotten

[c] A. reads, "*The Prayer and Our Father,*" &c. [d] Supplied from B.

Son, and to Thy all-holy, and good, and adorable, and life-making, and consubstantial Spirit; now.

People. Amen.

Priest. Peace.

[*People.* And with (thy) spirit [e].]

Priest. And ✠ may ✠ the ✠ grace ✠ and ✠ mercy ✠ of the holy, and glorious, and uncreated, and essential, and eternal, and adorable, and consubstantial Trinity be with you all, my brethren, for ever [f].

Deacon. Let us behold with reverence and awe. Spare, O Lord, and have mercy upon us.

Priest. Holy things are given for the holy and the pure.

People. The one Father is holy, ✠ the one Son is holy, ✠ the one Spirit is holy. ✠ Glory to the Father, and to the Son, and to the Holy Ghost. ✠ One they are from everlasting to everlasting. Amen [g].

Priest. May the one Holy Father, who formed the
world in His mercy, be with us. ✠ May the one Holy
Son, who redeemed it by His own grievous sufferings,
be with us. ✠ May the one Living and Holy Spirit, **67**
who is the perfecter and completer of every thing that

[e] Supplied from B.

[f] The crosses are supplied from B., which herein agrees with the rubric in Renaudot's translation, directing the priest to make six crosses as he had done before. See p. 48.

[g] Here B. adds: "*And he takes up the paten and elevates it: and putting it down, he takes the cup also, and elevates it: and after the elevation, he holds them up, the paten in his right hand, and the cup in his left hand, crosswise over the table, and says,* May the one holy Father, &c." Renaudot's rubric and the C. M. S. "Extracts" represent the elevation as occurring while the Sancta Sanctis is said.

is and hath been, be with us. Blessed be the name of the Lord, from everlasting to everlasting. Amen.

Deacon. The king's daughter standeth up in glory, ōı &c.

Priest. The Prooemium of the mother of God here: and he says[h], Let us all pray to that eternal Light which beamed forth from the Eternal Light, and sprang, the hope of life, from the Virgin's bosom and His mother's womb; to Him who magnified (and) exalted the memory of His mother in heaven and in earth; to whom belongs glory and honour, now.

68 *Sedra.* What tongues are sufficient to tell thy praises, O Virgin, full of all graces, mother of Christ our Saviour; who by His salutary revelation dissipated from us the darkness of sin and the error of corruption. Therefore we acknowledge thee the fountain of life, the source of our salvation, O blessed field, ladder that is an ascent unto heaven. At this we marvel as we say, Blessed art thou, O fleshly chariot, wherein the Lord of angels dwelt; blessed art thou, O famous bush, wherein was seen the ark of the Highest. And now, O thou that art full of grace, pray with us to thy Son who sprung from thee, so that He may blot out

[h] It is proper to observe that, not only is this Sedra wanting in the MSS. of the British Museum, but that it is not found either in B. or Dr. Mills' MS. The former reads:—

"*Deacon and clerks.* In offerings and prayers let us remember them.

"*Then.* By the resurrection of Christ the King.

"*The Priest covers, &c.,* as on p. 69."

Dr. Mills' MS. has "A Prayer for the Sick" in the form of a Litany extending over two pages and a-half. It terminates with the Lord's Prayer, after which comes the form "Make me worthy, &c." as on p. 69.

our sins in His grace, and do away our wickedness in
His mercy, and may make us and our dead meet for the
mansions of Jerusalem, and for the bosom of Abraham:
so that from the mouth of all of us we may send up 69
glory and honour to Him, and to His Father, and to
His Holy Spirit, now.

Deacon. Like as a father pitieth his children, οι̅ &c.

The Priest covers[i] *the Mysteries, and takes the spoon, and places it on the cup, and falls down before the altar, and kneeling before the table of life, prays these prayers.* Make me worthy[k], O my Lord, to eat Thee in holiness; and by[l] the eating of Thy holy Body may my lusts be driven away, and by the drinking of Thy Cup of life may my passions be extinguished; and by Thee may I be made meet for the pardon of offences and the remission of sins, O our Lord and our God for ever. Amen.

Another. Make us worthy, O Lord God, that our
bodies may be made holy by Thy holy Body, and our
souls made bright by Thy propitiatory Blood: and
may It be for the pardon of our offences and for
the remission of our sins; O our Lord and our God 70
for ever.

Another. Make us worthy, O Lord God, to eat Thy

[i] The word 'covers' (for which a space is left in A.) is supplied from B. Renaudot's rubric (p. 23) concludes with the words, "*dicit has orationes secreto, cum corde affecto, lachrymisque et suspiriis.*"

[k] In these and similar cases the verb rendered 'make worthy,' might be rendered 'vouchsafe,' (Lat. *dignari,*) as the Greek word ἀξιώσῃ is rendered in 1 Thess. i. 11, (margin).

[l] Lit., by the hand of the eating, an idiom of frequent occurrence.

holy Body, and to drink Thy pardon-giving Blood; and may we have an inheritance in Thy heavenly kingdom, with all who have been pleasing to Thy will, O good our Lord and God for ever. Amen.

And he ascends the step, and taking the COAL *from the cup in the spoon, he says,* I am holding THEE: I am holding the uttermost bounds and limits: I grasp THEE, who orderest the heights and the depths: THEE, O God, do I place in my mouth: by Thee may I be delivered from the fire that is not quenched, and be made meet for the remission of sins, like the sinful woman, and like the thief; O our Lord and our God for ever. Amen.

And when he partakes, he says, A propitiatory Coal of
71 the Body and Blood of Christ our God is given to a sinful servant for the pardon of offences and for the remission of sins in both worlds for ever and ever. Amen.

And when he drinks from the cup, he says, By Thy living and life-giving Blood which was poured forth on the Cross, may my offences be pardoned and my sins be remitted, O Jesus, Word of God, who camest for our salvation, for ever and ever.

And when he communicates a priest with the spoon, he says, A propitiatory Coal of the Body and Blood of Christ our God is given to an illustrious priest; *or,* to a modest deacon; *or,* to a monk of St. Antony's order [m];

[m] A. has ܐܛܘܢܘܣܝܐ 'of Antony,' or 'Antonian.' B. has ܐܣܛܘܢܘܣܝܐ perhaps 'of the guards,' or 'watchers,' a religious order. Compare p. 3.

and then, a steward of God, for the pardon of his offences and for the remission of his sins. May his prayers be with us. Amen.

And the Priest takes the paten in his right hand, and the cup in his left hand, and as he turns to the right,
and as the mysteries are going forth, he says[n], From Thy 72
propitiatory Altar let there come down pardon for Thy servants, O Son of God, who came for our salvation, and will come for our resurrection and the renovation of our race for ever.

And he continues, Stretch forth Thy invisible right hand, O Lord God, and bless this multitude which worships Thee; which receives Thy glorious Body and Blood, for the pardon of offences and for the remission of sins, and for confidence before Thee, O our Lord and our God for ever.

And when he comes down from the steps, he says, May the love of our great God and Saviour Jesus Christ be upon those who bear these holy things; and upon those who give them; and upon those who receive them; and upon all who have laboured and have participated and are participating in them. The love of
God be upon them in both worlds[o] for ever. Amen. 73

[n] See Introductory notice, p. 145. It may be added here that, as soon as the curtain is opened, and the priest is seen with the paten and cup in his hands, ready to bring them forth for the Communion of the people, the bells are loudly rung, while he repeats the first two prayers. As the second prayer is being said, he makes the sign of the cross with the paten in his right hand. He then places the right arm over the left arm, and comes forward to the chancel steps, repeating the prayer in the text, "May the love of our great God," &c.

[o] 'Worlds' supplied from B.

And when he communicates the people, he says, To true believers for the pardon of offences and for the remission of sins for ever and ever. Amen.

And the recipient says, Amen [p].

And turning to the right, he says, Glory to Thee, glory to Thee, glory to Thee, O our Lord and our God for ever. O our Lord Jesus Christ, let not Thy holy Body which we have eaten, and Thy pardoning Blood which we have drunken, be unto us for judgment and for vengeance; but for the life and salvation of us all. And have mercy upon us.

Deacon. Let us stand decently [q].

People. We thank Thee.

Priest. The thanksgiving. We thank Thee, O Lord, for the abundance of Thy mercies, whereby we have been made worthy to partake of Thy heavenly table. O my Lord, let us not be condemned in the reception

[p] It has been stated (Introd. Notice, p. 147) that a hymn is sung in the Malabar churches during the communion of the laity. Renaudot's translation supplies the following version of it, (vol. ii. p. 41):—"*Interea dum communio administratur cum cochleari, Diaconus reliquis succinentibus clamat:* Fratres mei, accipite Corpus Filii, clamat Ecclesia: bibite Sanguinem Ejus cum fide, et canite gloriam. Hic est calix quem miscuit Dominus noster super lignum crucis: accedite mortales, bibite ex eo, in remissionem delictorum. Alleluia, et Ipsi laus, de Quo bibit grex Ejus, et puritatem consequitur. *Qui versus, ut et multi alii, juxta communicantium numerum minuuntur vel producuntur.*" Another form is given on p. 42, as being said by the priest, during the distribution of the Communion.

[q] This is not found in either form of St. James's Liturgy given by Renaudot, nor in the Ordo Communis. But it is contained in (at least) four of the oldest MSS. in the British Museum, and in both of my MSS.

of Thy holy mysteries; but, being worthy, may we be
partakers of Thy Holy Spirit: may we find a portion 74
and inheritance with all the righteous who have been from the beginning; and we will raise unto Thee glory and thanksgiving, and to Thy Only-begotten Son, and to Thy all-holy, and good, and adorable, and life-making, and consubstantial Spirit, now.

People. Amen.

Priest. Peace.

Deacon. After[r].

People. Before Thee.

Priest. O great and wonderful God, who for the salvation of our human race didst bow the heavens and come down, pity us and have mercy upon us, so that we may continually glorify Thee, and God the Father, who begat Thee, and Thy Holy Spirit, now and at all times for ever.

People. Amen.

Deacon. Sir, give the blessing.

Priest. Bless us all, O our God; keep us all, O our
Creator: shew unto us the way of life, Helper and 75
Lord of us all[s].

[r] The remainder is supplied by the Church Missionary Society's Extracts:—"*Dea.* Having received these mysteries in the presence of the merciful God. *Peo.* O our Lord, we bow our heads before Thee."

[s] Here ends the Anaphora of St. James, properly so called. After the prayer, "O great and wonderful God," B. has the following:—

"*Deacon.* Depart.

"*Priest. The Seal.* Bless us all, O God; *or,* The brother who wishes.

"*The Anaphora of James the Brother of our Lord is ended.* May his prayers be with us. Amen. Depart in peace, brethren and beloved, &c.," as on p. 80.

The words, "The brother who wishes," may probably refer to an

The Seal with the sign of Mar James. O God, God who dwellest in exalted heights, guard us all by Thy eye full of mercy; protect us all under the shadow of Thy glorious cross (lit., cross of light); and rain down upon this blessed company the love that is from Thee. From the mouth of all of us will we send forth all thanksgiving unto Thee; and to Thine unseen (lit., hidden) Father, and to Thy Holy Spirit will we hymn praise. May we sinners, who have partaken of this Thy Body, O my Lord, be pardoned thereby the sins and crimes which have been committed by us. And do Thou with Thy hyssop make white our follies and our stains; and our faults and our offences do not Thou remember, O my Lord. And the dead, who have departed from this world of woe, do Thou make joyful in
76 the chamber of light that doth not pass away. Set up Thy Church, and make firm her walls on a rock (lit., the hand of a rock); and the Shepherds who guide her keep Thou by Thy power; make her Priests illustrious, and the Deacons Thou hast planted do Thou also make honourable. Enlighten with Thy light the Subdeacons and the Readers: support the aged; make the men holy; the young men make strong; to the women give modesty; the youths and the children do Thou nourish and lead on. Strengthen the sick; heal the infirm; help the weak; satisfy the hungry; assist with Thy

anomalous custom which is said to prevail in Malabar, that the laity are not communicated when the rubric directs, (see p. 73,) but at some time afterwards. If this be so, the present seems a more probable time for their communion than that at which it is represented to take place in the Church Missionary Society's Extracts, viz. after the words "I will render my vows unto the Lord," on p. 83.

riches the needy and the miserable. Put far away
wrath from this place, and from every place wherein
Thy living and life-making name is remembered.
Make the sword and captivity, and famine and death
to pass from hence; and cause Thy peace, O my Lord,
to surround it like a wall. By the prayer of Mary the
pure Virgin, Thy Mother in the flesh; and of the pro-
phets who proclaimed Thy coming into the world; and 77
of John the star that surpasseth all the stars, and went
before the Sun of Righteousness shining at mid-day;
and (of) Stephen, who prayed for those who stoned
him, and said, O our Lord Jesus, remember not this
sin against them; and by the prayer of the Seventy
and two[t], and with them the twelve Apostles, and the
blessed Fathers three hundred and eighteen; and by
the prayers of the just and the priests and the martyrs
who endured tortures; and of the confessors who were
persecuted and shamefully entreated, and of the doctors
who have affirmed the doctrine of the truth in Thy
Church, and have overthrown and destroyed the doc-
trine of every heresy; Ignatius[u], who made the angels

[t] Alluding to St. Luke x. 1, where, however, all printed editions of the Peshito text (and therefore probably all known MSS. of that text) read ܫܒܥܝܢ, 'seventy.' I do not know what may be the Philoxenian reading. The Vulgate, following some Greek MSS., reads *Septuaginta duos;* and this reading was insisted on at the Synod of Diamper, Ac. iii. Dec. ii.

[u] I hoped to gather some additional particulars concerning the persons here commemorated, by reference to Asseman's great work, but my search, I regret to say, has been unattended with success, except in the case of those whose names are already more or less notorious. And even in such cases the uncertainty of identification is very great. Thus,

marvel by his fasting; and Dioscorus[x], who pleased
78 God by his excellent administration; Basillius (and) Gregorius, who dug in the vineyard from morning to evening, and watered the vineyard, and rooted out the tares; Mar Severo, who adorned Thy Church by his hymns (or melodies); Ævannis, who gave instruction and was illustrious by his interpretations; Mar Ephrem too, with Mar James, who spoke homilies; Mar Barsumas (Son of Fasting), who fasted and prayed and

turning to the name Ignatius, I find no fewer than *sixty-four* patriarchs, maphrians, bishops, or abbats, of this name, all of them mentioned in the second volume, *De Syris Monophysitis.* Indeed, it appears to have been adopted by the Jacobite Patriarchs on their elevation to that dignity, from the year of the Greeks 1604 (A.D. 1293) onwards. Again, there are *seven* of the name Dioscorus; *thirty-one* of that of Basil, exclusive of St. Basil the Great; *twenty* of that of Gregory; *seventeen* of that of Severo; while of that of John there are upwards of four folio columns. I speak of the Index only. On the other hand, there are some names in this list which are not mentioned at all by Asseman.

[x] It creates a sense of horror, almost approaching dismay, to find the names of Dioscorus and Barsaumo (Barsumas) retained with approbation among those of the saints. They will be remembered as the ringleaders in that terrible scene of violence and murder which caused what should have been an Œcumenical council to be afterwards known as "The Robber's Meeting," A.D. 449. See an account of it in Dr. Neale's "Holy Eastern Church." Barsumas, indeed, is said to have murdered Flavian, (not Proterius, as Renaudot has it, p. 99 of vol. ii.;) for he never recovered from the blows he received from either Barsumas or his followers.

It is indeed possible, and one would fain hope, that the Dioscorus and Barsumas here mentioned are others than the President of the false Council of Ephesus and his abettor; but Asseman speaks very decidedly to the contrary, at least in respect of Barsumas, vol. ii. p. 7. In that case one can only hope, either that these men were not really so bad as they are represented to have been, or that the Syrians do not believe them to have been so.

laboured and watched; and Mar John, who . . . . [y], and Achud his mother, who kept off death by the incense which she caused to smoke; and of Mar Matthew, with Mar Zacai, who dwelt in the cave; and Mar Abraham and Mar Daniel, who were companions with them; and of Mar Bahanam and Sechro his sister, who renounced the world; and of the four martyrs,—for
them the Lord entwined four crowns;—and by the 79
prayer of the martyrs who suffered cold in the midst of the lake; and Sargis and Barcus with the sons of Shamoni and Eliazar; and Mar George, who provoked (perhaps, defied) and despised all torments; and Theodorus, who looked down upon and disdained youth [z]; and Mar Kuricos and Sabatha his mother, who prepared the offering,—and by their contest Satan was vanquished, and [? the old one [a]] was driven away; and Barnegro and Shushan his sister, who broke the images, and suffered death at the hands of [lit., from] their father, and did not murmur; and of

[y] There has been a correction in one word of the Syriac which leaves it doubtful what the corrected word ought to be, and greatly increases the uncertainty of a conjecture as to the meaning of the passage. The words, as nearly as they can be represented in type, are the following:—

ܘܒܢܘܚܬܐ ܗܘܐ ܡܬܟܒܢܐ ܡܣܪ. The middle letter of ܡܬܟܒܢܐ (the corrected word or words) has a line through it. But the passage is of comparatively little importance.

[z] Here, again, I suspect that the Syriac is incorrect. By *youth* perhaps the follies of youth may be intended.

[a] Syr. ܘܗܦܟ ܐܬܛܡܪ. Can ܘܗܦܟ be a mistake for ܘܛܦܟ, ܗ for its cognate sound ܛ, as pronounced in Malabar? Then it would be, "and turning was dissipated."

Mar Zino and his sister Sara, who cried out and said,
The law in this world which shall cause to live, in the
world of the end doth not pass away; by the prayer of
all the circle (of those) who have loved Thee and have
kept Thy commandments, and of our elect Fathers who
preside over this blessed congregation; by the prayer
80 of our brethren, and of our masters of the spirit and of
the body; spare us all, and have mercy upon us, and
pity us and help us[b].

*The Priest places his hand upon the throne, and says
this Address, and forms three crosses on the people, saying,*
Depart in peace, brethren and beloved, seeing we com-
mend you to the grace and mercy of the holy and
glorious Trinity, with the viaticum and the blessing
which ye have received from the propitiatory Altar of
the Lord; those far off with those that are near, the
living with the dead, saved by the victorious Cross of
the Lord, illustrious[c] with the sign of Holy Baptism,
that it may obtain the pardon of your offences and the
remission of your sins, and may give rest to the spirits
of your dead. And may I, a weak and sinful servant,
81 obtain mercy and help through (lit., by the hand of)
your prayers. And depart in peace, joyful and glad.
Pray for me.

The Priest kneeling [shall say[d]] the Prayer, May the

[b] The pages containing this *Seal* are not so much thumbed as the other pages of this Anaphora; and at the close there is a twisted string fixed to the page to enable the Catanar to turn quickly to p. 80, containing the *Address*. Hence one may infer that the Seal is often omitted.

[c] ܡܫܒܚܝܢ: B. has ܡܛܒܥܝܢ, 'sealed.'   [d] Supplied from B.

Lord God be appeased by the offering which we have offered to-day; and His elect and holy angels[e]; and may He make by it rest and good remembrance to His mother and to His saints, and to all the faithful dead, and especially to him for whom, and because of whom, this offering has been offered to-day.

Another. Thy sacred and holy mouth, O my Lord, hath promised and said thus: Every one that eateth My Body and drinketh My Blood, and believeth in Me, abideth in Me and I in him; and I will raise him up at the last day. And we, O my Lord, who have eaten Thy holy Body, and drunk Thy pardoning Blood,—let it not be for judgment, nor for vengeance, nor for con- 82
demnation, nor for accusation to me and to Thy faithful

[e] Here the Church Missionary Society's Translation has, "May the Lord God, and the holy and elect angels, receive the sacrifice we have just celebrated, and by it give good remembrance, &c." If the Church Missionary Society's translator had the same Syriac words to translate that I find in both of my manuscripts, his rendering is most unfair; for it represents the Lord God and the angels as *conjointly* the subjects of the verbs *receive* and *give*, which in English are clearly in the plural. *This is not the case in the Syriac before me.* The singular and plural forms of the third person future are distinct in Syriac, and both of these verbs in Syriac are of the singular form, referring plainly to God alone. There is, therefore, nothing but the *position* of the words "and His holy and elect angels" to give the least colour to so shocking a sense as that contained in the Church Missionary Society's Extracts. The Syriac is, ܩܘܪܒܢܐ ܕܩܪܒܢ (B. ܩܪܒܢܢ) ܝܘܡܢܐ ܢܬܬܢܝܚ ܒܗ ܡܪܝܐ ܐܠܗܐ ܘܡܠܐܟܘܗܝ ܓܒܝܐ ܘܩܕܝܫܐ &c. ܘܢܥܒܕ ܒܗ, which Renaudot translates as follows:—"Per sacrificium quod obtulimus hodie, placetur Dominus et Angeli ejus electi et sancti, et per illud præstet, &c." Too much importance should not be attached to Renaudot's punctuation, which is often unusual, but which I have thought it right to retain here.

people; but for the pardon of offences and for the remission of sins, and for a blessed resurrection from the house of the dead, and for confidence before Thy fearful judgment-seat, O our Lord and our God for ever.

And gathering up[f] *the Body, he says this psalm:—*

The Lord shall be my shepherd; and nothing shall be wanting unto me.

And in pastures of strength will He cause me to dwell: and beside still waters will He lead me.

He converteth my soul: He leadeth me in the paths of truth.

Because of Thy name, although I walk in the valleys of the shadow of death, I will fear no evil: for Thou art with me; Thy rod and Thy staff they comfort me.

Thou preparest a table before me in the presence of
my enemies: Thou anointest my head with ointment;
83 and my cup inebriates as red wine.

Thy goodness and Thy mercies have followed me all the days of my life: and I will dwell in the house of the Lord for ever. (lit., for length of days.)

And wiping the paten with the Coal[g], *he says,*

If there be a member remaining, it remaineth to Thy knowledge which created the worlds: and if there be a member remaining, may the Lord be its keeper, and forgiving and indulgent unto me.

[f] ܡܟܦܪ, lit., 'wiping;' probably wiping the crumbs together.

[g] B. reads ܒܡܟܦܘܪܐ, 'with the corporal.'

And when he serves[h] *the Cup, he says,*

What shall I render unto the Lord, for all that He hath rendered unto me?

I will receive the cup of salvation, and will call upon the name of the Lord.

I will also pay my vows unto the Lord.

With the sign of Mar James: O Son of God,—who by His immolation saved the guilty,—by Thy living sacrifice dispel my passions,. and heal my infirmities.

Good (is He) that came: and they pierced His side 84
at Golgotha.—By the Blood and Water that flowed
therefrom, quench Thou my thirst[i].

And when he drinks the wine which has been mingled by (lit., *from*) *the Deaconess*[k], *he says,*

They shall be satisfied with the fatness of Thy house: and from Thy delightful valley shalt Thou give them to drink.

[h] This appears to be used as a technical word for doing what is necessary in the disposal of the remains of the bread and wine, and in cleansing the holy vessels.

[i] A remarkable instance of the confusion of persons in grammar which has been occasionally noticed. Cf. p. 72, "O Son of God, who came," &c.

[k] It appears from a note in Renaudot's work, (vol. ii. p. 124,) that in some of the Syrian churches deaconesses might, in the absence of a priest or deacon, "administer the Eucharist"—the elements having been previously consecrated of course—"to their sisters in the monastery, and might wipe out and wash the holy vessels;" but he says nothing about this being a part of their ordinary duty. Yet the rubric before us seems to point to some such custom, unless the word rendered 'Deaconess' be used as a name for the Cup. See note o.

This rubric is partly explained by the following note from the Church Missionary Society's Translation:—"Here the rubric directs the priest to wash the cup with wine, and drink it; but on account of the poverty of this people, they wash it with water and drink it."

For with Thee is the fountain of life: and in Thy light have we seen light.

Keep Thy mercies for them that are near Thee, and Thy righteousness for the upright in heart.

Let not the proud foot come against me: and let not the hand of the wicked move us.

Because there all the workers of falsehood are fallen: they are overthrown, and are not able to rise.

And when he serves his hands he says[l], May the living
fire of the Body and Blood of Christ our God extin-
85 guish the flame of the fire, and the dreadful and vehement torments, from my members, and from the souls and bodies of the faithful dead who have put Thee on by water and the spirit: and do Thou call them, and set them at Thy side and right hand at the last day, as Thou hast promised, O our Lord and our God for ever.

When he serves his fingers, first of the right hand three times, he says[m], Let my fingers repeat Thy praises, and my mouth Thy confession. By the nails in Thy hands and in Thy feet; by the spear which pierced Thy side, pardon me my offences and my sins.

And that (sic) *of the left hand, he says*[n], Keep me,

[l] "*Here the Priest, taking a little water in his hands, and washing them, lets the water fall into the cup, saying,* May the living, &c."—*Church Missionary Society's Translation.*

[m] "*Again, washing his right hand fingers, and letting the water fall into the plate, he says,* Let my fingers, &c."—*Ibid.*

[n] "*Then washing his left hand fingers over the plate, he says,* O Lord, preserve me, &c."—*Ibid.*

O Lord, from all deceitful things; and let Thy right hand help me, and preserve me from all left-handed works for ever. Amen.

And when he drinks the Meshamshonitho, he says [o],

They shall be satisfied from the fatness of Thy house, &c.

Wiping the Cup with the sponge, he says, 86

(*By Mar Ephrem.*)

Wipe away, O Lord, by the sponge [of Thy pity all my offences, and the sins which I have committed before Thee. Pardon me in Thy loving-kindness, O Christ the King, who givest us life, whose holy Mysteries I have ministered. Make me meet to serve Thee, O my Lord, with the just who have loved Thee and with the righteous who have desired Thee, in Thy heavenly kingdom which is everlasting; perpetually, O my Lord, and Amen, now and at all times for ever [p].]

[o] "*Here the Priest pours the water from the plate into the cup, and drinking it, repeats again from the 8th to the last verse of the 36th Psalm.*"—*Church Missionary Society's Translation.*

The translation of this short rubric—ܘܟܕ ܫܬܐ ܡܫܡܫܢܝܬܐ ܐܡܪ: —has caused me not a little anxiety and hesitation. If we might suppose ܫܬܐ a mistake for ܫܬܝܐ, which is the ordinary form of the feminine participle active, it would then agree with ܡܫܡܫܢܝܬܐ, and the clause might be rendered, *And when the Deaconess drinks.* Otherwise, I should be disposed to think that the word ܡܫܡܫܢܝܬܐ, 'M'shamshonitho,' i.e. 'Deaconess,' is here used to signify the *Cup.* We use the word *service* in a somewhat analogous sense, in the expressions *a service of plate, &c.*; and the word *waiter* (= a tray) would present a yet closer analogy.

[p] The part in brackets is supplied from B.

And he washes his hands, and says,

Judge me, O Lord, for I have walked in mine innocency: I have trusted in the Lord, I shall not move.

Examine me, O Lord, and prove me: and try my reins and my heart.

For Thy mercies are before mine eyes: I have walked in faithfulness.

And I have not sat with evil men: and have not gone in with the foolish.

I have hated the congregation of evil men: and have not sat with the wicked.

I washed my hands purely: and went round about Thy altar, O Lord.

That I might make the voice of Thy praise to be heard: and might tell of all Thy wondrous works.

87 O Lord, I have loved the service of Thy house: and the place of the habitation of Thy glory.

Destroy me not with sinners: and my life with men of blood.

In whose hands is deceit: and their right hand is full of gifts.

But I have walked in my innocence: deliver me, and have mercy upon me.

My foot standeth in my integrity: and in the Church will I bless the Lord.

And he wipes his hands, and says,

Bring young rams unto the Lord: bring unto the Lord glory and honour.

Bring unto the Lord the honour (due) unto His name: worship the Lord in the hall of His holiness[q].

The voice of the Lord is upon the waters: the glorious God thundereth: the Lord is upon many waters.

The voice of the Lord is in power: and the voice of 88
the Lord is in glory.

The voice of the Lord that breaketh the cedars: yea the Lord breaketh the cedars of Lebanon.

He maketh them to skip[r] like a calf: Lebanon and Sanir like young unicorns.

The voice of the Lord that divideth the flame of fire.

The voice of the Lord that moveth the wilderness: yea, the Lord moveth the wilderness of Cadesh.

The voice of the Lord that moveth the hinds[s], and uprooteth the thickets: and in His temple every man speaketh glory.

The Lord turneth back[t] the flood: the Lord sitteth King for ever.

The Lord will give strength unto His people: the Lord will bless His people with peace.

[q] Eng. Vers., "In the beauty of holiness," or, "in *His* glorious sanctuary." Vulgate, "In atrio sancto Ejus."

[r] Here my MS., as it originally stood, had ܪܩܕ, so agreeing with the Hebrew. The word has been clumsily altered to ܪܩܩ, which was probably intended for ܕܩܩ, 'maketh small,' the reading of the printed editions. The Vulgate has 'comminuet.'

[s] Here my MS. had at first ܐܝ̈ܠܬܐ, 'hinds,' or 'oaks,' (Heb. אלח,) as in 2 Sam. xviii. 9, 10. The latter signification would best correspond with the 'thickets' of the next clause.

[t] The Syrian translator appears to have read יסב, not ישב, in this place.

And he sets the Sedra of the Dead.

First the Prooemium.

Let us all pray. Glory and thanksgiving unto Him
89 who by the hand of His death hath abolished our death, and by His being sacrificed for us hath made propitiation for all the children of Adam; the Good unto whom we shall be brought; and whom we will glorify at this time of this divine perfect Eucharist, and in all feasts and times, now.

And the Sedra.

O Thou who awakenest the dead, and makest them that are buried to rise again, receive Thou, O my Lord, the souls of these Thy servants, whose memorial we have this day performed. Make them dwell, O my Lord, in the blessed mansions of the Father's house, with Abraham, and Isaac, and Jacob Thy beloved; and with all the faithful and the saints who sleep in Thy hope. Awaken them, O Lord, and set them on Thy
90 right hand, and let Thy mercies abound upon us all. And we will all send up glory, and will give thanks unto the Holy Trinity, now.

The voice.

O our Lord Jesus Christ. Let not Thy Body and Thy Blood which we have received be unto us for judgment and for vengeance, O my Lord, but for the pardon of debts, and for remission, and for standing with confidence at Thy right hand.

And from Thy sweet valley shalt Thou give them to drink. May Thy Body, O our Lord, which we have received, and Thy Blood of life which we have drunk in faith, be a bridge and a passage whereby we may be delivered from fire and from hell, ōı and may inherit life.

Glory. Let not the hands which have extended their palms, and have received the earnest of the new life from Thee, be drawn back in the house of judg-
ment at the last day, through the violence of the 91
flame: ōı yea, by Thee may they be stretched forth.

From everlasting. From the top of the tree at Golgotha, our Saviour heard the low voice of the dead; and He was deeply moved, and descended and brake the yokes of death from the necks of the buried, ōı and comforted them.

The Smoke. May this offering which we have to-day offered unto Thee in behalf of Thy servants and Thy handmaids, O Lord, be a sweet perfume for them. May Thy pleasure, O my Lord, be appeased thereby: and give them rest in Thy mercy.

Examination. If, by the blood of beasts, Moses gave life to Reuben who sinned; how much more shall the faithful dead be pardoned by the sacrifice of life [the living sacrifice] that hath been sacrificed for them!

Kūr. Kūr. Kūr. [i.e. Kyrie eleison, Kyrie eleison, Kyrie eleison.]

Have mercy upon us, O our Lord: spare, O our
Lord, (and) have mercy upon us. O our Lord, receive 92
our service and our prayers, and have mercy upon us. Glory to Thee, O God: glory to Thee, O Creator: glory to Thee, O King Messiah, who hast pity on Thy sinful servants.

Sir, give the blessing.

Our Father, which art in the heavens, &c.

And he takes leave of the throne, and says, Remain in peace, O holy and divine altar of the Lord. I know not whether I shall return to thee hereafter, or not. May the Lord make me meet to see thee in the Church of the First-born that are in heaven: and on this testament do I trust. Remain in peace, O holy and propitiatory altar of the holy Body and pardon-giving Blood which I have received from off thee. May it be
to me for the pardon of offences and for the remission
93 of sins, and for confidence before Thy dreadful judgment-seat, O our Lord and our God for ever. Remain in peace, O holy altar, table of life: and entreat our Lord Jesus Christ for me, that my remembrance may not cease from Thee, henceforth and for ever.

The order of the Corban is complete without defect.

Again: the Prayer over the blessing of the Bread. Glory to the Father, and to the Son, and to the Holy Ghost; who hath stretched forth His right hand, and blesseth this bread which is placed in our hands by His grace and by His abundant mercies for ever. Amen. O good Dove * * * *[u] who givest food to Thy servants
in the fairness of the seasons, stretch out Thy invisible
94 right hand and bless this bread in Thy holy name;

[u] Syr. ܝܘܢܐ ܛܒܐ ܩܘܠܣܢ ܚܣܝܐ ܦܠܚܦܢ ܡܪܢܝܐ. The passage seems to be corrupt.

and cause Thy satiety, and Thy blessing, and Thy nourishment, and Thy fulness to abide therein; so that it may be to us, and to all who receive and partake of it, for the sustenance of the body, and for the pardon and healing of the soul, and for the viaticum of the way everlasting; and for the giving of thanks and praise, and for the glory of Thy holy name for ever. May the power of the Father, and of the Son, and of the Holy Ghost, come and descend upon this blessing, and bless it; and may the love of God be upon him that giveth and upon him that receiveth it, and upon all that have laboured and have partaken of it, and are partaking of it, in both worlds for ever and ever. Amen.

THE
ANAPHORA
OF
ST. PETER,
CHIEF OF THE APOSTLES.

"Aliæ inter illas quas enumeravimus, augustis veterum sanctorum nominibus insignitæ, Melchitis, quantum adipisci potuimus, ignotæ sunt, et Jacobitis propriæ. Apostolorum duodecim, Petri, Marci, Lucæ, Joannis Evangelistæ, aliorumque Apostolicorum virorum, etsi ab illis scriptæ dici non possunt, tamen supposititiæ non sunt, cum in antiquis exemplaribus multis reperiantur."—*Renaudot, Lit. Orient. Coll.*, II. x.

THE ANAPHORA OF ST. PETER.

Again the Anaphora of St. Peter[a], *prince of the Apo-* 95
stles.

The Prayer of the Peace. O Lord, God of peace and Lord of quietness, grant unto us all, and make us meet, to embrace one another with a guileless kiss, in a spirit that is not severed from love[b]; and we will send up unto Thee glory and thanksgiving, and to Thy Only-begotten Son, and to Thy Holy Spirit, now.

People. Amen.

Priest. Peace.

Deacon. Let us give.

People. Before Thee.

Priest. Unto Thee, and before Thee, O Lord God, we bow the necks of our souls and bodies; so that we may receive of Thee blessings and assistance for our weakness: for Thou art the helper and the house of refuge of all; and to Thee we send up glory and
thanksgiving, and to Thy Only-begotten Son, and to 96
Thy Holy Spirit, now. *Amen.*

Now also Thou art the Lord: cause Thy face to shine upon us; and deliver us from all enemies that hate us; and blot out and forgive all our unlawful deeds; that we may raise unto Thee glory and thanks-

[a] This Liturgy is almost word for word the same as that which Renaudot has translated under the title *Liturgia Petri II.*

[b] "Misericordiâ tua," R.

giving, and to Thy Only-begotten Son, and to Thy Holy Spirit, now. *Amen* [c].

Let us stand.

Priest. Thou art the Rock [d].

Priest. The Love.

People. With.

Priest. Upward.

People. They are.

Priest. Let us give thanks.

People. It is meet.

Priest. Depression. Truly it is meet and right that we should glorify and exalt Thee, the Maker of all creatures that are above and that are beneath.

Elevation. We glorify Thee, O Lord, with angels
97 and legions of archangels, calling out in words of praise [e], and saying,

People. Holy.

Depression. Holy and full of mercies art Thou, O Lord, for in Thy love towards man Thou didst send Thy Son into the world; and He was incarnate of the Virgin Mary for our salvation.

And he raises his voice. And when He willed to taste death, and to perfect the Passover in the evening [f],

[c] This is apparently the Prayer of the Veil; cf. p. 47. In Renaudot's translation of this liturgy, the prayer "Unto Thee, &c.," stands first; then the prayer "Now also, &c.," and after these the Prayer of the Peace; contrary to the order constantly observed.

[d] Renaudot does not give any part of this form.

[e] Lit., in the daughters of the voices of praise.

[f] Lit., the Passover of the house of the evening. A similar use of the word ܒܝܬ occurs not infrequently; cf. p. 90, and Ezek. xxiv. 17.

He took bread on His hands; bless ✠ ✠ ed, and sancti ✠ fied, and brake, and gave to the order of the Apostles, and said, Take, eat of it, for the remission of sins, and for life eternal[g]. *Amen.*

In like manner also the cup, when He had mingled (it) of wine and of water, He bless ✠ ✠ ed, (and) sancti ✠ fied, and gave to His holy Apostles, and said,
Take, drink of it, all of you, for the pardon of offences, **98**
and for life eternal[g]. *Amen.*

This He commanded them, and instructed them, that whensoever ye perfect these mysteries, ye make a memorial of My death and resurrection until I come.

Thy death.

And as we commemorate Thy salutary coming, and that second (coming), O Lord, we offer praise with supplication unto Thy lordship; so that in that fearful and great day of judgment, when Thou makest examination of the just and the sinful, Thou mayest not deliver us, according to our sins, unto the fire and the burning of weeping and lamentation; and that we may not be vexed and tormented because of our evil deeds and our faults. Spare, O Lord, and have mercy
upon us, and turn Thy face from our sins, and help us; **99**

[g] Renaudot gives the complete forms, "*Hoc est Corpus Meum, &c.,*" "*Hic est calix Sanguinis Mei, &c.,*" having found them apparently in some MS. of this Anaphora. But he observes that most copies represent the words as they occur in the text; and he endeavours to account for the anomaly by the supposition that the well-known forms were generally represented in this liturgy by the initial words only, and that then, some ill-instructed scribe, so finding them, had carried on the sentence by appending the final words in each case, leaving the form incomplete; and that his copy, so deteriorated, has been followed by most others. See note, p. 124, (Anaphora of Barsalibi).

for this Thy Church and Thy flock makes supplication unto Thee, and through Thee, [lit., by Thy hands,] and with Thee, to Thy Father, saying,

[*People.*] Have mercy.

[*Priest.*] And we also.

[*Deacon.*] How fearful.

Priest. The Invocation of the Holy Spirit. Have mercy upon us, O Lord, have mercy upon us, and send down Thy Holy Spirit upon us and upon these offerings, and sanctify these Mysteries; and may He also assist and pardon me.

Priest. Hear me.

Deacon. Koor[h].

And he raises his voice. So that He may come down, and make this Bread the Bo ✠ ✠ ✠ dy of Christ our God. *Amen.*

And may perfectly make this cup the Bl ✠ ✠ ✠ ood of Christ our God. *Amen.*

A. So that they may be to those who partake of them for the purification of souls and bodies from all stains,
100 and for the remission of sins, and for eternal life. *Amen.*

Receive our supplications and prayers, O Lord, and grant rest unto Thy people, and peace unto Thy flock; and preserve the true shepherds with the priests and deacons, and help all the clergy of Thy Church.

B. *And he raises his voice.* O Lord, make them firm (and) strong, and adorn[i] them with the quietness and help that is from Thee; so that they may be suppliants and intercessors for us, that we may raise to Thee

[h] i.e. Kyrie Eleison.

[i] "confirma," R.

glory and thanksgiving, and to Thy Only-begotten Son, and to Thy Holy Spirit, now.

Depression. Again vouchsafe, O Lord, to remember those who have charged us to make mention of them, and those who willed to come, and were not able.

Elevation. Remember also, O Lord, those who assist C.
Thy holy Church: be Thou to them a protection and 101
house of refuge; delivering them from all machinations of devils and of evil men: for Thou art the Saviour of all, and to Thee we raise glory and thanksgiving, and to Thy Only-begotten Son, and to Thy Holy Spirit; now and in all.

Depression. Remember faithful (i.e. believing) kings, O Lord, and put into their hearts thoughts of peace[k] towards Thy people.

Elevation. Appease, O Lord, the designs of those D.
who desire to rule over us, and deliver us from the hands of the envious and the hostile; so that we may raise to Thee glory and thanksgiving, and to Thy Only-begotten Son, and to Thy Holy Spirit.

Depression. Again, vouchsafe, O Lord, to remember
the holy Virgin Mary, and with her, all the prophets 102
and apostles, with the martyrs and confessors, and the rest of all the saints; and help us by their prayers.

Elevation. By their prayers and supplications help E.
us, O Lord, and make us meet for their portion and their lot; so that with them and among them we may raise to Thee glory and thanksgiving, and to Thy Only-begotten Son, and to Thy Holy Spirit.

[k] "consilia pacifica," Renaudot. Syr. ܡܫܝܢܝ̈ܬܐ.

Depression. Remember also, O Lord, those who in the house of the saints have gone before, (and) sleep, and are at rest, holy fathers and doctors; so that by their prayers and their intercessions we may be delivered from the wiles of [him who is] the adversary, and from evil sons of men.

F. *Elevation.* And those, O Lord, who have diligently
103 borne Thy Gospel in all the world, and have confirmed Thy holy Church in the orthodox faith. By their pure supplications, assist us all, and confirm (us) in Thy lovingkindness; so that we and they may raise to Thee glory and thanksgiving, and to Thy Only-begotten Son, and to Thy Holy Spirit.

Depression. Make good remembrance, O my Lord, by the hand of this sacrifice which is offered unto Thee by our sinful hands, to our fathers, and to our brethren, and to our masters, and to our dead, and to all the faithful dead who are here and in all places.

Elevation. O Lord, O Lord, lover of mankind, in the bosom of Abraham make them to dwell who have finished their lives in the true faith, putting away all iniquities and transgressions (both) theirs and ours;
104 for there is none free from sins, save only our Lord and our Saviour Jesus Christ; through whom we also trust to find mercy and remission of sins, for His sake, both for us and for them.

Put away.

Pardon and remit, O Lord, the errors and follies of Thy servants and of Thy handmaids, (those) which are secret and (those) which are open, delivering us and them from shame before Thee; so that by us and because of us and by reason of us Thy blessed name may be glorified and praised; with (that) of our Lord Jesus Christ, and the Holy Spirit.

Deacon. As.

Peace.

With.

May (the love, &c.) be.

Deacon. The Catholic[1].

The Priest breaks and signs.

The Prayer of Our Father which (art) in the heavens.

We make supplication unto Thee, O God and Father, Consoler, and Comforter of our weakness; cleanse
us from all stains of guilt and of the defilements of 105
sin; and receive these offerings which we offer unto Thee for our sins; so that with one equality of breath we may cry out unto Thee and pray, and say,

Our Father, which (art) in the heavens,

Hallowed be.

Yea, O God benign, lead us not into the trial of temptation; for we have not power to endure it; but according to Thy abundant mercies, rescue and deliver us from all strokes of wrath: for Thine is the power and the kingdom; and to Thee we offer praise and thanksgiving. *Amen.*

Peace.

With.

Before.

Before Thee.

[1] Renaudot here reads, "*Diaconus.* Credimus." Comp. p. 235.

O God, bless Thy servants and Thy handmaids, who bow the necks of their souls and of their bodies before Thee, and make supplication unto Thee: make them
106 meet for (Thy) love, and for the forgiveness of sins; for Thy love is abundant: and Thou art Almighty, and to Thee we send up glory and thanksgiving.

Amen.

Peace.

With.

May.

Let us behold.

Holy things.

The one Father.

Deacon. We confess.

Priest. The Prayer of Thanksgiving. We confess unto Thee, O Lord God, and we give thanks unto Thee for this gift which Thou hast given unto us although unworthy. Lay not upon us the confusion of our sins; but help and save us from opposing spirits that contend with us: and together we will raise unto Thee glory and thanksgiving, and to Thy Only-begotten Son, and to Thy Holy Spirit.

Amen.

Peace.

With.

After.

People. Before Thee.

Priest. Send down, O Lord, Thy right hand, and bless Thy servants and Thy handmaids, who are here
107 gathered together: keep them by Thy cross; be Thou

to them a protection and house of refuge from all adversaries, secret and open; and fulfil them with the abundance of Thy blessings; so that we and they may send up unto Thee glory and thanksgiving, and to Thy Father, and to Thy Holy Spirit, now.

The Anaphora of Peter, chief of the Apostles, is complete.

THE ANAPHORA

OF

THE TWELVE APOSTLES.

THE ANAPHORA OF THE TWELVE APOSTLES.

Again, the Anaphora of the Twelve blessed Apostles: and it is ascribed to Luke the Evangelist, as that which was from the mouth of all the holy Apostles[a].

The Prayer of the Peace. O merciful and holy Lord,
who by the hand of Thy Only-begotten Son hast pre-
pared this spiritual table for us, receive from us the 108
oblations of this unbloody sacrifice, and vouchsafe unto
us the gift of Thy Holy Spirit, and make us all meet
with pure heart to give peace one to another in love
divine: and we will send up unto Thee glory and
thanksgiving, and to Thy Only-begotten Son, and to
Thy Holy Spirit.

People. Amen.

Priest. Peace.

With.

Let us give.

People. Make (us) meet.

After.

Before Thee.

Priest. May Thy tranquillity, O our God, and Thy peace, and Thy true love, and the mercies that belong to the nature of Thy eternal divinity, be with us and among us, even to the end of the world: and we will

[a] "Mira est Codicum hujus Liturgiæ diversitas, quæ ex comparatione variorum Manuscriptorum conciliari nequit. . . . . Unde manifestum est nullam aut exiguam esse titulorum fidem."—*Renaudot.*

raise to Thee glory and thanksgiving, and to Thy Only-begotten Son, and to Thy Holy Spirit. *Amen.*

109 Before Thee, O King of kings, and Lord of lords, do we adore and entreat, making supplication that Thou wouldest look mercifully upon us. And make us meet to approach Thy holy altar in purity of heart, and in holiness of soul and of body; and we will raise to Thee glory and thanksgiving, and to Thy Only-begotten Son, and to Thy Holy Spirit. *Amen.*

Let us stand.

Mercies.

The Love.

And with.

Upwards.

They are.

Let us confess.

It is meet.

The Priest, kneeling. Verily Thou art holy, O God and Father, and giver of life; and to Thee glory is due, and praise pertaineth unto Thee; for Thou art blessed, with Thy Only-begotten Son, and Thy living and holy Spirit.

And he raises his voice. For before Thee there stand
110 around the four-faced Cherubim, and the six-winged Seraphim, and pure voices and divine strains, praising and vociferating and calling out, and saying,

People. Holy.

The Priest, kneeling. Holy, holy, holy Lord, full of mercies: Holy is Thy Only Son also, our Lord Jesus Christ, God who is over all; and Holy is Thy holy and life-making Spirit also. Holy art Thou, and the giver of good things; whose Only-begotten Son was incarnate of the pure Virgin Mary, mother of God, for our salvation; and by His divine dispensation saved (us) and delivered us from captivity.

Elevation. Who, when for our sake He had become
the Son of Man, without change[b], came unto the cross, 111
and, before His life-making sufferings, took bread in His holy hands, bless ✠ ✠ ed, and sancti ✠ fied; brake, and ate, and gave to His disciples, saying, Take, eat of it: this is My body, which for you and for many is broken and given for the remission of sins and for eternal life.

Amen.

So also the cup, after they had supped, He mingled of wine and of water, and bless ✠ ✠ ed, and sancti ✠ fied, and when He had tasted, He gave it to His disciples, saying, Take, drink of it, all of you. This is the New Testament in My blood, which for you and
for many is shed [c] for the pardon of guilt
and for eternal life. 112

Amen.

As often as ye eat this Bread and drink this Cup, ye make My memorial until I come.

Thy death.

For this cause we also, Thy weak and sinful servants, remembering Thy dispensation, entreat and implore

[b] Observe this expression in its bearing on the tenets of the Jacobites; cf. Appendix A. p. 168.

[c] This mark probably indicates some commemorative or symbolic act to be performed by the priest. See note x, p. 227.

Thee, O lover of men, when Thou arisest in the end of times, and renderest justly to every man according to his works, spare and have mercy on Thy worshippers, and save Thine inheritance; and all Thy Church offers supplication by Thy hands to Thy Father, saying,

And have mercy.

And we also.

How terrible.

Priest. The Invocation of the Holy Spirit. Have mercy
113 upon us, O Lord, have mercy upon us, and send to us from Thy holy heavens Thy Spirit the maker of life; and may He brood over this offering, and make it the life-making Body; and may He pardon and sanctify us.

Hear me.

Ko͡or.

Priest. So that by His descent, He may make this Bread the Bo ✠ ✠ ✠ dy of Christ our God.

Amen.

And the mixture that is in this Cup the Bl ✠ ✠ ✠ ood of Christ our God.

Amen.

A. So that these holy mysteries may be to us for the pardon of offences (debts), for the sanity of soul and of body, and for the strengthening of the mind: and let not a man perish from Thy believing people; but make us all meet, that being led by the Spirit in
114 purity, we may send up unto Thee glory and thanksgiving, and to Thy Only-begotten Son; and to Thy Holy Spirit, now.

Depression. We offer unto Thee, O Lord, this divine

sacrifice in behalf of Thy flock; namely, for the blessed fathers, our Patriarch Mar *Such an one*, and Mar *Such an one*, and our Bishop Mar *Such an one;* with the rest of all the orthodox bishops.

Elevation. So that in blameless life they may govern **B.**
and conduct Thy flock in purity and in holiness, and may present unto Thee a faithful people, a spiritual flock, that pleaseth the honour of Thy name, and may together raise to Thee glory and thanksgiving, and to Thy Only-begotten Son, and to Thy Holy Spirit.

Depression. Remember, O Lord, Thy people and **115**
Thine inheritance, those who have offered these offerings unto Thee; and spare this congregation which is now gathered together before Thee.

Elevation. So that they may live continually without **C.**
blame before Thee, and may be prepared for the good things which by Thee are provided for them in Thy presence, by the mercies wherein Thou hast compassion upon them, as a good and very gracious Lord: and we will raise unto Thee glory and thanksgiving, and to Thy Only-begotten Son, and to Thy Holy Spirit.

Depression. Remember, O Lord, faithful kings who are good to Thy people, and merciful to the sheep redeemed by Thy name: and strengthen them in Thy might; and let them not be overcome by their enemies.

Elevation. And send armies of Thy holy angels to **D.**
their help, O Lord; and deliver them from tyrannical **116**
plots, and from Belial of noted fame [d]; and may they

[d] ܡܠܝܢܢܐ: "spirituali," Renaudot. So elsewhere.

be delivered from the snares and machinations of the enemies of Thy faithful Church; so that in tranquil quietness and in concordant peace, we may confidently raise unto Thee glory and thanksgiving; and to Thy Only-begotten Son, and to Thy Holy Spirit.

Depression. Remember, O Lord, those who from the beginning have pleased Thee; to wit, Mary the holy mother of God, the apostles, and prophets, and martyrs, and confessors, and John the Baptist, and Stephen the head of the deacons; and all who have overcome, and have been made perfect and complete in the contest of their Father.

E. *Elevation.* Make us partakers in the prayers[e] that
117 appease Thee, O Lord; and make us meet for a portion with them, and grant unto us that we may be made joyful in the kingdom of Thee their Father, and we will raise.

Depression. Remember, O Lord, the flock of true fathers and orthodox doctors, those who did not change Thy truth, and bore and endured afflictions for the sake of Thy Church and Thy people.

F. *Elevation.* And grant unto us, O Lord, that we may walk in their upright footsteps, and that their truth may not be deceitfully and perversely changed by our lips; but that, in the simplicity which Thou lovest, we may walk innocently in Thy straight paths: and we will raise to Thee glory and thanksgiving, and to Thy Only-begotten Son, and to Thy Holy Spirit.

[e] Probably intended for "their prayers," the affix having been carelessly omitted. Renaudot's translation omits this entire page (117); but it is necessary in order to make up the twelve portions into which the Great Intercession is commonly divided.

Depression. Remember, O Lord, the faithful dead who have gone before unto Thee; and receive these offerings which are offered unto Thee in their behalf; cause them to rest in Abrahamic and blessed bosoms. 118

Elevation. In the hope of Thy loving-kindness have all the dead been made to rest, and expecting the mercies that are from Thee, O our adorable God: make them meet for the joyful voice that calleth and leadeth them, that they may be invited to Thy kingdom: and grant unto us a quiet departure in Thy grace, and blot out our offences in Thy loving-kindness. For there is but One who was innocent[f] upon the earth without sin; Thy only Son, by whose hands we also hope to find mercy, and remission of sins for His sake, both for us and for them.

Remove.

Remove, O Lord, the burdens of sin from us and 119
from them, and in Thy mercy pardon those who have transgressed against us; and be Thou, O Lord, a pardoner and remitter of sins both to us and to them; so that in us, and for us, and by reason of us, Thy all glorious and blessed name may be praised, and glorified, and had in honour, with (those) of our Lord Jesus Christ, and of the Holy Spirit, now.

As.

Peace.

With.

[f] ܕܐܬܚܣܝ. Renaudot seems to have read ܕܐܬܚܙܝ, 'qui visus fuerit.'

May . . . be.

The Deacon [*says the Catholic*[g].]
The Priest breaks and signs.

The Prayer of Our Father which art in the heavens.
O merciful Lord, who art celebrated, and exalted, and glorified above all, make us Thy poor and lowly servants meet purely and holily to pray and cry out and say, Our Father, which art in the heavens,

Hallowed be.

Yea, O Lord, merciful and loving towards man, turn
120 not away from us, (so) that temptation get dominion over us; but deliver us from the rebellious evil one, and from his tortuous and perverse ways: for Thine is the kingdom, and Thy only Son's, and Thy Holy Spirit's, now and in all times for ever. *Amen.*

Peace.

People. Before[h].

Bless Thy faithful people, O Lord, who bow before Thee; and deliver us from temptations and injuries; and make us meet to partake purely of these holy Mysteries; and may we be pardoned and sanctified by them: and we will raise to Thee. *Amen.*

[g] Supplied from Renaudot.

[h] Here follows, in red ink, the word ܩܕܡܬܐ, which is evidently a blunder, probably for ܩܕܡܝܟ, 'Before Thee.' This correction would require the transposition of the two preceding words, thus:—
Peace.
Before.
People. Before Thee.

Peace.

With.

May . . . be.

With.

Let us behold.

Holy things.

The one Father ————[i].

We confess.

Priest. The prayer ————————[k]. We confess to Thee, O Lord God, and we render thanks to Thee, entreating and making supplication, that
this divine communion may be to us for the pardon 121
of offences and for the remission of sins, and of all our transgressions, and for the glory of Thy holy name, and of Thy Only-begotten Son, and of Thy Holy Spirit. *Amen.*

Peace.

With.

After.

People. Before Thee.

Priest. O Lord God of our salvation, who for our sake didst become the Son of Man, and didst deliver us by the sacrifice of Thyself, deliver us from every destroying corruption, and make us temples for Thy holy name: for we are Thy people and Thine inheritance; and to Thee belongeth the glory, and the honour, and

[i] A blank in the MS. about ¾ in. long; compare p. 66. After this follows the Communion; see pp. 67—73.

[k] Another blank about 1½ inches long.

the power, with Thy Father, and Thy Holy Spirit, now and in all times for ever.

The Anaphora of the twelve holy Apostles is finished. By the hands of me a sinful and vile man. Yea, Amen.

THE ANAPHORA OF MAR DIONYSIUS,

METROPOLITAN OF AMID,

(OTHERWISE KNOWN AS JACOB BARSALIBI.)

THE ANAPHORA OF MAR DIONYSIUS.

Again the Anaphora of Saint Mar Dionysius, Metropolitan of Amid, who is Jacob Barsalibi[a]. 122

First. The Prayer that is before the Peace. Love, and concord, and perfect tranquillity vouchsafe to us in this time, O Lord, that we may raise unto Thee glory and thanksgiving, and to Thy Only-begotten Son, and to Thy Holy Spirit, now.

People. Amen.

Priest. Peace.

People. And to (thy) spirit.

Deacon. Let us give.

People. It is meet.

Deacon. And after.

People. Before Thee.

Priest. And bless us all with Thy blessings that cannot be taken away, and make us meet to do Thy will, and (that) of Thy only Son, and of Thy Holy Spirit; and we will raise to Thee glory.

People. Amen.

Priest. The Prayer of the Veil. And drive away every
impure thought from us by the hand of this sacrifice 123

[a] "Brevitas hujus Liturgiæ facit ut eam a Barsalibio compositam judicemus, eo fine, ut cum Baptismus moribundo infanti administrandus esset, haberent sacerdotes formam, quam sequerentur, ne dum, ut ipsis præcipitur per varias constitutiones, officium in breviores orationes contrahunt, necessarias quasdam omitterent."—*Renaudot.*

which we offer unto Thee, O Lord; and by it do Thou enlighten our souls, and by it do Thou sanctify our bodies; that we may raise unto Thee glory.

People. Amen.

Deacon. Let us stand.

People. Mercies.

Priest. The love.

People. And with.

Priest. Upward.

People. They are.

Priest. Let us give thanks.

People. It is meet.

Priest. Depression. It is meet and right that we should glorify and confess the Father, and the Son, and the Holy Spirit, One true God.

Elevation. And, with thousands of thousands and myriads of myriads of the fiery (host) who stand before Thee, and praise Thee unceasingly, may we be made meet to glorify Thee aloud, crying out and saying,

People. Holy.

Priest. Depression. Holy is the Father, Generator
and not Generated; Holy is the Son, Generated and
124 not Generator: Holy is the Holy Ghost, who Pro-
ceedeth from the Father, and Receiveth from the Son;
One true God, who saved us by the hand of His mer-
cies, and His grace.

Elevation. And when he was prepared for His salutary suffering, the Bread which He took He bless✠✠ed, and sancti✠fied, and brake, and named it His holy Body, for eternal life to them that receive it.

People. Amen.

Priest. And the Cup, which He had mixed of wine and of water, He bless ✠ ed, and sancti ✠ fied, and thoroughly made it His precious Blood, for eternal life to them that receive it [b].

[b] Only two signs of the cross are marked in the MS. in the blessing of the cup, the third being omitted probably by mistake.

But the words of this prayer or commemoration of institution present a much graver subject of remark.

It has been already observed that the Anaphora of St. Peter is defective in the corresponding passage of the Liturgy, in consequence of the omission of the words "This is My Body, &c.," "This is My Blood, &c.," which have generally been considered essential to the valid consecration of the elements.

A similar defect, in a yet more striking form, is presented to our notice in the Anaphora before us, and in that which bears the name of Xystus. (See p. 134 of the MS.) The Anaphora of Matthew the Shepherd is likewise defective in the form of blessing the cup. But these, it is believed, are the only four Anaphoræ, out of the large number in use among the Jacobites, in which this anomaly occurs. How is it to be accounted for? Can it be conceived that a defect of this kind would be deliberately permitted in order to produce a little of that variety of diction which is a remarkable feature of all these Anaphoræ, cast as they are in one general mould? (See Introd. Notice, pp. 184, 185.) A supposition of this kind might *perhaps* be admissible in the case of Anaphoræ which, although bearing weighty names, may yet have been the compilation of inferior authors; but it can hardly be admitted in regard to that of Barsalibi. For he flourished, it is thought, at the most only seven hundred years ago, (when Jerusalem was in the hands of the Franks,) and there seems to be little doubt that the Liturgy before us was arranged by him.

Moreover, Barsalibi was a man of great learning and theological attainment, as is evident from the works that he has left. Among these is a commentary on the Liturgy, in which he distinctly declares *that the priest "pronounces the very words which our Lord spoke in the upper room when perfecting that mystery, in order to make known that it is Himself who, through the will of His Father, and the operation of His Spirit, sanctifieth the fruits now placed on the altar, by His priest who forms the crosses and pronounces the words. For not he who minis-*

People. Amen.

Priest. And delivering them to His holy Apostles, He also commanded them, saying, Thus do ye, for My
125 remembrance, until I come.

People. Thy death.

Priest. Thy Church, therefore, remembering all Thy salutary dispensation, O Lord, and Thy second coming full of terror, wherein every man shall be rewarded according as he hath done;—yea, for this cause Thy penitent Church and Thy flock maketh supplication unto Thee, and by Thy hands, and unto Thy Father, saying,

People. Have mercy.

Priest. And we also.

People. To Thee.

Deacon. How dreadful.

Priest. The Invocation of the Holy Spirit. Have mercy upon us, O Lord, and send upon me and upon these Oblations that are set forth Thy Holy Spirit, who by His incubation perfecteth all these mysteries of the Church.

He raises his voice. Hear me.

People. Kūri. [i.e. Kyrie eleison.]

126 *Priest.* And may He perfectly make this Bread the Bo✠✠✠dy of Christ our God.

People. Amen.

ters, but He who is invoked, He it is that sanctifieth."—Renaudot, vol. ii. p. 84.

It is not likely, therefore, that Barsalibi would designedly omit the words of Christ in his own Liturgy; but it is conceivable that they may have been indicated only by the initial words, and the sentence afterwards completed by some ignorant scribe according to his own fancy.

Priest. And may he change the Mixture which is in this Cup to the Bl ✠ ✠ ✠ ood of Christ our God.

People. Amen.

Priest. So that they may be to all those who partake of them for the forgiveness of their offences; and by them may they inherit eternal life: and we will raise unto Thee glory. A.

People. Amen.

Priest. Kneeling. We offer unto Thee, O Lord, this sacrifice for Thy holy Church which is in every place, and for Thy believing people, and for the sacerdotal clergy.

Elevation. Grant to Thy holy Church, O Lord, tranquillity and peace, and to her governors good and honourable old age, and appoint in her shepherds who may divide the word of truth: that we may raise unto Thee glory. B. 127

Depression. Remember, O Lord, all honest workers, and have compassion upon and succour all that cry unto Thee, and take refuge in Thee, in the belief of the truth.

Elevation. And vouchsafing the assistance that is from Thee to all them that are afflicted with want and poverty, keep those also who extend to them the hand of help: that we may raise unto Thee glory. C.

Depression. The kings who aid Thy holy Church, do Thou remember, O Lord, and them that are good to Thy faithful people.

Elevation. And turn away from us, O Lord, the well-known enemy, and his tyranny; and deliver us from the hand of unpitiful lords: that we may raise unto Thee glory. D.

128 *Depression.* Remember, O Lord, all Thy saints, and the mother of Thy only-begotten Son, and deliver us and help us by the prayers of Thy blessed ones at rest.

E. *Elevation.* And protect us under the wings of Thy saints; and rank us in their congregation; and with them and among them we will hymn glory unto Thee.

Depression. Remember, O Lord, our shepherds true, those who have preached to us the right faith, approved fathers, and orthodox doctors.

F. *Elevation.* And keep us, O Lord, in the orthodox faith; and make us not wanderers, and not guilty, O Lord: that we may raise unto Thee glory.

Depression. Remember, O Lord, all the faithful (and) true dead, who sleep in Thy hope; and give rest in
129 Thy mercy to those who have been redeemed by the blood of Thy Only-begotten Son.

Elevation. And looking upon them in love, pardon their offences, O Lord, and remit their faults, for the sake of the Body and the Blood of Thy Only-begotten Son hidden in their members; by whose hands we also [c] hope to find mercy, (and) remission of sins for His sake, both for us and for them.

Put away.

And make us and them meet for the Christian end, not remembering our follies and theirs; so that in this as in all these things, Thy all-glorious and blessed name may be glorified and praised and had in honour, with (that) of our Lord Jesus Christ, and of Thy Holy Spirit.

[c] "We also" added in the margin by a later hand.

As.

Peace.
With.
May . . . be.

Deacon. The Catholic.
The Priest breaks and signs. **130**

Priest. The Prayer of Our Father which art in the heavens. To Thee, O God, the receiver of prayers, and answerer of petitions, do we make supplication; and before Thee do we pray this dominical prayer, which Thy Only-begotten and holy Son taught us; with contrite heart calling out and saying, Our Father which art in the heavens,

Hallowed be.

And deliver us from evil, and from every kind of iniquity; and remit our sins and follies; and to all those who have injured us in any thing soever, be Thou a pardoner to us and to them; that we may raise unto Thee glory.

Amen.

Peace.

Deacon. Before Thee.

Priest. Send down, O Lord, Thy right hand and pour forth Thy blessings on Thy people, and on the sheep of Thy flock, which is expecting to receive the
Body and Blood of Thy Only-begotten Son: and sanc- **131**
tify our souls and our bodies, that we may raise to Thee glory.

Amen.

Peace.

And with.

May . . . be.

With.

Let us behold.

Holy things.

The one Father [d].

Let us stand.

We confess.

Priest. We confess and adore Thy love towards man, O Lord: do Thou therefore confirm and help us all; support also and set us up; and pardon us all and give us rest, by reason (lit., the hand) that we have been made joyful from off this spiritual table: and to Thee we raise glory and thanksgiving, and to Thy only Son.

Amen.

Peace.

With.

After.

O Christ, the true Bread which came down from heaven, and was for us food that doth not perish, keep our souls and our bodies from Gehenna that may not be extinguished, and from the worm that dieth not:
132 and we will raise unto Thee glory and thanksgiving, and to Thy Father, and to Thy Spirit.

Amen.

Bless, O my Lord.

Priest. Bless us all.

It is finished.

[d] Here follows the Communion.

THE
ANAPHORA
OF
MAR XYSTUS,
PATRIARCH OF ROME.

THE ANAPHORA OF MAR XYSTUS.

Again, the Anaphora of Saint Cesustos (Xystus), Patriarch of Rome.

First. The Prayer of the Peace. Let tranquillity, and peace, and perpetual love, be continually with Thy Church, and Thy sheep, and Thy flock, O Lord, that we may raise unto Thee glory.

Amen.

Peace.

And to thy spirit.

Let us give.

People. Before Thee.

Priest. In Thee, O my Lord, may we all be blessed, 133
and made meet for the good end which is for men of peace: and we will raise unto Thee glory.

Amen.

May these mysteries be to us the alienation of sinful passions, and the domestication of works of righteousness, by the hand of this Anaphora (or Oblation) which we present unto Thee, O Lord: and we will raise to Thee glory.

Amen.

Let us stand.

Mercies.

The love.

With.

Up.

They are.

The Priest, lowering (his voice). With heart, mind, and tongue, we give thanks unto Thee, O Father, and Son, and Holy Ghost, who art one true God.

Elevation. With unseen multitudes, and unnumbered ranks, spiritually and seraphically joins all Thy be-
134 lieving people, O Lord, and loudly[a] praiseth Thee, and calleth out, and crieth, and saith,

Holy.

Holy art Thou, O God the Father; and holy is Thy Only-begotten Son; and holy is Thy all-holy Spirit:—for the incarnation of Thy Son[b] saved the world from error and from sin.

And he raises his voice. Who, when He was prepared for His salutary sufferings, in the Bread, which by Him was bless ✠ ✠ ✠ ed, and broken, and divided unto His holy Apostles, gave His propitiatory Body for eternal life.

Amen.

In like manner also in[c] the Cup, which by Him was

[a] ܬܠܝܬܐܝܬ, perhaps three times. Renaudot has *ter*.

[b] Lit., "Thy Son's being the Son of Man." I am inclined to suspect that the preposition ܒ, 'by,' has been omitted, and that the words should be, *for, by the Incarnation of Thy Son, Thou savedst the world, &c.* The second person masculine of the verb, and the third person feminine, are of the same form, the latter being usually distinguished (in the absence of the vowel points) by a dot over the last letter. This dot is wanting here.

[c] I have ventured to alter the preposition here, as the reading of my MS., ܠܟܣܐ, is almost certainly incorrect.

signed, and sancti ✠ ✠ ✠ fied, and given to His holy Apostles, He gave us His propitiatory Blood for eternal life [d].

Amen.

And with these He joined this admonition, saying, 135
As often as ye communicate herein, make ye remembrance of My death and burial and resurrection until I come.

Thy death.

For the amazing miracles of Thy salutary dispensation are not to be forgotten by us; with the terrible signs of Thy second coming (wherein [e]) Thou renderest to every man according to His works, O Lord: by reason whereof Thy Church and Thy flock maketh supplication unto Thee, and by Thy hands, and with Thee, to Thy Father, saying,

Have mercy.

And we also.

How dreadful.

The Priest, lowering (*his voice*). *The Invocation of the Holy Spirit.* Be propitious unto me, O Lord, be propitious unto me, and unto all Thine inheritance; and

[d] In Renaudot's translation of this Anaphora the words of institution are given entire. The clauses *Hoc est nempe corpus meum, &c., Hic nempe est calix sanguinis mei, &c.*, were found by him in two copies of the Anaphora, which, he admits, are of comparatively recent date, though free, as he believes, from interpolation by any one connected with the Western Church. Of these two, however, only one contains these clauses in the text; in the other they have been added in the margin.

[e] The word ܕܒܗ seems to be omitted.

136 be Thou pleased to sanctify[f] these Oblations by the descent of Thy Holy Spirit, who proceedeth eternally from Thee, and receiveth essentially from Thy Son[g].

Hear me.

Ko͡or.

Priest. And may He perfectly make this Bread the Bo ✠ ✠ ✠ dy of Christ our God. *Amen.*

And may He thoroughly make this Cup the Bl ✠ ✠ ✠ ood of Christ our God. *Amen.*

A. And may they make these ourselves who communicate in them partakers of the joy that is with Thee, O Lord; that we may raise unto Thee glory.

Depression. Be Thou, O Lord, to the pastors a tongue not to be conquered by the evil doctrines of heresy.

B. *Elevation.* And the mouths of heretics, wherewith they speak wickedly against us, do Thou shut and put to silence, O Lord; that we may raise unto Thee glory.

137 *Depression.* Be Thou a rewarder, O Lord, to them that work that which is good; and a Saviour to them that are bound in difficulties.

C. *Elevation.* And from the sigh of the evil-entreated,

[f] *Placitasque habe, et sanctifica,* Renaudot.

[g] This remarkable expression has been already alluded to in Appendix A, p. 173. "Hinc apparet," says Renaudot, "illud quod de Spiritu Sancto a Christo dictum est, *Ille de meo accipiet,* non de donis in fideles conferendis, sed de Processione per Filium, Orientales interpretatos fuisse. Et sane, cum errores Francorum enumerant Petrus episcopus Melichæ, Paulus Sidoniensis, et alii, non doctrinam illam, sed additionem particulæ *Filioque* symbolo factam reprehendunt."

A similar expression occurs in the Liturgy of Ignatius, Patriarch of Antioch, and in some others of Eastern origin.

and the supplication of the poor, and the tear of the afflicted, and the torments of the persecuted, turn Thou not away, nor (lit., and) keep silence, O Lord; that we may raise unto Thee glory.

Depression. Be Thou a fortress, O Lord, to every city, and place, and kingdom which believeth aright, and taketh refuge in Thee.

Elevation. And them that number[h] by circuit the towers of Thy illustrious[i] Sion, do Thou terrify and disperse, O Lord; that we may raise unto Thee glory. D.

Depression. Be Thou, O Lord, a support and help to those who participate in the memory of the Mother of Christ, and of Thy blessed saints at rest.

Elevation. And make us also, and our faithful dead, E.
meet for the prepared good things that are reserved 138
for them in Thy grace, O Lord; that we may raise unto Thee glory.

Depression. Be Thou, O Lord, a decoration incorruptible to those who, having honourably ruled Thy flock, are gone unto Thee with seemly piety.

Elevation. And from the neighbourhood of their pious paternity, whereby we became sons of Thy grace, do not remove and repel us, O Lord; that we may raise unto Thee glory. F.

Depression. Be Thou, O Lord, one who giveth rest, and propitiator, to all the faithful dead, who have been saved by the death of Thy Only-begotten Son.

Elevation. And being saved from death by Thee,
O Lord, and being delivered from the grave (*Sheul*) 139

[h] An error in the Syr. word is suspected here.

[i] Renaudot always translates this word "spiritualis."

and shaken forth from the dust; may the grace of Thy only Son prevail upon us; by whose hands we also trust to find mercy, and remission of sins for His sake, both for us and them.

Put away. (or, *Give rest.*)

And with the renewal of the general resurrection, make us and them, in Thy grace, O Lord, meet for the joy which is in Thy spiritual kingdom; so that herein, as in all things, Thy all-glorious and blessed name may be glorified and praised by all, with that of our Lord Jesus Christ, and Thy Holy Spirit; now.

As.

Peace.

With.

May . . . be.

Deacon. The Catholic.

The Priest breaks and signs.

The Priest. The Prayer of Our Father which art in the
140 *heavens.* O Lord, open our mouths and our lips; and sanctify the souls and bodies of us all; and purify our minds and our thoughts hereunto; that we may suppliantly cry unto Thee, O God, Father of mercies, and may pray and say, Our Father which art in the heavens,

Hallowed be.

And all those things which injure us and cause us loss, do Thou quickly and swiftly change for us, O Lord, to those which may do us good and cause us to abound; that we may raise unto Thee glory. *Amen.*

Peace.

With.

Before.

Priest. May all Thy graces, and all Thy blessings, and all Thy gifts, come and descend and be poured forth upon Thy Church, and upon Thy sheep, and upon Thy flock, O Lord: that we may raise unto Thee glory. *Amen.*

Peace.

With.

May . . . be.

Let us behold.

Holy things.

The One Father.

Let us stand.

Righteous[k].

Our mouths, accustomed to the food of herbs, give 141
thanks for this grace, whereby we are made meet for this divine gift, which is the Body and Blood of Thy Only-begotten Son, by whom and with whom is due to Thee glory, and honour, and power, with Thy Holy Spirit. *Amen.*

Peace.

With.

After.

People. Before Thee.

Priest. O Christ, the heavenly Bread, which came down, [and will be for us[l]] food that doth not perish,

[k] ܟܐܢܐ; perhaps a mistake for ܟܗܢܐ, 'Priest.'

[l] I am convinced that there is an error here in the MS. The reading is the following: ܕܠܐ ܗܘܐ ܡܬܚܒܠܐ, literally, 'which will not

make us not to be devoured at Thy second coming, by the fire that is not extinguished; that we may raise unto Thee glory, and to Thy Father, and to Thy Holy Spirit; now.

The Anaphora of Saint Xystus, Patriarch of Rome, is finished.

be food, &c.' A slight alteration would make the expression similar to that at p. 131, by reading ܘܠܢ instead of ܕܠܐ. I have ventured to adopt this alteration in the text.

σ̄

The Gospel of John[a], *for the Corban of every day.* 142

At that time Jesus said to His disciples, and to the multitude of the Jews, (For) My Body is meat indeed, and My Blood is drink indeed. Whoso eateth My Body and drinketh My Blood abideth in Me, and I in him: as the living Father hath sent Me, and I live because of the Father. And whosoever shall eat Me, he shall also live for ever. This is the bread that came down from heaven. It is not like that manna which your fathers eat, and died: whosoever eateth of this bread shall live for ever.

The Gospel of Mark[b], *for the Commemoration of the Mother of God.*

And there came His mother and His brethren stand- 143
ing without, and they sent and called Him unto them. Now the multitude sat about Him, and they said unto Him, Behold, Thy mother and Thy brethren without seek for Thee. And He answered and said unto them, Who is My mother, and who are My brethren? And He looked on them that sat by Him, and said, Behold My mother, and behold My brethren. For whosoever shall do the will of God, the same is My brother, and My sister, and My mother. And peace to you all.

[a] Chap. vi. 55—58. [b] Chap. iii. 31—35.

The Gospel of Luke[c]*: the Vocation*[d] *of Bishops.*

Jesus said unto him, Who then is the faithful and
wise steward, whom his lord shall set over his service,
to give the portion of meat in its season? Blessed is
that servant whom his lord when he cometh shall find
so doing. Of a truth I say unto you that he will set
him over all his goods. But if that servant say in his
heart, My lord delayeth to come; and begin to beat
144 the servants and handmaidens of his lord; and begin
to eat and to drink and to be drunken; the lord of
that servant shall come in a day that he expecteth not,
and in an hour that he knoweth not, and shall separate
him, and appoint his portion with them that do not
believe. And that servant who knoweth his lord's will,
and prepareth not himself according to his will, shall
be beaten with many (stripes); but he that knoweth
not, and doth things worthy of stripes, shall be beaten
with few stripes. For unto whomsoever much is given,
of him shall much be required: and to whom much
hath been committed, at his hand will men ask the
more.

The Gospel of Mark[e]*, for the Commemoration of Martyrs.*

And Jesus called the multitude with His disciples
and said unto them, Whosoever will come after Me,
145 let him deny himself, and take up his cross, and follow
Me. For every man that will save his life shall lose
it: and every one that shall lose his life for My sake
and for the sake of My gospel, shall save it. For what

[c] Chap. xii. 42—48. [d] Syr., ܦܪܢܣܐ. [e] Chap. viii. 34—38.

is a man advantaged, if he gain the whole world, and lose his soul? or what shall a man give in exchange for his soul? For whosoever shall be ashamed of Me and of My words in this sinful and adulterous generation, of him shall the Son of Man also be ashamed when He cometh in the glory of His Father, with His holy angels. And Peace.

* * * * * * *[f]

When Jesus had called His twelve Apostles[g], He
gave them power and authority over all devils, and to
heal diseases; and sent them to preach the kingdom of
God, and to heal them that[g] were sick. And He said
unto them, Take nothing for (your) journey, neither 146
balance[h], nor bread; nor let there be unto you two
coats apiece. And into whatsoever city[g] or house ye
enter, there abide[g], and from thence depart. And
they that[g] will not receive you, (and[g]) when ye go
out from that city, shake off the very dust from your
feet for a testimony against them. When they were
gone forth[g], they went about the country[g], preaching
and healing in every place.

[f] In the MS. one line is left blank, apparently for the insertion of the Rubric, which has been forgotten. The gospel that follows is taken from St. Luke ix. 1—6.

[g] In all these places the expression differs from that of the Peshito version.

[h] ܡܪܣܘܦܐ, 'balances' or 'balance-case.'

DEDICATION OF ALTAR VESSELS, &c.

The Prayer over new vessels that are offered for the Altar.

O Lord God Almighty, holy and giver of holiness,
who art ever holy, and dwellest in light that no man
147 can approach unto; whose glory and holiness filleth
all things, and who hast not left Thyself without some
to praise Thee, but didst create multitudes of fiery
(hosts), that they might glorify and hallow Thy ma-
jesty: not as though Thou needest hymns of praise,
but that they who hallow Thee might be magnified by
Thee. Yea, Thou didst create the world in Thy good-
ness; and didst appoint chief priests for Thine honour;
and didst accept the temporary tabernacle for Thine
abode; and didst adorn it with glorious vessels; with
plates and with censers, and candlesticks and cups,
together with the rest of all the Mosaic service, which
he commanded. Now also, O Lord, we Thy servants,
saved by the cross of Thy Only-begotten, do entreat
Thy mercy, that Thou wouldst hallow these vessels
which are placed on our hands; which are offered for
the service of Thy altar; that they may be for the
honour of Thy temple, and for the praise of Thy holy
name. And receive, O my Lord, the freewill offering
148 of those who present them, and of all that have par-
taken and are partaking in them: by the prayer of
Mary the Mother of God; and of Mar *Such an one;*
and of all the saints, now and at all times for ever
and ever. Amen.

Again. The Prayer over an Altar or Church which has been polluted by the heathen or by heretics.

The Bishop first signs the Altar with a cross without chrism, and says,

Sealed, and purified, and blessed be this altar and this table, and the holy church, and all its ornaments and appurtenances, and its vessels, and vestments, and pillars, from all heretical stain, and from pollution of the heathen, and from all noisomeness of the wicked, and from every fornicator that transgresseth law: In the name of the Fa ✠ ✠ ther. Amen. And of the ✠
Son. Amen. And of the living and Holy ✠ Ghost. 149
For hallowed sanctification and renovation from above. Amen.

And he goes down to the west of the church, and then to the north and to the south, and signs in like manner (as before) crosses without chrism, saying,

Cleansed be this church from every stain and abomination, and uncleanness, and pollution, heathenish and heretical; and let it be blessed and renewed. In the name of the Fa ✠ ther. Amen. And of the ✠ Son. Amen. And of the Holy ✠ Ghost: for renovation and perfect cleansing. Amen.

THE ANAPHORA

OF

MAR EVANNIS (JOHN),

OTHERWISE KNOWN AS

JACOB OF THE MONASTERY OF MAR HANNANIA.

THIS Anaphora is found in Renaudot's work, under the title *Liturgia Sancti Joannis, quæ in Missali Chaldaico Chrysostomo tribuitur.* There does not, however, appear to be the slightest ground for supposing that St. Chrysostom was its author; the practice of ascribing their Anaphoræ to one or other of the eminent saints of the early ages of Christianity being, it would seem, not unfrequently resorted to by the Monophysites.

THE ANAPHORA OF MAR EVANNIS.

The Anaphora of pious Mar Ævannis of Haran, and 150
Havuro, and Nisibis, who is Jacob of the Monastery of Mar Hannania.

First. The Prayer before the Peace. O God, who art great and eternal, who art tranquillity, and peace, and love, and fount of mercies; give peace, O Lord, to Thy Church, and keep all the world in Thy grace: that we may raise unto Thee glory, and to Thy Only-begotten Son, and to Thy Holy Spirit; now.

People. Amen.

Priest. Peace.

People. And to (thy) spirit.

Deacon. Let us give.

People [a].

Priest. Send down, O Lord, Thy loving-kindness, and stretch forth Thy right hand full of blessings, and bless Thy servants and Thy worshippers, who now bow before Thee; that we may send up.

People. Amen.

Priest. Strengthen us, O Lord, hereunto, that we may present unto Thee this spiritual and unbloody sacrifice, for the sins and offences of Thy flock, so that
Thou mayst blot out and pass over our unlawful deeds: 151
that we may raise.

People. Amen.

Deacon. Let us stand.

[a] A word is evidently wanting here.

People. Mercies.

Priest. The love.

Priest. Up.

People. They are.

Priest. Let us give thanks.

People. It is meet.

Depression. To Thee, O king of worlds, God the Father, with the Son and the Holy Spirit, all thanksgiving is just and due.

Elevation. All heavenly ranks and orders and powers, Angels and Archangels, Cherubim and Seraphim, Thrones and Dominions, invisible and innumerable, unceasingly laud and honor (Thee); as with mouths incorporeal and voices unutterable they praise (Thy) victorious glory, and cry aloud and shout and say,

People. Holy.

Depression. Truly Thou art holy, O God the Father, and Thy Holy Spirit, who is ever sanctified with Thy holy Son, Jesus Christ our Lord.

152 *Elevation.* Who, when in His love He had become incarnate for our sake, and for our salvation was willingly made low [b] and suffered in the flesh, in the night of sufferings took bread in His holy hands, ✠ and blessed, ✠ and sanctified, ✠ and brake, and gave to His disciples, and said, Take, eat of it: this is My Body which is given for you for the remission of sins, and for the new life which is for ever.

People. Amen.

Priest. In like manner He took the cup also, ✠ and

[b] The word used in Phil. ii. 7, corresponding to the Greek ἐκένωσε.

blessed, ✠ and sanctified, ✠ and gave to His disciples, and said, Take, drink of it all of you, for the pardon of offences and for the new life which is for ever[c].

People. Amen.

Priest. And He forecharged and admonished them, saying, As often as ye delight in these mysteries, be ye commemorating My death and resurrection until My coming.

People. Thy death.

Priest. We, O my Lord, Thy sinful and offending
servants, bearing in mind all the circuit of Thy salu- 153
tary dispensation, and Thy second terrible and glorious
coming, whereat we tremble and are afraid, offer prayer
and supplication unto Thee, and by Thy hands and
with Thee we implore Thy Father, saying,

People[d].

Priest. And we also.

People. We glorify Thee.

Deacon. How terrible.

Priest. The Invocation of the Holy Spirit, kneeling.

Send Thy Holy Spirit from Thy holy dwelling-place, O Lord, and let Him come down and abide upon this Bread and Mixture which is set forth, and sanctify them: and may He make me pure and sincere.

[c] A Malabar MS. of this Anaphora in the Bodleian Library (B. O. 626) reads, "In like manner He took the cup also, and blessed, and sanctified, and gave to His disciples, and said, Take, drink of it all of you. This is My Blood, which is shed for the pardon of offences, and for the remission of sins, and for eternal life."—Fol. 42, 43.

[d] The initial word omitted. The answer would doubtless be, *Have mercy upon us*, as in the other Anaphoræ.

Hear me.

[*People.*] Kur.

Priest. And may He pronounce[d] this Bread the Bo ✠ ✠ ✠ dy of Christ our God.

People. Amen.

Priest. And may He thoroughly make [d] the Mixture which (is) in this Cup the Bl ✠ ✠ ✠ ood of Christ our God.

People. Amen.

A. *Priest.* So that every one that partaketh of them
may be an inheritor in Thy kingdom of heaven, and
154 may be made joyful in the new life with the saints.
And we will raise to Thee glory.

People. Amen.

Priest. Depression. The pastors and governors of the Church, and all the sacerdotal state, remember Thou, O Lord.

B. *Elevation.* Enlighten us, O Lord, with the light of Thy divine doctrines; and grant unto us good times, and a quiet and abundant life in peace; that we may raise unto Thee.

[d] It may be interesting to compare the expressions used in this part of the Invocation in the different Anaphoræ:—

In the Anaphora of St. James, the words are ܢܥܒܕ, 'faciat,' and ܢܫܡܠܐ, 'perficiat.' Of St. Peter, ܢܥܒܕ, 'faciat,' and ܢܫܡܠܐ, 'perficiat.' Of the Twelve Apostles, ܢܥܒܕ, 'faciat,' (no other). Of Barsalibi, ܢܓܡܘܪ, 'perficiat,' and ܢܫܚܠܦ, 'transformet.' Of Xystus, ܢܓܡܘܪ, 'perficiat, and ܢܫܡܠܐ, 'perficiat.' Of Evannis, ܢܚܘܐ, 'annunciet,' and ܢܫܡܠܐ, 'perficiat.'

People. Amen.

Priest. Depression. Thy faithful and orthodox people that are here and in every place, remember Thou, O Lord.

Elevation. The harassed and the persecuted, the C.
afflicted and the sorrowful, the poor and the needy, foreigners and the miserable, those in bonds and the solitary, orphans and widows, do Thou govern and lead on in Thy loving-kindness, O Lord, that we may raise.

People. Amen.

Priest. Depression. Faithful and powerful kings, doers of Thy will, remember Thou, O Lord.

Elevation. And to us grant Thou, and vouchsafe in D.
Thy goodness, O Lord, that we may live quiet and
pleasant lives before Thee, and may be looked upon 155
in love by the eyes of those who govern us: and we will raise unto Thee.

People. Amen.

Priest. Depression. And Mary the Virgin Mother of God, and John the Baptist, and Stephen the Deacon, and all Thy blessed ones at rest, remember Thou, O Lord.

Elevation. By the prayer and supplication of those E.
who by administrations of justice have conciliated Thee, vouchsafe unto us a portion and lot with them, O Lord; that we may raise.

People. Amen.

Priest. Depression. Holy fathers, and approved doctors, and them that have shewn the mysteries of the truth, remember Thou, O Lord.

F. *Elevation.* And on the rock of the orthodox faith of the three holy synods[e], confirm us all in Thy goodness, O Lord, that we may raise.

People. Amen.

Priest. Depression. And our fathers, and our brethren, and our masters, and all the faithful dead, remember Thou, O Lord.

156 *Elevation.* And pronounce them not to be delivered to the powers of darkness; and rescue them from the grasp of evil spirits; and deliver them from torments and afflictions; and cause to arise upon us and upon them the light of Thy Only-begotten Son, by whose hands we also trust to find mercy and remission of sins for His sake, both for us and for them.

People. Put away. [or, Give rest.]

Priest. Hear us, O Lord, because of the abundance of Thy mercies; and deliver us from the judgment to come, and from the torments that are kept (in store) for the wicked; so that herein, as in all these things, Thy blessed Name may be glorified and honoured, with (those) of our Lord Jesus Christ, and of Thy Holy Spirit: now.

People. As.

Priest. Peace.

People. And to (thy) spirit.

Priest. May . . . be.

People. With.

The Priest breaks and signs.

Deacon. The Catholic.

[e] i. e. the first three Œcumenical Councils, viz. those of Nicæa (A.D. 325), Constantinople (A.D. 381), and Ephesus (A.D. 431).

Priest. The Prayer of Our Father, which art in the heavens.

O God, great and powerful, who, in Thy love to- 157
wards man, didst call and bring us to this divine gift, that we might glorify Thee, O Father, in its [mysteries?[f]] and worship the Holy Spirit, and sing the Dominical Prayer of Thy Only-begotten Son; with sincerity of mind, and cleanness of tongue, and purity of body, and with soul prepared with confidence, we will be bold to cry unto Thee, O God of heaven, Holy Almighty Father, and we will pray and say,

Our Father, which art in the heavens.

People. Hallowed be.

Priest. Yea, O good and merciful Father, who[g] hast vouchsafed unto us to be called Thy children, deliver us from temptations hard to be borne; and rescue us from the evil one, and from all his power; and from the machinations of evil men: that we may raise.

People. Amen.

Priest. Peace.

People. Before Thee.

Priest. O great and Almighty King, under the sceptre of whose dominion all creatures bow, send Thy bless-
ings on Thy Church which now boweth before Thee, 158
(that) she may raise.

People. Amen.

[f] My MS. has ܕܒܐܪ̈ܙܝܗ̇ which is perhaps a mistake for ܕܒܐܪ̈ܙܗ̇; but Renaudot has simply "donum hoc divinum, *per quod*," which would have been ܕܒܗ̇.

[g] Here ܗ̇ܝ is probably a mistake for ܗܘ.

Priest. Peace.

[*People.*] And with.

[*Priest.*] May . . . be.

[*Deacon.*] With awe.

Priest. His holy things.

People. The One Father.

Priest. The Prayer of the Thanksgiving. O God, we offer thanksgiving, and praise Thy Name, who hast made us who are unworthy, meet for this divine gift of the Body and Blood of Thy Only-begotten Son, and we will raise.

People. Amen.

Priest. Peace.

[*People.*] With.

Deacon. After.

Priest. O Jesus Christ our God, who by Thy will, and (that) of Thy Father, and of Thy Holy Spirit, wast sacrificed for us, and hast fed us with Thy living Body, and caused us to drink Thy pardoning Blood; confirm us in Thy love, and fill us with Thy fear, and establish us in Thy faith; adorn us with unblameable conduct, and forgive our sins, and (the sins) of our dead; so that we may continually and in all times glorify Thee, and Thy Father, and Thy Holy Spirit: now.

People. Amen.

Deacon. That we may go in peace, give the blessing to us all [h].

[h] Here ends the MS. of this Anaphora at the bottom of p. 158. The next page is blank, and possibly a word or two may be wanting to complete the Anaphora: but it is evident that very little is wanting.

SEALS AND SEDRAS

USED UPON SEVERAL OCCASIONS

IN THE COURSE OF THE LITURGY.

NOTE.—These prayers appear to be more or less corrupt in many places; but it seemed desirable to attempt a translation, in order that the MS. might be presented entire, so far as it goes: and notwithstanding the roughness of the translation (which here, as elsewhere, adheres as closely as possible to the original), it is hoped that it will not be found entirely devoid of interest.

A SEAL OVER THE DEAD.

Again, in the might of our adorable Lord and God, **160**
we write the Seal, with the sign of Mar Ephrem, over the
Dead.

O Christ, who wast the offering for (this) offending
world, and by Thy death did[st] become (its) Redeemer,
receive this offering, ✠ like the offering of Abel, and
of just Noah, and Samuel, and Abraham, and Isaac,
and of Jacob blessed at Bethel; ✠ like that of glorious
Melchisedec, and Enoch, and Elijah the prophet, and
Elisha the pure virgin [a], and of the children of the
house of Hananiah, ✠ and of Moses the great, and
Aaron, Joshua the son of Nun, and of Gideon, and of
Hezekiah, and of Solomon, and Father Mark and Aleth-
son, ✠ and of David, Heart of God [b], in the threshing- **161**
floor of Oran (Ornan) of Jebus; and the offerings of
Peter, Paul, and the elect Apostles, of Justus; ✠ and
like the offerings of the Prophets, and of the Judges,
and the Maccabees; and the widow's mites; and the
first and the last. ✠ In like manner, O our Lord, by
the hand of Thy mercies receive Thou the offering of
us Thy worshippers, and pardon thereby the sins of

[a] ܒܬܘܠܐ. So *παρθένος* is applied to both sexes in the New Testament.

[b] Syr. ܠܒܗ ܕܬܐܘܣ, lit., Heart of ὁ Θεός, perhaps in allusion to 1 Sam. xiii. 14; Acts xiii. 22.

Thy servants, through the prayer of Thy people and of Thy saints: ✠

And if he is offering for a man:—And spare Thou, and
in Thy goodness have mercy upon the soul of this Thy
servant, who put Thee on by Baptism, and believed
and confessed in Thy hope, ✠ for whom this offering is
presented unto Thee to-day. May it be dealbation for
his stains, and a propitiator for his offences. ✠ Mingle
him with the assemblage of the righteous, and make
him joyful with the saints, and bring him unto Thy
162 kingdom, ✠ and invite him to the chamber of light. ✠
Place him with just men, and set him on Thy right
hand, and make him whiter than snow; receive him
into the mansions of Eden.

And if he is offering for a woman:—Spare Thou, and
in Thy goodness have mercy upon the soul of this Thy
handmaid, who put Thee on by Baptism, and believed
and confessed in Thy hope, ✠ for whom this offering is
offered unto Thee to-day. May it be dealbation for
her stains, and a propitiator for her offences. ✠ Mingle
her with the assemblage of the chaste, and make her
joyful with the virgins; and bring her to Thy kingdom,
and invite her to the chamber of light. ✠ Place her
with the wise; set her on Thy right hand; and make
her whiter than snow; unite her with Shemvani and
163 her children, ✠ with Hannah, Mary, Martha, and
Sarah, and simple Rebekah, and Susanna, and Elisabeth
the barren, and all saintly women. ✠

And make us all meet worthily to glorify Thee without ceasing; and mercifully set us on Thy right hand with joy. ✠ O Christ, just Judge, have compassion upon us in grace and in mercy, the loving-kindness of Thy merciful Father, and of the tenderly-loving Spirit of holiness. ✠ ✠ ✠[c]

Another Seal.

To Him who pardoneth our offences by His Body, and blotteth out our sins by His Blood, ✠ to Him be glory in His Church, and among you, O ye His blessed people, sheep of His pasture. ✠ May He pour forth His grace upon you, and make His mercies and His blessings to abound unto you, ✠ and may He cause His right hand and His care to overshadow you, now and at all times for ever. ✠ ✠ ✠[c]

A Seal with the sign of Mar Ephrem, on the First Day **164**
of the Week, and on a Festival.

✠ O Father, who art full of indulgence, Sea of mercies and of grace,—receive this offering, which we offer unto Thee to-day, ✠ like the accepted offering of Abel oppressed and slain, and of just Noah in the Ark, and of Elijah on Mount Carmel; ✠ and as (that) of Melchisedec the Priest, who offered bread and wine, which were mysteries of this Body and Blood of Thy true Son: ✠ and as [those] of blessed Abraham, and of Isaac the son of promise, and of Jacob high in valour, [so] may this offering be accepted; ✠ and as that pure offering of David the king and prophet, on
the threshing-floor of the Jebusite, whereby Thou wast **165**
reconciled, O Lord; ✠ and as the mites of the desolate and poor widow, [so] receive, O my Lord, this separated

[c] The MS. contains five crosses in this place, that number exactly filling up the line.

sacrifice from the sons of the Church: ✠ and be Thou pleased by the sacrifices and offerings which Thy poor servants have offered, as did the blessed Apostles and sacerdotal Fathers: ✠ and be Thou reconciled by their offerings, and pardon and remit their faults; and heal and alleviate their sorrows, and blot out and do away their stains. ✠ Be Thou appeased, O Lord, by their vows and their firstfruits and their tithes; and preserve their sons and their daughters, and have mercy upon their dead: ✠ by the prayer of Mary, the holy and blessed Virgin, Mother of God in truth, [even of]
166 Jesus the Lord of glory; ✠ and by the might of the cross of our Saviour Christ, who is the Lord our Righteousness, who hath delivered us from evil and death, and hath raised us to the foremost place: ✠ by the prayer of Prophets and Apostles and Martyrs slain and immolated; and noted just and righteous men, who were inspired by the Spirit of holiness; ✠ and by the prayers of the Fathers, and holy men and holy women; and true synods, mighty defenders of the Faith. ✠ And from all of us, as one assembly, priest and holy people, praise and glory and oblation, to the Father, and to the Son, and to the Spirit of holiness. ✠

Another Seal.

By the prayer of the blessed Mother, full of blessing, full of graces and modesty, in purity and holiness; ✠
167 and by the might of the victorious cross whereon the Son of life was crucified; and blood and water flowed therefrom, and were the propitiation of the world:— ✠ O God, as Thou receivedst[d] the offerings of the

[d] Lit., He received.

Fathers, Abraham and Isaac and Jacob and the righteous, children of the kingdom, ✠ receive also, O my Lord, their offerings and their vows and their tithes, and bless the work of their hands, and their vines and their tithes. ✠ And bless us all, O God; and keep us all, O Creator; the way of life do Thou also shew unto us, O Thou that art the Helper and Lord of us all. ✠ Bless ye the Lord, all of you; both your great ones and your little ones, men and women alike, and the whole assembly with one consent: ✠ and Mar John (and) the Baptist, and Mar Stephen the Deacon, and
Mar Barsumas the blessed[e], and Mar Severus the 168
illustrious, ✠ and by the prayer of Antony, and fiery Ignatius, and noble Gregory, with great Basil. ✠[f]

By the power of our Lord Jesus Christ [we are beginning] to write a Proœmium. ✠ ✠ ✠

To the Bread of life which came down from heaven, and was made manifest of a daughter of David, and was broken upon Golgotha, and is divided in the holy Church, [lit., the Church of holiness,] and given to the faithful people, and sufficeth for the living and the dead, that it may make (them) joyful in His goodness: to whom belongeth glory.

The Sedra[g].

Before Thee, O God of gods, and Lord of lords, before Thee, O Judge of judges, and terrible above princes;

[e] See note x, p. 252.

[f] Here are seven crosses, apparently to fill up the line.

[g] This Sedra will be recognised as occurring in MS. B., shortly after the reading of the Gospel. See note a, p. 215.

169 at whose glory the fiery tremble, and at sight of whom
the spiritual are moved; before Thee, O my Lord, do
we worship, and make supplication unto Thy divinity,
(seeing Thou hast vouchsafed[h] unto me[i] the service of
the holy seraphim, and hast made me[i] partaker in the
adorable mysteries of Thy divinity,) that Thou wouldest
be propitious unto us in Thy abundant mercies, so that
we may stand holily before Thee, and before Thy holy
altar, and may carefully perform the priestly office unto
Thee upon Thy spiritual table; and wouldest send Thy
Holy Spirit, and wouldest sanctify this bread and wine
which is set before us, and wouldest glorify our bodies
and our souls, and wouldest sanctify our minds and our
thoughts, and wouldest cleanse from us all defilements
of sin, so that we may offer unto Thee sweet and un-
polluted sacrifices, and be made meet, we and our dead,
for the blessings which Thou hast promised to Thy
saints: and together with them, and among them, we
170 will raise to Thee glory and thanksgiving, now and at
all times for ever.

Proœmium. ✠

Blessed be the desired Oblation, and praised be the sweet Fruit, which was offered in our behalf, and hath wrought our pardon, and by its sanctifying immolation hath sanctified us; the Lamb, sprung from the Virgin sheep, which ascended the cross, and redeemed us, and delivered us from the sacrifices of dumb animals: to whom belongeth.

[h] Lit., who has vouchsafed.

[i] B. reads "us." See pp. 32, 33 of that MS.

The Sedra.

O Lord God Almighty, who receivest sacrifices of praise from them that cry unto Thee with all their heart, receive these spices from the hands of us Thy unworthy servants, and bring us unto Thy holy altar; and purify us that we may present unto Thee offerings and spiritual sacrifices for our sins, and for the offences of Thy people; and vouchsafe unto us that our sacrifice
may be acceptable; and let Thy good Spirit abide upon 171
us, and upon these offerings that are set [before Thee], and upon all Thy people which believe in Christ Jesus our Lord; to whom, with Thee and with Thy Holy Spirit, belong glory and honour and power, now.

Proœmium.

To that Cup of thanksgiving and redemption which was mingled on the height of Golgotha, whereby sinners are pardoned and cleansed from iniquity: to that pardon-giving Blood which was poured forth upon the heights of the cross, whereby the nations are redeemed and are delivered from death: to whom belong glory and honour and adoration, with His Father and Holy Spirit, in this time of this divine perfect Eucharist, and in all.

The Sedra. 172

O Christ our God, Creator and Disposer of all, the very saving Breath of the world, pure Salve of incorruption, and glad Savour of immortality; the sweet savour of whose divine knowledge filleth our hearts, and maketh us, abject and earthly creatures, meet to stand before Thee, and to minister, and in priestly office to perform, the service of Thy divine and ineffable

mysteries, into which the angels also desire to look: deliver our souls, O my Lord, and set them free from the service of sin, and from wandering after vain things; and grant us, under Thy light and pleasant yoke, to serve a good and perfect service unto Thee, so that we may live before Thee, in watchfulness of soul
173 and of body, and in stedfast conversation, all the days of our life: and bring us to the good end, and to the life of angels, far from that of woe and misery and sighing; by Thy grace and by the good pleasure of Thy blessed Father, and the goodness which sent Thee for our salvation, and the operation of Thy all-holy and good and adorable Spirit; now and at all times for ever.

Proœmium.

Glory without ceasing, and thanksgiving that faileth not, and laud without intermission, and honourable and splendid exaltation, on sweet and pleasant psalteries, may we be made worthy to present unto that true Shepherd who feedeth His flock with His own holy Body, and quencheth His Church's thirst with His precious Blood. Joyful are all our mouths which are hallowed
174 by His Body, and all our ranks made glad by His Blood, and all our crowns worshipping His honour, and all our peoples hymning His praise; to whom is due adoration from all tongues, in this time of Eucharist.

The Sedra.

The heavenly Lamb, whom the earthly Virgin bore in wonder, and whom Bethlehem Ephratah honoured in joy, and the river Jordan, in her gladness, looked unto with delight, and Golgotha exalted on the cru-

cifixion tree, of His own will was sacrificed for the redemption of the created, and by His immolation procured pardon for all peoples and tribes, and by the hand of His death gave life to all families and generations. Yea, and now also, O Lord, by Thy abundant
love towards man, and Thine unutterable grace, and **175**
by the prayers of the blessed and holy Mother, heard and accepted, and of all the [? assembly[k]] of Prophets and Apostles, and Martyrs and Fathers, be gracious unto Thy faithful Church; bless Thy reasonable flock; sanctify Thy priestly inheritance; keep Thy poor congregation; let Thy tranquillity dwell upon created things, and let Thy peace reign upon the earth. Command deliverance to the captives, and liberty to them that are bound and to them that are in bondage. And make good remembrance to Thy blessed and holy Mother, and to the Prophets and Apostles, and Martyrs and Confessors, and to the faithful dead who are gone before and sleep in Thy hope in the belief of the truth. And to me, O my Lord, Thy sinful servant [? and minister, to whom Thou hast entrusted this ministry, grant a conversation * * *]

[Here ends the MS. in its present state. From the condition of the binding and folding of the paper, it appears probable that two more leaves existed when the MS. was perfect.]

[k] Syr. ܣܝܥܬܐ.

INDEX.

n. signifies note.

Ahatalla, 45.
Alanghat, the meeting at, 45.
Alexander of Palakomatta, 48.
Alfred, King, and the mission of Bishop Swithhelm, 8, 21.
Allepie, Church Missionary Society's Mission at, 66.
Altar, the, in the Syrian Churches, 123 n, 127, 186.
Analysis of the Ordo Communis, 182.
Angamalé, the ancient seat of the Metropolitan, 23; ceases to be the Metropolitan see, 44.
Antiquity of the Church in Malabar, 8.
Archdeacon George, 29—34.
Assembly's Catechism, The, used at Cottayam, 93, 96.
Athanasius, Metropolitan, 67, 154; communicates with Bishop Heber at Bombay, 68; his violent proceedings, 68—70; expelled from the country, 83.
——— the present Metropolitan, 154—156.

Backwater, The, described, 2.
Baliarte, the Christian king, 22.
Barsumas, 252 n, 333.
Books, destruction of, by the Portuguese, 41.
Breach between the C.M.S. and the Syrians, 94—100, 104—107.
Bread, The Eucharistic, 187.
Buchanan, Dr. C., 56—60.

Catholicus, meaning of the title, 25 n.
Celebrations of the Holy Communion in the Mission Stations, 92, 100, 115.
Ceremonial in the East, 177.
Chattanoor, visit to, 118—124.
Church, a portable, 164.
Church Missionary Society's Mission in Travancore, The, established in 1816, 87; the missionaries' work appreciated, 66, 88; they establish schools, 88; and a printing press, 89, 90; translation of the Bible, 89; Sunday at Cottayam, 91; proceedings subsequent to the rupture, 107.
Churches of the Syrian Christians, described, 123, 125—128.
Climate of the Malabar coast, 5.
Coadjutor Bishop, election of a, 65.
Communicants, posture of the, 146.
Consecration, defective forms of, 295, n.
Conspectus of the six Anaphoræ, 184.
Cottayam, the College at, 61, 63, 66; course of study in the College, 93; Syrian Churches at, 153. (See Church Miss. Soc.)
Cranganore, 9, 24, 44, 48.
Cyril of Agugnúr, 53, 54.

Diamper, the synod of, 36—41.
Dionysius, Metropolitan, 53—58; his interviews with Dr. C. Buchanan, 56—58.

Entrance, the Great, 131, n.; 196, n.
Errors of the Syrian Christians in Malabar, 175.
Eucharistic Office described, 130—147, 179—185.
Evensong at Mavelicara, 149.

Grant to the Christians in Malabar, 13, 17, and Pref.
Gregorius, his arrival in Travancore, 49.
Heber, Bp., his letter to Mar Athanasius, 71; his letter to Mar Philoxenus, 75.

Holy Communion in the Mission stations, 92, 100, 115.
Hospitality of the Syrians at Chattanoor, 120.

Iconoclastic zeal of the Missionaries, 97, 98.

Jacob, Catanar of Chattanoor, 117.
Jacobite ascendancy, 20.
Jacobites, their distinctive tenet, 20, n.
Jacobitism, what it is, 168.
Jesuits, interference of the, 24.
Jews at Cochin, The, 161, 163.

Kanúnkalum, Church Missionary Society's Mission at, 115; Syrian Church at, 116.
Kayencolum, visit to, 125.
Kerr, Dr., visits the Malabar Churches, 58.
Koorillos Joachim, Metropolitan, 162.

Liturgical modifications made by Abp. Menezes, 39; introduced by the Church Missionary Society's Missionaries, 105.

Maphrian, the title of the Jacobite Patriarch's Suffragan, 25, n.
MSS., account of, 124, and Pref.
Mar Abraham, 25—29.
Mar Joseph, 24—26.
Mar Simeon, 27.
Mavelicara, Syrian Church at, 149; Mission Church at, 150.
Melchites, The, 20, n.
Menezes, Alexius de, appointed to the Archbishopric of Goa, 28; Abp., character of, 30, 42; his ordination of thirty-eight Catanars, 33; his letter to Archd. George, 34; his interview with the Rajah, 35.
Metropolitan of the Church in Malabar, The, its sole Bishop in early times, 29, n.

Nestorian missions, 18.
Nestorians, their distinctive tenet, 20, n.

Pantænus, 15.
Paroor, 165.
Philoxenus, Metropolitan, 64.
Procession of the Holy Ghost, 173.

Robinson, Archdeacon, his letter to the Patriarch of Antioch, 78.
Romo-Syrians of Malabar, 51.

Syrians of Malabar, 51.

Thomas Cannaneo, 15—17.
——— St., said to have planted the Gospel in India, 9—14.
Thomas's Mount, St., 11.
Trisagium, The, 157.

Vasco de Gama, 7.
Vestments of the Catanars, 132—134.

Wilson, Bp., his visit to Travancore, 100—104.

CPSIA information can be obtained
at www.ICGtesting.com
Printed in the USA
LVHW040029180422
716440LV00005B/354

9 783752 594966